FORGET ME KNOT

THE POISONVERSE

MARIE MACKAY

Copyright © 2023 by Marie Mackay

Edition 1.0

All rights reserved.

Cover made by Marie Mackay

Copy Edits done by Jessica Gilly

No part of this book may be reproduced in any form or by any electronic or mechanical means, including information storage and retrieval systems, without written permission from the author, except for the use of brief quotations in a book review.

To Erin.
My best friend, and someone with as much fire and passion as Onyx. Who has survived so much, and still come out a fighter. A protector. A beautiful person.
Keep shining.

CONTENT

> HOLD UP! Is there anything I should be aware of as a reader?

Yes! Let me get you a list so you know what you're getting into:

This is an MMFMMM, a scent matched pack including a male omega who is a part of the scent match.

Home invasion, stuffing omegas in metal vaults for their own safety, somewhat consensual kidnapping, and stalkers.

References of human trafficking and backstory of sexual assault entirely off-screen.

> Anything else?

Not quite done! Discussion of infertility and a woman's role in society but without touching on grief associated with infertility. Gun and knife violence. References to murder of omegas. PTSD and grief.

Also for spice tastes: there are group scenes, MM, and spanking.

Oh, also! I write in British English (Realize/realise) I was born in England and now live in Canada. Sometimes my language and dialogue has some funky flavour (I've given up fighting it)

Cheerio, let's have a cuppa, eh bud?

...

Thanks for giving this book a shot, and enjoy the ride!

ONE

ONYX

You truly are your own worst enemy, Onyx.

My dad's warning felt far too prophetic right now. I sat in the backseat. A folder stuck from the emerald handbag I clutched to my chest as my driver pulled away from the Institute.

"There's been a mistake." The words rang in my head.

It had taken me too long to come, and now that I had, I wish I'd never risked it because the plan had worked so perfectly it was almost laughable. Until it hadn't.

I'd found a scent match.

Detective Ash's last piece of advice wasn't something I'd been able to shake. *It's not a problem you can throw money at. You need to find a pack, a scent match, if possible, so they will claim you even if they learn the truth.*

I didn't need to see the text to remember it. The message was burned into my brain. And I'd done it. Against all of my instincts, all of my better judgement, against the weight of the guilt dogging me, I'd done it.

That text from Detective Ash had been sent a week ago. I'd

spent every night warring with guilt, terrified of turning the corners in my own house, terrified every time I entered a room with a light off until finally, I cracked.

And so there'd I'd been, just moments ago in the Valentine Division's lobby tapping my heel anxiously as I waited. I was due the report on the scent I'd identified—the pack I'd just *damned*—when a mousy-haired beta approached and said the thing that had turned my day upside down. No. My *life* upside down.

"A mistake?" I'd asked, mind reeling. What could that mean? "I *know* they were a match."

I'd been in a room with so many scents, and one had called to me. It had been unmistakable. *Could I have been wrong?* For a moment, the relief almost choked me.

It was wrong of me to come here. Cruel and selfish. I dug manicured nails into my favourite emerald purse and I almost reached for the little pocket within.

"C-correct ma'am." The woman before me wrung her fingers anxiously, her face pale. "The mistake wasn't whether or not you got a match."

"What other possible mistake could there be?" I had what I came for. Now I just needed what was inside that file she was so desperately clutching.

A pack was in there, waiting. I'd only been exposed to packs who found my other ailment acceptable, though that particular *issue* was one the Institute was all too aware of.

But also it meant the pack in that file might actually... *want* me.

I wanted to stand, but I couldn't move as I stared up at her. "Tell me."

She swallowed, a shaky hand patting her pencil skirt flat as she searched for the words. "Well..." She took a breath. "Our pack database is broad. We keep scents from all over—not just the ones from eligible packs looking for an omega—"

"What happened?" I snapped, panic rising in my chest.

"It seems there was a mix-up."

"A mix-up how?"

"The scent you matched with. It wasn't supposed to be in that room."

"What other kinds of pack scents do you have here?"

Scent matching was a strange thing that no one quite understood. It was theorised each omega had many potential scent matches across the globe—something about chance and proximity. But the moment either pack or omega experienced a complimentary scent, it locked in. That was it. Fated mates. I wouldn't get a scent match with any other pack.

With money like I had, I could pay for the Institute's special database in hopes of finding a pack closer to my status.

I was playing the odds.

"It's like fingerprinting, ma'am. When packs have a history in the system, we log them. The vial was mixed up with another database."

"Another database?" My voice was weak.

The woman nodded.

"Which database?"

"The..." She cleared her throat, and her next words were barely a rasp. "C-criminal division, ma'am."

I stared at her, the words saturating my brain much too slowly. "Criminals?" I asked. "You're saying... You just exposed me to the scent of a criminal pack—and I matched them?"

The woman's mouth worked for a moment, but she settled on a quick nod.

"But... It's forever." Forever or until death. I shook my head. "Check again. There's been a mistake."

"W-we have, ma'am." Her voice had descended to nothing more than a wisp.

No. She didn't understand how much I needed this to work, this wasn't *love* or *romance*. It was blind desperation.

"I'm so sorry." Finally, the woman opened the folder before her, and from it she pulled a few photographs.

I took them from her, heart in my throat.

They looked... Well, they looked exactly as I had expected a pack of convicts to look. There were three of them, each wildly different, and none looked like the kind of alpha I would go near.

Malakai St. James

King Hansen

Arsenal Gray

Small, as packs went.

Malakai had mid-brown skin with black eyes and his dark hair was tied up in a bun. He had a slender face of sharp angles and his nose was strong and straight. His head was tilted back just slightly and he looked bored.

King had tan skin, a blond sweep of hair with contrasting dark brows and a nose that could only be described as cute. Even in this shot, he managed to look pretty, but the expression in his sharp green eyes was drawn and dead.

Arsenal's skin was pale, and he had a wide set to his jaw, a strong nose, and dark hair that swung just to his brows. His tattoos stretched up his neck, a few reaching his face. There was a downward arrow beside his ear and a tattooed cross just beside his temple. His lip was curled just slightly in the photo, a half snarl for the camera.

"What did they do?" I asked. The woman's face, if possible, went even paler. "I... I'm not supposed to say."

"You can't tell me?"

"And I'll need... them back—the pictures. I shouldn't really have shown you at all."

"What?" I asked, trying to keep up. "Part of the package I purchased was a folder with my match's information."

"R-right, but this pack wasn't registered in our Valentine System. They didn't consent to have their information handed out."

"You just matched me with a pack of criminals, and now you won't tell me anything about them?"

"It would be a violation of their rights—"

"*Their* rights?" I could hear the edge of panic in my voice. "You just stole my chance at protec—at a pack. I'll never match another."

Primal terror was seeping into my blood, the world suddenly dizzying. I didn't realise I'd gotten to my feet, my aura leaching out into the small room. The woman's mouth dropped open as I stepped toward her, and I had no idea what my expression might look like right now. She barely fought me when I grabbed the folder, only holding on for the briefest moment.

"You're really not supposed to..." She trailed off as a low growl rose in my throat, and then the folder was in my hands and I was striding from the room. There was no security—I was an omega after all, not an alpha—and the exit was just around the corner.

"I have to report this—" Her voice carried after me. I spun on her before catching myself.

"Yes, you do need to report this. And make sure to mention my lawyer will be in touch."

I slammed the door and fled.

Now I was home, leaning on my balcony as dusk crept across the cloudy sky. The file was open with all the details I wasn't supposed to have.

Murder, armed robbery and... another murder.

The only glimmer of good news—which the woman hadn't mentioned—was that they'd not gone to prison. They'd gone to Middle Gritch Juvenile Justice Centre. The crimes they'd committed had been when they were teens. Their pack, it seemed, had met in juvie and formed after they were all released. The file had the bare bones only but, despite the crimes listed, none of them had been transferred to an adult detention centre after they came of age. That gave me hope, and I clung to it.

I teetered on the brink of the decision squaring me up. Their address was right here in front of me. They lived in the middle of the Gritch District, the most dangerous part of New Oxford.

Danger? For me right now, that word was irrelevant. There was nowhere I could tread without it following.

I turned, scanning the cold, still apartment behind me, ice creeping through my veins. I was alone, the space within designed by the best with descriptors like velvet, hand carved, marble, and leather. I'd let them get on with it. Now the space felt too big.

The mirror hanging across the open concept room reflected the duchess back at me. Tonight, my hair was sleek and dark, my lips a rich red. I held myself well. To the world, I was the ideal omega in every way but one, and, because of that, the only value I offered was when I was hanging from a muscular arm.

My phone buzzed.

I was out of time to decide; the text was from the company providing my ride, and they were here. Truthfully, I knew already what I was going to do; I'd taken the scent dampeners five minutes ago. A double dose, in fact, because I knew nothing of this pack, and I wouldn't risk them discovering what I was to them until I had more information. The dampeners were strong enough to hide something as potent as a scent match—but they'd only last a few hours. That was fine. I would be in and out.

I took a steadying breath. Even if they didn't know who I was, what I was about to do was dangerous. I hugged my purse close to my side, fingers rubbing together the interior silk to settle my heart as I left the space that no longer felt like home.

When I reached the lobby, I scanned the space for my bodyguard, Devin, a reaction of pure instinct, before I remembered.

My stomach dropped like a stone, my blood chilling.

He'd been on my payroll that night a month ago. I was with trusted company, and so I told him to go outside for a break—I knew the stress he was under. He was a single father, navigating the minefield of new information after his daughter had just perfumed as an omega. But then it had all gone wrong.

Dead...

Jumped outside the bar...

A random murder...

Except, I knew differently.

Me and Devin had been downtown last year when he'd noticed he was missing his earring. I'd laughed and given him one of mine—a golden stud. Only, he'd never taken it off. But the night after he died, I opened my jewellery box in my bedroom and found that very same earring waiting next to its pair.

I'd been called to identify his body, and sure enough, his piercing was missing. It wasn't enough of anything for the police.

But *I* knew.

I'd been alone since, too scared to hire another bodyguard.

And that had just been the beginning.

I hurried through the lobby, not meeting anyone's eyes and trying to forget how much I missed Devin striding quietly at my side. Mist hung in the night air as I stepped onto the street. Instantly, the jitter in my heart settled, and I found myself brushing the tattoo on my forearm. It was a delicate depiction of a flower, a forget-me-not taunting me with its irony for what I was missing.

I took another deep breath, inhaling the cool evening mist. With each second that passed, my fear settled. Nothing in the world could soothe my heart like the scent of icy mist.

There was only one way to tell if mates were more dangerous than the threat I was fleeing. I had a lie concocted and a fool's plan.

Tonight, I would meet them myself.

TWO

KING

The doorbell rang.

That was odd. No one used the doorbell.

I got up from the couch, not missing the look of confusion on Malakai's face as I took the three steps to the hall and made for the front door.

It was Saturday evening and we were only expecting one guest, but Riot *certainly* didn't use the doorbell.

Or did he? Maybe to off-balance us? Seemed a little unnecessary for a man like him. I opened the door to a woman who looked a million miles from home.

"Uh..." I stared at her, losing my words for a moment. My mind was reeling. She... was captivating.

She had on a dark trench coat and heeled boots. Glossy brown hair was tucked behind her ears and covered with a black woollen hat. She had a large, jade purse clasped in her hands, and I could see a folder sticking out of the top of it.

It was her eyes that caught me, though. Bright sapphires that held mine with confidence as she smiled, removing a glove and holding a dainty hand out.

"Veronica Smith," she said. "I'm here for a building inspection."

I stared at her, eyebrow raised. There was no way. The perfect nails and the general... put-togetherness of her just didn't quite scream building inspector to me.

She was a beta, I thought, though I couldn't scent much on her at all. It wasn't unusual for even betas to use scent dampeners on this side of town, though.

"At this time?" I asked, trying to pull myself together. I felt like I was free falling into those sapphire eyes with their much too alluring lashes.

She frowned, and it was just the slightest downturn of her rosy lips. This might be the most beautiful woman I've ever looked at. That thought came as a shock. I'd never been into the rich-girls-with-heels type. Far from it, actually. But then again, it was safe to say I probably hadn't ever had a good sample size in the shit-hole I called home. I was quite sure, right now, that I'd been missing out on something.

"Right." I cleared my throat. I had to say something comprehensible. What had she wanted? An inspection? "We actually can't right now. We have a visitor coming in an hour."

It wasn't just important, it would be dangerous for anyone to get caught with us when Riot arrived.

"Oh." She swallowed, then her voice dropped. "I could be quick. I just got this job, they said this area doesn't get looked at much..." She hugged her handbag to her side, looking up at me with hopeful eyes. I rubbed my jaw, unable to drag my gaze from hers. "Uh..." The others would be so pissed... But they didn't get what it was like to start a job, desperate to impress. And her put-togetherness was over the top for a place like this. How badly did she need this job? "You have to be quick, and I warn you, it's a mess."

She rewarded me with a smile enough to steal my breath.

I led her in, and she stepped by our mess of shoes carefully as she peered around at the cement walls that closed in the hallway.

She didn't take her heels off as I led her up the steps to the main room, but stopped halfway up the stairs, clutching her handbag as she stared into the space beyond. It was a bit of a tip, and probably nothing like what she expected.

"Pack lead said something about residential permits, but that was a while ago," I said. "But I'll make your life easier, it's all probably off code. You can tell 'em that, but they don't give a shit at the end of the day. Not anywhere past the railway tracks."

She was still looking into the large room. "It's... nice."

I laughed, but then realised she didn't actually look like she was joking. I glanced at the garage. It was a clutter of odd wall hangings nailed into concrete—from here I could see the old Coca-Cola poster on the wall.

The whole place was interconnected, and not built for a living space. The only separate room was the nest, which was beneath a trap door currently hidden by a small rug. Even our bedrooms weren't really rooms; they were what seemed to be old offices, tucked around corners. Then, beyond the railings and down the few steps was the workshop. We had a nice big rolling door we could crank up so people could bring their broken bikes in for fixing, but it was great during summer, too.

The ceiling was made of industrial beams above, most of the windows were too high to clean, like there'd been another floor above our heads at some point, and the kitchen was a clutter of appliances we'd managed to make fit.

"I did most of the uh... design, if you can call it that." I found myself with a lot more time than the other two with how often I was between jobs. I caught the tiny curve of a smile on her lips at that, and had to war with a juvenile elation lighting in my chest.

"What's this?" Arsenal stood from where he was working in the shop, peering over the ledge from which railings separated the living space.

"Says she's an inspector."

"Why did you let her in this late?" Arsenal demanded, tools clanging before he took the steps to the main floor.

Veronica collected herself. "It's really quite important—"

"Make it quick. We got a visitor in an hour. You can't be here." He was glaring at me, though.

"He won't be here for a bit..." I trailed off, scratching my head. Shit.

But Riot wouldn't be early, right?

"Of course," she said. "Right, well, when was your last inspection?" Her manicured nails thumbed her pen.

"Five years ago," Arsenal grunted.

"Okay..." She scratched something on a notepad, and then looked around again.

Arsenal had a snarl on his face as he jabbed his finger at me and mouthed, 'you *idiot*'.

But it was at that moment that the trapdoor opened, and Ice decided to surface from his nest. He didn't even look our way, heading over to the kitchen for a snack.

"Oh, who's that?" Veronica asked. Her eyes were trained on Ice, who was rummaging around in the kitchen, shifting one stack of dirty dishes onto the next, looking for something.

"Ice," I replied.

"I put it away," Arsenal snapped across the space. "Before you get any ideas." Ice didn't turn, lifting his middle finger at us all as he dropped the metal pans with a clatter.

I snorted. Couldn't have a knife out in our own pad, not even just for cutting up a goddamned apple.

Ice scowled, nose crinkling in that irritable way that I might find endearing if it wasn't always parcelled with his attitude. He grabbed his tub of ice cream from the freezer and skulked to the couch to devour it.

"You... have an omega?" Veronica's voice had an edge to it.

"Yup." I said, glancing back at her. She was staring at Ice, bottom lip caught in her teeth, her brows drawn in a perfectly mesmerising frown.

"Why?" Arsenal asked. "Do we need a special zoning permit for rodents?"

I winced. Could they not keep it together while she was here? What was she going to think of us?

But she'd barely reacted, her eyes still fixed on Ice.

ONYX

They had an omega.

Ice.

And he was beautiful. Much too beautiful.

He was tall for an omega, with a slender frame, pale skin, and a sweep of messy ash blond hair. He had a scattering of golden piercings along his ears and wore a crinkled button-up with the sleeves rolled up and buttons undone half way. With him came the sweet aroma of cookies and roses. None of that was what caught me. He had a golden ring around his pupils and it marked him gold pack as much as the bite on his neck marked him theirs.

Gold pack omegas were bottom rung in society. They were omegas who hadn't gone to the Institute within the first year of perfuming. On that visit, omegas would get an injection. Fail to do so, and the ring of gold appeared in their eyes at the one year mark. Those omegas weren't bound to the laws that kept society safe, and, as a result, they were also expelled from the protections the Institute offered alphas and omegas. In short—this omega was an outcast. Unprotected.

And as a member of the pack already, he was my mate as much as they were.

My eyes slid down to the bite mark again. It *was* a normal bond—had to be, since I had scent matched them. Plus, it didn't have the signature darker scarring of a dark bond. Those were bonds of control, and dark bonding a gold pack omega was completely legal.

That was a good sign, though? If he didn't have a dark bond...

Only... what had their *pack lead* just said about him? I couldn't have heard it right.

I glanced back at Arsenal. He was much more intimidating than King; built like a tank, with a few more face tattoos since the photo I'd seen, with what looked like it might be a permanent scowl on his face and a sweep of dark hair brushing his eyebrows. His scent was subtle right now, not a contender with the roses and cookies of the omega in the room, but I could pick out honeyed chestnuts. *Not* suited for an alpha who'd just called his own omega a *rodent.*

"That's... very inappropriate." My voice was weak.

Ice looked over sharply and his eyes locked on me, seeing me for the first time. I held his curious gaze for a long moment, just as Arsenal said, "You know who's inappropriate? The aura gods when they decided that little shit should be an omega."

"*You* chose to bond him."

Ice hopped up from the couch to perch on its arm, eyes darting back and forth between us curiously. Arsenal looked like he might crack his tooth with the clench of his jaw. "We did at that, didn't we?"

"The bond isn't registered," I said. There'd been nothing in the file about Ice.

"Registered?" Arsenal barked a laugh. "The Institute and us aren't exactly on the best terms."

"It's technically illegal—"

"Listen, lady. I don't know what it's like where you come from, but around here, no one bothers much with the Institute because the Institute doesn't bother much with us. You're here to inspect, right?" Arsenal waved at the massive room. "Inspect away, and keep your nose out of our pack business."

My pulse skittered through my veins as I glanced back around the room.

An omega?

At the Institute, I'd requested only packs without another omega. But then... the reasons for that didn't apply here, did they?

Still, I couldn't think straight. It felt like they were all staring at me, and suddenly this place, and their scents, were overwhelming. I took a step back, almost bumping into King, who was still hovering at my side. Perhaps my distress was showing on my face, because King said, "Don't mind them, they're just—"

"If she wants to leave, let her leave," Arsenal snapped.

"He's right," I cleared my throat, strengthening my voice. "I should go."

King's beautiful emerald eyes regarded me with perfect concern and I felt myself caught by them. His scent of apricots and champagne was soothing. It was high end, too. There were alphas in my circles who would kill for a scent like that. Even his voice was low and melodic and much too attractive.

But this man was a murderer.

I knew that. Yet, everything I'd read on that file had crumbled the moment the door had opened and I'd met them. I should leave. Now.

This was too much.

Arsenal was a prick, that much I was sure of, but King? I was drawn to him, dangerously so. And Ice... the golden-eyed omega who I couldn't even stand to glance at for how my heart sped up.

For as long as I could remember, alphas had been a means to an end. Because of that, I hadn't been prepared for my own reaction.

"You think you have enough to keep them happy?" King asked, eyes darting to the notebook. I nodded, a little caught up by the fact that he seemed completely invested in my venture to impress my new fake boss in my new fake job.

Really not what I'd expected.

I nodded.

"Good," Arsenal muttered. "Out, before—"

There was a loud bang at the door.

Everyone froze.

"Fuck..." King muttered, turning to Arsenal. "It can't be him. He said it would be an hour..."

"What?" My voice was higher pitched at their clear nerves, but they weren't paying any attention to me.

"What do we do?" King demanded.

"Vault," Arsenal muttered. "No choice."

"Vault?" My voice was high pitched. King was crossing to the kitchen, though, ripping a drawer open and grabbing a key. "What do you mean?"

"Just until he's gone."

Ice's eyes were wide as he glanced between us. For a moment, I had to contain myself, my aura almost leaching out into the room—though all that would do was burn through the dampeners I'd taken.

Arsenal had me by the arm and was dragging me across the room.

"Hey!" I tried to rip free, but he didn't let up.

"For your own safety." King's expression was apologetic. "I swear, it's better this way." The next thing I knew he was opening the door that was tucked into the kitchen wall. Behind it was a big metal crate.

My blood went cold.

"What the hell is—?"

"You have to hide. Just for a bit, okay?" King said. "The guy outside, if he sees a lass like you in our pad he'll get all the wrong ideas.

"No, *wait*—I'll leave—"

"Too late," Arsenal growled.

"I can't..." Terror saturated my voice. I threw myself against Arsenal's grip, but it was completely useless.

"Really sorry." King winced as Arsenal shoved me into the enclosed dark space. "It's for your own safety."

"Wait—" I tried to launch myself at the open door, but Arsenal shoved me back in. "NO!" My voice was a scream.

SLAM!

I was left, braced against the door, chest heaving.

A faint flickering light sent an unpleasant haze of dim light around me. Other than that, the small space was empty.

A box.

They'd put me in a box.

How long would they leave me in here?

And my scent dampeners? How long before they wore off?

I hugged my purse, sinking down to the floor, trying to stifle my whimper.

I needed to stay calm or I'd burn through the drugs. If that happened, the moment they opened the door all they'd realise that the woman in their box, who now smelled like brownies and lavender, was their scent match after all.

THREE

MALAKAI

What. The. Fuck?

"Why the hell is that woman in our fucking pad right before—?"

"I thought—She just... Shit..." King looked uncertain. "I don't know what I was thinking."

"Not with your head," Arsenal snapped. *"Ice!"*

For once in his life, Ice didn't argue with Arsenal. In fact, the slender omega was already halfway to his nest. He hoisted the trap door and vanished inside. I crossed the room to it and shifted the rug over the trap door. Riot knew we had an omega, but we weren't giving him extra details if we could help it. Ice was on the same page—no one in their right minds crossed Riot if they didn't have to.

And shit, if he caught that petite, fancy looking 'inspector' woman in our house when he visited, Riot sure as shit wouldn't chalk it up to coincidence.

I'd only caught a glimpse of her for a moment, an *image* of pretentiously well-dressed panic as Arsenal had shoved her into the vault.

Tonight's meeting was causing me more anxiety than I'd admit, but I take one fucking night to plug in to an old game to de-stress before the most important meeting we'd had in years, and *everything* went to shit. So now we had one of the most notorious criminals in the city on our doorstep, and a woman locked in our vault.

Fucking great.

And Riot wasn't someone to be fucked with. Everyone was fucking terrified of him. He had dirt on half the city, enough of it to turn top-siders bottom and launch bottom-siders top. When he chose to drop a bomb, you could be sure as shit that's exactly what happened.

Better for her that she wait it out, even if she didn't know it.

"Fucking idiot," Arsenal muttered. "What the fuck was he thinking letting her in?"

"He wasn't," I snorted. "Just saw a pair of pretty blue eyes and lost his last brain cells."

Riot's booted footfalls hit the steps as he entered our garage.

He was a huge alpha, wearing his signature trench coat which hooded his face almost half way. His scent hit the room in an instant, even though his aura wasn't out.

Burned ebony and gunpowder.

Riot wasn't just a threat: he was uncomfortable to examine. What he'd done, who he had become, it didn't make anyone want to consider too long. Especially not us: alphas and ex-cons to boot.

"You know what you need?" Arsenal was asking Riot. He could do what we wanted, but he'd been holding out on telling us if there was something we could offer him in return.

Riot rolled the cigarette in his teeth as he dug in his pocket, smoke billowing around him. "Institute check soon, yeh?"

Arsenal nodded. "In nine days." We were required by Institute law to go for our last yearly check in with the Institute—part of our 'rehabilitation' program after juvie.

"That goes into a computer in the criminal division. Don't care how," he said.

I stared at the tiny black USB he was holding between his fingers.

"That's it?" Arsenal asked, mirroring my thoughts exactly.

It was less work than I was expecting. Sure. We'd be right back to prison if we failed, but I hadn't expected any request Riot had to be above board. What he could offer us, it was worth that a thousand times. King slid onto the barstool at Arsenal's side, eyeing the USB Riot still held.

Riot cocked his head, bright eyes fixed on Arsenal from beneath his hood. He didn't say anything else.

"Done. But we can't change the date of our check in," Arsenal said. Riot watched him, waiting. "Your end gets done before that."

I didn't hold my breath. Sure enough, Riot flashed his teeth. "Nah, see, that won't work for me."

"We need—"

"I know what you need." Riot's eyes flickered to the rug that covered Ice's trapdoor. My stomach turned, and I felt the shift of discomfort through my bond with Arsenal and King.

"You don't trust we'll do it?" Arsenal asked.

"Don't take it personal."

A long silence stretched.

I might have asked why he'd come in person for something so simple, but I already knew the answer. Riot didn't get where he was by letting others be his eyes. He was more limited these days, I knew, but for whatever reason he'd decided this job was worth the visit. Either he considered us a threat, or this job was very important. I would guess the latter. My pack weren't trouble-makers in the Gritch District.

Even if we were, we'd do nothing about this visit.

The Institute wanted him detained, but it wasn't happening. Last month a pack had tried to rat on him when he'd turned up at their door. No one responded to the call, and Riot had walked away without a scratch. The next morning the pack woke to their omega gone. She'd turned up in their own basement nailed to the wall, a dead rodent jammed down her throat. She'd died slowly and painfully and right beneath their noses.

I shut my eyes, shoving the thought away.

I wouldn't survive that.

None of us would.

Shattered bonds, even under normal circumstances, were enough to drive anyone insane. Sure enough, three days later, the rest of the pack had been found dead, shot by their own pack lead before he'd taken the gun to his own head.

No. We had no intention of getting on his bad side. Although he might have proven himself a monster, he wasn't a liar, and if he said he could get us what we needed, then he could. We did what he wanted, kept it clean, then he wasn't a threat.

"Anything else?"

"Nah. That's all." He straightened.

"The USB?" Arsenal asked.

"This thing is too valuable. I'll drop it back here in a few days."

"When?" Arsenal demanded.

Riot didn't answer. When he passed, he clapped King on the shoulder. "Night, lads."

The tension in the room vanished the moment the front door closed.

"That's all he wants?" King asked.

I shrugged. "Not a small ask. Think about it. Might be easy for us, but the Institute's a fortress. The Institute only lets us in because we've never violated our terms. We're perfect choices."

King still looked a little pale as I walked over to Ice's nest door and stomped on it a few times.

"Right." King looked back at us. "Ready to deal with her wrath?"

Fuck. What the hell was up with that? I still didn't know the whole story.

We'd heard nothing from the woman locked in our vault; with the second door closed, it was completely soundproof.

"Give it a few minutes," Arsenal sighed. "Don't want her storming out and Riot seeing her anyway."

I was still stuck on the job. It felt too easy. I didn't care how much it made sense; it was impossible to look at the deal Riot had just offered, and not be suspicious. What he said he'd do, it was everything. It was a new start.

There had to be a trick. The universe was never that kind.

VIPER

I had lost.

I was a broken alpha. My pack bonds had been shattered, and my once-mate had long forgotten me.

Right now, I sipped an energy drink in the old car, a finished noodle box from a nearby takeout at my side as I watched a rundown garage poorly lit by flickering street lamps.

Onyx was in there right now.

The woman I loved.

The woman who didn't remember me.

There was no way for me to know if she was safe, but I only had four days left, and today everything had gone all wrong.

Money wasn't an issue. I'd picked the car up in an old lot today, knowing it wouldn't stick out in the Gritch District. I had her electronics covered. My hacker, Kai, was on it. He was good, not to mention all I could find without my father discovering what I was doing. Discretion was necessary, because if my father so much as heard Onyx's name, this would all be over. I wouldn't survive it, not this time. Or worse, *she* wouldn't survive it.

But Kai's pack owed me, and it was the only sure thing I had on my side. He had her phone, laptop, and the surveillance cameras in her house locked down. The problem was, this stalker ruining her life, he was good. Good enough that he hadn't found a trace of anything. My skin prickled at the thought of him, my aura wanting out like a storm shuttering old, worn windows.

It had been like that all day, ever since Kai had found an update I hadn't been expecting. She had gone to the Institute to match a pack.

I wanted to be sure she was safe, so finding out she was actively searching for a match... I could shove back the part of me aching for blood, desperate and furious at me for letting her go. I could focus on the reality that when I was gone, there would be no one else to look out for her.

I read the updates as Kai sent them. I knew the candidates the Institute had offered, and I knew the mistake they'd made with the vial.

I knew that Onyx was now trapped between two impossible choices.

She had pushed away everyone after the accident, focusing on nothing but her job. She had no one watching out for her, no one but me. Now threats were closing in, and my time was running out.

"You burned down the Oxford mansion." My father was a tall, slender man wearing a neat, dark suit as he rested against the wooden countertop in my kitchen, setting a bottle down. He didn't fit here. He was wealth personified, and this place—this was a place money couldn't touch.

Behind me, two of his thugs took up the doorway. I barely spared them a second glance.

"You tried to buy me into a pack with a dark bonded omega," I snarled. "It was fucked up and I was never going to—"

"That's not your problem, Viper." My father's sharp voice cut me off. "Whether the omega was dark bonded? No. You've sabotaged every attempt I have made to set you back on the right path. This is the last straw."

"What are you going to do now?" I tried not to let on how much I had been dreading the answer. I knew I was out of chances. "Have you found another terrorised omega you want me to bond with?"

My father just stared at me coldly. "I booked you a flight to England."

I paused, having not expected that. "I won't get on it."

"You will." He plucked a stem of lavender from the pot on the window. I watched him, stifling a growl, my heart racing. "Or I'll be forced to change tact." He snapped the flower in two.

I took a step toward him, a snarl on my face, but the two brutes in the doorway shifted forward, drawing me up. "You won't go near her." My voice was low.

I'd known that this would be the outcome one day.

"Board the plane, Viper, and never come back."

"Don't make me leave this place." This house—small and worthless to someone like my father—was everything. But he knew he'd won. That he was the one threat I wouldn't be able to protect her against. "It's mine," I rasped. It was theirs as well, not just mine. The pack that now existed only in black ink upon the arm of a woman who remembered them no more.

Remembered me no more.

But I'd stayed for them all. Hart had been left the house by his grandparents. His family wasn't rich like mine, but this place was everything we wanted.

Everything she wanted.

"And the Oxford mansion...?" My father said, tugging a match box from his pocket and knocking over the bottle he'd brought. Clear *liquid spilled onto the wooden floors as he struck a match. I stared at it, confused until I caught the powerful scent of gasoline.*

"NO!"

My aura struck the air, but the two thugs were ready and I barely made it a step.

I was too late.

The match tumbled to the ground as my father strode past where I was being held back, speaking to me as he passed. "The Oxford mansion was mine."

The memory shook me to the core. I blinked away the rest of it. The pain as I'd twisted my arm free from the bodyguards' grip and crashed into the cottage. The way the smoke burned my lungs, aura shivering in the air around me, threatening to get away.

Danger, it whispered.

It was broken. Strength and endurance. That's what an aura was made of. I had one half left, but if I overused that strength, I might not survive the aftermath.

I hadn't cared as I'd shoved through burning wood and creaking walls desperate for... For *what?* My knees crashed to the floor, my vision blurring. I was too late.

Too late, again.

For them.

For her.

I'd lost. My father had finally won.

So I was left with four days to rid New Oxford of anything that threatened her before boarding that plane and removing the final danger she didn't even know she faced.

It was late. I wasn't very good at this whole... surveillance thing. Not in real life.

But I had to know she was safe, and I didn't care what it cost me. There was nothing left for me to claim from this world, but she deserved happiness.

Kai had pulled up every scrap of information he could on the pack Onyx had matched with, apparently not a huge task, since he and one of his packmates had grown up in this area and knew of Arsenal Gray.

On the seat beside me was his folder with all the gritty details.

Each of them had been bundled into a juvenile detention centre before they hit 18, which—it appeared—was where they'd met. After release, they'd packed up.

But their pasts weren't pretty, and Onyx was still in that building with them. Again, I glanced down at the papers, rifling through them like they might offer me some comfort.

King Hansen: Incarcerated at fourteen years old for murdering his twin sister. King was found beside her body and confessed at the scene.

Malakai St.James: Incarcerated at the age of fifteen for armed robbery. Kai's scrawl across the page read *'Classic Harpy Gang: He fucked up, they cut him loose'*.

Arsenal Gray: Incarcerated at twelve years old for losing control of his aura and killing one of his pack fathers. The body was almost unrecognisable after being bludgeoned repeatedly with multiple blunt kitchen objects, including an iron.

There were more bits and pieces. A long list of jobs they'd taken after release, most short-lived—their past catching up to them. Kai had also added another little tidbit that grated a little every time I looked at it.

Upon his release at eighteen, King was welcomed back into society with the Steamy Aura's Weekly Vote: New Oxford's Hottest Bad Boys.

I was drawn from that thought as I saw another figure approaching the garage. It was a tall man wearing a trench coat and hood. He took the steps before tugging a hand from his pocket and banging loudly on their front door.

He entered and I waited.

Could it be one of the pack members returning home?

I glanced around the street. It was quiet, flickering streetlamps illuminated cracked pavement and graffiti. For a brief moment, my gaze snagged on my own face in the mirror of the car. My dark hair was buzzed short, and I wore an oversized hoodie that covered most of it. My skin was sallow against sharp cheekbones and there were bags beneath my bright yellow eyes—the colour that had given me my name.

Would Onyx have even been capable of loving what I'd become?

Nothing.

Hollow.

Silent.

I dropped my gaze to the old tattoos that wound up my fingers as I tapped the steering wheel.

A tiny little heart blurred on my knuckle, tucked into the design.

Her addition.

She'd wanted to get tattoos together that day. That was so, so long ago now...

A long time passed, and I turned on the car's engine to run to heat up, only for all of the vents to choke up the space with burned dust. Coughing, I rolled the windows down for a moment to vent the space. After that, it took a while for the car to heat up in earnest.

The tall, trench-coat man left, gravel crunching under his boots as he slipped away in the night. A visitor then?

I waited.

She had to come out soon. Not that I could do anything, unless she was in real danger. She could never see my face.

I hadn't slept properly for days, not since I learned my flight was booked, and the warmth of the car was getting to me. I had to drag my eyes open a few times.

Where was she?

Was it possible she wouldn't come out? That she'd taken one look at them and fallen in love?

I hugged my propped up knee to my chest, fighting the hammering panic in my chest at that thought.

If that happened, Onyx would have finally replaced me completely.

FOUR

ONYX

Scent blockers and adrenaline didn't mix. Adrenaline had a tendency to burn away the drug like salt in water. Even trying my best to remain calm, I dreaded that my own scent was rising in the small space.

I sunk down once more in the dim light of the pale bulb above, my handbag in the crook of my arm as I ran my fingers along the silk that lined it for comfort. With my other hand I traced the lines upon my forearm.

A scar and a forget-me-not.

Over and over I followed them, the stems, the leaves, the petals, and then the thin silver line of a scar down my arm at the forget-me-knot's side.

The longer the time stretched, the more I traced the lines, desperate not to think about what would happen when the door opened. Finally, after what felt like hours, I heard a faint bang outside. Then the sound of creaking metal.

Okay.

I dragged myself to my feet. The blockers... Perhaps they

hadn't worn off completely. I could just slip by them and leave straight away.

If I told them I was afraid, I could ask them to stay back so I could leave.

That would be reasonable. They had to listen.

Right. *Says the woman shoved into a metal box.*

They were clearly *super* reasonable human beings.

Brighter light from the garage beyond flooded the space, and it was King that met me, along with his heavy scent of apricots and champagne.

Fuck.

His mouth dropped open and his eyes widened.

"Fuck... me."

I was pressed into the far corner, but clearly it wasn't enough to stop the very thing I feared.

"Shit." His hiss was low, but carried to me all the same. "Oh... *Shit.*"

We stared at each other for a long, long moment.

"What's going on?" I heard a voice call.

I shook my head desperately. He collected himself enough to reply. "They're going to know. Your perfume is *heavy*."

I swallowed.

It was over.

I'd just... wanted to come to see them. I hadn't considered the possibility that they might find out. It wasn't just embarrassing, it was dangerous. They were a pack of alphas with no obvious regard for laws. Alphas like that sometimes let their possessive sides go too far.

King registered the terror on my face. "You're going to be okay."

I heard Ice's voice closer now. "What are you on ab—?" He cut off as his figure appeared behind King.

His mouth fell open.

"Fuck. Me." Ice sounded as dumbstruck as he looked. He didn't look like he could find the words as he stared at me. His pupils had blown, clearly tense.

It was over. The last shred of my denial crumbled away.

Then Arsenal appeared, tugging the door open. They were all staring at me like a rabbit in a cage. A rabbit that also scared them a little.

"Alright, back up, you oafs." Ice shoved Arsenal and King away.

"But..." King couldn't take his eyes from me. "Not... possible."

Arsenal hadn't said a thing. His eyes were fixed on me, his mouth still parted slightly. Ice, who was clearly paying more attention to my discomfort, closed a fist around Arsenal's sleeve.

"Give her some fucking space. All of you. Back the fuck up," Ice hissed.

"What is going on?" It was a new voice, and it came with an earthy aroma that reminded me of cloves and walks along the riverside. I wasn't in a state to be soothed, no matter the scent.

I took in the last member of the pack who was leaning against one of the pillars at the edge of the kitchen.

He was tall, with mid-brown skin and his black hair was tied up in a bun. I recognised Malakai from the picture, but in real life he was show stopping. Now he was here, I identified the last scent in the garage: riverside and clove.

It was lovely.

I didn't know if it was the hormones colliding with panic, but I had to catch a laugh from bubbling up my throat at the wild thought that popped into my mind as I stared at him. He'd have a 20 foot wing-span—at *least*—if he were a character in the magical books I read before bed. Just missing the strange coloured eyes. He *would* look good with purple, though. I think I had one in my handbag right now to compare descriptions—

"A mate?" Malakai demanded, turning on Arsenal and King.

"Why the fuck is our mate in our vault, and no one decided to mention it."

The word mate seemed to drop the reality right on Arsenal's head. He turned on Malakai. "We didn't fucking know when we shoved her in there."

"We don't have time for a—"

"Don't you think I know that?" Arsenal snarled.

Those words were an irrational blow that snapped me back to myself.

Right.

"I should go." But the moment I made a move, every eye in the room snapped to me.

Shit.

This was why this had been a dangerous plan. Of course, it would be illegal for them to keep me here against my will, but I didn't exactly know them as law-abiding citizens.

Society could dress it up as much as it wanted to—civilised we were, and refined. In control, so says the Institute. But right now that was stripped away. I was an omega facing up against three massive alphas, who had all just realised I was their mate.

I saw a flash of something in Arsenal's eyes that had me taking another step back. It was gone in a moment. Same with the others. King took a step away from me, as if to give me space, but he looked wounded.

"Wait." It was Ice that spoke first, moving around King to take a step toward me. "Could you… stay a bit. Just let us figure it out."

"Figure what out?" My mouth was dry.

"Veronica—"

"It's Onyx," I corrected Ice before I could stop myself. "Onyx Madison."

"Right. We believe you this time," Arsenal said, the darkness in his eyes from more than the raven sweep of hair shadowing them.

I should be backing out of the door right now, but instead I was fumbling in my bag. I found my wallet and tugged out a card, handing it to him. He scowled down at it. I didn't realise until too late that it was the Elite Valkyrie membership card that were handed out selectively. Oh dear... That made it look like I was bragging.

"A duchess?" Arsenal looked up at me, incredulous. "You're a fucking *duchess*?"

Shit.

"I..."

Dammit.

People didn't trust me when they found out I was a duchess. It was more than just a job, it was my title, and my aura carried evidence of that.

This was spiralling out of control.

"I... am, yes," I tried for more confidence this time as the elephant landed squarely in the room as my second chance mates —something most omegas never got—stared back at me, stunned.

A duchess was an omega who'd rejected her mates.

MALAKAI

Two weeks.

Two weeks we had to survive without doing anything to piss off the universe.

I'd expected a curveball, but the ashen-faced duchess in the middle of our oil stained disaster of a garage—well, *that* was beyond what even my cynical brain could have conjured up.

"Why are you here?" I asked.

"Why?" She looked startled.

"We're—"

"Scent matches. Right." I cut her off. "But why did you come? We'd have never found you if you didn't."

Scent matches or not, no woman from the other side of the tracks would willingly hunt down a pack like us. At least not one in her right mind.

King glanced between us, trying to figure me out. His bond was wide open in invitation. I took a breath, opening up mine, knowing all they would get from me was my unease and suspicion.

Onyx jumped at a loud clatter in the kitchen.

What the *fuck* was Ice doing? A filthy stack of pans almost toppled onto him as he wrestled a mug from its midst. It was bloody distracting. We needed to deal with *her* right now, not put teapots on to boil.

Our mate. A fucking rich duchess.

Onyx set her purse on the table, then straightened her top carefully before meeting our eyes. She was thrown off—this night was clearly going about as well for her as it was for us. Still, she levelled us all with gazes as if we were misbehaving school children.

"You're my mates. I don't take that lightly."

Arsenal snorted, drawing all eyes to him—well, all but Ice—who was currently rinsing the mug out in the sink.

"Is that so, *Duchess*?" Arsenal's voice dripped with sarcasm. I didn't blame him. If there was any omega in the world I'd believe put less stock in mates, it was a duchess. A duchess omega was born of declining a princess bond. Rejecting her mates. But then... that begged the question; how had she matched with us if she already had mates? The only way she would have another chance, was if the last pack were—

"Think we'll be an easy catch?" Arsenal's voice halted my thoughts. "Looking to double your title?"

A flicker of fury crossed her eyes as Arsenal cracked her perfect demeanour.

"Nah. I don't think so." Arsenal didn't give her a chance to speak. "We *have* an omega. You aren't welcome—"

Arsenal cut off as Ice slammed a mug onto the counter with a snarl. If it wasn't metal, it would have shattered. "She *is* welcome."

I paused, glancing at King. I could feel his confusion through the bond. Ice didn't like visitors. He didn't like anyone.

Arsenal bristled. "Now you're fucking social?" he demanded of Ice. "I'm pack lead. She's out."

"I'm the omega. I'm *homemaker*. If I say she's welcome, she's fucking welcome."

"Homemaker?" Arsenal's hateful voice was twisted with incredulity. As if in agreement, the tower of filthy pots Ice had just agitated groaned as it swayed threateningly.

The kettle's whistle grew.

Arsenal was on the brink of losing control of his aura, we could feel it through the bond; it was why he never closed it completely. I tensed, ready to reach him if needed. Out of the corner of my eye, I saw King do the same. The teapot got louder, rattling violently as Arsenal went on, though I only caught a few words over the clamour. "You—" He jabbed a finger at Ice. "...A little rat... leeching off..."

Onyx's mouth dropped open, and she took a step back from where Arsenal stood. Ice looked furious, but he spun to grab the teapot from the burner. I'd never seen someone aggressively pour a cup of tea, but Ice managed it. Then he turned his back on Arsenal, and when he stepped toward Onyx, his whole demeanour shifted.

Ice took her hand in both of his, his touch brushing up her wrist affectionately. Despite being an omega, I'd never seen him initiate affection with anyone in his life outside of heat. "Ignore them. Sit with me?" he asked, voice gentle. Onyx might have forgotten there was anyone else in the room at all by the way she looked at him.

Worse though, was that every single one of my alpha instincts switched to overdrive when I saw the two omegas together. Something fell into place. Something that was absolutely not allowed to fall into place. We had nine fucking days to get through. No disruptions. No tempting fate. Of course, Ice didn't know about our plans with Riot, and he couldn't. But *two* omegas?

Onyx was fucking trouble. I was sure of that—as sure as I was that it was Ice who'd switched all of my dust jackets the last time I'd left the pad.

I glanced at the other two.

Arsenal's jaw ticked and King's head was cocked slightly as if puzzling out what he was looking at.

Ice led her to one of the wooden bar stools while his touch lingered on her lower back, and she didn't seem to mind at all. I couldn't stop staring. Ice moved the cup toward her and then poured his own, settling in beside her, hand still lingering on her waist as he flipped Arsenal the bird.

Arsenal looked like he was warring with himself. Ice was challenging his authority *and* ignoring us all. He could let it slide, but then... that would set a precedent for Onyx, right? But he didn't want Onyx—we *couldn't* have her. So why did he care about that?

He could chuck her out, but that would piss off Ice. Ice lived in a perpetual state of pissed off, but he did get pretty fucking nasty if he had a tantrum. Ice was capable of ruining it all before the nine days was up—even if that sabotaged it for him, too.

I sighed. What Riot offered was more important than anything we'd done. It was our ticket to freedom from this miserable fucking life.

Arsenal turned and stalked back across the garage, taking the two steps down to his space, and I heard a clatter or two as he prepped to work on his bike. I relaxed, and I felt the same from

King. Working on broken bikes unwound Arsenal better than anything else.

King shrugged, and sat back down on the couch, but I noticed he picked a spot that made it easy to eye the two omegas. I understood that. I didn't want to take my eyes off them either—but only because it was goddamned suspicious, the whole damn thing.

FIVE

ONYX

"Here's the thing," Ice said. "They're not nearly as bad as they look—even when they're in bad moods. Swear it. Bit rough around the edges, but they're good."

I clutched my mug, letting his words settle me.

The cat was out of the bag. I could stay, just for a short while.

The others had drifted off. It was me and Ice, and I felt... comfortable. I always got comments about how standoffish I was for an omega, very picky about contact, even with clients. But I didn't care one bit that Ice's hand was still lingering on my arm—in fact, goosebumps trailed up my skin every time his touch shifted. Perhaps it was because he was an omega, too? He would know the importance of touch, and I felt I could trust him with it. I hadn't been near omegas very much since the academy.

Okay. So perhaps another omega wasn't a bad thing after all.

Up close, he was even more stunning. I could see the faint blush to his cheeks and a scattering of freckles.

His hair was just long enough to tuck behind his ears, though it hung in chaotic messy waves across his face and he kept nudging it out of the way. His nose was curved, and he had cute pointed canines that flashed when he smiled. He could be a poster boy for male omegas. His outfit was... Well, it was curious. He wore light, baggy jeans, and that half unbuttoned shirt. My eyes kept getting caught on the pale skin of his chest and lines along his upper abs that the buttons revealed. It was low-key, and extremely seductive in a messy way. Everything about him was, and not just because he was an omega.

I hadn't considered the possibility of an omega mate; they were much less common, but everything about him made me feel comfortable down to his scent of roses and cookies.

"Malakai—bit of a misanthrope, but you'll get used to him," he was saying. I bit back a smile, peering back to find Malakai shooting us both a dark look from the couch, but he said nothing.

"King's got a shell, but he's a softie once you crack it. And Arsenal..." Ice trailed off, and I noticed his eyes dart toward the huge alpha, who was still working on his bike.

"What?" I asked. Had that been fear in his eyes?

"He's fine. You just gotta be careful."

"Careful how?" My voice was low.

"His aura's a bit all over the place. I mean, you know what he was in for?"

I nodded. Arsenal had one of the two murder charges.

"Well..." Ice was pale. I noticed the alphas in the room were stiff. Each was obviously paying attention. "He's fine most of the time." Ice swallowed. Had he not noticed the others were listening? He was fixed on me so intently. "You just can't always tell mid-fuck, you know, and I have a mouth on me." He lifted his top and I had to stifle my gasp, my hand jumping to my mouth. Across his rib cage were silver scars that looked like angry claw marks.

I was on my feet in a moment.

"Don't worry." Ice was much too calm as he lifted his hand. "Said it was an accident and all—"

I jumped at the sound of metal clanging on metal. Arsenal was staring over at the two of us. The tool in his hand had slipped to the floor. There was murder in his eyes—pure, unadulterated murder. Then he was making for us, a snarl in his chest.

King and Malakai were on their feet in a moment to intervene. Arsenal was fixed on Ice, though.

"You lying piece of shit!" he snarled. "I'm going to fucking kill you—"

"Oi!" King grabbed Arsenal by the shirt, blocking him. Malakai made for Ice, who staggered back, and I didn't miss the fear in his eyes. "Nest. Now!" Malakai snapped with cold eyes, looking ready to pounce.

"Hey!" I stepped between the two of them. "Don't touch him!"

Malakai glared at me and rolled his shoulders as if not sure what to do with me. *"Ice."* He spoke through gritted teeth, a warning in his tone.

Ice's breathing was ragged. Then he darted around the kitchen counter as if fleeing. Malakai shoved past me, making a break for him. Behind Malakai, Arsenal pushed King free. He cut Ice off on the other side of the island. Ice, who had been more distracted running away from Malakai, didn't see Arsenal until the alpha had him pinned against the kitchen counter. I heard the crack as Arsenal shoved him hard against a stack of old plates.

"NO!" I tried to launch after him, but Malakai caught me. Ice was tall for an omega, perhaps six foot, but Arsenal was massive, and his tattooed muscular frame dwarfed Ice's slender one.

"You lying piece of shit!" Arsenal snarled. "Take it back!" He was all but shaking Ice now.

"Let him go!" My voice was desperate, blood roaring in my ears. I couldn't think straight. This was abuse, right in front of my eyes. Did they think they could lay hands on him because he was gold pack?

"I take it back." Ice's wide-eyed gaze found mine. "I was lying."

"Arsenal!" King had a hand on Arsenal's shoulder, but his eyes were darting between the two of them, clearly confused.

Arsenal was lost to fury. "More convincing, or you're going in the vault."

"I believe him, alright!" I was still fighting to escape Malakai's grip.

"P-please," Ice choked out. "I'm sorry. D-don't put me in there." His voice cracked.

I couldn't believe what I was watching right now. I tried again to fight from Malakai's hold. To my relief, Arsenal's grip loosened as he recoiled from Ice.

"The *fuck* are you playing at?" Arsenal demanded. Ice was glancing between all the alphas now, his breathing ragged.

Then, without warning, he reached for Arsenal, drawing himself intimately close and slipping his head beneath Arsenal's chin for a moment. I felt his aura tremble in the air, his scent—roses and cookies—leaching into the space, even if it was laced with anxiety.

We all froze. Had he just... *scent marked* Arsenal? It was a desperate, vulnerable thing for him to have done, but he *was* desperate, even I could see that. Arsenal, however, let out an enraged sound. I gasped as his aura split the air. It was laced with fury and violence. King dived for him—just in time, since it looked like he was going for Ice's neck.

"Don't!" I shouted. I'd never seen an alpha respond like that to being marked by an omega. His *own* omega.

"Arsenal!" King was trying to haul Arsenal back. "Calm down!"

Arsenal's aura was thick in the air, and he barely noticed King's attempts.

"Let him go!" I begged. I couldn't see anyone but Ice and his terror.

"You don't come in here and tell us how to deal with our omega," Arsenal snarled. His aura was the most aggressive thing I'd ever felt from an alpha before. I'd been around auras, but Arsenal... His was untethered. "Get her the fuck out!"

"No!" I fought against Malakai's grip, but he was hauling me across the room. "D-don't! *Wait, just don't hurt him!*"

King had pulled him back a bit more, but Ice was still cowering. Arsenal clearly didn't want to do anything in front of me, but... what would happen the moment I was gone?

KING

The moment the door slammed, Ice went limp in Arsenal's grip. He was shaking. I rubbed my face with both hands. "Fuck."

Slowly, Ice's breathless choked laughs rose across the silent room.

"Just... fuck," I groaned, ripping Arsenal back from Ice. His grip came free with ease now. "You can't take bait like that."

Now she was gone, Arsenal looked dumbstruck, his aura vanishing as all his rage was swallowed by shock. Beyond all reason, he cared what Onyx thought. *That* much was now painfully obvious.

Well.

It was too late; she was never coming back.

Ice slipped by me, tears of mirth still rolling down his cheeks. I grabbed his shirt. "You're playing with fire, you little shit."

Ice raised his hands defensively, expression much too smug. "Hands off alphahole, or *are* you like those other lowlifes after all?" His eyes twinkled with the dare.

It was one of the things we swore to him when we bonded him: that we'd never hurt him. Easy goddamned promise—or it *should* have been. At the time, we had thought it was about self preservation. I'd since concluded it was a challenge.

Ice, it turned out, was fucking insane, and there was no bear he liked to poke more than Arsenal. The guy's aura wasn't fucking stable—we all knew that. "He *is* going to lose it one day. Pull shit like that, it'll be your fault."

Ice just grinned as he picked up the half finished mug from the table and dumped the rest in the sink.

"Go shower," I muttered to Arsenal. I could smell Ice's scent mark on him. Roses and sweet fucking cookies on steroids. Everything Ice had just done was the perfect set up. Of course Arsenal had lost it when Ice had scent marked him; we lived in a bond with an omega who didn't want us. One who took great pleasure in rubbing that in at every turn.

Sleeping with Ice's scent was fucking torture. As in 'wake up with a frustrated hard on every goddamned hour' kind of torture.

Somewhere down the line, Ice had figured that out.

"Two for two." Ice practically sang the words as he crossed toward the trapdoor and pulled the wooden hatch open.

"What?" Malakai asked, returning to the room.

Onyx was gone.

"Omegas that'll never fuck Arsenal." Ice saluted with a grin before disappearing into his nest, Onyx's empty mug clutched in his hands.

SIX

ONYX

It had been ten minutes since Malakai shoved me outside. My voice was hoarse from screaming and my fist bruised from banging on the door. I was sitting on the broken down concrete steps, hugging myself when I heard the crunch of gravel. I looked up to see a car pulling into the broad lot that surrounded the building.

I squinted at it.

A cab?

It idled, lights on as if waiting.

Finally, the door behind me opened. I jumped to my feet in an instant. "Where's Ice?"

Arsenal folded his arms, leaning against the door frame. "Why do you care?"

I took a tentative step forward, not wanting to look afraid, though my scent was likely giving me away. Everything about him was more frightening now—his massive frame, the scatterings of tattoos across his face. I spotted a knife above one of his eyebrows.

None of it mattered in the face of what I'd just seen. "If you don't let him out, I'll—"

"What?" Arsenal asked. I lost the ground I'd been making up. "Call the cops? You think they'll give a shit what's going on between us and our gold pack omega?"

I stared at him in horror. "Is it about that for you?" I asked. "Why not dark bond him then?" If they'd wanted control over their omega, they could have dark bonded him.

Arsenal snorted. "Get in the cab, Duchess, and don't come back."

I swallowed. "I won't leave until I see him."

"Not your business what goes on in my pack."

"I'll make it my business. I'll bring the press, make a—" I cut off as Arsenal straightened, closing the remaining distance between us in a moment. It took everything I had not to stumble back down the steps. I'd seen what he had just done to Ice—how unhinged he'd been.

"Bring a single eye down on my pack and it will not go well for any of us. Not you. Not me. And certainly not Ice."

A threat.

And I knew I couldn't win. They had him in here with a bond on his neck. No matter how I came at it, police or press, Arsenal would have the upper hand. He had an all male pack, and Ice was a male gold pack omega. Vilifying him to society would be all but impossible. His face was twisted in a snarl as he glared down at me.

I fought another urge to flee.

"I c-can pay you." I just had to know he was okay. I opened my purse, rummaging in it for a moment. Arsenal groaned, running his fingers through his dark hair.

"Would you just leave off—?"

"No. Here." I pushed my cash toward him. I'd almost emptied my purse before coming, knowing I shouldn't be walking around a place like this with a lot of money. "I have more. I can get it to you—"

"Put that away!" He looked startled, fist coming over mine as he tried to shove my hand back to my purse. "Can't be flashing cash like that around here. Why are you even—?" He cut off, nose wrinkled.

I frowned, looking down at the money. It was only two hundred.

"Just. Get. In. The. Cab."

"I have to know he's okay." My voice cracked despite my best effort.

Arsenal hesitated, re-evaluating me for a moment, but then he clenched his jaw and patched up his hostile expression.

"He's fine." He grabbed my wrist, dragging me unceremoniously down the last three steps before hauling me across the gravel.

"No—" I tried to rip my grip free. "That's not good enough. Let me see him."

"You're not seeing him, or any of us, ever again." He reached the cab and pulled open the door.

I grabbed his arm, furious as I stared up at him. "I won't get in."

"You *bloody* well will!" He tried to bundle me into the cab. I grabbed the edge to stop him, but he was fumbling to unhook my grip. In a panic—and all dignity forgotten—I threw myself at him, clinging onto his enormous bicep and not letting go. "Would you —? *Fuck!*"

He tried to bend down so he could pry me off while also shoving me through the door. *"NO!"* I pulled myself closer, wrapping my legs around his waist. I could barely see a thing, my hair was loose, my handbag swinging wildly from my elbow, and my world swept up in honeyed chestnuts. Angry honeyed chestnuts, if that was a thing.

"Ow! Your fucking heels—"

"Let me *see* him!" I hissed, digging my heels in harder—I wasn't sure where, either his back or ass? It was hard to tell, he was a big pillar of solid fucking muscle. I hoped the latter.

Arsenal grunted in pain, then straightened.

"Fine!" he snapped. I froze, still attached to him with less dignity than I'd displayed in years—and boy did I know some reporters that would weep if they knew the scene they were missing.

Arsenal had taken a step back from the cab, still trying to pry me off. We were far enough from the open door that I felt safe letting go.

The permanent scowl on his face was more dire than ever as he glared down at me. I recovered my balance, dragging strands of hair from my mouth. He punctuated his next sentences with a jab of his finger. "You'll come inside. You'll see he's fine. You'll leave us alone."

Relief flooded my system as Arsenal slammed the door shut. Then he moved to the open passenger's window, pulling a crumpled bill from his pocket and tossing it onto the seat. "Sorry Rob. I'll get her home myself."

I heard something from within, either a grunt or a chuckle.

Arsenal spun back on me as I was straightening my coat and fixing my hair in hopes it would calm me. My scent was mortifyingly strong. "*You* are a pain in my ass."

"Good!" I snapped.

He turned, storming toward the door and muttering something that sounded like 'omegas' and 'the death of me'.

VIPER

I was still warring with my fight with fatigue when she finally appeared again. The door opened, and I saw her first, blinking like I always did when I saw her on the off chance she would vanish from my vision. Then I straightened, a growl sounding in my chest as I saw one of the alphas—Malakai St. James—with his hands on her.

I was gripping the car door without realising, every hair on my body on end, but... he only seemed to be removing her, not hurting her.

My heart was pounding in my chest. Were they mad?

They... didn't want her?

I felt no relief. This pack *had* to work out for her.

Kai and one of his pack brothers had grown up in this area. They'd told me Arsenal Gray was a good guy growing up—he was protective, and known for looking out for vulnerable kids. The only grief the community had felt when he'd killed his father, had been at the fact he was locked up for it.

I didn't realise how much I had been leaning on that glimmer of hope until I saw Malakai slam the door in her face.

I could hear her yelling from here. Banging on the door desperately.

I stared, unsure what to make of any of it. It went on for a while until she finally slumped down on the steps, leaning into the door, head resting on the railing as she buried her face in her hands.

She was in pain.

The world blurred, time flickering, my aura straining to be free.

I was outside my car, the door wide open, and three strides toward her before I drew up.

I forced myself back.

One.

Two.

Three paces.

She *couldn't* see me. It would destroy her. Everything she'd built. Every step she'd taken from the moment that still held my world in a vice.

I got back into the car, breathing shaky as I closed the door, then locked it, as if that would matter.

From there, I watched and waited.

Until a taxi arrived, and then another of the alphas appeared.

At that point, I cracked the window, enough to overhear the conversation. "...Just *get* in the cab!" the alpha—Arsenal, I thought—was snarling.

I strained to hear more. If I loosed my aura here, they'd feel it.

"I won't get in." Her voice was resolute, even in the face of the huge alpha squaring her up.

That was my Onyx.

The situation devolved quickly once he tried to bundle her into the cab. He had no idea what he was dealing with. Anyone that looked at Onyx and thought she was a prissy, rich girl was in for a shock. She leaped at him like a cat, a tangle of arms and legs he couldn't seem to find the end of. He turned once, twice, comically, and I winced for him as I saw her heel lodge firmly into his ass cheek. He cursed and I realised there was a grin on my face.

Once he'd stopped trying to get her into the cab against her will, she dismounted with a reasonable amount of grace. He was furious, snarling something and jabbing his finger in her direction as she loosened her bun and fixed it with a straight back. Not that she needed to. She was beautiful regardless of the state of her hair, but she had always loved being put together.

I rested back in my seat as Arsenal stormed back to the garage, Onyx on his heels as the cab pulled away.

Somehow *thinking* of her with the other pack had been harder than seeing it. There was still a faint smile on my lips when the scent hit me. Lavender and brownies.

Cracking the window was a mistake.

My vision blurred, the smile falling from my face in an instant.

Time vanished as I bowed over the wheel of the car, holding onto it as my mind crowded with a thousand memories.

One won out, as it always did.

The day that should have been a beginning.

Wet hair stuck to her cheeks, joining the glittering diamonds of rain illuminated in the lamplight.

Onyx swayed in my arms as the song on my phone played out. It was late. We'd been walking home in the warm summer when a flash storm broke above us.

The rain continued to pound against the walkway. Where we danced, only a few branches of a sycamore shielded us from the downpour. I rested my hands on her hips, staring down into gleaming sapphire eyes as she stepped from me, letting me twirl her around.

She wore a soaked, silken, jade dress that clung to mesmerising curves as she danced in puddles, feet bare but for stockings. She had a dazzling smile on her face before she fell back into my arms, back pressed against my chest.

I leaned down, tugging her closer and pressing my lips gently to her neck, inhaling her scent, the nighttime rain tangling with lavender and brownies.

She reached up, taking the back of my head in her hands as she tilted her chin up and drew me into a deep kiss.

"You're perfect."

It distracted me from the slow sway of her rain-soaked dance, even if her hips still swayed, not missing a beat as the phone in my pocket continued its tune.

She'd always been elegant, even before perfuming. There had been three years between when my aura showed and hers didn't. I'd spent them all formulating every plan possible to ask her out, researching the benefits of betas in packs to convince my father that it wouldn't be a scandal.

Then her aura had shown, and I should never have doubted.

Onyx was born to be an omega.

And then... Even now, a lump formed in my throat. The bond with my packmates was three months young, and the news that followed had knocked the wind from my lungs. Onyx wasn't just an omega we could bite in with a normal bond.

She was our omega.

SEVEN

ONYX

I was only focused on one thing as I followed Arsenal back into the house.

Ice had been terrified.

The goosebumps across my skin were from more than the cold.

Was it because he was gold pack?

I'd admit I was sheltered. I perfumed at 14 and registered days later. I excelled in everything the Institute threw my way. By the time I graduated, I had applications spilling from overstuffed folders. I'd *heard* about the poor treatment of omegas less well off than me, of gold packs, but I'd never seen it. I'd never seen an omega manhandled like that before in my life—not outside of the bedroom, at least.

My thoughts flashed back to being trapped in that awful box.

Ice was still in there.

How long would they leave him?

I couldn't get his terrified whimpers from my head. He'd been through that before, it was clear. And he was trapped with them.

My mates, I realised, were monsters.

But Ice was my mate now, too, and I wouldn't leave him.

The moment I was in, I hurried toward the vault, searching for the keys. I opened drawers, desperately searching for them before turning when I heard a thump. Arsenal was standing over a ratty rug, stamping his boot loudly. I blinked, unsure. King was frozen, watching me from the couch, and Malakai had reclined his computer chair, eyes narrowed as he observed.

They were doing *nothing*. "You said you'd let him out."

"I said—" But he cut off as I turned back to the drawers, searching through them.

"Could you slow down for just a fucking second!" Arsenal's footfalls sounded, and then his hand closed around my wrist, where I was about to rip another one open. I spun on him.

"You can't treat him like that just because he's gold pack—"

"He's gold pack?" Arsenal asked. "I hadn't noticed."

"You're all *sick*!"

Arsenal's lip curled, whole frame tense. "And the universe chose us for *you*, Duchess. What do you make of that?"

"*You* are a disgrace of an alpha."

"What did you think you were going to gain by coming? Thought you could train us into being a white picket fence pack to show off to your friends? Tame the criminals and have cute little fated babies—"

SLAP!

The world was blood red, my vision narrowing as my palm collided with his cheek. It was a mistake. I knew it the moment I'd done it, my hand jumping to my mouth.

His pupils blew wide, an inky black as his aura shattered the room.

Hands slammed against the wall on either side of me, caging me in, the impact powerful enough that I heard a crunch of wooden panels. His face was twisted in a snarl. It was, perhaps, one of the most frightening things I'd ever experienced, because his rage was directed at me.

Rightfully directed at me.

MALAKAI

Me and King got to Arsenal at the same time. The second time in one night we had to peel him from an omega. No doubt there'd be a rut coming soon.

Fuck.

"I'm s-sorry," Onyx stammered. She was still tense, one hand clutching the other as she gazed up at Arsenal in fear. "I shouldn't have... I don't..."

"Get out, Duchess," I snarled at her. "Before you get hurt."

"I c-can't." She swallowed. "I *won't* leave him in there."

I examined her closer for a moment. Her face was white as a sheet, her eyes darting between us, but she was still here. For Ice. I'd met alphas bigger than me who crumbled beneath Arsenal's aura in a heartbeat. She didn't move, despite having an open path to the door and a clear desire to flee.

King hauled Arsenal back a pace, scowling before cuffing him across the shoulder. "The fuck, mate? Get your pride in check, you didn't tell her he's not—"

"I don't have to explain shit to bratty fucking omegas coming into *my* pad, accusing me of—"

"What the shit is going on?"

Ice was poking his head out from his nest.

Perfect fucking timing, as usual.

Onyx made a strangled noise—half sob, half whimper—and I turned in time to see her expression crumble. She took a quick step toward him, but then caught herself.

Ice's eyes widened. "What are you doing?" He looked stunned.

"She wouldn't leave since she thought you were in the vault," I said through gritted teeth.

I could see the remaining blood drain from Ice's pale face. For a flicker, there was definitely panic in his eyes before he flattened his expression. "I... uh..." He swallowed.

Arsenal let out a low, angry sound, tearing from our grip and stomping back past us all. He stopped by Ice, expression furious as he jabbed him in the chest hard enough that the slender omega staggered back a pace. "Put her out of her goddamned misery." He glared back at Onyx. "Ten minutes and I'm taking you fucking home."

I exchanged a look with King that said neither of us would be leaving Arsenal alone with either omega right now without an escort.

King followed Arsenal's lead and vanished back over to the couch, but I was too invested at this point. I wanted to know what Ice was going to do. He did very poorly when forced to confront his own issues. I sank down onto a barstool.

Onyx looked lost, and for a moment, I couldn't help feeling sorry for her. She ran her nails along the flower tattoo on forearm, glancing between me and Ice as if needing one of us to say something.

"I feel I've..." She swallowed. "I've made a bit of a fool of myself." Her voice was the faintest dry whisper.

Well. *Almost* correct. *She* hadn't made a fool of herself. Ice had made a fool of her. She and Arsenal both, just like he did best. I knew the look I shot him conveyed that, but I was surprised to see his face was already a mask of discomfort.

He crossed toward where she still stood, rubbing the back of his neck. Again, Onyx reached out to him with a shaky hand, as if she wanted to touch him, and then withdrew. Instead, Ice reached out to brush her cheek with his knuckle. Then he frowned and withdrew, as if unsure why he'd done it at all.

What was this? A strange omega mating dance?

The touch, it seemed, was all Onyx needed to crack. She took a shaky step toward him and then threw her arms around his neck.

Ice looked completely stunned, hand rubbing her back, and for a moment he glanced at me as if for help, before blinking and looking at the wall.

Not that I *would* have helped. He'd dug this hole for himself.

"I'm sorry." Onyx drew back, her voice a bit thick. She didn't put much distance between herself and Ice, though, I noticed, peering up at his face, hand still lingering at his cheek. "I'm not... like this usually. I thought..." She swallowed. "Are you hurt?"

"Never..." He cleared his throat. "Never in any danger, actually."

He glanced at me, clearly pissed I was still here. But, oh no, no, no. If Ice was about to choke up an *apology*, I wouldn't be missing it for the world.

"On all fronts, I might have exaggerated—"

I coughed.

Ice gritted his teeth. *"Lied,"* he amended. "About Arsenal and all that shit I said."

"Oh. Okay." Onyx nodded, but I could see by the pinch of her brows that she didn't understand at all.

"All theatre. Arsenal gets on my nerves. I like to poke him. Shouldn't have put you in the middle of it. Wasn't fair." Ice was talking faster now, the creeping of mania in his voice. He took a step away from her. "Anyway. Totally understandable that you don't ever want to see me again, so I'm just going to—" He turned on his heel, clearly about to make for his nest, when Onyx caught his wrist.

He glanced over his shoulder to her, a sweep of ash blond hair covering his eyes.

"I'm glad you're okay," Onyx said.

Ice nodded, and I could swear there was a flush in his cheeks.

"And I don't... not want to see you again. Though... I mean..." She straightened, letting go of his wrist and wringing her hands. "I think this whole meeting went rather poorly."

I snorted, which got a nervous glance from her.

"I can see this pack is... uh... content as you are. You have no need for me."

For one insane moment, I felt the first rumble of a growl click in my chest at the very notion that we didn't want her. Then I shoved it down, because every rational brain cell I had remaining agreed entirely with what she'd just said.

Ice said nothing, just staring at her as if his brain had short-circuited.

"Right. Well..." she said. "I think it's best if I apologise to Arsenal and go."

ONYX

Arsenal was crouched beside his bike, wiping off a tool with an oily rag. He glanced up at me as I approached. "You ready?" There wasn't a hint of anger in his voice. Quite the opposite. He was perfectly neutral.

"Actually, I'm here to apologise."

"You already did."

"I'd like to apologise properly."

He sighed, tossing the metal wrench onto a scratched up work desk and getting to his feet. He eyed me wearily.

"It was very inappropriate of me. I don't know what came over me..." I swallowed. It was the truth. I'd never slapped anyone in my life. "I'm *very* sorry."

"It's fine." Arsenal shrugged. "Barely a scratch, really. Shouldn't have reacted the way I did."

I nodded, the smallest amount of tension from the night ebbing from me.

"There'll be no need to drive me home," I went on. "I can call another ride."

"Nah. Rob got off ten minutes ago, and I don't trust the midnight drivers."

"I have a company on call—"

"You'll take the ride," he said, jabbing the oil stained rag at me. "And not say another word about it." He tossed it aside and grabbed a clean one to wipe his hands off.

I was too tired to argue. Emotionally, I felt like I'd been put through the ringer tonight. Flutters of panic still skittered in my veins as I thought of Ice, even though I knew now he was fine. He'd always been fine.

I nodded mutely.

He grabbed a set of keys from the desk and started toward the door. "Right then. Be back in—" He cut off as I followed. "What are you assholes doing?"

The three others were grabbing coats as if readying to leave.

"The fuck, Ice?" Arsenal asked. "You never leave."

"It's dark out, anyway. And I want to know where she lives."

"And you?" Arsenal glared at King and Malakai.

King grinned. "BetaBatter's Waffle truck is at the Crimson Bullet until 3am tonight."

"It's a food truck," Arsenal said flatly. "It *travels*."

"Come on, it never crosses the tracks—they *lie* about that."

"I'll bring it home." Arsenal said, hustling me out of the door. The other two were not deterred.

"Like fuck you will. I want it fresh." Malakai grabbed a pair of boots that were out on the porch.

"Don't even know if she lives in that direction."

"Don't kid yourself, Arsenal," King scoffed as Malakai turned one of the boots upside-down, letting a few old leaves fall from it before jamming his foot in. "She don't live anywhere but Westside. Isn't that right, Duchess?"

Arsenal glared at me, but I shrugged with a self-conscious nod.

"Fuck. Fine."

EIGHT

ICE

She'd come back for me. And now we were taking her home.

That felt wrong, but there was no other option. I knew that. We were all looking at the same woman. She wouldn't last five minutes in our world. Except… she'd come back for me.

Guilt twisted in my gut, and I tapped the jeep's panel because Arsenal really fucking hated it when I did that.

Why had she done that? Come back for me?

It threatened a whole lot of walls I'd put up.

And then there was the fact she'd searched for us. There was no reason I could think of that a woman like that would seek us out, scent match or not. In fact, most women like her—if they discovered they had a scent match like us—would run in the opposite direction. They'd never risk the idea that we ever caught a whiff of her.

Instead, she'd hunted us down.

Which meant she was hiding something.

My anxiety loosened. That was good, because she couldn't be as perfect as she'd been today.

It meant it was okay to drop her off, even though the idea of it was insane. I couldn't take my eyes from her in the rear-view mirror. She was crammed between Malakai and King, and I had to war with the little bubble of warmth that rose in my chest at the sight of it. As if it was right, somehow.

As Arsenal drove us closer to the address she'd given him, I noted Onyx change. It was subtle at first, almost impossible to tell. She straightened in her seat, her hands that gripped her coat and bag were taut, nails digging in just slightly to the bag. Her scent, though, that was what I noticed first. It shifted. She hadn't exactly been relaxed before, but it wasn't like this. Now, though, she was outright terrified.

My gaze shifted to Malakai and he shared a narrowed eyed look with me, his eyes darting subtly to the side, scanning her.

She was scared, doing her damndest to hide it from us, too, but it was becoming impossible. It was getting worse the closer we got to her home.

Eventually, even Arsenal noticed, glancing back at me with furrowed brows. Onyx, by this point was staring at her knees, handbag clutched in her arms, clearly trying to compose herself.

I saw her glance up to the window, clearly calculating where we were. She took a breath, but her scent became outright bitter. She caught me looking and offered me the slightest smile that tried too hard to be reassuring. Arsenal glanced to me, then into the mirror where he caught King and Malakai's eyes. We were all watching him.

There was a long, long pause, and then he screwed up his face, stretching out his scowl and nodded.

I knew what that meant.

Onyx was more scared of her own home than she was of us—the pack of criminals that had just terrorised her to almost tears.

And, by the tenseness of everyone in this car, that wasn't something we were willing to let lie. Could be anything; something private or personal that we couldn't fix, but none of us were comfortable dropping her off and leaving.

I tapped on my phone and opened up the app we needed, letting it load up.

"Arsenal'll walk you up," King was saying to Onyx as we pulled in. On her other side, Malakai tugged a bag from the trunk and dug around before slipping Arsenal the little box he needed.

Onyx nodded, trying to focus, then paused as if King's words were just catching up to her. "Oh. No need."

"Not our way, Duchess, bringing you home and not making sure you get to your door safe."

She stared at King, opening her mouth, and then shutting it again. "Alright. The door only." Her voice was quieter than before, all the command gutted from it. I wasn't expecting the flare of anger in my chest at that. Something waiting for her in her home was frightening her enough that it was stealing away who she was.

"Course," Arsenal grunted, hopping down from the jeep and striding around it to meet Onyx on the other side.

"Well." Onyx gathered her bag against her chest as she turned back to us. "Lovely meeting you all."

There was something wispy and unfocused in the words. Pure formality—and obviously a total lie. Her mind was far from present right now. There was no colour left in her cheeks.

I nodded, trying to shoot Arsenal a look that said 'don't fuck this up'. It was unnecessary. If there was one thing that could be said for Arsenal, it was that he was the most protective alpha I'd ever met. If I was feeling like this, he would be boiling over.

The door shut and I waited until the two of them had walked away before turning to the others.

"She's fucking terrified," King murmured.

I nodded. I looked at neither of them, instead tapping away on my phone furiously, setting up exactly what we needed. I was already halfway there, shifting a view around. A few more moments and the cam software went live. This was good tech—most of which we'd borrowed a while back to do a monitoring job for one of Arsenal's contacts in exchange for some better tools for the shop.

The bug might be small, but Arsenal was going to have a time finding a way to put it on her.

ARSENAL

I could be honest. Whether or not it was completely primal, whatever was making Onyx frightened left me blindingly full of fury. Simmering rage *would* put an edge to my scent and give me away to Onyx, except for the fact my scent was always a little charred.

I wasn't a rogue, but my aura had come out early from a traumatic event. It was unstable as fuck, and anyone who met me knew that. Right now, the strings holding it in place were taut.

Onyx said nothing as we stepped into the elevator, nor as she led me down the hall to her place. A few times I thought of asking her, but dispelled the thought. We were strangers, and she was working hard to keep her fear from us. If I asked, and she didn't want to share, she'd be on alert.

"Thank you for walking me up. Good of you," she said.

I stared at her, unable to rip my gaze away. It would be too easy to get lost in those eyes, to forget exactly why I'd come up. I could take her praise for being the kind of alpha that would walk her to her door simply for the sake of being a gentleman. I breathed a laugh, coming back to myself.

I wasn't that sort of alpha at all, and I had a job.

Very slowly, so that she could see every move I made, I lifted my hand to her cheek. Her brows furrowed, as if she couldn't understand what it meant. But then, for the briefest moment, she leaned into my touch.

She wasn't a touch deprived omega—couldn't be. She was a duchess, with alphas at her beck and call—even if that thought twisted the knot of rage just a little. But I *was* a touch starved alpha. Ruts spent alone, a scar scabbed over a million times. And that slightest motion undid me, peeling back a thousand layers to the need beneath.

She drew away, as if sensing the shift. A bit embarrassing, really, but my job was done. The small black bug was fixed to her earring.

She fumbled with her key for a moment, her scent shifting just a bit, and for a moment the fear diluted in lieu of something else... Sorrow...? Want...?

For me?

I almost shook my head to dispel that thought. No.

She'd come to us with intention, not desire. She didn't want us and we didn't want her.

The moment the door opened, it was as if I didn't exist. I noted when she stepped into the space, she didn't turn her back to it, instead sliding in sideways. She threw one last glance back to me with a nod, and then the door closed with a click.

KING

I held the ancient radio in a tense grip.

We were all staring at Ice's screen as Onyx headed into her apartment. Arsenal would have a view of her on his phone, waiting at the door.

I was wound too tight as I stared. I could feel the tension of my brothers through the bond. Ice, who had his bond locked down at all times, was absolutely fixed on the screen, but his sweet scent of roses and cookies was flooding the car, giving him away.

Onyx had taken a few steps into her apartment and stopped.

She turned her head side to side, examining the whole space. Was there someone else waiting for her?

My thoughts flashed to a partner, someone who would be angry she was gone. But that wouldn't make any sense.

Slowly, she stepped into the room. It was open concept, with high end finishes and furnishings. With too much caution, she set her coat down on a barstool.

She didn't move, her head turning side to side occasionally. A minute passed, then another.

"What is she doing?" Malakai asked.

Ice shook his head with a shrug.

Finally, Onyx stepped into the lounge. She hadn't taken off her shoes, I noted. Too distracted? Or was she not planning on staying long?

She crossed the room and adjusted the curtains that hung from a huge window. It was sheer fabric and closed for privacy, though it let a bit of light in from the street outside—her apartment was only a few stories up. I peered across the street on a whim, scanning the apartment block, and sure enough I could see movement in one of the windows, the shape of her a shadow against the curtain. My heart tightened at the sight of it.

Not doing much of anything with the curtains, Onyx moved to the couch and sat on its armrest. Again, she stopped, though this time she pulled her phone from her pocket.

I saw then that her grip was trembling. I glanced up to the others, and this time Ice even caught my eyes, his brow furrowed, that sharp mind of his working quickly.

She opened her phone and opened up her texts. The first she went to was a contact named Detective Ash. She began typing.

> Onyx: I fucked it up, Jane. I'm not even wanted by a pack of—

. . .

I heard Malakai release a breath of a laugh, leaning back slightly and shooting me a 'I knew it' look, but then Onyx was deleting the words until there was nothing remaining but the first four.

> Onyx: I fucked it up.

She left it there for a long time, fingers hovering buttons. Then slowly she typed another sentence.

> Onyx: I fucked it up. I don't have anything to offer them.

Sorrow tangled with my tenseness momentarily at seeing those words. Mal had gone silent, too.

What could she mean?

There was another pause, then she set her phone down and crossed the fancy kitchen for a bottle of wine. She poured herself a glass, and sat back down, the drink clutched in her hand as she stared at the unsent message. She took two large sips before deleting it and typing out another message, this one quicker.

> Onyx: Do you know how small my selection was at the institute? There were 23 packs left that might want me. Out of how many? This pack didn't even get to opt out. They didn't need to know a damn thing about me to know—

Onyx placed the phone down to finish the glass of wine. Then she picked it back up and deleted the whole text.

Instead, she scrolled back through walls of conversation that moved too fast for me to read them. Finally, she paused, and Ice snapped a screenshot with each frame as she lingered. They popped up on the screen and he cropped them quickly so we could read. One after another, until the conversation pieced itself together.

> Ash: Have you considered what we discussed last time?

> Onyx: I thought about it.

> Ash: Look. Let me level with you. This threat is no joke. Our hands are tied. The detail sat at your place for days but it's not a permanent solution. A bodyguard at least is a must.

> Onyx: I can't. Not after Devin.

> Ash: There are agencies that provide special training.

> Onyx: You haven't caught a trace of this guy. How is training going to help if the police can't touch him?

> Ash: Please think about what we talked about.

> Onyx: This guy won't just vanish because I find a pack.

> Ash: I've dealt with duchess stalkers before. I can't emphasise enough how much a bond might change things. Studies show that if an individual is already unbalanced at this stage, things can be driven by more than just emotions. Auras can't be understated.

> Onyx: You're convinced this is an alpha.

> Ash: Not considering that possibility would be too dangerous. You're an unbonded omega.

> Onyx: I don't want to find a pack this way.

> Ash: I know it's shitty, but right now, escalation is the only outcome I can see.

> Onyx: Couldn't I be putting them in danger too?

> Ash: I don't have a better option for you, Onyx. I'm speaking as a family friend, not a professional. I've never seen anything this bad before, not without any leads.

> Onyx: How am I supposed to approach a pack like that? What do I do? Lie to them until it's too late and they're stuck with me?

That was where the conversation cut off. Onyx had scrolled down a few pages until she rested on a list of things that Detective Ash had given to keep herself safe in her home.

I glanced up at the others.

"A stalker?" That was Arsenal through the comms.

"How bad are we talking?" Malakai looked torn. It looked bad to me, but... bad enough to get involved? I was glad it wasn't my call.

"Did we just read the same thing?" Ice asked. "She's fucking terrified—enough to turn up on our doorstep after reading your files. And if I recall, they all show your ugly mugs, too."

I was barely paying attention. While we were talking, Onyx had gotten to her feet and made her way to her bedroom. She looked to be searching for something before she paused, turning toward a bathroom. From here I could see the door was cracked open.

"Alright, but—" Malakai began, but I cut him off.

"The fuck is that?" My voice was hoarse. Onyx had frozen in the doorway, staring into the large bathroom. It was, like the rest of the apartment, all fancy with marble and fluffy bath mats and towels. But it was in disarray. Drawers were ripped open, their contents spread across the floor and countertop. That wasn't the thing that made my heart sink in my chest.

The mirror was split, as if it had been punched, cracks webbing out from the centre. Across it, in red, five words were scrawled.

"You will never escape me."

Every hair on my body stood on end. I heard the little whimper through the cam's audio.

Onyx's terror.

The stalker... They'd been in her house—could *still* be there.

I was smashing the comms button.

"Arsenal—" I began, but it was unnecessary. I felt his own fear and rage rocketing through the bond.

NINE

ONYX

I couldn't move.

The words scrawled across the mirror—written in my lipstick—pinned me to the spot. Terror was like shards of ice spiking my veins. It was a terror I'd felt before, and no less paralysing for it.

They'd been in my home while I was gone.

And they were angry. *Furious.* It was etched into each crack of the mirror and sharp edge of shattered bottles.

Could they still be here?

Then I heard a sound from the living room. My doorknob turning.

My breath caught.

My body moved before my mind. I had one chance. I raced to the kitchen, ripping open my drawers, where was—? The lock clicked—*fuck*. All the other locks that I'd slid into place still held. They had been expensive to install—the best on the market.

Shit. Shit. Shit.

The door thundered as if someone had just thrown their entire weight against it. I let out another whimper of terror. I should have gotten the set under my pillow... Easier to access than this. Why hadn't I gone there first? Then I saw them, a set of brass knuckles.

No knives. That's what Ash had warned.

In a panic, I raced to the other side of the door, slipping them onto shaking fingers. My eyes darted to my phone. Still on the kitchen counter.

Too late.

Escape: that was my priority.

Engage only if necessary. Get to the hallway. Get to people.

From here, I might be able to startle them enough to slip out.

Again, someone threw their weight against the locks and I felt the powerful aura of an alpha blast through the air. My breath caught, vision narrowing as I lifted my shaking fists. This time, with a crash, the locks splintered, and the door flew open.

ARSENAL

My vision was red with rage as I loosed my aura completely and slammed my weight against the door. It burst open so hard I had to steady myself—

CRACK!

Pain split my face so hard I saw stars. I let out a growl of rage, lashing out. The fucker was here, *challenging* me?

I'd snap him in-fucking-two.

But then my swimming vision came back, and I realised it was Onyx, sprawled across the marble floor, scrambling away, her face a mask of terror.

Damn, I'd just—but I didn't get a chance to think on it because her expression crumpled as she recognised me. She was on her feet in a blur of wild dark hair and glittering jewellery before she flung herself into my arms.

I held her without thought, the bloodlust pounding through my veins fighting with the urge never to let her go.

"I-I'm sorry," she sobbed. "I thought—"

"It's okay. I'm not leaving." I could practically sense the shift in her at those words. I'd not noticed how small she was until she was trembling in my arms with no stubborn fury making her larger than life. "The others are coming," I murmured. Whoever was terrorising her, they could still be here.

It didn't take long before King, Malakai, and Ice were crashing into the apartment.

Ice and King drew up at the sight of Onyx clutched in my arms, but Malakai entered without pause, barking at the other two to get moving as he began searching the place.

For a moment, I was torn, but then, wasn't it perfectly reasonable for me to leave the searching to them in lieu of her obvious need for comfort? It was the right thing to do, and she didn't seem likely to let go of me, anyway, so I moved to the couch as the others did a sweep.

I winced.

Alpha instincts. That's what this was. But I wasn't willing to give them up. She was my mate, for fuck's sake. I would make sure she was okay.

"You alright?" I asked. She nodded slightly, face pressed into the crook of my neck. She was shaking from head to toe, her breathing short and sharp.

Definitely shock.

It might take a while for it to wear off.

"You see anyone?"

"No." She shifted back.

"Take your time. The others are searching the place."

She nodded, her grip digging in once more, and I could feel the metal between her fingers.

"What are you doing with a knuckleduster, Duchess?" I asked, trying to lighten the mood.

"The detective said…" She cleared her throat, drawing back a little more, chin still tilted down, her dark hair obscuring her face. "B-bring a knife and there's a weapon in the fight. A-alphas are more likely to survive a stab wound than I am."

Well… Not bad advice, actually. She was tiny. I couldn't imagine feeling threatened even if she was holding a blade, not unless she knew how to use it.

"Well. You got me good." I could feel the trickle of warm blood trailing my cheek now.

I looked up as Malakai strode from her room, expression dark.

"What?" I asked.

Onyx finally peered up, furiously wiping the tears from her face as she glanced at what Malakai was holding.

"What are these?" he demanded, waving a wilted flower in her face.

"Slow down," I growled as Onyx tensed.

"They're…" She cleared her throat, shifting back from me as if she was going to stand. My grip on her tightened; King and Ice weren't back and we didn't know if the place was fully safe yet. She glanced at me nervously. "They're forget-me-nots. They're left every time… every time they break in."

Malakai's expression twisted with rage. Then he whipped the dead flower across the room, his own aura shattering the space.

Onyx went stiff, her terror back.

"Calm the *fuck* down," I snarled.

"No." Malakai spun back to her. "You reckless *idiot*, not thinking for one second what you were bringing to our doorstep."

"Mal." My tone was a last warning. Onyx's face was pale as she stared up at Malakai.

He slammed his boot onto the coffee table and was fumbling

with the laces. What the fuck was he—? But then he ripped something dry and leaf-like from it.

He held it out for me and Onyx to see.

My blood went cold.

In his palm was the same dead flower. Onyx's hand jumped to her mouth.

"In my boots outside our door, scattered across the entryway."

Shit.

Her stalker had already followed her to our place?

I turned where I sat, still clutching her, but I had to know. King and Ice were entering the living room, settling the panic in my chest.

"What?" King asked.

I took a breath, trying to tear my eyes from Ice before the fucker got too smug about it.

He was safe. He was with King. Of course he was safe. I looked down to find Onyx pulling from my arms earnestly this time.

"What's going on?" King asked again.

Malakai went off, ranting about the flower, but I was focused on her. She was staring between Malakai, King, and Ice, fear still written all over her face as she absently tugged the knuckle dusters from her fingers. Despite the faint traces of tears down her foundation, her makeup was pristine and the dark hair that now tumbled to her waist, still glossy.

"It's not her fault—" Ice began.

"Like fuck it isn't. She knew exactly what she was doing."

"H-he's right..." Onyx's voice was faint, but she seemed to be collecting herself at last. "I shouldn't have... I knew how dangerous this was..."

"He's *following* her," Ice spat.

"Look. I should call the police. I appreciate you coming in..." She trailed off, brows furrowed. "How did you...?"

Ice reached out and plucked the little camera from her earring and tucked it into his pocket.

Onyx stared at him, her lips parting in shock. "You bugged me?"

"Thought you were in trouble," he said, as if it were the most obvious thing in the world.

"And we were right," I added, because I saw something indignant creeping onto her expression.

She folded her arms, eyes narrowed. The shock was clearly wearing off as she looked around at us. "Well. Thank you for checking the place. Like I said, I should—"

"Go with King and Ice," I told her. "Pack a bag."

"I'm sorry, what?" she asked, her eyebrows shooting up.

"You're coming with us." At my words, I felt a flare of rage from Malakai through the bond. His eyes flashed, but he kept his mouth shut. Onyx had a similar expression.

But *this* was the only solution. We had nine days to survive. If all the damned omegas in my life wanted to make that as difficult as possible, I'd be keeping them under one roof.

"She is?" Ice asked, a grin spreading across his face.

"I *certainly* am not." Her voice had lost its tremor, and she was straightening her dress. She'd gone from frightened little omega to spoiled duchess in the blink of an eye.

Really?

All of this—dragging a fucking stalker to our door for protection, and now she didn't want it?

"You want to stay here?" King asked.

"Golden Tooth has last minute rooms. I can—"

"Do absolutely nothing of the sort." I folded my arms and leaned back on the couch, fixing her with my best *'I've no patience for bullshit'* look. Because I didn't. Mal was right. She'd brought this danger to us. To Ice. "You'll pack a suitcase. And forget the cops. For all the fucking good they've done you."

Her eyes turned dark, her nostrils flaring. "I don't appreciate your tone."

What the fuck had she just said to me? All that sweet, cuddly protective alpha bullshit that had been warming my chest—and making me an idiot—vanished in a second flat. I got to my feet.

But she had the gall to turn her back on me, stalking over to the kitchen island and grabbing her phone.

The last of my patience flickered out. In the absence of her magical omega tears making me soft, the stress of the night crashed back.

I was having none of it. She'd made this my pack's problem, and that meant I called the shots. I needed only to give King one glance, and he was after her in a second.

He plucked the phone from her and tucked it in his pocket before she could do a thing, then dragged her back over to me.

"Get your hands *off* me!" she snarled. King didn't flinch at her struggles, tugging her arms behind her back and forcing her to face me.

I wore a cold smile as she glared up at me. "There's a whole pile of shit not to be appreciated tonight, Duchess. I promise my *tone* is the least of your worries."

"How dare—"

I cut her off, temper still getting the better of me. "The first thing you should be worried about, if you *don't* pack, is that Ice'll do it for you. So unless you want to be tramping around our pad in nothing but lace, I suggest you do as I say."

"You are *mad*."

"And *you* need protection. You're out here on your own."

"I have people I can stay with—"

"Liar." I snorted, cutting her off. "Or you wouldn't be talking about staying at hotels."

She drew back against King, affronted, but she couldn't seem to find a response for that.

"You came to us. This is how we do things."

"I didn't mean for you to—"

"You still came." I took a step closer to her. I was so high-strung, the collision of fear and anger from the last few hours setting my aura on edge. It came out now in my tone. I took her chin so she wasn't tempted to look at any of the others for help. "You endangered my pack, Onyx, and that's not something I *appreciate*."

"I *never* meant to put anyone in danger."

I believed her, truly. And it didn't matter one bit. Plus, my cheek fucking hurt. "Perhaps, in the future, be more careful what you wish for."

I nodded toward her bedroom door and stepped away, slumping back down on the couch as King began dragging her to her room, ignoring her indignant protests. Ice, much too gleeful, followed them. I turned to Malakai who looked like he was going to crack a tooth.

"Spit it out."

His response was instant. "This is a *shit* plan."

"All our options are shit."

"You trust her?"

"No. But it all makes sense now, doesn't it? She doesn't *want* anything to do with us, she just needs protection. It's simple. We give her it, sort out this fucker, and she goes away."

"Why are you offering at all?" Malakai asked.

I stared at him, knowing there was a bitter expression twisting my face. "If it was your call, would you leave?"

Perhaps it was low to ask that. Once upon a time, it would have been his call.

"Yes." He said it through gritted teeth. I snorted, feeling the conflict within him even as he said it.

"Right." As if he'd not been right at Ice and King's side charging into her apartment. "If that makes you feel better."

"What if she fucks anything up with—?"

"She won't." I knew why he was on edge. Riot was about to hand us the world. As long as we got in for our check in. As long as we stayed on the right side of the law. "Look. We won't do anything below board—nothing that could get us in trouble. Even if that means we keep her with us to make sure she's safe, wait this fucker out, and then deal with him on the other end of it."

"She's going to be living with us, Arsenal. She's a *scent* match. How do you see that going?"

I laughed. "Mal. Look around. There is nothing that could happen in nine days that will make a woman who comes from *this*—" I glanced about at the luxurious apartment sprawling around us. "—belong in a pack like ours."

TEN

KING

Onyx was clearly flustered as she rifled through her stuff and tried to pack a suitcase.

Did I feel bad? Maybe a little. But Arsenal wasn't wrong. And... we did get to bring her home. My alpha hindbrain had no arguments about that.

Nor with the idea of the alternative, which was to leave her for this fucker alone. Arsenal's methods were... harsh, but it wasn't my business to question that shit.

I stood at her side in her closet as she rifled through outfits. Everything about her was fucking intoxicating. Her scent, the little concerned furrow to her brow at the treatment Arsenal and Malakai were delivering her, and fuck, she was physical. Every opportunity she had, her fingers brushed my forearm with muttered questions like "Which should I bring?"

What the fuck gave her the impression I'd know if she should pack noir or crimson silken scarves? None of us would know—

"Crimson. You've packed too much black already."

Ice. Of course. I could already see the little shit sucking up to her—and getting in on her little touches.

"Black's easy to match, though."

"Right, but you'll be left with a dozen different shades, and then what?"

She chewed on her lip with a nod before neatly folding the crimson scarf and placing it into the suitcase.

She was hot. Hot and totally out of our league. No. She wasn't out of our league. She was in another stratosphere. But... I was hot, too—way more than those two other grumpy pricks, so maybe she'd overlook the whole... criminal thing? She was still wearing that shirt with a low neckline, and my eyes were constantly snagging on her cleavage or the side of her breasts.

It was a fucking scandal.

And don't even get me started on her scent.

She was deadly.

But what Onyx didn't know was that we were more proficient than any alpha in resisting the seduction of a sweet omega. No other alphas on the planet were forced to live with Ice's rose fucking cookies only to get frozen out at every goddamned turn. And most often accompanied by a middle finger and a smirk as he vanished into the nest he'd banned us from. No, if that little shit had given me anything good in this world, it was ironclad self-control.

Just like Ice, if we allowed an inch, she'd take the rest of our goddamned world, and we couldn't afford that. Not with how close we were to freedom.

Two omegas, though?

I watched her hand brush Ice's again as she sifted through her obscenely sized wardrobe.

He caught me watching with narrowed eyes, and I realised my nose was wrinkled in a scowl. Only, Ice was fully aware of what that meant. He ran his fingers through the loose waves of his ashen blond hair, that cocky half grin on his face.

I almost bared my teeth at him, but it was an overt reaction which would tip him off to exactly how damned hot I found him. And once Ice got a tip, he stored it in his little box of pins so he could needle us with it later.

That box was full to the brim, and if he got even the slightest whiff of the fact that watching the two of them together felt like someone was injecting boiling hot water into my veins? It was game fucking over.

I tried to stop staring. Tried really hard. But they looked so goddamn good together. They were opposites, almost to a T. Onyx was elegant, dark hair, smooth and glossy, outfit deliberate, sexy and tight-fitting. She wore delicate jewellery, a thin golden necklace, a few slim rings, and two pretty dangling earrings.

Ice wore baggy jeans, tattered boots, and a wrinkled button-up with only one sleeve rolled up. His hair was messy, and the buttons on his shirt were done up wrong—also hanging open almost to his mid-chest.

Comparatively, Onyx was refined. Sure, I couldn't stop my eyes from snagging on the low neckline of her shirt, but it had a way of pretending it was decent that made me feel like a pig every time. Ice demanded attention and he knew it too, the little slut.

How were we going to deal with two omegas? And what if their heats synced?

Well... Ice didn't let anyone but Malakai touch him during his heats, which would leave me and Arsenal for her.

Two alphas for an omega in a pack of five?

We were screwed.

My imagination was getting ahead of me, though. We were protecting her and then dropping her off. Scent match or no, she didn't belong with us. Even now, I couldn't take my eyes from the golden necklace that perfectly complemented the smooth skin of her neck. She was everything an omega was supposed to be, and we were a bunch of degenerates that society had left behind. Me most of all.

She wouldn't share her heat with us. She would never have looked twice if scent matching hadn't left us her only option.

The quicker we dealt with the stalker the better.

Ice turned up at the door with a fluffy dressing gown.

"Won't fit," I grunted.

"Well make it. It's important."

"It's what?" I scoffed, but then I realised he was right. Her scent, lavender and warm brownies, was everywhere in here, but the dressing gown was the closest thing to scent marked I'd come across.

She glanced between me and him and there was a guilty look on her face. "I would..." She swallowed. "Prefer if we could bring it."

I rolled my eyes, then nodded. "Alright. Shove it in."

MALAKAI

"Go and do your... brain thing, alright?" That had been a dismissal from Arsenal if I'd ever heard one.

Now, I leaned against Onyx's bathroom door, staring at what was inside.

A puzzle.

There was rage in this room. Fury that chilled my blood when I imagined it levelled at Onyx.

I hated Arsenal's call, but I hated more that I understood it. That there was no way we could walk away from this. I was just grateful that it was him that had to do it so I could still cling to this fucking frustration that we were here at all.

He'd fought me for the right to make that call. I'd lost that fight, bloody as it had been, and never regretted it a day since. I knew he regretted it every day.

This asshole had come into her space and taunted her. It was a violation, and it was by design. He'd done what he could to make sure she felt as unsafe as...

Wait.

I peered around her bedroom, then did another loop of the apartment. I'd already taken the whole space in a dozen times, but I needed to see it once more. Sure enough, I didn't find what I was looking for. Not even a measly pile of laundry stashed in a corner.

I pushed open the door to her obscene walk-in closet. Ice was sitting in a pile of clothing and King leaned against a wardrobe as Onyx overfilled a huge cream-coloured suitcase.

"Where's your nest?" I demanded.

She looked up from the pair of leggings she was carefully folding. "My... nest?" she asked, like it was a crazy question.

"Yeh. You're an omega. You've lived here a bit. Where's your nest?"

For a moment, she looked anxious, and I could swear her eyes darted to Ice. "I... don't have one."

"What kind of omega doesn't have a nest in their own home?" I asked.

I might have punched her for the struck look on her face.

"Mate..." King muttered, glaring at me. "Leave off."

"Do you have any other place?" I asked. Sometimes, if they couldn't find a safe place at home, omegas would nest elsewhere. There were zoning laws keeping them out of public property as it could, on occasion, cause issues. Omegas could be territorial about their nests. They were supposed to be private and safe. There'd been a lawsuit a few years back when a bowling alley had found a nest in one of their back rooms from an omega who was suffering heavy abuse at home. Perhaps the company could have lived with it, if she hadn't become aggressive toward workers who passed too close.

"Could you keep the tone deaf questions *at least* until tomorrow?" Ice snapped.

"This prick's trying to get in her head. Nest would be the perfect place to target." The faster we solved this shit, the faster we could get rid of her. But then I caught Onyx's expression.

She'd changed, quite significantly, actually. Aside from the little blip when she'd been in Arsenal's arms, she was stiff as a rock, impeccable. Had been in the jeep when she was scared, and she was quite indignant in the face of Arsenal.

But there was true panic in her eyes as she looked around the room. Her eyes were flickering back and forth between the three of us, rapidly, as if she was unravelling before my very eyes.

"Shit," Ice muttered, reaching for her, but she flinched away, her breath catching. "It's alright—"

"Could I just..." Her fingers were squeezing the pair of leggings in her hands, her chest suddenly heaving. "I need a moment." Her eyes were wide and beautiful and pleading. I *wouldn't* fall for it—but King grabbed my shoulder and shoved me out while Ice shut the door.

"I don't buy it—" I began.

"You great, tactless oaf," Ice spat. "She doesn't have a nest *because* of this prick, alright?" He waved at the bathroom door.

"What?"

"There has to be *something* safe about a place to build a nest. Nothing here is, and you just rubbed it in her face while questioning her as an omega."

"I didn't *rub* it in." Or question her as an omega? Where was Ice coming up with *that*?

"As good as," King said.

I rolled my eyes. "Forgive me, but I'm more interested in

sorting this—"I waved at the bathroom. "—than sparing the sensitive feelings of a spoiled duchess."

"She's not weak, and she's not spoiled."

I turned on King, struck by that response. He was a roll with the punches kind of guy. Happy without the burden of responsibility, King had found his peace, even when the rest of us hadn't. He'd found it in the pack, as dysfunctional as we were, so there were very few things that could push him to make waves.

I narrowed my eyes, but he was straightening, tucking his hands in his pockets. "Her bodyguard died last month. Killed on a job with her. Random, or so it looked, but this shit all started right after that."

"Alright. So this guy's a killer, too. Wonderful."

"She's refused to get another bodyguard. Does that fit spoiled duchess to you?"

I stared at him, knowing my jaw was ticking. No. It didn't. Not at all. I'd have expected ten bodyguards at her side every time she stepped from this place.

Instead, she was alone.

"But *we're* disposable?" I asked.

"She didn't choose us," Ice hissed.

"Tell me where she went wrong?" King asked. "To me, it looks like she's stuck. She's done everything she can with what she's got. She tried to keep as many people out of it as possible."

"Until she cracked, and went to dump it all on a pack."

"That detective was right. Better pack than body guards," Ice said. "And I'm glad she matched us instead of some rich pricks. They'd have just tried to throw money at it. Wouldn't be enough."

"And you think *we* are?" I asked.

King squared me up like it was a challenge. "You don't?"

"Not if you weasels keep stopping me from asking her important questions," I snapped.

"Tomorrow, ask her whatever you want, alright?" King said. "Just give her a night. It's been rough for everyone."

"She asked if we could grab stuff from the bathroom; face wash, all that shit," Ice waved a hand. "And whatever makeup survived her makeup box after it got lobbed at the mirror."

"What?" I asked.

"Some of the fabric is jammed in the cracks."

I returned to the bathroom, staring around. Ice was right. Of course he was, bloody observant, as always. I'd assumed it had been punched.

I pulled my phone out and took a bunch of photos before salvaging what I could of her makeup from the shattered box. It had a jade velvet exterior and was made of wood.

I returned, a bag full of random stuff I had grabbed from the bathroom, and the door to the walk-in wardrobe clicked open. Onyx peered out cautiously.

"I'm all packed," she said stiffly. I handed her the bag and she took it, not even checking what was inside before turning back to her suitcase, which was way too full. Ice had to clamber on top while King zipped it up, but I kept my eyes on Onyx. Once more, she was picturesque, but this time she couldn't hide the fresh red in the whites of her eyes.

Fine. Maybe I could wait until tomorrow before asking the questions teeming in my brain.

"Can I have my phone?" she asked as King straightened.

"No." I said, right as King reached for his pocket. Fucking putz. He paused, glancing at me guiltily.

"I need to call someone to fix the door," she said. "If I don't, someone else will call the cops."

"Then give me the number."

"This is ridiculous."

"Take it up with Arsenal."

ELEVEN

MALAKAI

"Where am I going to sleep?" Onyx asked.

She was standing in the middle of the garage. All the confidence from her previous visit had slid away.

I refused to feel pity. If Arsenal insisted on keeping an eye on her constantly until this fucker was found, I'd do it, but I'd be glad he took first shift. She was... I shut my eyes and turned from her. She was too much.

"My bed tonight," Arsenal said.

"And you'll be?" Onyx asked.

"In my bed."

"I'm not sleeping with you."

"He was outside this place. I have no intention of waking up to an omega murdered on my couch."

He was right. I wouldn't sleep either if she was alone through the night. Given the situation, I didn't even feel safe leaving Ice to sleep alone in his nest. What if this stalker turned his attention to our omega? Ice slept in my room during heats, so it wouldn't be a huge deal.

"Hey," I tapped Ice on the arm as he passed me.

"Nope. Not a chance," he replied, before I could even formulate the thought. I swallowed.

Great.

I could insist on not giving him a choice like Arsenal wasn't giving Onyx, but there was no way it wouldn't start a pack war. Instead, I sighed, and remembered exactly what Ice's nest looked like to settle my heart. If the stalker got in there... Well, he'd regret it pretty quick. Omega or not, Ice knew how to use a weapon.

"I'm not sleeping with you," Onyx insisted, for all the good it would do her.

"Don't try and make it sound sexier than it is, sweetheart. It's just a bed."

I snorted, settled into my desk chair, and shifted my mouse so the computer woke up. It would be okay. I was usually up so late there were only a few hours between when I went to sleep and King woke. We would be able to keep these two imbecilic omegas safe. And Onyx would be safer than anything with Arsenal. He slept poorly, I knew that, woke at the slightest sound. Getting 3am snacks for myself usually saw his bleary-eyed self stumbling from his room and snagging a few before returning to bed.

"You can pick someone else tomorrow night."

"I'm not cycling through your beds like a whore."

King chuckled. "None of us are going to touch you. Unless you ask, and even then it's still a gamble."

I almost snorted at that, but he obviously felt my derision through the bond because he shot me a dirty look. Me and Arsenal, maybe, but King was having trouble not panting when he was near her.

Still, Onyx narrowed her eyes as if he'd just offered her a challenge. My mind wandered. What if she did choose me tomorrow night?

Onyx in my bed?

Ice joined me when he was in heat, never allowing me in his nest properly, but... Well, Onyx was different. I... knew Ice. There were barriers in our relationship. The others and him didn't get on, sure. But he was an absolute in my life. I knew that, and he knew that. It didn't make us sweet or friendly, but it was a constant. I could trust that even when I couldn't trust him. And he was attractive, sure, but his boundaries were clear. He didn't want anything from me unless he was in heat. And then I had my work cut out for me... Okay. Bad plan, thinking about Ice in heat at the same time as contemplating Onyx in my bed.

She was obscenely hot right now, following Arsenal who was dragging in her suitcase to his room. Even pissed off, her hips swayed—like a sexy strut of some kind.

She was a brat, that much was sure. Spoiled and rich, and I was sure she'd never had anyone but the more pretentious gits within the sheets. She'd not had anything like me. Like us.

That's why she seemed so confident that she could push us around. I kind of liked it. It was a flashing sign offering challenge. What would happen if she didn't get what she wanted? It made my cock twitch watching the simmering frustration in her gaze. The same look she'd get if I denied her. Showed her how I could take care of her and then snatched it away. Could I get her begging for my knot? For me to pin her down and—

Fuck.

If I did ever want that—which I didn't—this was a terrible fucking start.

It was her smell. That was all. Literal Heaven, just like Ice. I didn't actually know how the others survived, constantly drowned in his scent and never getting a taste... but I might have to go through that with Onyx.

I noticed Ice watching her curiously, eyes trailing her as she stalked after Arsenal. I'd never seen lust in his eyes as I did in that moment, his tongue pressing up against a canine, tilting his head just slightly.

He was smitten.

Heat speared my core, new imaginings stealing me away. Taking Onyx in front of Ice. Making him watch as I ruined her. Making him choke on my cock as I treated her. All those years of torment from the fucker, paid back in one.

Goddamnit.

I spun in my computer chair, glaring at the welcome screen.

I'd *warned* Arsenal this was a bad fucking plan.

ARSENAL

She took way too long to get ready for bed. I generally ripped off my top, grabbed some comfortable pants, and splashed my face with water.

She was in the bathroom for what felt like an age. When she returned she wore black, silken pyjamas which were appropriately pretentious. Her hair was down and loose in thick, glossy waves that tumbled to her waist. I had trouble looking away from it.

Fuck, she was beautiful. It didn't seem to matter if she was wearing no makeup, or what her hair was doing.

Her manicured nails fiddled with a dark wave of her hair. I glanced back down at my phone so I didn't stare too long. Only then, she crossed toward where I was sitting on the edge of the bed and nudged my phone away from my face.

When I glanced up, I got trapped in sapphire eyes as she looked up at me. Her bare face glowed with moisturiser, her eyes free of liner, and she looked... vulnerable. Softer and sweeter. The way those waves tumbled around her face made her look younger. She was a duchess; I'd assumed she was close to my age—twenty-six or twenty-seven, but now I was wondering more if she was maybe in her early twenties. She chewed on her plush bottom lip anxiously, and I noticed the faintest scattering of freckles across the bridge of her curved nose.

"I appreciate the offer of protection," she said. "But it's absolutely unnecessary for me to share a bed with you, not to mention inappropriate. I'll sleep on the couch if you'll just provide me a blanket…"

I considered her. How much younger than me was she? Could she be right about this being inappropriate? When I didn't say anything, she shifted closer, taking my hand in both of hers.

"I *am* grateful. I do understand the impossible position I put you in."

I ripped my gaze back to hers, away from the traces of circles she was running across my palm. The goosebumps that rippled across my skin, however, I couldn't mask. I just hoped my tattoos did a good enough job making them less obvious.

One touch and I was reacting like a teen alpha virgin for fuck's sake. God, I was weak, worn thin from years of violent ruts and an omega who didn't want a thing to do with me. But she was mesmerising down to the heavy scent of lavender and brownies in the air. What the hell was up with all of these delicious smelling omegas? Couldn't the universe give me one that didn't make me crave fucking food?

"You're doing the best you can," she went on. She lifted her hand toward me. To do what? I didn't know. Perhaps to cup my cheek or to sweep the dark strand of hair away from my eyes so she could ensnare me without barrier. I never found out, because I caught her wrist.

No. My decision wasn't just about the arrangement tonight. If she was younger—not that I'd expose my insecurities by asking her—then it meant she needed the protection more. But she was staying in our bloody garage, and if I wanted to get ahead of this—because I knew the power omegas could seize if you *blinked*—then she'd need to understand the rules here and that I made them. What I said, goes.

"You misunderstand," I told her. "I'm not doing this for your gratitude, sweetheart. But I don't do things by halves, and I won't have you dead or taken on my watch."

"I won't be." Her voice was tight.

I didn't say anything else. She glanced at the duvet on the bed, but then seemed to decide better than arguing. Instead, she stood and stalked from the room. Turned out silk pyjamas did wonderful things to swaying hips.

I snorted as she vanished around the corner. I'd been waiting for her to climb into bed first. It might have given her a sense of control to let her pick her side, her space, and I'd fit in around her. But if she insisted on being a brat, she'd be treated like one.

I climbed into the bed and settled under the covers until I heard the expected sound of her outrage drawing nearer.

From the corner of my very comfortable and warm position in bed, I saw King entering with Onyx slung over his shoulder. The light silk of her pyjamas clung for dear life over that divine ass that I couldn't help but eye. She was fighting King tooth and nail and he had to shift his head to the side to avoid her clawing hand. He laughed, patting her firmly on the ass—to a shriek of rage—before tossing her onto the bed at my side.

She let out a high-pitched sound of derision as she landed. She drew herself up, trying to compose herself as she glared from me and back to King, who'd folded his arms, waiting for what she'd do next. Her glossy hair finally looked a little wild, and her cheeks were much more red than usual.

I noticed Ice leaning against the door, clearly delighted at watching another omega get the brat treatment for once.

"You can't—!"

"Into bed, sweetheart," I said. "Or next time he'll tuck you in and read you a story."

Onyx's cheeks flushed even brighter.

"This is..." Oh, I could see the duchess act dissolving, and this time it wasn't for fear. She searched around her and grabbed one of the pillows. "*Stupid!*" she snarled, throwing it at King with all of her not-so-frightening-omega-might. King caught it, shot her a cheeky grin, and then departed with a salute, pillow still under his arm, shooing Ice out with him.

I didn't reply, content to watch the cogs in her brain turn as she spun on me, clearly working through the options she had left. There weren't many. We still had her phone, and I wouldn't be giving it back until I was sure she wouldn't do something stupid.

I grabbed my pillow, turned on my front and got settled, watching with satisfaction as she realised her next problem.

"What kind of savage only has two pillows?" she demanded.

"Night, Duchess." I watched her search the room for a substitute before closing my eyes. It would be a long time before I was asleep, but darkness calmed me. It was more necessary than usual, with her omega scent heavy in the room. And she wasn't in *soothing* omega mode, either. My heart sank as I felt the faint stirrings of my aura's agitation.

A rut was coming.

Two irritable omegas was enough to draw it out sooner.

I shoved down the nauseating turn of my stomach and the flutter of dread. Would have happened sooner or later, anyway.

There weren't many things that could shake me these days, but enduring my ruts would shake anyone.

My aura had broken upon surfacing.

I had never *regretted* the murder that sent me to juvie. The act hadn't just wiped that violent piece of scum from the face of the earth, it had also led me to my brothers. But deep in the throes of dark, agonising ruts was the closest I ever got to regret.

I was ripped from my thoughts as I felt her touch on my arm. My eyes snapped open to find sapphire blue irises much closer than I'd expected. All my senses went on high alert.

"What?"

"About my job," she whispered.

"What about it?"

"I can't miss my appointments or my clients will leave."

"And *what* appointments would those be?" I focused on her, razor sharp, not daring to even draw my hand from her touch. It would give away how much she was getting to me.

"I'm a duchess."

Right, we all knew what that meant. She was hired out to hang from the arms of rich alphas so they could feel powerful. I certainly understood it, though. They said duchess auras were different than normal omega auras, and it was a war not to tumble into that trap. I could only imagine that for alphas less on guard than my pack, she could make them feel like the centre of the world. I was warring with that right now.

"You can go with a bodyguard."

"He died—"

"I told you. We aren't letting you out of our sight."

"*You* want to be my bodyguard so you can watch me spend the night with another alpha pack?"

The growl rose in my throat before I caught it, and she flinched back. I cut it off instantly, settling my expression.

"We will do what is necessary," I said through gritted teeth. "If that means bodyguards, it means bodyguards."

There was a pause. "It will have to be Malakai or King," she whispered.

"Why?" My voice came out harsher than I meant it to.

"They look less..." She trailed off, and suddenly she wasn't meeting my eyes.

"Like criminals?" I asked.

She chewed her lip again, guilt in her expression.

"Does it scare you, Onyx? How I look?"

She stared at me, and all the hazing of her scent fell away. "I don't... feel unsafe around you."

Huh. Well. I didn't know what I'd expected, but that wasn't it. Right.

"Good."

"It's just... to my clients... You'll stick out."

"I stick out everywhere."

Her hand was still against my skin.

There were more problems with inviting Onyx into our home than just the asshole stalker tailing her. I was unbalanced and a touch from Onyx was stirring up embarrassing shit within me. The edges of my aura were just the faintest bit fuzzy, like I got when I started to spiral.

"A bit friendly," I said, eyes tracing where her hand touched my arm. "For a woman trying to run out of here a minute ago."

Her expression tightened. "I said it was inappropriate—which it *is*." She emphasised the last word. "Not that I couldn't handle it."

"Good night, Duchess."

Very deliberately, I took her hand and drew it away. "You'll have to convince them yourself. I'm not ordering them on a pro-bono bodyguard trip."

"I would never expect them to do it for free."

I paused, hating how my brain snagged on that. How much did Onyx pay her bodyguards? How much could my brothers make by going with her? How many dangerous jobs would it make up for?

Everything always came back to money. I hated it just as much as we were bound to it. And she was free of those laws entirely.

I said nothing else, flipping onto my other side and staring bitterly at the wall. Before I closed my eyes this time, I texted our pack chat.

> Me: do we know how old she is?

> Ice: asking after you climb into bed with her?

> Ice: what if she's not of age and you just kidnapped her?

> Me: go fuck yourself. She's a duchess, she has to be, idiot.

> Malakai: she's Ice's age, according to the articles I'm reading.

I'd been right, then.
Fuck.

> Me: christ

Twenty-two? That four year age gap felt a lot larger now she was tossing and turning *in* my bed.

> King: Damn. I thought for sure she was older than us.

That, I could agree with. I sighed, refusing to turn, even when she was clearly shifting around behind me just to be annoying. But it would still be hours before I went to sleep. Sleep and me, we were old enemies.

ONYX

The problem *wasn't* the hulking alpha murderer who'd decided making me sleep in his bed was in my own best interest. The problem was that, despite the insanity of it, my foolish omega brain felt absolutely safe. Enough that I fought burning tears as I reconciled how fear had been hounding every second and every breath, now I felt its absence. It was a fist slowly releasing my chest.

And its absence was dark and warmth and silence, but for the slow breaths of his slumber.

TWELVE

KING

"Bless her lying, little omega heart," I murmured, leaning against the door frame of Arsenal's pad in the morning.

Arsenal slept terribly but woke like a raging beast if prodded, so I usually just left his coffee by his bed and let it stir him. I'd made two this morning, as it only seemed polite, but the sight I found halted me in my tracks.

Arsenal was curled up right at the very edge of the bed, as much as was possible without him falling out, and facing the wall, his back toward Onyx. Strangely, on her side of the bed was her purse, as if present for comfort. She, on the other hand, had left most of the remaining space untouched. She was curled up against him, arm over his side. More than that, though, I could hear the faintest light rumble, rising and falling across the space.

She was purring.

Fucking purring. While asleep.

The moment I set the mug down, Arsenal's eyes flew open. His expression was tight as he glared at me, as if I'd kicked his cat or something.

I grinned. "She's purring?" I mouthed.

"All goddamned night," his voice was a low whisper.

"Oh, *poor* you."

"Can you just..." He mimed at her hand, which was balled into a fist at his shirt. I reached out, carefully tugging her grip free and lifting her arm gently. Arsenal ducked out of the bed. I reached out, grabbed a pillow and tucked it beneath her arm where Arsenal had just been. She clutched it to her chest, her brow coming down in a little bunch.

I left her coffee on the other side table, then went to hand him the other, only to catch him adjusting the duvet over her properly. He didn't look the type to be gentle—especially not right now: a canvas of black tattoo upon corded muscle—but people got him wrong all the time. He was maybe a little over protective, impatient and not at all happy about his role as pack lead, but he *was* a good person. If he wasn't, he'd never have ended up in juvie with the rest of us.

Onyx's response to him told me that maybe she sensed that, too. I stifled my smile as he straightened and took the coffee from me, a scowl on his face.

We were just leaving the room when I realised something.

"What?" Arsenal asked.

I looked back at her, listening intently. The room was quiet. "She stopped."

Arsenal's scowl deepened.

To my surprise, Malakai was in the kitchen when we returned. He went to bed late, which meant he hadn't slept much. Not that I'd be able to tell by looking; he was just one of those guys who was always well put together. His bun of thick dark hair was still the perfect amount of messy he preferred, and his morning complexion was like smooth russet clay—while I was still blinking sleep from my eyes, my hair sticking in a dozen directions.

"We should talk," I said, taking a barstool. The missing mug beside the sink meant that Ice was up, but probably on the roof where he drank his morning coffee.

"Yeh. Right. Okay, I did a lot of digging last night—" Malakai began.

"Hold up. Digging?" Last I checked he was pissed—and I'd felt his anger until he'd shut the bond down last night. "We should be on the same page."

"We are on the same page," Arsenal said. "She's staying, we sort the fucker out—nothing below board, not until we've done Riot's job—and then she's gone."

Malakai nodded curtly, even if his expression was tight. I rolled my eyes. "How many grunts did it take the two of you to sort that out?"

Malakai snorted.

"Seven," Arsenal replied, downing the rest of his coffee. "Now, spill. What do you have?"

"It's not what I do have. It's what I don't fucking have. I don't have any info on the pack she rejected. I don't have any info on what ended her up in the hospital—"

"Hospital?"

"Right. Four years ago Onyx Madison turned up at a hospital on the westside with injuries across her whole body and—so she claims—no memory of what happened. It was during the assessment that one of the seers noted her aura had shifted. Soon after, she was designated a duchess."

Arsenal scratched his chin. "Wait. She doesn't remember how she became a duchess?"

"Not the pack. Not the rejection. Nothing," Mal said. "Which is a problem."

"Why?" I asked.

"Because she matched with us."

"And?" But I knew the answer as the question came from my mouth.

"And so she couldn't have matched with us if her old pack was still... intact."

"So..." I winced. "Either they fell apart, or they died." Most likely the latter. The full breakdown of established packs was rare —even having *one* member cleave was rare. The complete breakdown of a pack—enough to collapse its scent (and associated scent matches)—was unlikely without death. By causation or repercussion.

"You see the problem?" Mal asked, glancing between us as if it were obvious.

"I mean... I see a problem for her old pack." I said.

Malakai rolled his eyes. "She's got a stalker, missing memories, and a pack she rejected."

"You think it's connected?" Arsenal asked.

"Only thing Onyx woke up with in that hospital was a tattoo and a scar, both on her arm. And the tattoo was of—"

"The same flower." I'd seen it. A delicate piece across her forearm, and not a flower I'd recognised until I'd seen the dead ones left scattered across her bathroom. I'd just assumed it was the stalker taunting that he knew more about her.

"How do you know about the tattoo and scar?" I asked.

"Pieced it together. She doesn't talk about it publically much, but Ice got hold of hospital records a fan leaked last year. They were all but wiped from the internet, but there are a few copies still hanging around."

"Ice?" Arsenal sounded surprised.

"He was going manic last night," Malakai said. "Came up after she went to bed and started grilling me on everything I'd checked already—" He cut off as Malakai's phone pinged and he snorted flashing it at us. "Keeps sending me anything he can find."

"Right. Well, anything else?" Arsenal asked. "Otherwise we can just, you know, ask her when she wakes up?"

Malakai snorted. "I want to know she's telling the truth. Though—Ice's been sending me *pages* of duchess and duke fan magazines shipping her with the rich alphas she's seen out with, alpha's she's not seen out with, and other dukes—but, this one, you might be interested in."

Malakai pulled up something on his phone and tossed it to me. I read through the bright article, Arsenal peering at it too.

It was a mix and match voting game for famous duchesses titled 'Build Them the Perfect Pack'. And there, along with a number of famous alphas, was my face with the tag 'King Hansen—Voted sexiest bad boy! Our readers think Onyx is up for a challenge'.

Arsenal snorted.

"It's the rich boys I wouldn't play nice with," I said, eyeing the rest of the votes for Onyx's perfect pack. All well known last names. A Lincoln, Oxford, Rife, and a Kingsman.

Huh.

I had hated the attention that stupid magazine had given me, but right now it was hard not to feel a little puffed up.

"There's something else, too," Arsenal said.

"Yeh?" Malakai asked.

Arsenal rubbed the back of his neck. "I told her she could go to work, but only if one of us was with her."

"To... work?" I asked.

Malakai choked on his coffee. "You want to watch her go on dates with another pack?"

A spike of heat hit my veins at those words, and I had to slam the bond shut real quick. I lifted my coffee to my lips as Malakai shot me a funny look.

"Actually..." Arsenal wrinkled his nose. "She said I wasn't an option."

He made it sound like they'd chatted last night. I tried to shove down a little flare of jealousy. Ice had bonded—just barely—with Malakai, leaving me and Arsenal out of it entirely. What if Onyx connected with Arsenal? Would she have room for me?

"Not an... option?" I asked, shoving the thought away. It was hard though, now I'd closed the pack bond down. Knowing they couldn't sense anything I was feeling, I let all my insecurities run rampant.

Arsenal waved at his tattooed face, expression impassive. "It'll have to be one of you two."

Malakai opened his mouth, an incredulous look on his face, when a silken voice sounded behind us. "I would pay you, of course. I could have my lawyer draw up a last-minute contract."

I turned in my chair, and Malakai spun where he stood. She was wearing that plush cream coloured dressing gown and matching fluffy slippers. The golden tan skin of her legs was smooth and perfect, and instantly drew my eye. Her hair was bundled on top of her head in a bun, and her face was bare of makeup and glowing. The mug of coffee I'd left for her was clutched in her hands. The aroma of lavender and brownies drifted into the room with her.

"But," Onyx went on, stepping closer. "I would need my *phone* for that." Something had changed about her, but I couldn't put my finger on it yet.

Malakai glared down at her. "I wouldn't be caught dead tailing around after my scent match on a date with another pack."

"I didn't get the impression you cared much about the scent match designation."

"Apparently, we cared enough to fucking save you," Malakai grumbled.

She slid into the chair around the table's corner from mine. "You insisted on saving me against my will, because you think I'm a damsel, and you three..." She slid her forearms forward along the counter so that her dressing gown popped open just enough that I got a glimpse of the smooth skin almost to her— "...Are primates," she finished.

I scowled, snapping back to her sapphire gaze, but the raised eyebrow look she was giving us all said that I wasn't the only one who'd just felt an obscene gravitational pull on my eyeballs.

"It's just a job," she said, holding my gaze. "Will you do it?" She paused. "Since *Arsenal*—"There was a bitter slant to her tone at his name."—says I can't go without, and it's my work. I can't just stop turning up."

"Work," Malakai huffed, stomping away.

I barely heard, though, swallowed up in her gaze. She rocked back and forth where she leaned on the table, and that gravitational weight shifted with her. "I... uh," I cupped the back of my neck as the golden skin of her cleavage flashed once again. "Yeh, I mean... I wasn't doing anything tonight, anyway. How hard can it be?"

A dazzling smile appeared on her face, and she leaned back in her chair, gripping my forearm and sending goosebumps across my skin. "Thank you." She sounded so earnest.

Feeling his sourness, I couldn't help but glance at Arsenal. He was resting his chin on his fist, absolute disgust in his gaze as he watched me.

"About the pay," Onyx drew my attention back to her. "I consider it more dangerous after Devin. I'll make sure we're in and out quickly... I usually do fifteen percent, but if we called it twenty, would that be fair?"

"Yes. Sure, if you really need to." It felt weird, getting her to pay me, to be honest. I'd do it anyway. I got why Arsenal insisted she stay, but stopping her from working wasn't fair. "Uh... What does that mean?"

"Twenty percent of what I make. I know it's not the way everyone does it, but I always felt better with a fair cut."

"What's twenty percent of a duchess' wage?" Arsenal asked.

"For the night..." She thought on that. "About eight?"

"Eight what?" I asked.

"Grand."

My mouth fell open at the same time I heard a loud crack behind me. Dazed, I glanced behind to see Malakai, frozen halfway down to his computer chair, shattered coffee mug in his fist.

"If you let me have my phone to text my lawyer, I can be more specific on that, though."

Eight grand?

That was the taxes on this dump for the year sorted. Then the loan Arsenal and Malakai got out to start the shop... And maybe we could get a proper room for Ice sorted. He insisted on living down in his nest, but he needed more space than that—

"Fifteen. He won't go for less."

I spun on Arsenal so quick I got a crick in my neck. I winced, grabbing it as I glared at him.

"Shut the fuck up," I snarled. He was a prick, and she was stubborn. He'd ruin it without a thought.

Arsenal's eyebrow rose as he glanced at me. "Eight is fine." My voice was hoarse.

He didn't fucking get it.

Malakai and him pulled in enough with the shop. The worst he looked like was some goddamned gang runner with all of his tats. And what did people care if they worked out who he was? He'd murdered his fucking dad, a notoriously violent alpha. People praised him. But me? They only saw a child killer. It didn't matter that I'd also been a kid when it had happened—I was an alpha. When fear got involved, they didn't see a kid anymore.

I was between jobs.

Again.

Finally Malakai and Arsenal were training me on the bikes,

but I was shit at it—and years late. And I took up too much time with them trying to explain shit to me over and over just so I could fuck it up.

I was stressed anytime I was working without one of them watching me. I'd cost us almost a grand because last time they'd left me alone, and the bike had ended up more broken than it had started. They kept telling me it didn't matter, but how could it not fucking matter?

Arsenal would never say it, but he was tense about me being shop-side when his clients came into the garage. Just in case. They could look the pack up and I'd be listed, but best not to draw attention to it.

Now, I was the only one who said I'd go tonight. She wanted to pay me more money than the other two would see in months—and he thought he would ruin it?

My blood chilled.

She hadn't wanted Arsenal because of how he looked. What if I...? What if someone recognised me while I was with her? I wasn't famous enough that I was spotted on the street. Well, not often, anyway, and I'd be standing back. It... should be fine.

"Alright." Onyx took another sip of her coffee. "Well. The date's at seven. We'll leave an hour early so we can get you an outfit on the way."

"What am I supposed to wear?"

"A suit."

"I have a suit."

"A *decent* suit," she said. The curve of the smile on her lips as she set her mug down wiped away any offence I might have felt at that comment. "Don't worry. I won't deduct it from your pay."

Shopping?

How ridiculously... mundane. I caught Arsenal's eye roll beside me and kept my expression neutral as I shrugged. "Sure."

Yet, inside, I was warring with a childlike excitement I hadn't felt since... Well, since before my sister had died.

ONYX

Malakai's scent of riverside and clove was far too soothing for an alpha as cold as he was. I was straightening my hair in one of their small bathrooms when he came to grill me.

"Want to ask you a bit more about the stalker," he said, folding his arms and leaning against the doorway.

I nodded, glancing at him. He was unfairly gorgeous up close. His skin was a smooth, brassy brown, and his nose was too straight. His lean face was a host to some good cheekbones, cut by two strands of black hair loose from his bun. The furrow to this strong brow seemed fixed in place.

"You set up any cameras?" Malakai asked.

"Yeah. I had them around the apartment," I told him. I'd been over this with the police a few times already, so I was expecting it. "They caught nothing, but a few times they'd been shut off."

Malakai's brow furrowed. "Before the break in?"

"Seemed that way, but I could never tell if it was before or during."

"So he was hacking your stuff?"

I considered that. "I think he was. But when I paid someone to take a look at my devices, they said he was good enough there was no trace."

"Damn..." Malakai muttered. "What did he do when he came in before?"

"The first time he returned something—the earring I'd given my bodyguard as a gift. After that, he'd come in and take my things."

"How did you figure that out?" Malakai asked.

"The forget-me-nots." They were left every time, scattered

across the place he'd stolen from. Each time I saw them, my heart would sink. Sometimes it would take me a while to figure out what was missing, but a pattern emerged.

"And those match... the tattoo?" Malakai was looking at my arm. I lowered the straightener to show him. He examined the tattoo beside the long thin scar.

"Police said it was a taunt, most likely."

"What sort of things did he take?"

"Any gifts I was given by the packs I date. It's why the police think it's definitely an alpha. If one of my dates gave me a gift, it would be gone or smashed in a week."

"What about messages?" he asked. "Any others like the one on the mirror?"

"No," I said, returning to my hair with the hot iron to distract from my tremor of fear. "That was the first one he left."

It was one thing knowing someone was watching me, and another entirely to know he had a voice.

I saw him nodding to himself from the corner of his eyes. "We have an old camera already at the door. I'll get it hooked up again just in case it catches anyone. Footage is grainy, but seems worth a shot."

Well, it couldn't hurt.

He looked about to leave when he paused. "How did you find us?" he asked.

"I..." I chewed on my lip, even more fixated on my hair than before. "Well... the Institute had a file on you—"

"And they *gave* it to you?" He sounded sharp.

"No..." My voice was quiet all of a sudden. "Well, they... showed me the pictures. But then I took the file."

"You... took it? As in—"

"I stole it, alright?" I said quickly, glancing at him. The look he was giving me was far too judgemental. "Who wouldn't have?" I demanded.

He raised an eyebrow, but didn't respond. I swallowed. "Where's Ice?" I still hadn't seen him, and I'd rather change the subject.

"In his nest. Was upstairs earlier."

"Upstairs?"

"We have a roof... deck... sort of thing."

"Is he... upset?"

"At who?"

"At me?" I asked. "I was in Arsenal's bed."

The first smile crept onto Malakai's mouth as he ducked from the room. "His words were, and I quote: 'if one of you oafs can seduce her she'll be more likely to stay, but I'm not holding my breath'."

I frowned "Then why is he—?"

"Hiding?" Malakai asked. "Not that he'll ever admit it, but he's shy."

ICE

I could go up any moment.

She was there. With my pack. And yet I was holed up down here, and I couldn't move as I hugged my knees to my chest, leaning against my wall. The room around me felt colder than ever, doing the job it was designed to do, while she was up there with them right now.

A sick feeling twisted my gut. There was so much I wanted that I could never have. She couldn't stay with me like she was the others because no one could see this place.

The room was musty, with no windows and peeling wallpaper.

Today, another girl had been shoved into my room. She was too fragile for a place like this. She was in the corner, huddled up on her bed. She had perfectly straight hair, soft features, and couldn't be older than fifteen.

An omega with the scent of blackberries and orange.

She was too young.

Taken, just like me. The room was small and grimy, the peeling wallpaper a weak attempt to distance it from the truth of what it truly was.

I wanted to ask her a million questions.

What year was it? Was it summer or winter outside? I didn't even know how old I was anymore.

But... that wasn't fair.

"What's your name?" I asked instead.

She just stared at me, terrified. So I told her stories about anything I could think about that wasn't here. The same ones I told myself so I wouldn't forget. I'd grown up in the Gritch District, and those streets had character and a whole lot of tales. I'd been a no one until I'd perfumed, an idiot street kid just surviving.

I didn't tell her the other parts. That becoming an omega was the worst thing that ever happened to me. That I would have gone to the Institute in a heartbeat if I hadn't perfumed in the wrong place at the wrong time.

Finally, she shuffled a little closer, whispering one word to me.

"Hannah."

I decided in that moment I would get her out. What had happened to me wouldn't happen to her. I hadn't had a chance to contemplate an after, but maybe she had. Maybe, if I got her out soon enough, she would chase dreams I couldn't.

Her eyes weren't yet gold. Perhaps, if I got her out, they never would be.

It had been in this room that I'd woken up one day to find the gold ring around my eyes. Once upon a time, becoming gold pack would have been my worst nightmare, marking a life as an outcast. A life in which my freedom could be stolen at any moment.

In here, that was a threat made of nothing.

Clinical sharp silver glinted back at me from all around. A constant threat that calmed my nerves. I reached out, running my finger along a sharp edge, not enough to break scarred skin, but enough to remind me of the truth. Onyx wouldn't want me. Not really. I had tried to sabotage her even when she fought for me. It was worse that she still wasn't even mad.

This was different to anything before. And I couldn't fight the fact it might be something good... Only I didn't deserve something good.

I reached out and clutched the mug from the side table. It wasn't a good object for hosting scents, but I could still smell her lavender and brownies on it, diluting the poison of my own scent that touched everything down here.

I could feel the draw to her, and the terrifying notion that I didn't feel afraid when she was near.

And that was the most dangerous thing of all.

THIRTEEN

KING

Onyx was relaxed around me.

Hired muscle or not, it was surreal to be strolling down the street at her side. I didn't do normal—couldn't have it. If I was out with the pack, I was wearing hoods, constantly worried someone would recognise me. But the man in a suit staring back at me in the mirror—*I* didn't even recognise him.

It gave me confidence I wasn't used to.

We ducked into the back of the limo, and her driver pulled away. The more distance I got from my brothers, the more I shed the weight of their expectations that we alienate her. It was stupid and shortsighted. The universe had given me two good things up until yesterday. Of the two, only my brothers loved me back, so I couldn't afford to fuck this up with Onyx.

Most people in the world would be horrified at having me as a scent match. But somehow, she wasn't. In fact, she was sitting close, peering up at me like I was a puzzle.

Malakai was already doing a good enough job of making her

dislike us. He'd grilled her all afternoon. Was there anything the police could have missed? Was she sure she'd done everything she could to catch him? The guy had been stalking her for over a month and it was getting worse, didn't Mal think she would have done everything in her power to make it stop?

She reached up and touched the silver sword earring dangling from my left ear, cutting me from my thoughts.

"Does it have a meaning?" she asked.

"Not really," I lied. Much too heavy to bring it up, and would beg questions I wasn't ready to answer.

A gift from Sarah. I'd had my ear pierced while she got both done on our birthday. That was the last shared birthday I'd ever had.

"Should I... take it out?" I asked her, trying not to sound like the idea wounded me. I didn't want to, but it was just one night and I didn't have room to screw this up, not with that kind of money on the line. Again, my stomach twisted at the thought of it. At the thought of giving something back to my pack at last. Of not being a burden.

It still felt too good to be true.

"No." Her brow furrowed. "I like it."

Somehow, she wasn't anxious or uncomfortable at all. Not outwardly, anyway. This whole day felt surreal.

Yesterday, I hadn't known we had a mate. Now it felt to me like Onyx was the centre of the world.

ONYX

King was actually a ridiculously good bodyguard.

He was quiet, and I barely had to give him any instruction on where to stand—or how to stand, or anything. Once I was settled into the pack, he all but vanished into the scenery.

King had given me my phone back at last, but I was ashamed to say I'd not had the faintest urge to contact anyone. I didn't know exactly what I'd say or what I'd ask for. Arsenal was right, I didn't have anyone. I had been so career focused the last few years, my family and friends had drifted. And this pack was—in their own fucked up way—doing what I wanted.

Right now we were at a large lounge in the Khoven pack's choice of venue, with dim lights, and daybeds, and a coffee table of food and drinks constantly cycled in. Currently, sports played across a few TV screens, but the event was focused on the socialising. I couldn't stop my eyes from finding King. I'd never been anxious on these dates, not since my first, but today I found myself off balance.

Taking him shopping before the date had been pleasant. I would be lying if I said it hadn't surprised me. I'd seen his file. I got a little flutter of horror in my stomach every time I thought about it actually. I could ask him about it, but what would it matter what he said?

He could deny he did it, tell me he did, or a thousand things in between. I was stuck with him either way. Perhaps it was the hormones talking, but I didn't feel he was a danger. I knew danger. I knew paranoia, and this wasn't it.

There was what I saw, and what I read.

The King I knew was the man who'd stared, wide-eyed, at himself in the mirror in his new suit with a blush on his cheeks. The man whose apricot champagne scent left me with an unreasonable sense of safety.

Ink printed on paper described a different King. A boy found beside the body of his sister. No reason. Just a confession. The perfect enigma for the world to gape at.

Just like I was.

The duchess with no memories. No pack had come forward.

No history revealed. So the world was left to muse on a wound that I was told I couldn't cradle. Couldn't dream of. Because how *dare* I throw away something others wanted so dearly, and dream of them, too.

I was more of a dreamer than those who reduced fate down to scents and science. I believed there was more to scent matches. Let's say there was a chance—just the smallest, tiniest chance—I could have this bond the world had told me I didn't have the right to dream of...

That was worth a little faith.

No use fearing a thing until you had reason to, and King had given me no reason to at all.

The Khoven pack was my date tonight; they were a pack of four alphas—Lor, Nixon, Percy and Evan—each pompous and rich. I was in contract with a few different packs. They had all requested me—along with many others—and I let them fight over the contracting. My manager informed them I went on eight dates a month, no more. If they wanted more than another pack, they paid up. I went out with the Khoven pack twice a month. They were my least favourite, often dull and a lot more about political manoeuvring.

Lor, the pack lead, was a tall, dark-haired alpha who had—in the last few months—gotten a little more comfortable with me than I liked. Not physically; the boundaries in the contract were airtight, and he was a man who played by the rules. Rather, he had taken to dropping hints about opening the contract further. I'd informed him I had no interest, yet his pack had continued to make offers on my time. They'd even explicitly requested physical boundaries within dates be broadened.

Last week he'd even made a rather obnoxious bid on a particular intimate request. It might have been sweet, I supposed, but I still wondered if he'd been drunk. As it stood, the hand Lor currently had rested on my waist as we sat together was as far as he was allowed to go, and he never failed to take advantage. I couldn't help shooting a glance over at King every time he did it, but my alpha mate was rigid, hands clasped, eyes drifting between me and the rest of the occupants in the room impassively.

Strangely enough, I had to stifle a wave of disappointment. Which was foolish, because it wasn't as if I wanted him. *Or a scene*, for that matter.

Tonight, I knew, was a big night for the Khoven pack. The Khoven pack's company dealt with shipping, and they were trying to entice a new contractor that they claimed would change the game. He'd informed me on our last date that my presence was an absolute must. Not just for status, but Lor Khoven liked that I knew the finer details of their company's process. I took my job seriously enough to do my research. They found it rather effective when I spoke to any of their prospectives about the opportunity they were offering.

During this date, there was a particular issue they'd asked I jump in on if concerns were raised—conflicting schedules between them and a fellow sub contractor. They could say what they wanted, but the truth was clear to me. They asked that I speak on the solution to their biggest concerns, because if a hired duchess could see the solution, then it was *obviously* a non issue.

A few packs arrived early, and though some had omegas, there were no other duchesses hired in. But now, the star guests, those visiting packs, were filing in, presenting gifts—mostly bottles of wine—and greeting everyone. Every time eyes snagged on me, which wasn't an uncommon occurrence, I practically felt Lor puff up at my side. They settled, and one rosy-cheeked alpha who went by Endrick Jr, could not seem to keep his eyes from wandering back to me or the hand Lor had on my waist. Lor made a point of turning to me with a smile.

"You know, we brought you a gift tonight, Onyx. I can't believe I forgot earlier."

Nixon, a blond alpha from the Khoven pack who was equally smitten, if a lot more respectful, stood. "Right, of course." Then he hurried from the room.

"You didn't have to," I said, placing my hand on Lor's arm.

He smiled, eyes twinkling. "I won't hear it."

Nixon returned with a thin black box that he handed to Lor.

Lor opened it before all of the guests. "Oh..." My hand jumped to my mouth. Within the box was a stunning diamond necklace. "It's..." Completely and utterly ridiculous, as was the notion that this wasn't a contrived display for their guests. "...Beautiful, Lor..." I looked around at the others. Nixon was practically glowing. I might actually believe, of all of them, he perhaps *did* think they'd simply forgotten until now.

"Let us see it on, won't you?" Percy asked, and Nixon, who was usually least interested in these events, had perked up, watching my reaction.

I smiled, glancing back to Lor, who was already freeing the necklace from its home. "Of course," I told them, turning so Lor could place it around my neck. The eyes of the entire room were on me as Lor swept loose wisps of hair away and placed the necklace around my neck. I let a contented smile drift onto my face as I felt the weight of it rest, hand coming up briefly to touch it, as if it were the most precious gift in the world.

Finally, when the whole room had been given time to witness the ordeal, I turned back to Lor.

"Thank you," I told him, then glanced at the rest of the pack. It was important to balance my attention. Distribute between them, ensure you have respect for each of them as a pack member, while also respecting the hierarchy. It was different with every pack, and I'd learned to get a feel for it quick. In the Khoven pack, deference to Lor as leader was paramount.

"You look perfect, Onyx," he said, as I returned my attention to him. He'd stepped back slightly, admiring me. That's what I was tonight, walking proof that they had enough money to toss around. Even if I happened to be privy to the knowledge that most of that money didn't come from their company at all.

I reached up and placed my hand on his arm; an offer of contact that drew a smile on his face. There were strict limitations of the kind of contact they could offer me, but they had long since abolished all boundaries for what I could offer them.

When we sat back down, for the quickest flash, my eyes caught King. I was finding I couldn't help it with every new turn of events, as if I was worried I'd look up and he'd be gone. From here I couldn't catch his scent of apricot champagne—especially not since he'd used a spritz of mild scent dampeners.

He was there, though, with his not-entirely-tamable mop of blond hair, and honey tan complexion, looking much better than any other alpha in this room—even if his suit was trying not to be eye-catching. Honestly, he looked like the kind of guy you'd catch on a sunny beach with a surfboard, rather than in a suit at all.

His bright green eyes flickered to mine, and I realised I'd been lingering on him perhaps a little longer than I should. Usually, I could contain my internal eye roll at the more ridiculous parts of my job, but somehow tonight, with a witness to the pomp, it was harder.

What would he think?

His mate, the shallow barbie with money and wealth and alphas. What business did I have coming to his pack and putting them in danger?

Only, I thought, for the briefest moment, I caught the faintest curve to his lips before he returned his attention to the rest of the room.

Aside from the cheeky grin he'd offered me as he stole my pillow last night, I hadn't seen him smile. That one time stuck in my mind, as irritated as I might have been. He was beautiful, miles more beautiful than any other person in this room. I wanted to see him smile more. Just... not here. Not like this.

I had to catch the frown forming at that thought, in case I appeared ungrateful for the gift I'd just been given.

FOURTEEN

KING

"Tell me, why do I feel I recognise you from somewhere?" That question drew me up. It was one of the omegas passing back toward the cove of seats on which the few visiting packs were sprawled.

She was peering up at me curiously. "One of those faces," I said quickly, but my heart rate picked up.

I straightened at my post, clasping my hands, not glancing at anyone else as she kept walking.

It was fine. She'd get distracted and forget.

Time passed slowly as I watched Onyx flirt with the Khoven pack. I used it to determine which rich prat was the worst of them.

"Come now, how long until your next heat?" the pack lead, a dark-haired alpha named Lor, simpered at Onyx. So far, I was pretty sure he was also lead prick. I hadn't known Onyx for more than a day, and I could see she wasn't interested in him. Not really. She was pretending well, but her smile was rigid and fake compared to what she'd offered me earlier.

Onyx breathed a laugh. "You ask that as if you haven't already put a bid in."

Lor worked his jaw, the smile on his face stiff. "At least tell us *which* pack seems to so consistently outbid us."

Onyx winked at him, sipping her wine and saying nothing.

"Just think on it." Lor shifted closer. "We don't have to go through this. Think what we could offer you? These occasions wouldn't be a few times a month. We could treat you every night for the rest of your life."

"Come now, what would your babies look like?" one of the bonded omegas asked with a sigh.

Onyx stiffened, but no one else noticed.

Lor's arm rested so delicately around her, his palm brushing her arm. "They would be beautiful. The specimen of alpha would be obscene. We've got better genes than the Wren pack you sometimes go out with, at least. You have to agree."

"Those hooligans," another alpha snorted.

"Besides," Lor went on, peering down at Onyx. "You're going to have to settle down sometime soon. You can't slip from pack to pack forever, can you? It'll catch up to you, eventually."

Onyx's eyebrows lifted, and there was a flash of something in her eyes. Before she could answer, the omega from before who had recognised me, raised her phone triumphantly. "I was right. It *is* him." She was waving straight at me.

"Who?" Lor asked, clearly irritated at the change of topic.

"Your bodyguard Onyx, King Hansen. I knew it."

The whole room turned to me. I could hear the whispers flooding the space, things I'd heard a million times before. My ribcage felt too tight all of a sudden.

"The criminal?"

"Killer?"

"... How did it happen again...? Lost control of his aura?"

It didn't matter how much time passed, I would never get used to having that day shoved in my face by people who hadn't been there. They hadn't seen my sister's ashen skin and glazed eyes. My twin. Unmoving, no matter how hard I tried to wake her—

"There's a *killer* at my event?" Lor's voice was dangerous as he got to his feet.

Shit.

This was going all wrong.

Like always, it wouldn't just cost me. It would cost the people I was with, and today that meant her. Eight grand, she'd said, and I'd lost my mind. But what the fuck had I been thinking?

"He's in my employ," Onyx said quietly.

"*You* brought him in here?" Lor sounded stunned.

I couldn't move a muscle as I clasped my fingers before me, bracing for what was to come. She was going to tell me to leave. I'd embarrassed her.

Would she be the type to be angry? Or pretend she wasn't?

I found out eventually with everyone. Once they realised the curse I carried, the one I couldn't escape, they left.

Ice liked her, Arsenal was losing his mind over her, and even Malakai couldn't take his eyes away when he thought no one watched. And I'd ruin it for them, just like I ruined everything for them. Again, they'd tell me it didn't matter. It wasn't my fault. Anyone who couldn't deal with it wasn't worth the pack anyway.

But I didn't want to do it again. Not over her—

"I brought my bodyguard." Onyx's voice was smooth, pulling me from the spiral. "As I do quite regularly."

She was trying to save face. It wouldn't work. When she realised she couldn't, she'd distance herself from me instead and tell them she hadn't known.

"What company allowed this?" That was the blond alpha, the one smitten with her, he sounded as if he were trying to smooth it over. But the pack lead, Lor, was fixated on me.

"Company?" Onyx asked.

"They didn't tell you they hire out killers?" I didn't see who asked that, unable to take my eyes from her.

There it was.

I gritted my teeth, knowing exactly what she was about to say. Bracing for it. It shouldn't hurt, I barely knew her, but my throat was tight and I realised I was holding my breath.

When she spoke next, her voice had dropped. I almost missed what she said. "Are you questioning my competence, Lor?"

All other sounds around the room died.

The alpha, Lor, glanced about, eyes lingering on me for just a moment before looking back to Onyx, a half smile on his face as if trying to find the joke. "Are you telling me you knew, and you brought him anyway?"

"I wasn't aware the contract allowed you a say over my employees." She glanced at the rest of the pack. Her voice was cold, spun silk, not one sharp edge to it, and it was enough to send a shiver down my spine. "Did I... miss something?"

"Onyx..." the blond alpha still had that mediating tone to his voice. "You can't blame him—*us*, for being shocked."

"You *believe* I would bring someone into your house who posed a threat?"

"You did," Lor corrected.

"His time is served and slate clean. He poses no threat."

"You *knew*?" Lor spluttered. There was a dangerous silence as Onyx pinned him with a gaze cold enough that he visibly shrunk. She let the silence stretch and Lor seemed off balance. "I mean, you can't tell me you *trust* that?"

"If *your* trust in my professionalism is so low, perhaps we should—"

"Wait, wait!" The blond idiot was on his feet. "Let's not be rash. I'm sure you have an explanation."

"*If* I needed one, I wouldn't owe it to you," she breathed.

"We didn't mean—"

"I don't care what you meant, Richard." Onyx got to her feet, clasping her emerald handbag shut with a neat click. "I'll be leaving."

Onyx crossed for the door, but Lor was after her in a second, his expression dark. "You insult us, and now you think it appropriate to *walk* away?" His hand closed around her arm. I was already moving toward her with barely a grip on my aura at the sight of him laying hands on her. But she spun, her eyes flashing dangerously. As I reached her, she held her hand out to me, drawing me up.

Her next words were low, and there was enough distance that the rest of the guests—who were all staring—couldn't hear. "Less than a minute, it would take me, and no duchess in the city will come near you, not for all the money in the world."

Lor released her instantly, jaw clenched.

"And it will take *less* time to find better company with far less insult."

His face was red, and it wasn't just the wine anymore as he tailed her. One of his own security guards had moved to his back, eyes on me. "You aren't all that, Onyx," he spat. "You are only as relevant as we make you."

Her lip curled. "Your foul soul leaves you paying for affection since you can't have it any other way. Offering me a thousand dollars for a kiss?" She let out a cold laugh.

His jaw clenched, fury written all over his face. Once more, his eyes darted to me. "Careful what information you divulge—"

"Your desperate bids are *not* in our contract," she spat. "And your obsession with me is—"

"Obsession?" Lor spluttered.

"Aside from your hand-me-down wealth, Lor, how much are you worth?" Her fingers closed around my shirt, tugging me closer, and then I was staring down into stunning sapphire eyes. A storm of fury and—right now—demands. "Let me show you."

I stared at her, my mind racing as I tried to understand exactly what she was asking. She leaned up and I felt her fingers tangling in my hair. At that moment, I thought I knew. It was obvious. Or at least I *thought* it was.

I took her chin and drew her into a kiss.

Then I realised I must have lost my mind. *This* was definitely not what she—but her fingers gripped my shirt tighter, pulling me closer. The scent of lavender brownies and her lips on mine sent all my thoughts scattering.

When I drew away, she was breathless. There was a flash of want in her eyes as she stared at me, her porcelain performance of the night shattering.

Okay... Good.

I had been right.

She turned back to Lor, a curl of a smile upon her perfect, plush lips. Then she ripped the necklace from her neck and pressed it to his chest. "Keep your money."

I finally dragged my eyes from her to see the snarl on Lor's expression as he glared between us. I didn't know much in that moment, but what I did know was a thrill as I stared at a man who had everything that was so impossibly out of reach for me. A man who had all of my dreams.

And she had just handed me his.

It was probably wildly inappropriate to be grinning like an idiot right now. Lor looked like he wanted to strangle me, but with my wrist in her sharp nailed grip, she dragged me from the room. I followed, utterly dumbfounded. I recovered a bit of my senses when the cold outside air slammed into me.

I didn't know what to think.

"You didn't need to do that..." I said. "Will they cancel the contract or will you be able to keep them on—?"

"*Keep* them?" She stopped, blazing eyes turning on me with such ferocity that I shifted back a pace. "They wish," she hissed, reaching up and tugging the hair tie from her bun. I followed the waves of her hair as they cascaded down her shoulders. "And Lor put his hand on me, the *brute*. I'll ruin them, and I'll get collateral on top. That contract will tear them to shreds." She was fumbling with her purse, trying to get the clasp open, but her hands were shaking so hard she couldn't open it.

Okay.

Not faking, then.

Not even close.

"Duchess..." I reached out, undoing the clasp for her, but she just seemed more anxious.

"How *dare* he!" She snatched the purse back, rooting around in it. It was a decent size, and clearly quite full since it took her a moment to find her cigarette and lighter, taking the broad steps down to where there were limos parked along the entryway. "How *dare* he make a judgement like that about you. As if he thinks he can know a person from one line on a piece of *paper*—"

"Hey!" I halted her, and when she looked up at me, I could swear there was a faint glistening of tears in her eyes as she fumbled with her lighter. I tucked her hair behind her ear. "It's okay. I get it everywhere." I winced. "I shouldn't have taken the job."

"*You* have done nothing wrong."

Those words were enough to stop the world.

I'd never heard them spoken with such conviction, such honesty, as the furious, trembling omega before me.

She hadn't noticed I'd stopped, still rushing down across the entryway. I caught up to her as she finally stopped beside our limo to cup her hand around her lighter.

"I... don't understand." I couldn't even conceive of the money she'd just lost for me. "I'm not worth your job."

"You don't deserve that."

"You don't know what I deserve."

"That's *not* how it works." She was back to being furious as she jabbed me in the chest, cigarette lowered so she could square me up. "I don't have to know anything to demand better."

I stared at her, still absolutely off balanced. "You... kissed me."

"*You* kissed *me*," she replied as if it were that simple.

I snorted, staring at her, but the way her furious sapphire eyes glittered killed all retorts from my brain.

I had to get it together. "You don't have to pay me for that shit show."

"I'll be paying you double for fucking damages."

I snorted. "I'm not taking the money." It might hurt to say those words, but it was the right thing. "I just lost you a contract."

"*They* lost themselves a contract. Do you know how many packs would fill that spot in a heartbeat?"

Something coiled tight within me, threatening a growl. "What if—?" I cut off, stifling the response that just leaped to my tongue.

"What if what?" I didn't know what had changed, but all of a sudden, there was static between us.

I waited, and the silence between us stretched, and lavender and brownies filled my senses as her pupils expanded as she watched me. Next thing I knew, I had pressed her against the limo.

She was the centre of the universe. Her aura—identifiable as intoxicating lavender and brownies—was like nothing I'd ever felt from an omega before. It was strong, absolute, and sure. She was a goddess. Even with a cigarette in shaking fingers. And she was trembling in anger for me, her blazing gaze holding mine, still making dares of me.

I took her face between my hands and kissed her again. Brownies and lavender curled in the air around me, wiping my mind clean as her lips parted for me. Her tongue pressed into my mouth as if she couldn't get enough.

Back. Off.

I could almost hear Arsenal's command in my head. But I just... couldn't. She was too tempting and my brain was half off a cliff after what had happened in the club.

Not just what they'd said, resurrecting all of my monsters, but watching her with those filthy alpha's hands all over her. It was different, Ice prancing about the garage with loose, low cut v-necks and little seductive purrs. I didn't have to watch other alphas put their paws on him.

Well, Malakai, I supposed, when Ice was in heat. But that had always felt like a spark of hope, not competition.

Right now, I had Onyx pinned against the limo, and she wasn't fighting me. Her lavender scent spiked, her sapphire eyes daring. She reached up, tugging on my collar. "If *what*, Alpha?"

I almost groaned at that word on her tongue. My filthy hindbrain ran off with imaginings of hoisting that dress up and taking her right here. She never spoke without control, but I wanted to hear what she'd sound like with that word on her tongue; a plea, not a dare.

I leaned closer, each word a low growl. "What if I don't want any other packs to fill that spot?" I needed to watch my hormones, or I'd go into a fucking rut. Her grip on my hair tightened, and I reacted with those hormones, leaning down and pressing my lips to hers.

This woman had defended me, and never asked a thing. No explanation. No... nothing.

No one in my life had offered me that, and she had no idea what it meant. Not forcing me to speak those words one more time, even if I thought they might just be believed.

I didn't do it.

I'm innocent.

They carved out a piece of me each time. The baseline for everyone else in the world existed without those words, but for me, I could barely scrape normal together if I screamed them at the fucking night sky.

And she'd not made me say them.

I slipped my hand beneath her dress and the sweetest little whine rose in her chest. I was right. Seeing the wild omega side of her break past that perfect exterior was the hottest thing I'd ever witnessed.

"Did you like it?" I asked. "Making me watch?"

She groaned, lips parting further as I slipped a finger into her. I loved watching the way her pupils blew. It changed everything about her. She went from controlled, rich duchess to wild omega, pristine edges cracking...

"Your leashed criminal." I pressed a kiss to her neck with each word, driving my fingers into her. I didn't know why I said it. It didn't make me feel good. It was likely as much to turn her on as it was to degrade me. To remind me that no matter what was happening, no matter how much she might invite me in, I couldn't ask to go further. I need her to know how much I adored what she'd done, but I didn't deserve anything out of it.

Her fingers laced through my hair, dragging me to face her. "I don't believe that's all you want to be," she whispered.

I stared at her in shock for a moment.

It didn't matter, it's what I was—what we all were. Arsenal wore it like a badge of honour, but I never had. The others could tell me there was more that defined me, but the world recognised my face, not theirs, so it meant nothing. Yet, hearing it from her was different.

I tugged her fingers from my hair and sank to my knees. She looked adorably startled, but I didn't care. I drew her legs over my shoulders, pinning her to the limo with my palm, and then used my other hand to tug her panties out of the way.

I pressed my tongue to her little bud as I drove my fingers back into her, relishing in the little moan she let out. This was the singularly hottest thing I'd ever experienced. She was everything, her sweet lavender scent in the air, the way her heels dug into my back as she arched against me; it was all Heaven.

Whether it was the setting or the hormones, it didn't take long before she came apart against me, thighs clamping around my ears. I didn't let that stop me working her until every last shudder had died down and she was panting softly above me.

I let her down, standing and cupping her chin in one hand, while I pressed my two fingers to her lips, her scent and wetness coating them. She parted her lips, pressing her teeth gently to my skin. Then she took my hand in hers and directed my fingers to the limo's roof. She guided them, drawing a little heart that glistened faintly in the lamplight above.

I raised my eyebrows, confused.

"Our limo is over there." She nodded her head a few spaces forward.

"And this one?" I knew there was a grin spreading on my face, guessing the answer before she said it.

"Khoven pack's."

Rich or not, *this* was my dream girl.

FIFTEEN

ONYX

I was on the roof of their garage alone, a warm cup of tea in my hands while I huddled in my favourite fluffy nightgown.

Up here, like everything else, was makeshift—not meant to be enjoyed at all. But they'd made do with some rusting chairs beneath a rickety, wooden structure, on top of which was nailed a tarp. It wasn't raining now, so I leaned on the metal railings, gazing out across the city lights.

It was comforting, seeing the sprawling city around here. I loved looking at the city at night from my apartment balcony. I loved New Oxford. The city was always alive, like an old friend I could always rely on if I didn't want to feel so alone.

This was new and familiar all at the same time. The night was louder than I was used to, occasional cracks splitting the air and the sound of cheering, chatting, or laughter from passersby on the street beyond.

I took a sip of my drink, letting everything sink in. King made everything feel a lot more normal. I don't know how *that* made sense, given he'd just been a major part of upending my job before pinning me against a limo—in public—to give me an orgasm.

My thoughts wandered to Ice. I'd come up here hoping to find him—they told me this was his territory. But he wasn't here.

Which meant he was still in his nest.

Was he... okay?

He'd been the first one interested in me, but now...

Well, I was literally in his alpha's beds. No matter what he'd said to Malakai about me and his alphas, it had the potential to cause problems. I hoped I could talk to him tomorrow.

I was still processing what had happened between me and King.

It was just a physical thing. It could mean nothing... and yet it didn't feel that way; it felt like we'd just opened a door we wouldn't be able to close again.

Absently, I ran my palm along the tattoo on my forearm, feeling the bump of the scar. For a brief, startling moment, guilt gripped me.

Traitor.

A face flashed in my memories. He was looking at me. He had a heart-shaped face, chestnut eyes crinkled into crescent moons, and his grin was impish. His hair was sunny blond and tied up in a bun with wisps fluttering around his cheeks.

I froze, fingers pausing over the scar on my arm, my heart racing.

It was gone as soon as it appeared. My nails bit down on my scar, breathing picking up as I scrambled to get it back.

But my mind was a void, and I was left clawing at nothing at all.

KING

I'd just finished straightening out my bed when Onyx appeared in my room. Her hair was down, and she wore her fluffy dressing gown with her emerald handbag on her arm.

This whole bed situation was weird. It felt wrong. I got why Arsenal was getting protective, but my room was tucked into the back corner of the garage. There weren't any entrances near. "I thought I could sleep on the couch." If anyone got in, they'd have to pass me—and Mal—before they got to her. "If... If you want." My mind jumped back to this morning. She had been purring all night with Arsenal.

She stared at me, not saying anything as she crossed and sat at my side. I looked closer and realised she was different. There was a bunch to her brows and her face was paler than usual.

"Are you okay?"

She looked up at me for the longest moment, opening her mouth and then shutting it again. Then, finally, she spoke in the lowest breath. "No."

"Can I help?"

She looked like she was truly considering that. "I don't know."

"Do you want me to leave?" I didn't care if Arsenal gave me shit. She deserved my respect. But she shook her head, then looked a little confused as to why she had.

"Okay." I moved back on the bed, tucking myself under the blankets and sitting back against the headboard. She was watching me with calculating eyes, as if she was working up to a question.

"You know what I am," she said at last. "You haven't asked a thing about my past."

I shrugged. "You know my record. *You* haven't asked."

"It's not my business," she replied. That was debatable at this point, since she was being bullied into sleeping *in* my bed, but I shrugged.

"Likewise, Duchess."

A small smile crept onto her lips as I leaned my head against the headboard. Still, something nagged at me as she shrugged off the fluffy dressing gown for the silken pyjamas beneath. I dropped my gaze before she caught me staring.

"You'll still uh... let me around you?" I asked. Did she have any idea how much that set her apart from other human beings?

She shuffled to the side of the bed, setting her handbag down on the side table. Her reply came as if it were perfectly obvious. "Ice feels safe around you."

I choked a laugh. "Ice hates me."

She adjusted the handbag, leaning back and inspecting it. "I don't think there's anything simple about Ice, but he built a nest in your home."

"Oh." I'd never thought about it like that before.

It took a while before she was satisfied with the position of her handbag, then she shuffled under the covers and sat at my side.

"Why did you search us out?" I asked.

She couldn't bond with us. If she bonded us, she'd no longer be able to work as a duchess. Her aura would always have its duchess-y allure, but the bite on her neck would give her away.

She'd lose everything.

"Maybe..." She hesitated, and I saw a flicker of something vulnerable in her eyes, as if she was about to take a leap of faith. "Maybe I'm a fool, but I believe love is worth more than all the money in the world."

"With the kind of money you lost today just by kissing the wrong guy, you better be right."

She smiled, and I shivered as her touch brushed my arm. She turned my hand in hers, chewing on her lip. "I didn't kiss the wrong guy."

Again, I felt that thrill of pride. "He really offered you a thousand dollars for a kiss?"

"You should have seen their bids on my heat."

"You let alphas bid on your heat?"

"I'd be a fool not to, don't you think?"

I barked a laugh at that. "Aren't you worried the winning bid will be a pack you hate?"

"Darling." She breathed a laugh, giving me a pitying look. "The Khoven pack win every time. Their bids are getting—quite frankly—comical."

"But you—"

"I can *choose* whomever I wish."

"And you never tell them?" I grinned.

"It's not my job to teach them not everything is about money."

I chuckled at the image of those alphaholes tearing their hair out, wondering why nothing was working.

A silence stretched, and when I glanced at her, I saw that worry returning. Finally, she spoke. "Can I tell you a secret if you promise not to tell the others?"

"I can keep a secret."

"I've never said it to anyone. Not out loud but... It wasn't just the... stalker." For the briefest moment, her eyes glistened, but then she blinked. She looked so small. "I'm... alone."

I understood isolation. Loneliness. We all got it. How isolated had we all been when we were younger? Since the accusation all the way until I met my brothers... the only ones who accepted me. I remember the days were so silent, stretching to infinity.

A slow torture.

Right now I could see that in Onyx.

I pulled her into my arms before thinking. But the moment I did, she opened up more. "I can't tell anyone because I'm not supposed to be lonely."

That must be the most isolating thing of all. No one else

seeing it. It *was* a strange thing to consider—a lonely duchess. At one point, she'd had mates before us. Had she rejected them because they were awful? Awful enough to offer a princess bond...?

It was the best bond an omega could be offered.

No.

Something didn't add up, and I knew that was a mystery she lived with.

"I went to the Institute because... I don't know. I wanted change, but I was scared of it. So it seemed right to match with a well-off pack. It was safest. It's a world I know. But when I matched to you, this huge part of me was so..." She chewed on her lip. "So fucking relieved."

"Why?"

"All the rich people I know are lonely, just like me. Putting them together doesn't seem to fix that."

"We're appealing because we're poor as shit."

She shrugged, a giggle bubbling to her lips. "I know Arsenal *insisted* on this situation, but I've never felt less lonely than I have in the last few days."

I tugged her closer before I caught myself, and the faintest purr rumbled in my chest. It died just as fast, heat creeping up my neck.

Shit.

Had I really just done that?

I couldn't look at her. I thought she drew closer to me though.

"Just uh..." I cleared my throat, trying to make it less embarrassing. "You know... No one should feel alone."

We remained in silence for a few moments longer. "I didn't remember them," she said at last.

"Who?"

"My mates from before."

I stared at her, mind racing. *"Didn't?"*

"I... don't know... I thought today... after..."

Onyx went stiff in my arms. I withdrew, looking down. There was something strange about her. She blinked, her head shaking just slightly as if she were reading invisible lines of text.

"Onyx...?"

She didn't reply, eyes still flickering, her nails digging in where she clutched my arm.

"I can't... can't..." She looked like she was ready to throw up. "Talk about them."

I drew her chin up to face me. "We don't have to."

"I mean..." She gulped for air. "I can't because..." Something in her expression shattered as she found my eyes at last. "I don't know *why* I sent them away. I wanted a pack since I perfumed, it was my dream. And then... I woke up in a hospital a duchess. No memory, just a tattoo and a scar. Until I know the truth, how could I even consider having that again?" The words spilled out so fast I wondered if she'd ever spoken them out loud before.

Her *dream*?

I hadn't expected that. But suddenly, a lot more made sense.

"Onyx, I promise you couldn't have found a better pack if you're looking for second chances. It's all we're fucking doing."

Maybe... Maybe there was something more to scent matches than just biology. Maybe we really were perfect for her.

But... What was I saying?

What was *she* saying?

This was supposed to be temporary.

It didn't feel it. Nothing about this felt casual. And what if she *was* meant for us?

Usually hope scared the shit out of me; the fragments of shattered dreams I was forced to tread barefoot every fucking day served as a constant reminder. But it didn't right now. Not with her holding me like this.

I shifted until we were both lying in bed and held her until her breathing slowed.

I couldn't sleep, not for a long time. I was usually out the moment my head touched the pillow, but something stopped me. It wasn't until her sleep became deep enough and I heard the faintest, low purr in her chest, that I finally relaxed.

It was validation. So I just lay there, holding her against me, marvelling at the little omega that somehow felt safe in my arms. Something I'd long ago believed I could never have. It was hard to explain what a gift that was.

SIXTEEN

ICE

"It's your nest, isn't it?"

"What?"

I stepped up beside Onyx as she sat holding a morning tea on their garage top patio. She was ridiculously perfect, with a messy bun, soft, moisturised skin, glittering sapphire eyes with those dark lashes and a cream dressing gown.

Of course, in her arms was the green handbag. Her eyes dropped to it. "My... nest?"

"You take it everywhere." I pulled up a chair beside her and sat down on it with my morning coffee, trying to act like I wasn't nervous at all. It had taken me a number of attempts. They'd all replayed over in my mind before I'd sucked it up and hurried up the steps before I could change my mind.

"I *had* a nest," she said. "This isn't it."

"Okay." I said, sipping my coffee. "Can I see it?" I held my hand out.

She recoiled, a little flash in her eyes, her bag clutched closer than ever.

"Alright." I sipped my coffee again to stifle my smile.

She pursed her lips, eyes dropping to the bag in her arms. "It's... *possible*, I might be substituting certain comforts while I'm... between..."

Homes?

I saw the brief sadness cross her features, and decided to change the topic. "King's bed last night?"

Her eyes snapped to me. "Yes."

"Oh. You're blushing. What happened?" My heart rate picked up. Envy? Lust?

"We... Nothing— In his room, I mean. At work... We just kind of..." She was flustered. "Not all the way, and it wasn't planned—"

"I'm not with him." I cut her off. "You know that. He knows that."

"I know but... He's your alpha."

"The fact he doesn't fuck other omegas is entirely his choice. I never banned him."

None of the pack fucked other omegas. Or betas. Or anyone. It was a silent promise they made, knowing if *any* of us said it out loud it would all blow up in our faces. Just like I never told them I was grateful. Even though I was, and I don't know what I'd do if they ever changed their minds. Which was stupid, because I wouldn't commit to them so it was wildly unfair, but I wasn't ready to face that.

All that aside, Onyx wasn't *other*. I'd silently told *them* that when I'd demanded she stay.

Basically, it was a mess and our pack communication was top tier.

But they could fuck Onyx. I wanted them to, actually. She'd be more likely to stay, and I would be less likely to screw it all up.

She seemed a bit off balance, though. "So, uh... how did you meet them?" she asked.

I snorted, but something weary stirred within me. "Bit of a stupid situation, really."

She waited, sapphire eyes as disarming as ever, making me want to open up more than I'd wanted to in years.

"Secret for secret?"

"What do you want to know?" she asked.

"Won't tell until after."

She tapped her manicured nail on her cheek, thinking. "Alright then. Tell me."

"Hmm..." I sipped my tea, considering. I realised I'd never told the story before. I'd never spoken it out loud. "Started because I thought they had money."

"What?" Whatever she had been expecting, it clearly hadn't been that.

"I'd just got out of some... shady shit. I needed money to get away. I didn't have many resources. And look, I'm smart as fuck, right? But not good at reading situations."

"What do you mean?"

"Alright, so when you get out of juvie, they offer these programs. Start your own business and such to get you back on your feet. Anyway. Malakai started one, and it was doing really well. Like... *really* well. I didn't read between the lines."

"That what?"

"That Mal's from the Harpies. That kind of gang don't let you go easily, and there was no good reason for his business to be doing that well."

"Oh." Her eyebrows shot up. "Laundering?"

I nodded, scrunching my nose up. "He wanted out. It's one way they'll let you out. Something about the fresh start programs are actually really good for that sort of thing, so sometimes they lean on their old members. Do this for us, and you're home free, you know?"

"Ah."

"So, when I blackmailed them I had no idea I was launching myself right in the middle of a full-blown gang laundering scheme."

"Wait. You blackmailed the pack?"

"Uh. Yes. He was skipping some of the health and safety requirements and they'd been cracking down recently. Didn't need that much cash, besides. Only, they thought I was onto them about the laundering."

"Shit."

"Then Arsenal caught me—managed to track me down from the call. Next thing I know, I've got these three pissed off alphas in the attic I was hiding in. By that time, I knew about the laundering 'cuz it all came out, right? And Mal wasn't sure what to do with me. I knew all his dirt and if I spilled, he'd be in trouble with the Harpies. Arsenal thought bonding me was the obvious solution, but Mal didn't want an omega—"

"Wait, Malakai didn't?"

"Right. He was pack lead when I met them. For about five minutes."

"Oh..." Her eyes went wide. *"Oh."*

"Yup." I breathed a laugh. "Arsenal said he wouldn't risk Mal going back to jail for the sake of me. Mal didn't want them all to have to bond me just because he was tangled up in Harpy business. So, next thing, there was a violent alpha brawl in this tiny little attic. King barely dragged me out alive, because I swear Mal was trying to kill me."

"But you and Malakai are—"

"The closest?" I asked. "Yeh." Suddenly, I couldn't meet her eyes. *"Mal* didn't want to bond me." Mal hadn't wanted me at all.

I knew where he stood. I knew, if it came down to it, he'd leave me behind. And in that, there was absolute safety. It wasn't something I could explain, just like my nest wasn't.

"Also," I added, since I didn't want her to linger on what I'd just said. "I'm pretty sure he's straight."

"He's *what*?"

"Like... as straight as an alpha can be."

"But... your heats?"

"No... He does... And he's... Well, hormones." I shrugged. "He doesn't fake anything, if that's what you're wondering." He was into it, truly. It was one thing he absolutely let me feel from him, and I needed that.

"He's also great in bed. Likes to be in control." Mal was *hot* in bed. Way too fucking hot—not that I could afford to linger on *that* with my heat upcoming.

Onyx stared at me. Her cheeks were rosy, and she looked like she was scrambling to change the subject.

Oh. Cold Mal still intrigued her.

"So... you, uh, hate Arsenal because of the bond?"

"I could give you the full list, but we'd be here all day."

She raised her eyebrows as if she didn't quite believe me. "He'd have dark bonded me in a second, though. I'll tell you that."

She stared at me, shocked. "Why?" she asked. "Was he afraid you'd still tell on Malakai?"

Exactly that. A dark bond would have given him absolute control over me, one word from him and I'd not have been able to speak a word about Mal. A flutter of ancient terror rose in my stomach, along with a stirring of resentment. Onyx, with her beautiful blue eyes, born to money and freedom, she couldn't understand.

"Don't give a shit why he wanted to steal away my freedom. I just care that he did."

Onyx paled. "I... didn't mean it like that. I'm sorry. I was just trying to figure out why he didn't."

Because we'd struck a bargain. It was Mal who'd come up with a deal to offer me. That I take the bond and keep their secret, but that any physical affection at all would be initiated by me. I'd demanded two more things. I wanted to hear them swear off any threat of physical violence, and that I'd owe them nothing as their omega. No comfort, no aura management. No ruts. They'd agreed, and I'd taken the deal, knowing it was the best I was going to get.

And maybe... Maybe there was more to it than just that...

I cut the thought off. "I've got a silver tongue." And *not* because Arsenal was a decent person who'd been caught in an impossible situation. He was a giant, fucking possessive prick. I would stand by that.

Onyx leaned back in the chair, a smile playing on her lips. "Worse case I've ever seen."

I smiled, something loosening in my chest.

She'd not asked the obvious question. The one I always dreaded. *Why are you a gold pack at all? Why not go to the Institute and get the damn injection?*

"They said you don't leave this place often?"

"No. I'm not registered. There are still people after me." I winced, knowing that would open a can of worms.

"You're not registered?" She was back to horrified. Again, with her delightful tendency to miss the obvious questions I didn't want to answer. "That's so dangerous. The Institute—"

"Isn't everything it seems," I cut her off sharply, not willing to delve into that conversation.

Just go in, give them all your information and you'll get a shiny card.

It'll protect you, Ice.

What are you afraid of?

They had no idea. There were people at the Institute waiting for me to do exactly that. Sure, registration would protect me—if I made it. I never would. And the moment they had my details—my address—they'd turn up and I'd be taken away without a trace.

A dark, musty room with no windows and peeling wallpaper flashed in my vision, but I shoved it away.

I knew too much. They would never let my name end up in that side of the system. Onyx, to her credit, didn't push it, seeming to read the discomfort on my face.

"I was wondering why the pack wasn't listed with an omega..." she mused, instead.

"Ah. You thought you'd get the grouchy pack of ex-cons in their luxury garage all to yourself?" I asked.

She looked to be fighting a smile. "Silly of me."

"Okay," I prodded her. "Your turn."

"Right."

I swirled my drink, knowing I might be about to poke a bee's nest, but my curiosity was getting the better of me. "You said there were only 23 packs that were interested in an omega like you."

It didn't make sense. She was a duchess. She was beautiful, wealthy, refined... She was perfect. Was it because she'd rejected her mates before? No way. Assuming she was looking, that wouldn't be a disqualifying point. The packs could just offer her a normal bond and not take a risk with a princess bond.

Onyx's scent shifted instantly, something hostile raising its head. Her cheeks were pale.

"Don't." I held up a hand quickly. "I don't want to know anything you don't want to tell me."

She shut her eyes. "It's not..." She sighed. "It's fine." But I could see that it wasn't.

"No." I had been serious. Telling her my secrets hadn't been a burden. Actually, it was the opposite. I didn't need anything back for that.

She rested back on the seat, unsure. "How long has it been?"

"Since?"

"Since you joined the pack."

"Three... and a half years?" Had it really been that long?

She considered that, taking another sip of her drink. "Do you think you'll ever...?"

"Like them?" I snorted. "Look, I know this is hard to understand for most omegas. It's supposed to be in our blood and all, but I never wanted a pack. I don't want them or any kind of bond. I never wanted to be a fucking omega."

The words came out more bitter than I intended. More shocking, however, was that as I spoke out loud the words I'd clung to for years, I realised they were lies.

No. They *weren't* lies. I was just tired of the reality I'd never escape, trying to find fucking comfort in what I had left.

"What *do* you want?" she asked.

"To be alone." Again, I barely missed a beat, and again, something twisted inside of me at the idea of it. *Did I really want that? A world without the pack? Without touch—or even the possibility of it? And what about heats?* Then again, if this was a dream world, I wouldn't have them. I wouldn't be a fucking omega. I'd be a beta. Someone who didn't rely on others to survive.

And then I could be lonely and it would be fine. I would be safe.

She stared at me for a long moment, and then a twisted smile appeared on her face as she breathed a laugh.

"What?"

"It's just... you have everything I want, and I have everything you want."

I snorted and a strange quiet filled the air. "Can I, uh... see your nest?" she asked, at last.

I scratched my head, anxious all of a sudden. "It's not visitor friendly." That was a fucking understatement. I rubbed my fingers together, feeling the faint traces of scars along them.

"Tell me about it?"

"I... It's hard to explain. I don't think it would make you feel much better."

"Why?"

"It's... a mess."

"It's supposed to be a mess."

"I promise. There's nothing cosy about it. Not to other people, anyway."

She nodded, contemplating that, but I got the feeling there was something else on her mind. "About the... intimacy. I swear, I wasn't planning—"

"I know." I raised my hand defensively. But she really needed to stop bringing that up. Now I was trying desperately to bury the image of King's muscular form caged around her as he—

"It really doesn't bother you?" she asked, ripping me from it.

"Really." I wrinkled my nose. "Have 'em."

"Let's say I did... do anything with them." There was, I thought, the smallest hint of mischief in her voice. "You wouldn't want to be a part of it?"

A *part* of it?

"You wouldn't want to watch or... join in?"

Fuck, what the hell kind of game was she playing? I stared at her, shaking my head quickly as my heart pounded, my scent hitting the air like a beacon screaming *liar, liar, liar*.

She took a sip of coffee, something dancing in her eyes as she regarded me.

How could someone sipping coffee in a dressing gown with a messy bun look so fucking devastating?

"I mean, I would feel better if we both froze out Arsenal—" The prick."—but..." I rolled my eyes. "It's probably a losing battle." I cleared my throat. I was rambling in my attempt to salvage this. "I *could* be collaborative if they were the ones forced to watch."

Wait. *Why had I said that?*

My blood ran unreasonably hot at the thought, but... her scent shifted. Fucking lavender and brownies was smothering me. Was... Was my scent doing the same thing?

She was watching me from beneath those heavy lashes, her pupils blowing wide. So... Yes. Probably. But I couldn't stop. She was perfect. More than that, she was safe. She wasn't an alpha; she wasn't here to claim me.

She was my mate.

But then... not just Malakai, but King and Arsenal, too? Watching me with Onyx?

"Ah," she said. "Is that right?" I swear it sounded like a dare, and blood rushed to my crotch.

Did I really want that?

Okay. Maybe. Just for the sake of taunting them.

Nothing else.

VIPER

"You got room to fit me in?" I asked, hauling the shiny motorbike up the gravel toward the garage.

The huge metal door was open and I could see Arsenal just inside, working. I'd bought it today. I'd kicked it a few times, but it was pretty solid, so then I'd looked up ways to break a bike. Finally successful by the strange noise it was making when I turned the key, I had me and the bike dropped off around the corner and walked it up the street.

Arsenal got to his feet, wiping his hands off as he saw me approaching.

"Uh, yeh. You know the problem?"

"Not a clue." I halted, turning the key, proud of the strange sputtering noise it made. Arsenal dropped his rag as his eyes snagged on the black bike properly. Then he hurried over.

"Fuck... That's... Is that a '57 Hound?" I was surprised at his enthusiasm. He crouched beside it, hand resting on the seat. While he did that, I examined him. He was wearing jeans and a dark red shirt with the sleeves rolled up. By the stains of black, it was for work.

His hair was dark, a few loose waves tumbling down to his eyebrows, the sides cut shorter. He seemed more practical and down to earth than I was expecting, and not the thug that stared back at me from the picture Kai had given me.

He was covered in tattoos. I could see a rose down from the back of his neck to his collar. His face tattoos were more sparse, but I could make out a knife, a cross and an autumn leaf. I narrowed my eyes. I had tattoos down my arms. Onyx had sat in on some of those sessions. She liked them.

But face tattoos were a bit excessive, weren't they? She wouldn't prefer his, *surely...*?

Arsenal cocked his head, staring back at me, still rubbing his strong jaw with oil-stained fingers. His hazel eyes had more excitement in them than I was expecting.

Oh. He'd asked me a question.

The bike.

"Yes..." A Hound. I thought so. I didn't really know. Hound sounded right, though. I'd just asked for one that would make me look cool, and the guy had pointed me to some old models. The price tag had only been a couple hundred—not that I knew how much bikes were supposed to cost.

"And you trust me with her?" He was wiping his brow as he stared along the bike's body.

"Uh... Yes. I trust you with her."

"The parts are going to be pricey to order in."

"I'm just, uh... want her back in working shape." I clapped my hands together.

"Great... Yeh..." Arsenal still looked a bit dazed as he stared at the bike.

A good choice then.

At that moment, one of the others—Malakai—stomped down the steps toward us.

"Morning, sunshine," Arsenal said as he began wheeling the bike back into the garage.

"Guess what was outside on the porch before I went to bed?"

Arsenal paused, looking back at Malakai. "More of the damn flowers?"

"He's fucking *taunting* us, goddamned freak."

I froze, eyes darting between them both.

They were talking about her stalker? But I'd been out there all night. How had I missed him? Was it possible... Could they know who I was?

"What do we do?"

"I told you. Just lay low for now. He's not getting in and if he does, we'll gut him."

There was a pause as Malakai set up my bike in the shop, shifting around a few things to make room. I could see the frown of worry on his face.

"What's Kenneth's doing here again?" Malakai asked, examining the few bikes lined up.

"Just the tires. Tell him it was nothing and don't charge," he said. Malakai nodded as Arsenal pointed to the next one. "Engine leak." He pointed to another. "And rusted tank—I keep telling Chris she can't keep running it so low. I'm grabbing a break, then I'll take this one, not actually sure what's up with it—" He looked up at me after patting my bike.

"You left your number, yeh? I'll call to let you know what I think tonight. Don't worry, we'll get her back on the road." He smiled, but I could see he was thrown by what Malakai had just told him.

I nodded, taking a step back. "Thanks."

Before I turned, I darted one more look at Malakai's

towering figure as he got set up in the garage. His dark hair was in a messy bun, with a few strands loose around his cheeks. His nose was strong and straight, and his heavy brows suited his face. I wouldn't lie, I'd seen the article on King, but I was a little disappointed the other two were so good looking in person as well.

An hour later, I sat across the street from their shop, leaning against a grimy wall. I was far enough away that when I let my aura free, they wouldn't sense it. The world exploded with sound, and I honed it to the best of my ability. The garage door was wide open and I tuned in to what was going on.

"I fucked it up." I recognised the speaker as King, who had come out and was now sitting on the bike beside the one Malakai was currently working on.

"How?" Malakai straightened.

"I... was recognised in the middle of her date."

"Shit," Malakai muttered. "I'm sorry. What, uh... did she do?"

"She lost it."

"Damn. Sorry mate—"

"No. I mean... she lost it on them for calling me out," King said.

"She did...?" Malakai sounded unsure.

"Yeah, I mean really lost it. Kissed me in front of them—"

Malakai dropped his tool with a clatter as he sat up to stare at him. "She did what?"

"This rich prick was pissed she brought me, was obviously into her. But she uh..." King rubbed the back of his head. "Well, she kissed me in front of them all."

I straightened, a growl ripping from my chest. I had to hold myself back from crossing the street toward them..

No. This was what I wanted. This was good.

I shoved the wounded part of me back down so I could keep listening in.

"Ah." Malakai, somehow, didn't sound pleased. At least I thought not. It was hard to focus.

"Okay, but that's the problem. I sort of ruined her date. I can't... I can't go again."

Malakai grunted.

"So... Well, she has another one tomorrow. Since she can't take Arsenal—"

"No."

"Come on, man. I feel like shit. I lost her one job, and she's saying she'll pay me double."

"I'm not going to watch her fuck around with other alpha pricks."

"You feel alright losing her her job?" King asked.

"It's not my fucking problem."

"Why, cuz Arsenal said we were sticking with her?"

"Yeah, actually," Malakai said. "Not my decision, not my problem."

"You're a dick, you know that?"

"She brought a stalker down on our heads, and she doesn't seem to even think there's anything—"

"She was fucking terrified. And she *does* care. She feels really guilty."

"Bloody hell, King, one kiss and she's melted your fucking brain." There was a pause. "It... was just one kiss, right?" He sounded unnerved. "Jesus—"

"She's our mate. Besides, we didn't go all the way..."

I balled my fists, steadying my breathing.

This was good.

This. Was. Good.

"You fucking idiot—"

Both of the alphas visibly froze, and then they turned back to the rest of the shop—or home, actually, since it looked like they lived in the open space past the railings of the shop.

"Do you—?" King began.

"Yeh." Malakai sounded like he was speaking through gritted teeth, clearly shocked. Whatever they were hearing from inside the garage, I couldn't catch from here.

"Should we—?"

"Absolutely fucking not," Malakai growled.

"Sorry mate, but there is no way in hell—if that's what I think it is…" King was already hurrying back in and out of sight.

Malakai stood stock still for a long moment. Then he slammed the tool he was gripping down with a loud thud and a curse, and followed King, pushing a button on the wall on the way out.

The last thing I saw was the shop door sliding down.

SEVENTEEN

MALAKAI

The scent we'd caught from the garage hadn't lied.

There were absolutely two omegas on our couch, mid-fuck. It was a flowery aroma with an undercurrent of chocolate cookies.

Ice was seated on the couch. Onyx was straddling him, now wearing a silken nightgown. It was falling open at the front, swaying with each movement as her body moved lithely, impaled by his cock.

I was drawn to a halt, blindsided.

Her smooth, golden skin peeked from the silken gown. She was a work of art. That wasn't an exaggeration. They both were.

Ice was fixed on her, his lips parted with pleasure, his buckle undone and pants down just enough to free his cock so she could ride it with mesmerising skill.

What really threw me, though, was watching that expression of bliss on Ice's face, one given to him by someone else. Not one of my brothers like I dreamed. Instead, it was her. The woman who was slowly weaving herself into every corner of our pack.

The air was thick with lavender and brownie, tangling with Ice's rose cookies.

Our scent match and our omega.

I couldn't take my eyes from them.

This was nothing like what sex was like in Ice's heats. It could be rough, kinky, and hot, but it couldn't be sweet. Never. Not even a little bit. The moment I gave him the slightest hint that I cared about him beyond his needs, he closed off. Once he'd shut down enough that I hadn't been able to touch him for hours, despite his temperature skyrocketing. It wasn't until I'd pinned him down by the neck and told him I was going to fuck him, frigid and heartless, he had finally relented, trusting that coldness enough to let me.

This was different. Ice had one hand on her hip, the other trailing her cheek, tips of his fingers tangling in her hair as he held her close. It was passionate. Sweet. Everything I wasn't allowed.

Something inside me shattered.

Arsenal was in the kitchen and there was a glass of water in his grip as he stared at the show, absolutely frozen. King, obnoxious as he was, settled onto the couch just beside them. I scowled, wanting to tell him to piss off in case he broke the magic, but it was too late. Onyx shifted closer to Ice, her curtain of glossy dark hair obscuring Ice from view.

She whispered something to him before shifting back. Her eyes found me just as Ice tightened his grip on her hips, driving into her harder. She moaned, clutching the couch to steady herself and returning her gaze to Ice, eyes trailing down my torso and snagging on my crotch along the way.

I was rock-fucking-hard—because of course I was.

I could see glimpses of her body from here.

I'd never admit it to Ice, but like... tits were kind of my kryptonite. And hers were perfect and round, a good handful, and they kept peeking out at me from the opening in her gown. Could Ice fuck her harder so I could see what they looked like when they bounced?

Her haughty demeanour vanished, and she grabbed the couch with both hands to steady herself as Ice—for the first time in his bratty life—did something for me, seizing her hips and picking up his pace.

Her face was turned down as she kept her focus on Ice, but I could see the little scrunch to her expression, Ice's cock clearly doing some omega magic. The sensual, low whine that slipped from her was like a shot of lightning in my veins. I took a step toward them before realising it, then caught myself.

What the fuck was I doing?

This woman was going to be gone soon enough.

Ice was mad. King too. There *was* no getting attached.

ONYX

I knew this was totally insane.

Making dares of my scent matches was playing with fire, but there was something about Ice that was irresistible. I knew he was complicated, maybe a little off his rocker, and he had demons chasing him, but none of that mattered.

I was pulled by my instincts, as if I could see his wounds and knew how to offer them reprieve. But when our hormones collided, it was like we'd doused the room in a spell.

Now I could feel myself losing control. I didn't do that often. Even in heat, I always wanted to be present and as in control as I could be.

I'd never fucked an omega before, and Ice was my mate, so really, I should have seen this coming.

The whole pack was watching us. It had been the plan, but it was sending me over the edge—that, and Ice's tight grip on my hips as he took control.

I couldn't make the mistake of meeting Malakai's eyes again, his expression had been icy, but his pupils were wide. Seeing him turned on was hot. Way too hot. Arsenal was ahead of me and I didn't dare look at him even once.

Ice paused a moment before driving into me again, thumbs hooked around my thighs, tugging my legs apart further to take him. I'd planned on giving them a show, but now, with each whimper that slipped from my chest, it was hard to avoid the fact that I might *be* the show.

I kept my gaze on Ice, nails digging into their couch. The longer his skin touched mine, the more I felt the rest of them there, like anchors, drawn toward us. It felt like the most natural thing in the world that they be a part of this. Ice would deny it, but that was his wound. The one I sensed too clearly. He didn't know how to bridge the gap, but this was *his* pack. I didn't think he quite knew that—or that he was at its centre. He didn't see how the others were around him. How they all noticed when he entered, how—in their own ways—they were doing everything they could to give him what he needed.

I thought, perhaps, he considered himself a straggler instead.

I felt fingers brush my cheek and turned to find King beside me, tucking my hair behind my ear. "Let me help him ruin you, Duchess."

Ice drew out of me slowly this time, and I turned to him. His cheeks were flushed, his chest heaving, but his eyes darted between me and King. There was something desperate in them. Something unsure.

I unhooked my hair from my ear so that when I leaned close and took his chin, King could no longer see him. "Do you *want* to see him touch me?" My voice was barely a breath in his ear.

I leaned back, holding his gaze.

He stared at me, dumbstruck for a long moment. Then the faintest smile edged his lips, a flush rising in his cheeks. He nodded. It was faint, almost as if he didn't want King to notice.

I smiled, leaning forward and nipping his ear. Without looking back, I reached out behind me, finding the fabric of King's shirt to drag him closer. He was upon me in a second. He was tall enough that when he planted his knees on either side of my hips, he caged me in without crushing the space Ice had to fuck me.

"If I'm going to help you out..." King brushed my dressing gown back, rolling both my nipples in his fingers and getting a shocked whine from me. "You can fuck him better than that," he growled, pinching down harder.

I shook as I held myself up.

"Fuuuck..." Ice groaned as I began riding him harder, one hand pressed against his chest to steady myself, the other now reaching back, planted on King's thigh.

I could feel myself getting close as King's voice growled in my ear. "Come for me, Little Omega." It was a command. It seized me, and I didn't put up a fight.

I let out a low moan just as Ice did, and I felt him come inside me as my orgasm shook me. Ice's cum was like a shot of heat right to my core. It turned out male omega seed was made of something goddamned magical. It felt as though another orgasm rolled right from my core outwards.

King's weight pressed in behind me, impaling me on Ice right as one hand dropped to my clit, the other closing around my neck and dragging me against his chest. I saw stars, utterly overwhelmed, feral noises I'd never heard before coming from my throat.

I clutched his arms as he kept on, shaking from head to toe, sure that I was spent.

"I... finished," I panted, feeling my body about to give out between the two of them.

"You're not nearly undone enough, Duchess," he murmured, fingers still working my clit. My nails bit at his arms, eyes wide as I finally made the mistake of looking up at Arsenal. He was leaning forward on the kitchen island, unapologetically watching, head cocked, eyes fixed on me. I let out another indistinct sound as my body seized and another orgasm hit me.

Ice groaned, squeezing his eyes shut as my body clenched around his length, and I felt him spill into my core again.

This time, King released me, and I collapsed down onto Ice, a shaking mess. Ice held me tight as I panted in his arms.

EIGHTEEN

ONYX

It was completely necessary to shower. Ice came a *lot*.

When I climbed out in a fresh dressing gown, Malakai was lying on Arsenal's bed, hands tucked behind his head, clearly waiting for me.

He sat up as I entered the room. "I'll do the job tonight."

I raised my eyebrows. "You will?"

"Yeh."

"Because I let you watch me take your omega for a ride?"

Malakai chuckled. *"You* were not the one taking anyone for a ride, Duchess."

I raised an eyebrow, not finding a response with which to dignify that.

"You picked the game and then got played."

"Right," I smiled. "You got a show and *I* got nothing at all out of it. Not a bodyguard and three orgasms."

"Three orgasms, and they still weren't good enough?"

I paused, folding my arms.

He smiled, stepping by me and leaning close to breathe the

next words in my ear as he passed. "If it had been me, you wouldn't be walking straight for days."

A shiver ran down my spine.

MALAKAI

This was just as bad as I thought it would be.

It was a massive press event at a theatre, which meant I had to haul Onyx through a bunch of reporters at the front.

I'd been high-strung since I'd seen her straddling Ice earlier. How the fuck was I supposed to recover from that? I was on edge for more than that, though. The stalker had been back, leaving flowers outside of our home again. I needed to check the footage outside of our door, but it was an old piece of tech, and took an age to upload.

As I hurried Onyx up the steps to the event, I couldn't help scanning the crowds. He was good enough he could be here right now. There was no way for me to know, just looking, but I tried to commit as many faces to memory as I could. Any fucker with their eyes on her both outside and in the event as she got settled in.

King had mentioned it was torturous watching her in the arms of another pack, and he had been absolutely fucking right.

These goddamned omegas would be my ruin. Now, every time I saw another of the alphas touch her, I wanted to pounce. I don't care how much we needed it, I would *not* be paid for tonight. It was fucking degrading.

Right now there was a brutish alpha, with a neat chin strap and wearing an *obnoxious* wine red suit, with an arm around her shoulder. His thumb grazed her skin up and down. It was all I could watch—not that I gave a shit about the dancers prancing around on stage below me.

It wasn't that I wished to be the one holding her like that. It was the fact it felt like a taunt. We couldn't get out of a scent match no matter how we felt about it, but being forced to watch another alpha touch mine? Every once in a while, her gaze would slide over to me and our eyes would lock in the low lighting.

I could feel the heat rising up my neck. It took everything I had to keep the scowl from my face.

No one did this to me but Ice.

Ice? Do *not* think about Ice right now, you prat. Or Ice and her...

His heat was coming soon. He got so goddamned bratty when he was near heat, racking up the debt, making sure I suffered. And today had been on another level.

Heat with Ice should be a lot more challenging for me than it actually was. It was theorised that the more alphas an omega was bonded to, the more intense their heat. That meant alone, I should be absolutely exhausted dealing with it.

I theorised, however, that being held out on–like I was all the time—provided me as much energy as I needed to go as long as he needed. I didn't have data to back that up, but then, they didn't do studies on packs who had little shits like Ice for omegas.

Right now, as I watched, one of the alphas was tucking Onyx's hair behind her ear. Then he leaned closer to whisper something. I contained my growl as he pressed a gentle kiss to her cheek. She'd told me this pack was more hands on than the one King had seen. She smiled warmly, but even from here I could tell it was totally fake. This was an act for her, a job, and it made me feel a spark of pride that I could see that so clearly, because whatever she was offering us... Well, maybe it wasn't so fake.

Pride?

I think watching my two omegas fuck had broken my goddamned brain.

I froze.

My omegas? Had that thought actually just gone through my head?

I forced my gaze back to the stupid dance.

She was trapped with us. We were the mates she didn't want. I couldn't forget that. She was stuck with us only because she was more afraid of the alternative—even if she was giving us live events in the middle of our living room.

Still, as the alpha's touch brushed her arm again, I couldn't help imagining it was me. Imagining what it would be like if she did stay. Would Ice want her during his heat? If today was anything to go by, then yes. Would she... maybe want me by then?

And then... Well, there was *her* heat to think about. What if, in some crazy universe, she did decide she wanted us as a pack. Then she'd have heats to deal with, too. And unlike Ice, she'd want us all, or at least... I thought she would.

I could experience a heat with my brothers the way I wanted to so badly. I wasn't attracted to them like I was Ice, but that wasn't what sharing a heat was about. It was more. They were the other souls in this bond, and I'd never been able to experience that connection with them.

In a crazy world in which Onyx wanted us, I would maybe, just maybe, get that.

Fuck me. My rampant hindbrain was out of fucking control. I just had to get through the night. Right. So I could go back to the garage where I was smothered by lavender and bloody roses every moment.

I tried once more to straighten out my thoughts; to be reasonable and suspicious, just like I was supposed to be.

I glanced down to the performance below. Was there a story to all the jumping about? If there was, I wasn't following. Now I tried, as it was the only thing offering distraction from the alphas putting their hands on my mate.

By the time the curtains closed in the middle of the stupid show, it felt like my skin was prickling.

She led us through the crowds until we entered a private room she said the pack had reserved. What was it? A puff room? Something like that.

"They hire this out?" It was large, with a few velvety couches to rest on, and a whole line of vending machines that looked out of place until I realised they weren't selling food. There was everything from bottles of champagne to a rather astounding selection of sex toys.

"The Rypma pack doesn't believe in doing anything by halves," she said, standing before the mirror and doing up her lipstick.

"Evident," I grunted.

"You're miserable," she noted.

"I'm working. You had too much fun with King, obviously."

"And you're no fun?"

The words came out of my pent up brain before I could stop them. "King's fun. I'm too much for you, Duchess."

She lowered her lipstick, eyes narrowed. "What did you just say?"

I didn't reply, setting my gaze straight and leaning against the wall beside the door. I heard her close her purse and stalk over. When she stopped before me, I didn't take my eyes from the wall ahead.

"What did you say?"

A smile tugged at the corner of my mouth, but I didn't reply. When she reached up, as if to take my chin, I caught her wrist in a flash. Finally, I slid my gaze down to meet a furious expression.

"You can't handle me, Duchess."

"What can't I handle?"

I released her wrist and it fell away. I leaned down to murmur in her ear. "What I'd do for every instance I'm forced to watch my mate touch another alpha."

I practically felt her shiver. When I leaned back, her eyes were full of challenge. She held her chin high as she said, "Show me."

Heat slid through my veins at the dare. I considered, for one fleeting moment, that this really was an awful idea.

And then I moved quicker than she could react. I spun her, catching her wrists behind her back and shoving her up against the arm of the couch to our right. Then I slid my knee between her legs and lifted her wrists so she was forced forward with a little yelp.

I groaned, leaned back, and took in the view of her bent over the couch before me, wriggling slightly, but unable to get her footing. I had her lifted just enough that her heels only grazed the floor. The wall mirror stretched out before me so when she lifted her head, I got to watch the surprise on her pretty face.

"Are you going to tell me to stop?" I murmured. She turned her face to the side, her cheek was against the couch cushion. She was blinking rapidly, eyes darting about in shock, her chest heaving as I pressed her wrists into her back with one hand. She said nothing, so I slowly pushed the silken dress up her thighs until I was rewarded with a stunning view of her perfect ass. Her breathing hitched even more and she wriggled slightly, her sex pressing against my knee.

Still, she said nothing.

She was wearing black lace and a garter belt which I decided, in that moment, was my new favourite thing in the world. It was tight in this position, so the round flesh of her ass pressed against it.

"Six times," I whispered menacingly. She went still as my hand grasped the flesh of her ass. "You let one of them kiss you." I squeezed harder and was rewarded by a little whimper. Her scent rose in the air. Sweet goddamned brownies and flowers. Fuck, it was intoxicating.

I tugged on one of the garter straps and let it snap back against her skin. She jumped.

Once again, I massaged the tan flesh of her ass. Goosebumps had erupted across her skin and her scent was getting heavier.

Onyx knew what was coming, and she was absolutely hot for it.

ONYX

The first *crack* of Malakai's hand against my ass had my brain giddy with need.

I'd never been spanked before. No one had warned me how absolutely hot it was.

Between each one he massaged my flesh, exploring it just enough to leave me panting and desperate before his palm could come down again. Each time I would writhe, my heat pressed against his knee where he held me up. I had to fight to keep the whines in my chest. My cheeks were flaming, my dignity out the window enough already. I wouldn't give him more.

Finally his grip on my wrists vanished, his knee dropped, and his fingers wove through my hair as he drew me up slowly to face him. My dress tumbled back into place as I stared up.

"So?" he asked calmly, as if we'd just gone to coffee.

"W-what?" I tried to compose myself.

"Too much?"

"Not at all." It was the thrilling truth. Might that mean he wasn't done? I—with much more desperation than I'd ever let on —didn't want him to be.

"Well then, Duchess, don't want to keep your pack waiting. I suggest you go and fix your lipstick—again—and you'll need a scent dampener."

My cheeks flushed, but he was right. My aura was filling the space, scent out of control.

"Do you still want to stay in my room tonight?" he asked, arms folded as he leaned at the door while I quickly fixed up my smeared lipstick in the mirror. I held his eyes through the reflection.

"I... Yes." My mind raced. "That was the plan."

"Good."

What did it mean? I had to get my hormones sorted. I couldn't go back to the Rypma pack like this.

Malakai held the door open for me, and I had to stop myself from staring as I passed. His looks alone were enough to make my brain trip over itself. The sharp angle of his jaw, long straight nose, rich brown skin, and—right now—the faintest smirk on his face. His hair was still tied up in a bun, not a hair out of place. "I'm not much of a theatre guy," he said, "But I'm feeling much better about the second half. Aren't you?"

NINETEEN

MALAKAI

Standing at the back of the private theatre booth, it was much easier to watch rich pricks lay a hand on her now. Satisfying even, when her eyes would dart to me to check if I was watching—as if I had any interest at all in theatre. No, there was something beautiful in this room, and it wasn't the dancers below.

I was born to the Harpies, raised a gang runner, and sent to juvie for armed robbery in my mid-teens. There was nothing about my upbringing that could have warned me I had a thing for rich women.

Turned out, they were hot as fuck. Now, even when Onyx was haughty and aloof, it sent spikes of heat through my veins. I kept jumping back to the shock on her face in the mirror as I'd brought my hand down on her ass that first time, sending her pride scattering.

I was quite content until the end of the play, when she said goodbye to the pack and we exited the theatre.

I hadn't been turned on like this enough times in my life to be quite prepared. I didn't realise this lust high had an equal effect on my aura than any other possessive-as-fuck alpha instincts. It was as goddamned powerful as it was primitive. She let me touch her? She was mine.

I didn't just want her in my bed, I wanted to protect her. With years under my belt with Ice claiming the former while failing the latter, I went from ice-cold bodyguard to completely unhinged in the blink of an eye.

We took the steps through the crowds to get back to her limo, and we were swarmed with reporters, all asking questions. Fuck, this was... *wild*.

I heard King's name mentioned as I grabbed her arm, tugging her close while I shoved a pathway through the swarming leeches.

That was when a weaselly journalist shoved past the ranks, his nasally voice breaking through the rest. "How long do you think your popularity will last, rejecting alphas like you did the Khoven Pack? Isn't your value dependent on them?"

I saw red—and that was before he was jostled, his mic jumping forward, catching Onyx in the chest.

I lost it.

Completely lost it.

My aura exploded outward and my fist crashed into the asshole journalist's face before anyone could blink. He was thrown back into the crowd, cameras shattering, people crashing down around us.

I didn't care. It wasn't enough. Something ancient and hateful rose within me, my veins alight. I would *gut* him—

"*Malakai!*" Her voice ripped me back to the present. I blinked. She was clutching my arm, her eyes wide and scared. Around her, a wide circle was forming. A few people grabbed the beta—who had blood pouring from his nose—and tried to drag him away. Other people were running. A thousand cameras were flashing.

I'd just...

My ears were ringing.

No...

There was just over a week left before our check in at the Institute. I'd be charged, no two ways about it.

Ice.

I'd... failed him.

"Malakai!" Her hand touched my cheek. "Let's go, alright? It'll be okay," she said. Her sapphire eyes and the aroma of lavender anchored me.

The sound of the world—clicks and shouts and racing footsteps—all crashed back in.

Her hand slipped into mine, and she began tugging me toward the limo that was waiting. Onyx was on the phone by the time we got in, but I could barely hear what she was saying.

Ice.

The whole pack.

I'd just fucked us. Completely, totally and utterly f—A word from her startled me back to myself.

"...Right in my *tits*, *and* on camera... Definite contact. Not the first time. It was Connelly—Yes, that one. Fisher was in the crowd. Might be able to get pictures from him right now. He's usually on our side—And *Amber*—" Her voice became frigid. "He doesn't get a dime to settle or you tell him I'll sue him down to the freckles on his stupid fucking face. *Those* words—And make it class action. I have another dozen duchesses in the process of harassment suits with the Beta-Watch channel. They won't want another."

She listened for another moment, nodding along, then there was a click and she dropped the phone.

I stared at her.

"You lot," she sighed. "Are *high* maintenance."

"What... was that?"

She waved a hand. "Dealt with."

"Just like that?"

"This shit happens all the time. Devin once lost it on a nasty reporter too, and he was a hard bodyguard to crack..." She trailed off, frowning slightly, pain flashing in her eyes. She shook it away, a smile on her face. "Talk about anger issues. You looked like you were going to kill him. Gave him the shock of his life, but he deserved it. He was the one who leaked Victoria Washer's second address. She was keeping it secret because of her baby, for fuck's sake."

"Our..." I cleared my throat. "Last check in with the Institute is in a week."

She stared at me, eyes calculating. "Oh." Her brow pinched. "There won't be a whisper of a charge. I told her I wouldn't pay him, but if something happens I will. He's a greedy fucker at the end of the day. I'll make it go away."

I narrowed my eyes, a thousand suspicions leaping to my mind. "Why would you do that?"

"I hired you without training."

"Because we kidnapped you."

"Okay..." She nodded as if that was a fair point. "But you did kidnap me for my own good, and I am getting to-die-for omega sex out of it."

I felt the corner of my lip twitch up as I leaned back against the window.

We sat in silence for another stretch. I know she'd said it was sorted, but how could I not worry?

As if sensing my anxiety, her fingers traced my arm.

"I'll tell you my last resort if you promise not to tell anyone," she said.

I raised my eyebrows, glancing at her. "Alright, then."

"I have DMs of him on a Heat Match account begging me to go on a date. Worst case scenario, I'll wring him for a night of expensive drinks that'll cost him a month of his wages."

The still unhinged alpha in me reacted, a growl rising up my throat as I slipped my fingers through her hair and forced her to look up at me. I could see the shift in her demeanour the moment I did; the way her chest heaved, her eyes darting between mine, something needy in them. I leaned near, my breath close enough to tickle her ear.

"I would rather go back to jail, Little Omega," I breathed. And in that moment, I really wasn't sure it was a lie.

The limo was suddenly filled with the scent of lavender brownies.

I released her and straightened, not meeting her eyes as I rested back against my seat, satisfied with the obvious fidgeting I spotted out the corner of my eyes.

After another long silence, I tilted my head sideways toward her. "Nine," I murmured.

"What?" she asked.

"Nine times you let that pack kiss you while I watched."

"Oh." The word was a squeak. "They kissed me more because *you* made me smell like sex."

"Correction, Duchess. *You* made you smell like sex, because you found it hot when I spanked you."

The lavender brownies became intoxicating, and it took everything in my power not to pounce on her right now.

"You could do it here," she said, voice weak. "You know, there isn't a door on your room..."

"There isn't, is there?" I asked, meeting her eyes at last.

How was it I'd forgotten how impossibly stunning she was in the few seconds I hadn't been looking? I'd thought I had pretty solid self-control until today. With difficulty, I returned my gaze to the window, enjoying watching her shift even more in her seat as she contemplated what I might have planned.

When we got home, Onyx vanished up to the roof for what I could only surmise was her evening smoke.

"How'd it go?" King asked from the couch beside Arsenal. To

my surprise, Ice hadn't vanished to his cave yet, and they were settling in for TV.

I shrugged. "Alright."

"That's it?"

"Yeah."

"What did you think?" King pushed.

"Of what?" I asked.

"Watching her with other alphas?"

"Fine," I grunted.

"Surprised you didn't lose it," Ice snorted.

"Maybe I have more self-control than you imagine I do." My own lack of said self-control was so raw and recent I didn't much feel like talking about it yet.

"Yeh fucking right," Arsenal chuckled, flicking through TV channels for something to watch.

I lingered a while, trying not to stare too hard at Ice's presence. Was this a result of this afternoon? She had only been here a few days, and she was already changing us. I couldn't deny it was for the better.

Somehow that made it easy to lose the battle I was currently waging with my self-control. I crossed to her suitcase and rooted around until I found what I was looking for—well, *better* than I was looking for.

"What are you doing?" she hissed, taking the steps down the staircase.

"Can you explain to me why, when you were packing to join us at our *classy* garage, you chose to bring a purple one piece?" It was made of flowery lace.

Her eyes flashed, then darted across the room toward the others before snatching it from me. "I wasn't *looking*. I just shoved in a few handfuls. I'm not planning on *wearing* it."

"Now you are, Duchess, I think lavender is my favourite purple." I pressed it into her hands.

"You're out of your mind if you think—"

"You can wear what I choose, or you can kip with King or Arsenal again," I said with a shrug.

King straightened on the couch, hopeful. Arsenal was glaring at us both with narrowed eyes, as if he couldn't believe what he was witnessing.

Onyx stared at me. I doubted she wanted to opt into Arsenal's bed again—she still had a stick up her ass about him—but she liked King well enough. So I'd discover if she actually *wanted* to stay with me tonight.

I realised, in a moment of surprise, that I would be gutted if she didn't. I had yet to show her the most important thing I had to offer. The piece I'd been missing for so long...

She swallowed, eyes lingering on the lingerie. She glanced up to me and then to the side as if she were fighting the urge to look at the others. To my delight, she snatched the lace from my grip, then stepped toward the suitcase, reaching for one of the nightdresses I'd tugged out. I caught her wrist, halting her.

"I didn't choose those."

Her eyes flashed, but her voice was low. "I'll get cold without a nightdress—"

"Then I'll just have to keep you warm."

Her chest was heaving as she stared at me, those kissable pink lips turned down. Then she wrinkled her nose and stalked back to my room with as much dignity as she could muster with the lace clutched in her fist.

I didn't realise how far the smile had stretched across my face until I glanced back at the others. Ice's gaze had followed Onyx, but the other two were staring at me. King looked stunned, and Arsenal's mouth was slightly open.

"What just happened?" King's voice was dry.

I shrugged. "I think she might be into me."

MALAKAI

Lavendar lace clung across curves to die for.

Onyx's smooth, golden-tan skin that glowed in the low light, and a curve to her hips that tapered up into a pinched waist. The lace was thin enough that I could see the smoothness of her stomach. She had long legs and a slender frame, but her skin wasn't tight against muscles. Instead, it was soft. Perfect. Squeezable.

As always, her hips swayed beautifully as she walked. Now though, with so little obscuring her figure, it was more entrancing.

I'd glimpsed these treasures this afternoon, but in fragments or from afar. As she stopped before where I sat, I could enjoy it. I reached up, resting my hands on her hips, taking my time drinking in every last detail. The lace pressed against two full breasts, and right now her nipples were erect, pressing against the fabric. She was a goddess, loose strands of hair fluttering around the bun that had become progressively messier throughout the evening.

I drew her toward me, and she sank onto my lap, straddling me. "Take your hair down." I wanted to see it.

"I didn't have time to straighten it—" She cut off as I plucked the hair tie from her bun and tugged it away. The lion's mane of dark chocolate waves tumbled around her face. They were wild and messy and fierce, a perfect contrast to the thin golden necklace around her neck, and the little golden earrings in her lobes. I leaned back.

This was what she was supposed to look like.

"Beautiful," I murmured, shifting the mane of waves around her shoulders so I could see them frame her heart-shaped face. She swallowed and it was impossible not to follow the movement down her neck. I was unstable tonight, and for a moment I imagined sinking my teeth in right there, claiming her as mine.

"It's not the sort of look my clients want."

"*My* pack wants to see it."

"You're speaking for the others now?" she asked, a half smile on her face.

"Did you know I used to be pack lead?" I asked.

She considered me for a moment, then nodded. "Ice told me."

"Did he?" That surprised me.

"He told me how you met."

"Ah." Not the most appealing story. "All I'm saying is I absolutely have the qualifications to say this pack would all love to see your hair like that."

"I see."

I didn't want her to myself. I had Ice to myself and I felt lonely.

I wanted to share her with my brothers, and I thought she wanted that, too. Leaning forward, my teeth bit down gently on her nipple. She arched in my arms, a breathy sound slipping out.

"Stand up."

She considered me more seriously now, a little part of her warring with my commands. But she slipped from my lap and stood.

"Because of you, I'm turning in much earlier than I'm used to. So you're going to go and make me tea. My brothers will see how good you're being for me, then I'll give you the punishment you need and the praise you deserve."

Her breathing picked up. "I can't go out like this."

"I'm not interested unless they see you this beautiful, too."

If anything, at that, I thought I saw the conflict vanish from her eyes. Had her desire for me just become stronger?

Because... I valued my pack. She wasn't just interested in me. She was a pack omega, I could see it in her eyes.

It was difficult in that moment not to drag her back to me and claim her right now.

For being everything I'd ever dreamed of. Instead, I tugged her closer so she swayed forward just a step. "Will you do it?"

She nodded, unable to rip her gaze from me.

"Good girl," I purred. "First, though, turn around for me."

I had one last gift for them.

TWENTY

ONYX

I was swimming in sex hormones by the time I found the courage to enter the main room and cross to the kitchen. I was painfully aware of how very little I was wearing. It shouldn't have made me as hot as it did.

I was shamelessly desperate to play out Malakai's night. He was... captivating. Everything he did had me hooked, everything he promised or might do. If that meant taking the punishment he wanted to deliver, I would make him goddamned tea.

In front of the pack of criminals I'd met less than a week ago.

In a lacy, lavender teddy.

With an alpha's bite mark across my ass cheek.

Because *yep*... Malakai had just bitten me. Not a claim or a bond. Just a bite. And I thought it might be the hottest thing I'd ever experienced. I swear I'd almost come the instant I'd felt his teeth against my flesh.

Ice spotted me first as I was getting a tea bag ready. He did a double take, his jaw dropping open.

"*What* are you doing?" Arsenal asked through gritted teeth.

"Making Malakai tea," I said, as if it were the most obvious thing on the planet.

King turned, also doing a double take, his mouth working soundlessly for a moment. "I thought you were kidding about the... lace."

Ice got up from his chair and was crossing toward me, pupils dilated, the scent of roses and cookies heavy in the air. His eyes roamed me up and down, and I don't know how he managed without it feeling creepy, but he did. Perhaps because his eyes kept getting stuck on my hair, as if that was the most riveting thing.

"I love it," he croaked, fingers brushing the mane of waves that trailed down to my waist. "Where did it *come* from?"

"Seconded." King had turned around fully on the couch, watching my every move.

"Why are you doing what Mal tells you?" Ice asked. He shifted forward as if wanting to move closer, perhaps put his hand on my hips, then drew back nervously. Which was silly, since he'd been fucking me just this afternoon.

"You were right," I told him. "He's hot." It was more than his demeanour and ruggedly good looks. It was more even than the fact he'd punched out a leech of a reporter who'd been dogging me for months. There was more to him, I'd seen it in his eyes. Asking me to get him tea wasn't just about control. His pack was important, and from the little I knew of Ice's heats, he was the only one involved. He wanted more than that. He cared about his pack more than anything else, and somehow it was more attractive than all of the rest of it put together.

Even now I could feel the heat boiling in my core as I felt their eyes trained on me. The kettle boiled on the stove and I poured Malakai's tea before heading back to his room. I could feel every eye on me—on the mark Malakai had left—until the moment I vanished around the corner.

I paused when I entered. Malakai was sitting on the side of his bed, now topless. And holy hell, he was built like a chiselled god. His grin was cocky as he looked over at me, and I realised I was ogling him like... Well, like the others had just been ogling me.

He took the tea, then set it down on the side table before turning back to me. I waited, and I felt the last barriers I'd been clinging to fall away. I would do whatever he asked right now.

He stood, knuckles brushing my hair, eyes roaming it for a moment. I'd spent so much time with Ice today, I had lost track of the time and rushed to get ready. On my date I'd been worried one of the alphas would comment on it, even tied back as it was. But right now, beneath his gaze, I felt a deeper appreciation for the wild hair I usually spent so long taming.

I loved how much taller he was than me, his broad form dwarfing mine. I almost reached out to run my hands along the smooth ridges of muscle along his chest, but I held back. He wanted control, and I wanted to give it to him. His knuckles dropped to my chin and tilted it up gently.

"On your knees on the bed. Face the headboard." He dropped his hand, watching me with those stunning dark eyes. Butterflies took flight in my stomach the moment I moved to follow his command, kneeling on the centre of the bed, waiting.

Goosebumps lit on my skin as his touch brushed my waist. "Do you like it when I tell you what to do?" he asked.

I nodded as he shifted closer, his chest pressing against my back as his touch trailed up and down my skin.

"Are you going to take your punishment well?"

His hands came up to my breasts, squeezing them. My back arched, my voice breathy. "Yes."

"Yes, what?"

My brain short-circuited, and the next words were reactionary. "Yes, Alpha."

There was the faintest vibration of a rumble in his chest, and it sent a shiver across my whole body. "Good girl." His fingers pinched my nipples roughly and I let out a moan, arching further against him, lips parted in pleasure. I knew my scent was dousing the space.

I was soaked. I don't think I'd ever been this turned on from so little. But it didn't *feel* like a little. Every one of his touches was electric.

"If you take your punishment well, I'll reward you."

My mind went crazy. He was still rolling my nipples, but it wasn't enough. My fingers bit down on his thighs. "Take me however you want, Alpha," I panted.

Never had I wanted someone to fuck me as badly as I did right now. With wild, desperate desire, I needed him to pin me down and drive his cock into me. I didn't want warm up or warning. I wanted it feral and rough just like I knew he could give.

His fingers vanished. "Bend over for me."

I did it without question and no regard at all for how embarrassed I should be bent over, presented to him as if... Well, as if I was in heat.

With my cheek pressed to the bed and my fingers tangling in the sheets, I heard his soft groan of pleasure just from looking. It sent another shiver down my spine.

His touch found my skin again, running down my back to my hips, and coming too close to my heated core.

"You're soaked, Little Omega," he growled. Then I felt him tug the lace that reached up my back from between my thighs. The thin material slipped, getting trapped in the flesh of my sex. I loosed a whine as he tugged at it, sending a jolt of pleasure into my clit. I didn't realise I'd ground against him until he chuckled, releasing the lace and the pleasure it was bringing. "I didn't say you could move."

I froze, my breaths too laboured. "Sorry, Alpha."

"Good girl," he murmured. "Are you ready for your punishment?"

"Please," I whined. I'd planned on saying yes. Not that. But I couldn't think straight.

He laughed again. *"Nine* kisses." His palm brushed the sensitive place he'd bitten, and it was a war not to push back against his touch again. "From alphas outside of my pack."

His touch vanished, and my breath caught as he shifted back and to the side. I knew what was coming. He waited far too long, until I was shivering.

The first crack of his palm came down on the sensitive flesh at the top of my thighs. I whimpered again, fingers digging into the sheets, holding myself absolutely still.

"In the future, you will count every time you let that happen. And you will come to me after. Is that clear?"

"Yes, Alpha," I breathed.

His hands ran up my waist and stomach until his fingers found my nipples. When he pinched down, I arched against him with need but he was already drawing his hands away. He rested his grip on my hips again, caressing my flesh with his thumbs until his touch vanished entirely.

My breath picked up instantly as I anticipated the next strike.

He waited a long time again, and I almost looked behind. I let out another breathy noise as his hand came down. Once again, he worked his way up my body and tugged on a nipple until another moan escaped my chest.

He leaned back and waited. Goosebumps still pebbled my skin and I didn't know if this lace was enough to contain how wet I was.

SMACK!

This time it was so close to my sex that I jolted forward with a groan. His strong fingers massaged the spot, so close to my entrance that I shifted back once more. He let out a low laugh. "So needy, Duchess."

I couldn't argue. I'd completely given up on dignity for the desperate, coiling lust that was building in my stomach. I could feel the wetness slipping down my thighs.

By the time he hit nine, I was trembling. I knew my flesh must be raw, but I still didn't feel like I'd had enough.

"Sit up."

I did as he said instantly. He drew me up until I was on my knees, back pressed to his chest.

"You took your punishment so well," he murmured, nipping my ear, hands still massaging my flesh, working their way up my stomach again.

He returned to rolling my nipples between his fingers. They were so sensitive now that I moaned instantly.

"Fuck me."

"You've already been fucked today," he murmured in my ear.

"I want you," I breathed. "Please." I'd never begged before, but Malakai was my undoing.

"You will come for me, Little Omega."

I reached down between my thighs, desperate for stimulation, but his touch vanished in an instant. "Do you want me to leave you to it?" he asked.

I shook my head, biting my lip.

"Do you want to come?"

"Yes."

His fingers returned to my nipples with the slow torture, but I could feel an orgasm building as he worked them, even if it had me writhing and desperate for his touch in other places.

Finally, when my breath became heavy, he switched his pace, pinching hard enough to get a gasp of shock, tugging at them with sudden fierceness. I whimpered, nails biting down on his thighs as an orgasm shook me, tingling down from my nipples all the way into my core. He kept up his roughness until my last shudder died down.

"Was that enough for you, Duchess?" Somehow, his question felt like a taunt.

"It was." It had felt blissful, but the truth was I just felt more needy now.

He tilted my chin up and leaned down so I was looking up into his dark eyes. "Don't lie to me." A half smile crept onto his lips and he flicked my nipple lightly, getting a jolt and a breathy moan from me. "Omegas don't like it when their holes aren't filled, do they?"

I shook my head, holding his eyes desperately.

"But today you made sure I watched someone else fuck you, and another pack throw themselves all over you. I don't think you deserve my cock."

I blinked in shock, realising he was serious.

"Are you pouting?"

I measured my expression, trying to collect myself. But it was a strange experience hearing an alpha tell me I didn't deserve them. Usually, it was them begging.

He released my chin, slid from the bed, and crossed the room. He grabbed something from the side table. He nodded toward the head of the bed. "Lay up on the pillows, get comfortable."

I did as he told me, anticipation biting at me. Maybe he had been joking about no sex?

I'd never been denied sex in my life. This was a little ridiculous, considering he was my mate and I was spread out for him on his bed wearing a four hundred dollar piece of lace.

He returned to the bed, not in a hurry at all, and knelt between my legs before nudging them apart with his knees. He was holding a bottle, and I was embarrassingly disappointed to see that it was only moisturiser.

He squeezed some into his hand, and then swept up one of my

legs. Starting from my feet, he began massaging the cool cream into my skin. It was shockingly relaxing, and ridiculously sexy. His lustful, dark eyes roamed over my body as he worked, and occasionally he would press kisses on my calf or shin. He worked on my feet to my knees first, then told me to turn over.

I shifted onto my stomach, butterflies lighting again. His touch traced up my hips and to the tender areas of my flesh, which he squeezed softly, lingering on the bite. I couldn't help my moan, heat renewing in my core again.

His thumbs brushed the sensitive area where my thighs met, so close to my sex that I shifted back toward him without realising. I tilted my head on the pillow to meet his eyes.

"I want you." I tried to make it sound more seductive than whiny, but I was feeling damn whiny right now.

I jumped at the icy touch as he pressed more of the lotion into my skin, gently massaging my thighs and butt. I took it back. This wasn't romantic. It was fucking torture. And I got the distinct impression that he was very happy with his lot for the night, given the amount of time he was spending squeezing the flesh of my ass.

When he was done, I was panting. I'd had to stifle more needy moans as his thumbs came too close to my heat.

"You are divine," he murmured, as he draped the blankets over us and held me against his chest.

I finally got some evidence that he wasn't as in control as he appeared. There was a raging hard-on pressed against me as he held me close.

I wriggled against him hopefully, but he squeezed the bite mark on my ass. I let out a little squeak of derision, but he just chuckled.

"Behave." He nipped my ear. "Or I won't keep you warm."

I didn't realise how safe I felt until that moment, when a little purr shuddered in my chest.

"That's what I want to hear," he breathed. "Do that for me all night."

I smiled, relaxing against his back.

The last thing I noted as he curled up, holding me tight, was that he hadn't even touched the mug.

Because, for Malakai, it had never been about the tea.

TWENTY-ONE

KING

"I don't think she's real," Ice declared. "We're having one of those... shared pack hallucinations."

I snorted.

"How the fuck does Mal do it?" I asked. I thought she liked *me*, but she'd gone from frigid to wearing lace on one date with him. And he hadn't even been the one taking her on the date. "And he bit her?" That had *definitely* been a bite across the smooth skin of her ass.

I don't think I'd ever seen Arsenal blush before, but now his tattoos weren't enough to hide the richer colour on his pale cheeks.

I leaned back, a faint smile on my face.

I'd seen Onyx's ass.

She'd *let* me see it.

Fuck.

I adjusted on the couch for the hard-on that kept popping up every time I pictured it.

When we'd heard the faint sounds coming from Mal's room, none of us had turned up the TV. Not even Arsenal.

Malakai left the bond wide open and we could feel him.

Predictably, he was a boiling pot of lust, but there was more to it. Beneath the lust, I felt something from Mal that I didn't realise until this moment, I'd never felt before.

He was happy.

"This plan of yours has gone sideways. Fast," Ice said after no one had spoken for a long time.

Arsenal wrinkled his nose. "If you lot could keep your dicks in your pants—"

"What kind of oppressive bullshit is that?" Ice was affronted. "I'm an omega."

"Since when do *you* want to pull the omega card?" I asked.

"Since a slice of lavender heaven walked in."

He sounded smug, but then I caught the frown slide onto his face. His tone was taunting as usual, but what he was saying... I couldn't help glancing back at Arsenal. He was fixed on Ice with a curious look.

It was like we all realised at the same moment.

Ice had just taunted us with everything we had been trying to push for years. And it wasn't about getting sex out of it or anything like that. He had never accepted what he was. He hated it, and we all knew it ate him alive.

This was good, but it was also wildly dangerous: Ice and healthy conclusions were prone to blowing up in all of our faces.

And there was the other problem. If this hinged on Onyx, he might fall off of a cliff the moment she left. I could see that realisation on Arsenal's face, too. He glanced in the direction of Mal's room, calculation in his eyes.

"Well," Ice stood. "On that note, good night."

When he'd descended to his nest and I'd covered the trapdoor with a rug, I turned back to Arsenal.

His eyes were fixed on the rug, a thoughtful look on his face, which—because it was Arsenal—still somehow looked grumpy.

"We should talk to Mal tomorrow," I said.

"About what?"

"About her." I rolled my eyes, finishing the thought before he could shut me down. "We need to discuss offering a bond."

"That's a bit soon," Arsenal said. But his expression was too drawn, as if his heart wasn't in it. Was he tired?

"She's our scent match." I knew it was crazy, but I felt sure about this. And it wasn't uncommon with mates.

"If we make an offer that fast to a woman like that, we'll look desperate. She won't take us."

I frowned. We weren't discussing a high school romance. "She isn't like that."

"How do you know? You met her *days* ago."

I opened my mouth to reply, then cut off, realising something; Arsenal's side of the bond was shut down. I examined him closer. Ice had left, and so had the intoxicating perfume that hung in the air since the moment he'd seen Onyx. Now I could identify Arsenal's scent. It was always a little charred, but right now it was worse. "You... alright?"

He blinked, looking over at me like he'd forgotten I was even there.

"Yeh..." He drew his phone from his pocket as if needing a distraction. "The videos from the camera downloaded."

"Did they?" I asked that news dragging me from any suspicions. I moved to sit next to him.

"Yeah, few hours ago. I checked them earlier, but I've seen nothing yet."

"There were more flowers outside overnight, though?" I asked.

"Yup."

"Then they had to have come to the door."

"I've looked it all over twice," Arsenal grunted. "No one shows, aside from the occasional racoon."

I peered at his phone, watching the video footage with him. The old camera only recorded when it sensed movement.

"Mal said he's no good at tech security," I mused. "I don't know about this shit, but if he was on her phone, could he be in ours already?"

The thought gave me chills. If he was on our computer, what else did he have access to? For a moment I was grateful for our beat up, tech stunted garage. There was nothing much for him to hack in here at all.

Arsenal hadn't replied.

"You sure you're alright?"

He nodded, "Yeh. Think I'm uh... going to turn in." Then he stood and crossed toward his room. Not quickly enough that I missed that look in his eye.

There was only one thing I could think of that would have Arsenal scared—scared and hiding it from us, anyway.

Shit...

A long moment passed as I considered. Usually, I would respect a departure like that, but right now I was following my pack instincts.

I found Arsenal sitting on his bedside, face buried in his hands.

Shit.

"When?" I asked, sitting down beside him.

Arsenal dropped his hands and my heart twisted at how lost he looked, all hostility gone. "I can get through the night. Let them... I don't know, shack up or whatever they're doing before I ruin it."

"Fuck..." I breathed. But he wasn't wrong.

When Arsenal went into a rut, we were all miserable for days.

None of that even held a candle to the experience for him, though.

"And her?" I asked.

"She's going to have to stay, with this creep about."

"She won't like it." Not one bit. Not that any of us did.

"I know." Arsenal rubbed his face again, releasing a long sigh. "I don't know the right decision anymore. I think Mal was right. Bringing her here in the first place was the wrong choice if we didn't want to get involved with her."

"Really?" I asked, sarcasm dripping from the word.

Arsenal shot me a dirty look. "I didn't think there was a chance in hell she was... decent."

"She fought you *not* to get in a cab to make sure Ice was safe," I said, incredulously. That was when I'd known.

Arsenal groaned. "She still needed our help then. Thought it was an easy way for her to look good."

"Tragic. Our mate is actually a nice human being."

"It is tragic for her. Look at us, we're a fucking mess." He waved vaguely at the living room. There was the slightest tremor in his hand when he did it.

He caught me watching it and crossed his arms with a scowl.

"Do you think... because she's here, too?" I asked.

Living with an omega who wanted absolutely nothing to do with him was exactly *why* Arsenal went into such bad ruts. Mal was fine; he balanced it out during Ice's heat. I went into ruts sometimes, but they didn't last as long as Arsenal's and weren't near as bad. My aura was stable as fuck. Sometimes I could get away with one afternoon in the vault if I blew off enough steam at the gym. Arsenal, whose aura had surfaced too young in a violent, traumatic disaster the day he'd killed his dad, had one of the least stable auras I'd ever been around.

"I..." Arsenal wouldn't meet my eyes. He winced. "She probably had something to do with it. But it's good. It was coming anyway. Better to get it done. Didn't want it getting in the way of Riot's job."

I sighed, thinking of Onyx living through what our pack did every rut...

I took it back.

After this, she might never take a bond with us at all.

ONYX

"What are you doing?" I asked as I entered the kitchen.

I'd woken to Malakai tossing on a shirt in a rush and then darting from the room. I'd slipped into some casual clothes, grabbed my dressing gown, and followed.

"...Should have *told* me you were close," Malakai was saying. He was rummaging in a kitchen drawer. Arsenal was hunched on a stool, his breathing heavy as King leaned on the island, a frown on his face.

"Was a bit blindsided. Never been around two omegas before, have I—?" Arsenal cut off as he caught sight of me with a wince.

"You piss?" Malakai asked.

Arsenal just snorted, but didn't answer as Malakai tossed him the injection. He ripped the cap off with his teeth and then, with no warning, jabbed it into the solid muscle of his arm and injected the contents.

"What's going on?" I asked, shocked.

Arsenal flipped the safety, shooting me another glance that didn't hold all of his usual confidence. "Rut."

"What?"

"I'll be in a rut within the week."

"And so... what was that? Suppressants?"

"Nah. Too expensive."

"I can—" I began.

"And too late. Sorry, Duchess. Would have had to start them before now."

"So what *was* that?"

"Opposite," he grunted.

"What?" He was *trying* to go into a rut?

"Induce it early. Get it over faster—and I can't afford it screwing up any plans."

"But... I don't understand. If you're rutting...?" I trailed off. Usually alphas without omegas made plans with other omegas, or the Institute for... well, sex.

I heard a creak and spun to find King was opening the vault.

"You didn't think it was actually for Ice?" Arsenal asked.

I stared at him, my mouth dry. "But there are clinics...?"

"I'm not fucking some random omega just because my biology's a bitch."

"But...? You just wait it out?" It had to be agony. I couldn't imagine going through my heat, fully awake and alone.

"These two banned me from the pits."

"You nearly died," Malakai muttered.

"Fight pits?" I asked, my voice high.

"Only other reliable way to ride out a rut," Arsenal grunted, getting to his feet. He looked strained, as if whatever he'd just injected was hitting quick. "Right. Well. Catch you in a day or two."

"Are you serious?" I followed him, but King cut me off. "You can't go in there for that long?"

In a rut?

It would be torture.

"Nah, we leave the outer door open so we can hear if he needs to come out for a piss."

"But... That's it?" I was staring between them, eyes wide. "But you have..." An omega? I knew their relationship with Ice wasn't conventional. King just snorted before shutting the vault door. I couldn't take my eyes from it as I heard the lock click.

This wasn't right.

I stared between them, knowing there was horror on my face. King crossed to the couch and Malakai poured himself a coffee before following. I hurried after him, though I didn't take a seat as they flicked through channels.

"Where's Ice?" I asked.

"Ice doesn't show when we rut," King said simply. "Not his thing."

Not his thing? But they were *bonded*. Being in proximity to Ice with no affection would make them rut more often.

"We bonded him," Mal said quietly, clearly reading my expression. "He didn't get a say. Not his job."

Finally, when Malakai settled on soccer and I still hadn't sat, he looked up at me. "Come on, Duchess." He nodded toward the couch beside him. "It's going to be a long few days."

I hesitated but joined him, still feeling the shock of what they'd just done.

At first it was silent. Too quiet for too long.

"He could be dead in there," I whispered at last.

"He's fine."

It was a lie. A massive lie.

Next came the thumps. Quieter at first, as if Arsenal was pounding a fist on the walls. But then they got louder and stronger, as if he was throwing his full weight against the vault.

That was when the shouting began. A faint wave of his aura blitzed past the metal of the vault, making me jump. The next thump made the windows rattle.

"LET ME OUT!" He sounded enraged, frighteningly inhuman.

Malakai turned the TV up, jaw clenched. King was white as a sheet.

"You go first," Malakai muttered. "This is my—" He cut off,

wincing. I looked at him in time to see him shaking his head incrementally at King.

"What?" I asked.

King swallowed, glancing at me before looking back to Malakai. "It's no one's fault."

I felt horror settle in my stomach. "Is this because...?" My throat was dry.

"No." King shook his head.

I was glancing between the two of them. "You're lying."

Malakai screwed up his face with a sigh. "Truth, Duchess?"

"Mal—"

"Tell me." I snapped my angry glare to King.

"It's possible," Malakai said stiffly, "that seeing you last night might have been too much for him."

I felt the blood drain from my face as he confirmed it.

"The *bite* might have been the final straw," King added. But if he was attempting to lighten the mood, it didn't work. I couldn't take my eyes from Malakai.

"Hey," Malakai tugged me toward him, slipping his arm around my shoulder. "It's not your fault."

"It is."

"You know what?" King asked. "Fuck it. Bless the bite. If I was rutting I'd rather have that on my mind than the guilt of dreaming of Ice."

Another bang on the vault made me jump. "This... isn't funny." My voice was weak.

"I'm completely serious."

"He was going to rut one way or another, Duchess," Malakai said, thumb brushing my cheek. Then he glanced back to King with a nod. "Go on."

King nodded gratefully, slipping his remaining earbud in. I watched him turn the volume up on his phone. He shut his eyes, leaning back on the couch, but he still flinched every time the windows rattled or another wave of Arsenal's aura split the air around us.

I hugged my legs to my chest, grateful for Malakai's arm around me as the shouts devolved to howls. They turned from fury to agony until they were incomprehensible.

"This is barbaric," I whispered.

"It's life." Malakai didn't take his eyes from the soccer match, but he never turned it up too high so we could always hear what was going on.

When the howls became pleas, I broke, getting to my feet. "I can't do this."

Malakai was after me in a second. "You can't go, alright? We can't leave him, and you aren't safe."

"I didn't mean leaving."

Malakai opened his mouth, but his words were cut short by Arsenal's strangled shout.

"LET ME OUT!"

I jumped.

"PLEASE!"

The damn broke. Tears flooded my cheeks. "I mean we have to—"

"*What* Onyx?" Malakai's voice was raised and I could see fierceness in his eyes. "Don't you think if there was a better option, we would be doing it?"

But another thundering bang sent a jolt of fear through my veins, and I found myself shouting. *"I am your better option!"*

I knew, in that moment, it was the absolute truth. Every frayed edge of my aura calmed as I realised it.

Malakai drew up, staring at me as if not understanding what he was looking at. King had tugged the earphones from his ears. "No way." His voice was rough. "He'll snap you in two."

"No he won't—"

"Are you fucking crazy? Can you *hear* him?" King asked, now on his feet.

"Because he doesn't have what he needs." And that was me.

Because I was an omega.

It was strange and foreign to think, let alone say. For so many years, I'd been the wrong kind of omega. Nice to look at, but worthless for anything deeper. It was more than the fact I was a duchess, seen as untrustworthy and aloof. The matches I'd had available for me at the Institute, it had sealed the deal.

They had shown me the truth of what society thought of an omega like me.

But not in this moment.

Not here. With my mates.

"I'm going to open it."

TWENTY-TWO

ARSENAL

The world burned and I was alone.

I didn't know where I was. All I knew was that my blood was on fire and I thought I was going to die.

I could feel them. My family. There was a bond holding me with them, yet they weren't here.

I was in a prison. There was nothing in here but darkness and pain. I could barely breathe, but I couldn't stop trying to get out. I couldn't die in here. They needed me. We had a job to do and if we did it, everything would be better.

Ice.

King.

Malakai.

And... she was there, too. Not in the bond, but tangled with us all the same.

"I can fix it," I rasped. "Please..." My voice was choked. "Don't leave me, I swear I can fix it."

But it was too late.

They were gone. If they were here, they'd never leave me to die like this.

No one gets left behind.

That was the rule. If they *had* left me, it meant they were done and I was out of chances.

ICE

I hid in my nest, curled up at the back with my earphones in.

The rut would last a few days. I was prepared to wait it out.

As always, it worsened as the time ticked on. My nest was below the vault. It was sound-proofed, but the banging and shouts weren't the only issue.

Finally, I felt his aura scatter through the air.

The door from my nightmares shuddered. An aura I knew too well blitzed into the room. The lock began to turn.

I turned up the music until it hurt my eardrums, squeezing my eyes shut.

But it wasn't long before my nest shook, and it was enough to send a tremor through my bones. Enough for the memories to swarm back.

Nash's aura split the room before the door was even open. The instability of his rut filled the air.

Hannah was trembling.

"It's going to be alright, Hannah," I hissed. "Just don't say a thing." I was too close to getting us out to let anything happen to her.

The music was on max volume, and I hugged my knees closer as the nest shook again. The old wounds-turned-scars like white claws across my chest throbbed with phantom pain.

. . .

The door burst open. Nash's eyes darted from me to Hannah.

I followed the instincts I'd been trying to bury since the moment I'd come here. The moment I gave into it, it came without effort. My perfume tangled into the air with sickening ease.

His wild, feral gaze snapped back to me.

I reached out to one of the sharp edges around me. I pressed the silver scar at the tip of my finger against it until I was staring at a spot of beading crimson.

Instantly, my breathing calmed, the music loud enough to drown the world.

ONYX

"Is anyone there?" Arsenal's pleas were too much. Tears burned my eyes, something old stirring and creaking within me.

King was blocking the door.

"This isn't right!" I had the key clutched in my hand.

"It will *pass*," King said. "You *can't*."

"Please! I think... I'm dying..." Arsenal's thump on the metal was dejected this time. "Please...I need them...."

It was familiar. Too familiar.

"Where are they...?"

"...I don't understand... They were waiting... They were just there and I... have to tell them something important..."

"...No. You don't understand. They would never leave me."

"Stop saying that..."

"You're lying—Why are you lying? Tell me where I am so I can

get back to them. Please. They're waiting... I have to tell them something."

"Let me in," I snarled, trying to launch myself past him. My reality wasn't fitting together right, though. There were Arsenal's pleas and something else... *The world was empty and cold and quiet. It had been for as long as I could remember...*

"Get out of my way!" I'd *never* watch this happen to anyone else.

Arsenal needed me. It was like a fist around my heart, not letting go until I did something.

King wouldn't move. "I won't watch you get hurt."

"King!"

We both paused as Malakai put a hand on King's shoulder.

"Maybe... We could—"

"Don't!" King looked off balance as he stared at Malakai. "It's *too* fucking dangerous."

"We could go in first."

"And what if she's wrong—?"

My hiss of rage cut him off. "Don't you *dare* question my capacity as an omega."

Arsenal's low, wounded howl echoed around us, his aura present even through the vault. I was shaking, my vision blurred.

"But if you get hurt—"

"I *am* the solution. Not that fucking box."

King rubbed his face violently, looking back at Malakai once again, then groaned.

"I open it, you stay back, alright? Behind Malakai."

I nodded, swallowing and wiping away my tears.

Malakai stepped in front of me as King hauled the huge door open. I jumped as it leaped a pace, a feral bellow echoing across the room as Arsenal threw his entire weight against it, his aura crashing through the room. King's aura hit the air just in time for him to catch Arsenal. I saw only a flash of Arsenal's tattooed face split in a feral snarl, eyes vacant of all humanity.

There was a loud *crack* as King slammed him back against the wall with all of his might. Arsenal bellowed.

"*Mate!*" King had to shout, arms locked around Arsenal's chest, face buried in his shoulder. "It's me. It's King."

His fighting died down as King drew back enough that Arsenal could see him. His scent was off, burned chestnuts and honey.

"I'm here, alright?" King's voice cracked.

Arsenal still looked wild, eyes darting over King as if he didn't understand. "I... hurt." His voice was a whimper.

I couldn't watch this anymore.

"Fuck—*Onyx!*" But it was too late, I had slipped by Malakai, needing to get to Arsenal. Only, when I reached for him, touching his arm, he snapped.

King was thrown back, and with a pain in my back, Arsenal had me pinned against the wall. I could barely process what was happening before I felt the sharp pain of teeth at my neck.

Shit.

Shit.

"Arsenal!" I gasped. A strange, vibrating sound was stuttering from my chest. He froze.

Malakai and King arrived, grabbing him, but... "*No!*" I clutched him, holding on. He'd stopped. He wouldn't... He wouldn't hurt me.

His vice-like grip on my waist and shoulders loosened, his breathing ragged.

I realised that sound I was making was a purr. Contentment or fear could draw it out, and right then, with his teeth at my neck... I swallowed. He had an omega already. He couldn't dark bond me. Every other bond required consent.

"Onyx?" His voice was gravelly and strained.

Relief flooded me. He was back.

"I'm here," I whispered, shaking fingers finding his face. I wasn't ready for how shattered he looked. His hazel eyes burned, sweat beaded his skin. He looked through the wild tangles of dark hair that swung before his eyes. Despite all of that, his scent—honey and chestnuts—was more intoxicating than I had planned for.

His pupils blew as he took me in, and then he was shifting back, a low growl rumbling in his chest. I held on. King and Malakai still both had their hands on his shoulders, tensed and ready.

"Don't." It seemed to be all he could get out. I paused, relaxing and letting my aura seep into the space between us. He tilted his head back, loosing a low whine as he felt it. I could see each corded muscle along his tattooed neck. "Leave." He was shaking. "You have to—"

"I'm not going anywhere."

I was okay. I wasn't hurt. Again, I reached up, cupping his cheeks in my hands, keeping his eyes locked on mine. My aura spilled from me, easily tangling with his, compositions colliding and forming something new. His grip on me steadied.

I stayed perfectly still, staring up into wild eyes, letting my aura mix with his. I thought, perhaps, if we were bonded, it might be easier. If I reached up a little closer, I could have kissed him. But I didn't.

"We're going to your bed."

"I don't..." Arsenal swallowed. "I don't want sex. Not when I'm like this."

"Trust me, Arsenal." Sex might be the simplest solution, but it wasn't the only way. Right now I was, in as long as I could remember, truly confident in my abilities as an omega.

He breathed a shaky laugh. "You plan on cuddling me out of my rut?"

"Would you prefer I left?" His grip tightened around me incrementally at that. Then he was lifting me in his arms. I pressed my lips to the damp skin at the crook of his neck, fingers winding through his hair.

King and Malakai finally let him go, and he stepped from that horrible metal box. When Arsenal settled onto the edge of his bed, I knew what we needed.

I would treat this like a heat. Sometimes, in the worst part, it was best to have an alpha touching you all the time. Ruts were more frequent and shorter, but the principles were similar.

Right now we would focus on touch.

"Take off my shirt," I told him. I could do it, but I needed him to set the pace.

"No."

I took his chin in my hands and leaned close. "Have a little faith, Arsenal Gray, and take off my shirt."

TWENTY-THREE

ARSENAL

Glittering sapphires held me in place. They were mesmerising and soothing and safe. I relished every inch of her skin pressed against mine.

The ache was gone.

Never had I had a rut like this.

It had, for a while, been murderous rage splitting my brain. My body had ached, my soul ripping apart as I flung myself against the walls of the vault over and over. Needing blood. Needing sex. Needing fucking *something*.

And then she'd been there, cool water against a fresh burn.

I was still mid-rut, but I was laying in soft sheets, her skin pressed to me, her aura tangled with mine, and she was purring like a little motorbike. Lavender and hot brownies swept me away.

I'd never had a rut like this. *That* was truer than anything, but more than that, I'd never had *anything* like this. Not ever. Pathetic as it was, I'd never in my life been… held.

Without intention or need or demand.

I'd grown up with three pack fathers and two mothers, and they'd all been cold.

And somehow, that she didn't want sex *did* things to me. Like my throat was really thick and my eyes were stinging.

Hormones.

She was dumping omega hormones all over me. If I was teary-eyed, it was her fault. Eventually she settled, tucking her face into the crook of my neck. I was seated with my back against the headboard, and she was straddling me. It was impossible to avoid the fact I had a perfect view of her ass, hugged by black lace, her chocolate mane of hair just barely brushing it.

I couldn't remember why I kept pulling the blankets over her, but she kept tugging them back off, moaning about being too hot.

I heard movement and saw someone stepping around the corner of my room. A growl rumbled in my chest, senses going on high alert. My hands closed around her waist, holding her tighter as I grabbed the blankets and pulled them over her.

She was *mine*.

Oh.

It was just Malakai with a glass of water in hand. He fought a grin, his eyes darting across the room. I followed his gaze to see King lounging on one of the rusty chairs from the roof.

Right.

King was here. He'd been here the whole time.

Onyx was stirring, having been in and out of naps. She blinked blearily up at me, a little smile on her lips.

"Need anything, Duchess?" Malakai asked.

"A basin of warm water and some washcloths," she told them, voice smooth and undeterred. King sprung to action. Bullshit that omegas didn't have barks. She could do anything she wanted right now.

King and Malakai didn't argue, suddenly bustling around to

help. I noticed when they set the basin down, they still watched the two of us warily as if I might pounce.

"What happened? The rut end early?" Ice's voice overturned every ounce of peace that had settled upon me.

He stepped around the corner, but froze when he caught sight of us.

A red haze crept into my vision. The pain slammed back in, that ripping, tearing agony that sent every thought fleeing.

I tried to make for him but—Onyx... Onyx was still in my arms...

He was still there. I couldn't... *He* couldn't be here.

A growl ripped from my chest. The agony and panic was blinding. Fingers gripped my chin, dragging me to look down into cool sapphire eyes.

Roses collided with lavender.

My mind was tearing itself apart. My chest heaved. I was on the edge of my bed. My grip on her waist... it was too strong. I let go in a flash. I was hurting her. Still, she hadn't left, fingers winding through my hair, holding my chin steady.

When I looked up, Ice was gone.

ICE

Everything had stopped too soon.

I'd waited a long time, but there wasn't a hint of that aura, the shakes of the ceiling, or his yelling.

Worry warred with relief.

What had happened?

Slowly, I climbed my ladder to the main room, peering around carefully before clambering out. No one was there. I could hear movement in Arsenal's room, though.

No yelling. No aura.

Just the strongest scent of lavender and chocolate tangled with

Arsenal's honeyed chestnuts.

Had she...? But... that would have been insanely dangerous.

I made for his room, part of me still high-strung with terror, the other half needing to know. What happened to Arsenal was my fault. Every time. I knew that. If she'd fixed it...?

I peered around the corner into the room, unsure what I wanted to see.

"What happened? The rut end early?"

I didn't expect what I found.

Onyx was curled up against Arsenal who was sitting against his headboard, his aura calm. And somehow they weren't fucking.

King walked around the corner, washcloths in hand when he spotted me.

"Oh." He drew up, eyes darting to the bed. "You should—" But it was too late.

Arsenal's aura shattered the air. I went still; completely locked in place. His eyes went dark.

Everything happened in a blur. Arsenal went feral, a growl ripping from his chest. He tried to lunge for me, and the only thing that stopped him was Onyx in his arms.

Arsenal's aura shook, waning, waning. Then a wounded whine sounded from him as he dragged his gaze back to me. King grabbed me, dragging me back.

I was trembling. I had to get back to my nest. It was the only thing that felt safe right now. But... was it safe enough? I didn't feel—

"Ice!" King shook me. "What's going on?"

"Nothing," I hissed, trying to get myself together. "I just..." I shook my head. "I came up because I need... For my nest..."

I shot a glance at the locked box sitting on top of the fridge.

That... That would fix everything. There was a tremor in my soul, a clawing anxiety that only my nest could fix.

"We already gave you two for the month."

Panic rose like a tide up my throat and I seized my hatred to try to stay afloat.

Right. The quota. The fucking quota limiting me from feeling fucking safe. Goddamned fucking pricks treating me like a child.

I hated them. All of them. Especially that oversized tattooed *oaf* currently cosying with Onyx.

What did she see in him, anyway?

"You should go back to your nest."

"I fucking will, if you give me a—"

"No."

"Fuck you!" I spat, going for his throat. King caught my hand then shoved me against the wall.

"My heat is what... a few weeks away?" I snarled. "How easily could I set him off?"

"You'd put her in danger."

"I don't give a shit about her, or you, or anyone in your stupid fucking pack." Well... No. Onyx. I cared about her. But not them. Only... they were alphas and I was a stupid goddamned omega. She'd pick them.

Pick them? You're fucking trapped with them, you idiot.

My heart didn't settle at that thought.

Until they drop you.

It's coming. You just saw the truth for yourself. The same truth I'd been frightened of for years. *How long until you're finally too much and they call in on the bond. Decide it's better to leave you behind even if it cuts them up... And they'll have another bond by then. With her. It'll make it easier.*

Good.

That's what I wanted. What I was waiting for all this time.

I needed them to give me a goddamned—"Hey. Ice." It was Malakai. King let me go so he could step in. He was stooping his head, trying to get a read on me. He brushed my arm with his knuckle.

Trying to calm me? Trying to be fucking affectionate like I was a dog that could be trained? I caught his fingers in my fist, twisting them as I shoved them away. He didn't flinch.

"I *need* it," I spat. "You *don't* understand."

He stared at me. "It's not good for you."

"*Fuck* you!" My scent leached out like poison. Whatever omega shit Onyx was up to in Arsenal's room—the concoction of hormones that was settling him—this was the fucking opposite. I sent it into the space like a flood.

"Get it together." Malakai seized me.

"Give me—"

"*No.*" He wasn't backing down. "You fuck up Arsenal's rut? You're *still* not getting shit from us."

My chest heaved as I glared at him. Finally, I conceded, my mind already spinning backup plans. I ripped free from his grip and stormed to my nest.

ARSENAL

Onyx's lips brushed my jaw, trailing down my neck. Each soft flutter of her touch settled my heart rate. Her scent was drowning the room, smothering *his*.

Time passed strangely, and this rage took longer to fade. When it had, I was terrified of the amount of time that had passed. I tried to sit up, and she moved with me, still straddling my hips, keeping her skin pressed to mine.

"I..." My voice was a weak croak. "I need to find Ice."

I'd... Fuck. What had I done?

He'd been terrified. I'd never, until now, seen him during my rut.

When I went into one, his bond slammed closed with the shutters down. We never knew why, but after years, we suspected. We knew where he'd come from.

And now... I'd lost it on him.

"I think we should give him a bit of time." Her silken words made too much sense, even if I didn't want to hear it. But what if I lost it again?

How much damage had I done?

"He's been with us for years," I rasped. I knew what it looked like to outsiders. I knew she'd never believe it used to be worse. "Every change takes months. The smallest bit of trust at a time..." And now I'd ruined it.

How much had I just set us back? And with the job so close... I shook, and Onyx held me tighter.

"I didn't realise..." Her brows were pinched. "Why... are you so rude to him?"

Well, I wouldn't claim he wasn't sometimes infuriating, but it was more than that. "It's our... language. He gets freaked if we're nice. King tried to take him to dinner once. He stayed in his nest for a week."

She didn't have a reply for that, but I sensed discordance in her aura, as if that disturbed her just as it disturbed us.

"I need him to know... I wasn't angry *at* him."

I stared at her, trying to figure it out. I hadn't meant to do it. I just hadn't been out of my rut enough to keep control. "Seeing him... hurt."

But I *should* hurt. I deserved it. And yet I'd gone for him as if he was at fault for that.

"Why?"

"Because..." I swallowed. "Because I failed him."

Onyx drew back, fingers tracing my cheeks as she met my eyes in the low light. "How?"

"He wanted..." My voice was barely a breath. "He wanted freedom."

She waited.

"We had no idea what he'd just escaped—"

"What had he escaped from?"

I shook my head. It wasn't only the fact it wasn't my secret, but saying those words out loud made me sick to my stomach.

We hadn't known for the longest time, piecing together clues until the foul truth came clear.

He wouldn't take anything for his nest that didn't come from a very specific pawn store down the street. I couldn't understand it until Malakai finally did some digging.

A trafficking ring—right beneath our noses—with roots so deep we couldn't consider touching it. All we could do was keep him hidden and safe.

It was why he wouldn't register with the Institute. We'd confronted him about it once, knowing it might ruin our relationship—and that had set us back months. But during that fight he swore blind that the people that kept him captive had ties to a dark branch of the Institute.

Registration was thorough, they needed contacts and an address. If he tried to get registered, he believed they could come for him before the process ever went through.

In short, he'd seen too much.

What we *had* figured out was that he was never sold off to another party. Someone in the ring had taken a liking to him. He'd been kept like an animal.

My gut twisted.

Is it any different here?

"He escaped something dark," I said. "Can't imagine what it took to do that. He was barely out, and then he met us."

"And he... blackmailed you?"

"We had no idea who he was. All we knew was this crazy omega had discovered Malakai's Harpy scheme. He'd go back to jail if he was caught, so..." I shut my eyes. "It was me—*my* choice. I made sure he'd never be free again."

"You... didn't dark bond him," her voice was a breath. "You could have."

"Doesn't make a blind bit of difference. He was nineteen. Just a kid. And we were this pack of fucking idiots, thinking that the shit we'd seen was the worst of the world."

I was grateful that she said nothing, just running her thumb gently across my cheek as she listened.

"He's scared of our ruts. Won't admit it. Tells us he hates us, that he sends us into them on purpose, but we can feel the truth." I couldn't imagine how traumatic it must be for him if *we* felt it. He locked the bond down air tight. Anything that got through was colossal. "I need him to know I wasn't angry at him."

"Do you think I could talk to him? Tell him you're sorry."

I stared at her, heart racing at the thought that I couldn't go to him myself. Couldn't get on my knees to beg him to forgive me. That was a joke of a dream, anyway; a violation of every boundary he'd ever set.

"I... You can talk to him, but no apologies."

"Why not?"

We couldn't show the slightest bit of affection, which meant we certainly couldn't apologise.

Ice was broken.

His nest, the one we weren't good enough to free him of, was evidence of that.

But how could I explain to her that if I showed him I cared enough to be sorry, he'd spiral?

She just nodded. "Okay. No apologies. Do you think he'll see me?"

My breathing was calming at last. I nodded. He would see her. There was no doubt in my mind. "I barely ever saw him smile until you arrived, Onyx."

I realised, in that moment, that King had been right last night.

Onyx was the answer to everything.

TWENTY-FOUR

ICE

I'd snuck out while the idiots had been tending Arsenal.

Keeping my fear in check was a task. It had been a long time since I'd been out of the garage by myself.

These streets were dangerous for me. I could get spotted by the wrong set of eyes at any time. I'd sprayed some scent dampener on my jacket, but I didn't have any pills to take. The spray should be enough that I wouldn't be easily identified as an omega.

That would be good enough for my trip. I wouldn't be long.

This foul, coiling sickness within me, it wasn't going anywhere. Not until I was back in my nest with what I needed.

I hurried down the street, hands in pockets.

I'd be quick.

I kept glancing behind me, unable to shake the feeling that I was being followed.

There *was* someone walking behind me, but that was nothing to be paranoid over. Still, I paused, leaning against the grimy wall, waiting for them to pass just in case. I narrowed my eyes as the figure slowed down for just a moment.

My breathing picked up. *Had I been right?*

But then they carried on. I watched suspiciously, hand clutching my phone all of a sudden. He was as tall as Malakai, wearing his hood up, which wasn't uncommon around here. He wore a black mask over his mouth with sharply pointed white teeth printed across it. That was a bit odd, I supposed. I watched him cautiously from beneath my hood as he neared. I caught the faintest scent from him... mint and rain in the nighttime streets. An alpha, then? I tensed, but piercing yellow eyes flickered to me only briefly as he passed.

I waited until he'd turned the next corner, then carried on.

I had to hurry, my panic was rising again. Arsenal was back there right now, learning what the fuck I'd been holding just out of reach.

How many ruts had he spent in the vault? The pits?

This was it.

I was done now they knew what Onyx could offer.

I blinked. I had to get myself together. I shut my eyes.

"Not long now, Hannah."

She didn't talk. Her name was the first and last thing she'd ever said.

"We'll be out soon."

Every day we got closer as I dug a hole around the lock before covering it back up with wallpaper.

I took a breath and hurried on.

Time was strange. I was a street away. Then the door to the alley shop was right before me.

I stared up at it.

Ironside Pawn Shop

". . ."

"Shall we see if you can behave enough that I can take you out?" His hand gripped my chin, forcing me to look at him. "You want to be able to leave again, don't you, Ice?"

Had I replied? Nodded? That part was hazy. I remember hating him so much it hurt. But I got good, eventually, at hiding that.

I hadn't been back here, but I'd been explicit to the pack. Everything they gave me had to be from here.

This place was owned by *him*.

It couldn't be any other way, not if I wanted to sleep at night. I pushed the door open to the tinkle of a welcome bell.

The sound ripped me back to the last time.

It was torture seeing this shop, or any of the outside world again while knowing I would end up back there.

Hannah was my leash.

I knew what this was. I knew the only reason I'd never been sold was because he had taken a liking to me. But it kept us both safe, and worked to my benefit. I was learning the ways in and out. I'd planned our escape.

After that? I didn't know. But I had her to take care of, and that pushed me onward each day.

I didn't realise I'd entered the shop, but suddenly I found myself standing before a large glass cabinet. At long last, the world around me steadied.

ONYX

I knocked on the trapdoor to Ice's nest.

Nothing.

I tried again, waiting.

King watched me from the couch, concerned. When I heard nothing after the third knock, I looked up at him.

"He probably thinks it's one of us. Crack it and let him know it's you."

I undid the latch and opened the door. "Ice?"

I was met by roses and cookies, which I expected. But I hadn't expected to find the lights off, or how dull the scent would be. Not everyone could tell, but there was a certain scent to a nest when an omega was present.

Ice wasn't in there.

I glanced back to King. "Is he on the roof?"

"Uh..." King got to his feet. "I didn't see him leave." But he was crossing the room and hurrying up the stairs. I waited for a moment, but then King returned, shaking his head.

Did I need to check my sense of smell?

"Ice?" I took the ladder down to the space below, fumbling for the string light that caught me in the face.

"He not in there?" King was above me.

I tugged the light on, a sense of foreboding turning my stomach.

Warm light filled the space from a bulb hanging from the ceiling. I didn't know what I had been expecting, but this wasn't it.

It was small, with empty wooden shelves along the walls as if it was supposed to be a cellar. The width was just enough to fit the bed at the end, with a little space around the edges.

None of that was what made me gasp, a hand jumping to my mouth.

Along each side of Ice's bed were two thin wooden panels that stretched from bed to ceiling. And through the wood, each one facing the bed, were driven dozens and dozens of knives.

ICE

The glint of silver blades stared back at me from the display case.

The sight of them was enough to settle my heart. This was right where I was supposed to be.

For a moment, I was back in my nest. I counted the knives pointing back at me as I curled up. Each a promise. A threat.

Nash.

I couldn't sleep, not ever, unless I could see his threat. Each blade was made of that threat, made it tangible. If I could see it, I wasn't looking over my shoulder, waiting for the moment he was back. Waiting for the moment I woke up in my prison and realised this was all a dream.

Arsenal, King, Malakai... I caught my sob.

Onyx... She was definitely a dream.

"Can I help you?" a gruff voice behind the counter asked. It was familiar. I glanced up at him from beneath my hood. Gruff stubble, messy greying hair, slim with an oversized coat.

I remembered him from last time I was here. He'd laughed at something Nash had said and chatted for a while as I waited silently. I remember feeling like I could breathe for the first time. Not stuck in that room of peeling wallpaper. While they talked, I'd stared out the window to the street beyond, marvelling at the sunlight.

In the present, I nodded, keeping my head down and tapping on the glass.

"The blue handle." I didn't care which knife. I just needed one and I could leave.

The shopkeeper took it from the case, turning it in his hand. "Ah. This one's gone off. I'll give it a shine."

"It's fine."

"Won't have it reflecting on my shop." He was fumbling in a drawer behind him before grabbing a rag and a bottle. I tried not to fidget impatiently. He was taking too long. I glanced up at him, then dropped my gaze back down. My eyes would stand out.

"Do I know you?" he asked as he rubbed the blade with the cloth.

I shook my head, eyes fixed on the knife. *Just give it to me.*

"*Swear* I recognise you."

"First time here," I muttered.

He shrugged, then took wrapping from the shelf behind him.

"I don't need it wrapped."

"Ah... Son, that would be illegal."

It took too long, but finally he handed the bag to me.

The moment my fingers closed around it, reality slammed back in.

Terror gripped me.

What the fuck was I doing?

I'd just walked into the lair of the beast.

For a fucking knife.

But... was the knife the reason I'd come? Or was it because I knew, deep down, I never deserved escape at all.

"That's the one." *Nash ignored me completely. With his rut over, he was more composed than the last time I'd seen him. He pointed to Hannah.*

"Don't take her!" *My voice was hoarse. Despite the terror that shook me bone deep when I looked at Nash, I got to my feet. But others were entering the room. Alphas? They looked official.*

They shoved me aside, grabbing Hannah.

"NO!"

This couldn't be happening. I fought them, biting; scratching, doing anything to get to her.

I was a week away at most. The tiny metal pick I used to carve a hole around our lock blistered my fingers until they bled. My captors didn't care, thinking I was anxiously biting them. But it had slowed me down. I thought I had more time. But now they were taking her.

"NO!"

She was dragged from the room, fighting to get back to me, eyes wide.

I should have done more—pushed through the pain. Why had that mattered to me when the alternative was this?

"ICE!" Her terrified scream was the last thing I heard before I was thrown back and the door slammed in my face.

I turned for the door, blood roaring in my ears, unable to control my fear. I had to get hold of it. I was good at managing my scent—but I knew it was too late. The scent dampener wasn't enough.

How far was home?

Ten... maybe fifteen minutes?

What had I done?

It was at that moment that I realised something was wrong. My heart skipped a beat, and it was like I couldn't breathe.

The shop keeper had never asked for payment.

A familiar click sounded behind me, stopping me in my tracks, hand on the door handle.

His rasping voice was a drawl. *"Nash's little pet."*

I closed my eyes for a moment, blood roaring in my ears. Then I turned slowly to find a gun pointed at my head.

TWENTY-FIVE

MALAKAI

I was sitting in the chair in Arsenal's room, waiting with him while Onyx went to talk to Ice.

For every fix, the next disaster rolled in.

Arsenal looked distraught, seated on the edge of the bed. His rut had waned almost completely, fed and stabilised by Onyx's aura. That was a gift. But how long would it take for us to pry Ice back out of his shell? And last night he'd hung out with the others in the living room. As if... if he liked us.

Then King appeared in the room, eyes wide.

"He's gone."

"Who—?" But I cut off.

That was when I felt it.

Ice's side of the bond crashed open in a wave of terror. I felt him for the first time. Ice, in his entirety. Bound by a thousand cords of darkness and pain. Trapped. Silenced.

Alone.

And now, he was terrified.

I was on my feet in a moment, the world spinning, that one word echoing in my head.

Gone.

Something had happened to him, and he was out there, alone.

VIPER

Their omega left the garage alone.

I had suspicions that they had another, but I had no idea who it was. Who *he* was, I realised now as the slender, ash blond man slipped out a back window and began hurrying down the street.

I narrowed my eyes, hesitating only a moment, but my alpha instincts had kicked into overdrive the moment I'd seen him. There was something wrong.

Onyx was inside with the others, safe.

This omega, he was on his own, and something about the way he held himself, the way his shifty eyes darted around the street, set me on edge. I grabbed my mask from the dashboard, locked the car, and slipped after him.

If there were goddamned forget-me-nots outside their home after this, I would have my answer. The fucker was onto me. Tomorrow was my flight, and I was prepping for the worst—that I would be out of the country before I found him.

I was pinning my hopes on her new pack, and the Saint Pack —since Kai had sworn his pack would also look out for her if I had to leave before she was safe.

The omega ahead of me was paranoid. Super fucking paranoid. At one point he leaned against the wall and waited for me to pass. I'd had to hide around the next corner and wait to see what direction he took. I'd got the slightest glimpse of him as I'd passed. He was gold pack. He'd clearly sprayed scent dampeners on his clothing, but it wasn't enough to rid him of the aroma of sweet roses and terror.

My instincts were right. There was something deeply wrong. I tailed him into the doors of a back alley pawn shop.

I waited outside. Was this all he was doing? Buying something before heading home?

I hoped so.

I could see him inside, hood still pulled up, waiting at the counter. For every second that passed, my anxiety grew.

Then he was walking back toward the door and my breathing settled. His hand was on the handle when he froze.

A long moment passed before he turned slowly back to the shopkeeper within.

That was when I saw it.

A gun.

ICE

The world was made of a frigid, hollow silence as if my brain had yet to understand exactly what was happening.

"Don't try anything. He prefers you alive, but he doesn't care how." The voice was rough in my ear as the gun was jammed at my back, shutting off every plan my brain had been spinning for escape.

He flipped the open sign to closed, and we waited at the door.

"Drop the knife."

I stared at it. The blade's silver had a glow of orange from the lamp lights beyond. It was night. I stared through the window at the sky. The last time I'd stepped into this shop I'd marvelled at the daylight outside. Now I wouldn't see it ever again, and the sea of clouds above meant I wouldn't even glimpse the stars.

"*Drop* the knife." Blood roared in my ears at the idea of it. I couldn't... could I? I'd come for this? Yet the purpose of it was fading in the face of a nightmare catching up.

In the blade's reflection, I saw my own golden eyes as the gun was jammed against my skull.

It was over.

With trembling fingers, I let it go. The moment my fingers released the blade, the silence vanished for the nightmare that was here.

Viper

My aura was out: a thread stretched taut and crackling with energy that warred to get out. It was worse than it had ever been since my father had burned down my cottage to force me out of the city.

Minutes passed as I waited. The omega was still at the door while I waited across the street. I was able to see down the little alley well enough from where I was crouched behind a car. My senses were honed on him, unable to detach from the frightened omega at the shop door. His breaths were short and sharp, his golden eyes fixed on the street, darting around as if trying to find an escape.

I couldn't see the gun anymore.

I had to wait for the right moment. What were they waiting for?

Dread crept up my spine as time crawled by. At one point the omega tried to move, but the man behind him grabbed him and shoved him against the glass.

My aura shuddered, every instinct screaming as my focus finally shifted to the beta behind him.

Kill. Him.

I clutched desperately to the last threads tethering my aura to my sanity, dragging it back in. I had to wait, or he would die. The omega would die before I got there. It was enough, barely.

I heard the screeching of wheels. Doors opened, and I heard the clicking of guns.

Finally, the shop door opened with a bell's ring, and the omega was shoved out. "For you, lads. Tell him I want it in cash."

Five men had climbed out of the car. All alphas, but their auras shattered the street. Behind me I heard curtains drawn, as if people were peering out to see the disturbance.

"Go on." The beta shoved the omega forward, and he stumbled down two of the steps toward the alphas. Three were in the alley, two hung back.

"Look who it is," one crooned. He had silver-flecked black hair tied up in a ponytail. "Stupider than we all thought if you're back here."

He was tucking away his gun, though. The others lowered theirs. I narrowed my eyes. What a gift.

The omega glanced between them, wide eyes full of terror.

"Aren't you going to run?" Ponytail asked, twisted glee in his voice. He was the only one whose aura wasn't out yet. My rage burned through sense as the last alpha tucked his gun in his belt, a leer on his face just and the shop door chimed closed.

The omega jumped over the cracked brick wall as Ponytail's aura split the air.

My cue.

Thrill shocked my system as I launched for the three alphas closest to me. My aura was still sick.

I got a burst as I reached the first alpha. Ancient, feral instincts took over. He turned in time to see me, hand and gun jumping up too late. I was upon him, and he crashed to the floor, nails digging into flesh. He screamed, but it was stripped to a gurgle as my fingers found his throat. There was a squelch, and a snap, and then silence.

I got to my feet before my aura shuttered, vanishing to almost nothing. The next alpha landed a punch that sent me crashing into a car. The others would be upon me soon.

Fuck.

Survive.

Just hold out—he pinned me to the metal with crushing strength as the other fumbled for his gun.

Then my aura was back in a flare.

Just in time.

I head-butted the one before me. My memories of this would be blurry later, but I wouldn't forget the concave mess of a face as his body crumbled to the floor. I turned on the last alpha who was halfway to training his gun on me.

I dived for him, colliding just as a shot split the air.

I felt no pain of a wound, but my head exploded with agony as the noise turned my vision white.

Shit.

I crashed to my knees, holding onto the flesh of one of the alphas before me. I couldn't see anything. Couldn't think. I ripped at the fistfuls of flesh in my grip until there was no more movement.

Shit.

A sound filtered in over the high pitched ringing.

The omega's shouting. Desperate and hoarse. I caught the scent of roses edged with terror the likes of which I'd never felt. Each scream was like a shot of adrenaline through my broken body.

He would be taken.

I... couldn't stop them.

My aura had shuttered out again. I'd pushed too far. It wasn't coming back soon. I fumbled with my coat as the world reformed around me, dragging out my phone with trembling fingers. It was the one I had *just* for her. I coughed, edges of my vision turning black, brain not working right. It was open to the one contact it had. I couldn't... couldn't think...

My fingers fumbled with buttons, trying to make words

My ears rang, but I heard talking.

"...Nash is looking for alphas..."

I had seconds. I tapped out words. Did... they make sense? The screen was smeared with the blood on my fingers.

"I said grab him, you fucking coward!"

Another shock of adrenaline hit at the sound of the omega's scream, and the smothering inky blackness at the edge of my vision receded for a moment.

Enough to press send.

The phone was ripped from my hand and I watched it crack beneath a heavy boot. Something collided with my head and everything went black.

TWENTY-SIX

ONYX

My phone buzzed.

I tugged it from my purse desperately.

Ice?

He had my number. The text lit up the screen from the number I didn't recognise.

> Unknown: Omega. Pawn shop.

I stared at it.

"What is that?" It was Arsenal's voice.

I blinked, dragging my gaze from it with difficulty. "Pawn shop?" I asked, unsure.

All of them froze.

"No..." King's voice was hoarse.

Arsenal snatched the phone from my grip, eyes wild. "Who is this?" he asked, after his eyes had scanned the texts.

"I... don't know." My mind was racing. Malakai and King were both at his side in an instant.

Could this be my stalker? My blood chilled.

Had he come for Ice?

"Why would... he be there?" Malakai asked.

"I... It could be unrelated." King said. But none of them looked like they believed it.

"It says pawn shop. This *is* about Ice."

"W-what does that mean?" I asked.

King was shaken. "It's where we get his knives."

"I don't understand..." I breathed, trailing off in my panic.

Arsenal hadn't moved. His eyes were fixed on my phone screen, but he wasn't present.

"Is this the stalker or the—"

"I don't care who. If it's the pawn shop—If he's been taken, we know where he is." Arsenal was crossing to one of the tall cupboards, ripping it open, and unlocking a safe.

"We can't leave her," Malakai said.

"You want her to *come*?" King asked. "It could be—"

"What if this is a trick and it is the stalker? The moment we're separated, he could make a move."

My blood chilled to see Arsenal laying guns out on the table.

"So we take her into the human trafficking circle instead?" King demanded harshly.

"Shut up. Both of you." Arsenal growled. He was staring at me, eyes calculating. "She's safer with us." Arsenal said finally, tucking rounds of ammo into his pockets. King's face turned a sickly colour.

I opened my mouth, heart thundering in my chest, but then shut it. All formulations of the thought in my head hitting a solid wall. I realised the police had never helped. Not once. Not for me, and not for this pack. I felt safer with them—no matter what that meant—than I ever had anywhere else.

"I'll get in the way," I said as Malakai and King grabbed their own guns. "I could... go to a random hotel. No one will know where I am."

"This asshole's too good," Arsenal said. "We don't know this isn't him. I don't trust he doesn't have eyes on you right now. You're not leaving our sight." He was picking up the last gun from the table. "Can you use one, Duchess?"

"I..." *Shit.* "I learned." My voice was weak. A pack had visited a gun range a few times during our dates. Enough that I knew the basics. It was not enough to feel confident as Arsenal pressed the cold weight of a weapon into my hands. "Don't use it unless you have to."

I nodded, but it was more reactionary than anything else. Something shifted in the others as they saw me holding the weapon. Malakai especially, who was staring at me like he'd seen a ghost. But then Arsenal was making for the door.

VIPER

4 years ago.

It was a perfect night.

Onyx was our scent match. The universe had been leading me all along.

She rested against my chest, fitting against me perfectly as she continued gazing into my eyes as she swayed. She was shorter than me by a foot—something that was easy to forget for the presence she wielded. And I supposed I was holding her heels between my fingers right now.

I brushed her cheek, stolen away by this perfect moment as the song came to a close. My thumb grazed her lips before pressing into them just hard enough that her eyes shifted from delight to something more sultry.

I would have taken her right here in the rain, but tonight I had something so much more important. I was supposed to wait, but I'd never been patient—and much less so while trapped by starry sapphire eyes.

I felt the intent rise in my chest as the words slipped from my lips without refrain. "Take the princess bond."

There was a breath of silence, and then she tugged away, turning, all the smooth elegance gone for the shock on her face. She could feel the offer hovering in the auras between us.

I'd seen Onyx twist alphas around her little finger with ease. She was confident in her own ability to melt the brains of men, but in this, I had her stunned. A smile tugged at the corner of my mouth, I was proud to have off-balanced her.

But truly, what had she expected? It was the only omega bond she deserved—approval of my father be damned. He was pissed enough about my choice of packmates, besides.

Onyx's lips parted, eyes darting between mine as if trying to find the joke.

"What about the others?"

"We all want you to have it," I murmured, leaning closer until my forehead touched hers. "You're royalty, Onyx."

Princess bonds, of the three bonds omegas could host, were rarest. It created a powerful bond between omega and pack, in which the omega was firmly on top. It could only be offered to scent matched omegas, but there was risk. She could walk away from the bond and leave us shattered. Then her aura would shift, mark her a duchess ready to claim the riches of the world, becoming irresistible to every alpha that crossed her. Duchesses had power. A power some omegas dreamed of.

But Onyx wouldn't walk.

We were made for each other. Every member of this pack was a piece of me, and she was the final missing piece.

"I..." She trailed off, still caught off guard. Her fingers curled in my shirt, and the excited shift in her scent had my heart in my throat. "You know what I'll say, babe." She was fighting a smile.

"But I'll only say it with the others there."

Of course she'd wait. Because she loved us all. Because she was perfect.

"Then I must insist we get back to them." I took her slender wrist between my fingers and lifted it. I didn't take my eyes from hers as I pressed my lips to her forearm, and even though we'd fallen in love a thousand times already, even though the night was dim and the light warped by rain, I could see the flush rise in her cheeks.

My kiss brushed the only tattoo that graced her skin. A stem with five flower heads.

One for each of us.

The delicate lines of a forget-me-not...

My dream was swallowed away by the splitting pain in my head as I woke in a dim room.

A groan sounded, echoing off the thick walls. My groan.

I blinked, looking around.

This room was like something out of a movie. A cage. A prison. There were no windows, the striped wallpaper was fading, and the bed I lay on was rigid. The lightbulb hanging above me was clinical and white. I groaned, pushing myself up.

There were two beds in the room. I was on one, my wrists shackled to the wall. The omega knelt at my side—unchained—as he helped me up.

"Why?" He seemed angry. "Who are you?"

I blinked, staring at him. His hood was down. I could see him properly now. He had freckles, delicate pale skin, and messy ash blond hair. I hadn't thought, after Onyx, I'd ever think someone could be perfect, but... I reached up, the cuffs allowing me some movement, but he drew back.

"No one," I croaked. "I just—"

"Decided to get involved with a bunch of guys with guns?" he demanded. "Yeh. I don't think so."

"I tried... to save you."

"That's what's not computing, genius."

He wasn't fooling me. His eyes were wide and his perfume was spilling across the space, an edge to it that set my adrenaline pumping once more.

I reached out again without thinking, brushing the ash blond hair from where it covered a deep bruise on his forehead. An instinctive growl rose in my chest at the sight of it, but he flinched back from me, something hostile in his eyes.

I withdrew my hand again.

"What the hell is this?" he demanded, getting to his feet. "Your *brain* misfiring? I'm *claimed*." He pointed to the bite on his neck. I stared at him, still trying to orient myself.

It didn't matter. He was important. Too fucking important.

"What's your name?" he asked.

"Viper."

"I'm Ice. Warm welcome to the trafficking ring that lives in the underbelly of New Oxford. Settle in because there's no fucking way we're getting out."

"I'll get us out."

He choked out a laugh. "Why? Because you're an alpha?" he asked. "You think they're above selling tough guys like you? Put a collar around your neck and the asking price goes sky high."

"How do you know?"

If he was on edge before, it was nothing to now. His fingers dug into his scalp as he spun back on me. "Because this is where I fucking came from. The guy that runs this place, he's been looking for me—"

"Why?"

"Because I..." He trailed off, eyes darting to the door. "I know shit about this place, alright? Stuff that could ruin them."

"You're bonded. Your pack will come."

He just stared at me, and a manic laugh slipped out. "They aren't coming."

"Bullshit—"

"They hate me."

No. That wasn't right. I'd been getting all the intel I could on them. "They don't seem the type."

Silence hit the room, and Ice's fingers stopped wildly running through his hair.

Shit. He took a step back.

"It's not—"

"How the fuck do you know anything about my pack?" He didn't sound scared now, he sounded... protective, a little snarl curling his lips.

"Look, I just—"

"You just what?"

Well. What did it matter? We were fucked. "I was... tailing Onyx."

"Tailing?" Ice stared at me, shock written all over his face. "Like... Wait—"

"No." Shit. I could see how that sounded. "I'm *not* her stalker. I was trying to catch them, and I'm—was—running out of time."

"Right. Thanks for telling me you're not her stalker. That clears it all—"

"I love her." I was sitting straight in an instant and the world spun around me. I slammed my palm to the wall to steady myself. "I would never hurt her."

I squeezed my eyes shut, warring with the memories that threatened. I didn't realise I was falling until it was too late, but then Ice was there, holding me up by shoving me against the wall.

"What is another alpha doing tailing her around The Gritch District?"

"I... knew she matched a pack. Your pack," I croaked. Ice said nothing, watching me. He didn't argue with that assessment. He *was* their pack. That meant he was Onyx's mate. "I can't be with her. Not ever. But I had to know she was safe before I left."

"Left where?"

"I'm... leaving. I'll never see her again."

"Why do you care? What are you, one of those rich dicks she—" But Ice cut off, blinking as he regarded me. "She can't see you?"

I shook my head.

"You're... from her old pack?" Ice asked. "The one she rejected?"

"She didn't reject us." The words were out of my mouth, more angry than I'd meant.

Ice's brow furrowed, but he didn't question that.

But I felt the strength drain from me the moment I said it out loud—that it was over, that me and my brothers were a part of her past. Not present. Never future.

There was still calculation in his eyes.

"I just... needed her safe," I rasped.

There was a long silence. "She doesn't remember," Ice said quietly.

"I know. It has to stay that way."

"Why?"

"Because... this pain... She doesn't deserve it."

"They died?"

I didn't answer, but he was gripping my arm still. He would feel the way my whole body shook at those words. Infected, open wounds that weren't healed.

That *couldn't* heal.

Sometimes... Sometimes I could blink, and that living room would still be there, but *they* wouldn't be. No bodies limp and cold and unmoving. Hart wouldn't be there, on that couch.

The nightmare that never left.

"Alright." Ice's voice ripped me back to the present, and his nails bit down on my arm. "Shit. Okay. Look, you shouldn't be caught up in this. Nash..." He swallowed, and I saw a flare of panic in his eyes. "Nash is going to come. If I can give him—"

"You aren't doing shit for me," I rasped. "Your pack is coming. Until then, I'll—"

"You don't get it. You get taken by these guys, you vanish. Even if my pack was coming—"

"They *will*." He was crazy. "They're your—"

"They never wanted me!" His voice cracked. "They have h—" But he couldn't finish.

I stared at him, reading pain all over his face.

They have her?

He thought... Onyx had replaced him?

No no no.

I reached out again, and this time he didn't stop me as I took his hand in mine. That connection was like lightning in my veins, keeping me alert, and I knew the next words weren't a lie. "I won't let anything happen."

For a moment, Ice stared at me as if he wanted to believe me, something vulnerable in his stunning golden eyes. His fingers squeezed mine for just the briefest second. Then he choked a laugh, a wild smile on his face as he gestured to the room. "You can't stop this."

TWENTY-SEVEN

ONYX

I was huddled in the side seat of the jeep as Arsenal raced down the street.

We'd arrived at the pawn store first. King had stayed in the jeep with me while Arsenal and Malakai jumped out. I couldn't see much down the alley but was that… a body?

Malakai and Arsenal didn't take long. I saw Arsenal check the street while Malakai went to the pawn shop door and rattled it. Locked. When they came back, Arsenal was tense. I'd never seen Malakai disturbed before, but his eyes were wide, his expression sickened.

"What?" King asked.

"Massacre. Alphas involved."

"But Ice—?"

"If he was hurt, we'd know." Arsenal was already ripping away from the street.

"Why was he there?" I asked. It was hitting me now we'd seen it. "He knows who owns it."

King looked struck. "Earlier… We…" He swallowed.

"What?" Arsenal demanded.

"After he saw you, he asked for a knife..."

"A knife?" I asked.

"For his nest... I mean, you saw it."

"And?" I asked.

"Well he's supposed to get two a month."

"You... said no?" My voice was dry. "He saw me—another omega—with Arsenal during his rut, then asked for the thing that makes him feel safe, and you told him... no?"

Malakai was staring at me and for a moment, he just looked lost.

"We... didn't think about it like that," King whispered.

"Fuck," Arsenal muttered. He slammed his fist into the steering wheel. *"Fuck!"*

"He's not interested in your ruts, mate. Never has been. I didn't..." But King was running his fingers through his light hair.

"It doesn't matter," I whispered. I could imagine it. I knew that desperation. Right now, my handbag was clutched in my arms. It had to be near. If it wasn't—

"Tell me about the shop."

"It's where he asked us to get the knives. It's owned by—" Malakai glanced at the others before pushing on. "By the guy who runs the trafficking ring. He took a liking to Ice, kept him there for a long time before he escaped. He always asks us to get the knives from that shop."

"That's—"

"Fucked up. We know. Alright, we know how sick he is," Arsenal said. "That's all we're working towards. Trying to fucking fix it."

"I didn't think... You're saying he just walked out and went there by himself?" King asked. "He wouldn't do that."

I winced. "Omega instincts aren't a joke, especially if he isn't well. Hyperfixation, rash decision making, even dissociation all can be symptoms of an unbalanced omega."

King looked like he was going to be sick. I grabbed his hand, squeezing it tight. Malakai was looking out the window, so I didn't catch his expression as he spoke. "It doesn't matter. We're getting him back."

"Where are we?" I asked as we pulled up into a parking lot before a huge building.

"The people after him, they aren't a joke. When he told us, we did our research. They're based under the Gritch District, but when Ice escaped it was through an exit that came out in this theatre."

"You live so close—"

"We're trying," King breathed. "We need a pack house, but they're expensive. The garage was inherited, but isn't selling for much—and Ice panics if we talk about moving."

"I'm... sorry." I said, glancing out the window, guilt gnawing at me. "So we're going in?"

Into a trafficking ring?

"That's the problem, Duchess," Mal said.

"Leave you alone for the stalker, or take you down into one of the most dangerous places in all of New Oxford?"

"You're not going further than the theatre," Arsenal cut in. "King and I will go ahead. You stick with Mal. He'll be in charge of keeping you safe."

"We're splitting up?" Malakai sounded shocked.

"Then if anything happens—if we get caught—it won't be game over."

ICE

I would have known it was Nash without looking. His scent was simple soured lemongrass and might have been nice, but to me it had always been too bitter.

"Three fucking years," he laughed. "And now you turn up?"

He was exactly what I remembered. With his curly chestnut locks, crooked nose, and broad grin. He had always been well put together. Even now, he wore a black suit that stretched across his broad frame.

"Come," he said, folding his arms and leaning against the wall as the door shut behind him.

I didn't move, my fingers anxiously brushing faint scar against faint scar on my fingertips. The promise that had come with my freedom.

The promise of this.

"Come, or I'll skip the chat entirely." He lifted his gun and waved it in Viper's direction. I was on my feet in a moment, staggering toward him, ignoring the growl that ripped across the room from Viper.

I ignored the desire I felt to step back into that protection it offered. *"I won't let anything happen."*

An impossible promise. Yet he'd made it.

I didn't know why I wanted to believe it so badly. Alphas didn't want me. They didn't protect me. None but a pack who had no choice but to keep me around—and that was over, now. But Viper's beautiful yellow eyes had been filled with such conviction...

I shook the thought away. I couldn't be the reason he died or was taken like Hannah.

Nash lowered the gun, but didn't loosen his grip on it as he stared down at me.

"Now for the real question, Ice. Kill you or keep you?"

I stared at him.

Kill me.

I'd rather die today than become his for another second. But just like before, there was someone else.

A sneer curled on Nash's face as he tapped the gun against my cheek. I flinched, eyes darting down, old habits surfacing so fast.

The gun vanished for his touch and my flinch was more violent, but he gripped my chin and forced me to meet his eyes.

"Don't touch him!" Viper snarled. My eyes flickered to him, straining against the chains, desperate. Why... Why was he defending me?

Nash ignored him, still fixed on me. "Just as irresistible as ever."

I shut my eyes, hearing another violent tug on the chains behind.

"Is the alpha yours?" Nash asked, fingers dropping to the bite on my neck. "He made quite a mess. Do you know the kinds of money that might bring—"

"Don't..." My voice broke, my eyes snapping open. He was Onyx's. He didn't belong here. But Onyx felt so far away. A dream. "I'll d-do whatever you want."

"NO!"

This time I glanced back in time to see Viper flinging his weight against the chains, eyes wild.

Nash ignored him. "Leverage didn't work very well on you last time—"

"I didn't leave until you took her," I spat.

Nash paused, a snarl on his face, his fingers closing tight around my neck and squeezing. I grabbed his hand, staring into those hateful brown eyes as I gasped for air. "I can give you... what you want." The words were quiet enough that Viper shouldn't have been able to hear them, but he let out another snarl, throwing himself against the chains once more.

Nash's smile widened, then he stood, dragging me up by my neck. "Shall we go and see if that's still true? And maybe, just maybe I'll consider leaving him. For now."

I steeled myself, clutching his arm to loosen the pressure on my neck as he turned back to the door. Tears blurred my vision.

No.

It didn't matter. I had always been doomed to end up back here. I'd never been free. What was the difference, if my chains were with Nash or with them?

I trembled.

It didn't matter. The latch clicked as he was opening it. The space outside was too familiar. Concrete walls, clinical smell. Nash. Lemongrass.

Nightmares.

It didn't matter. I didn't realise how much I'd been clinging to that lie until this moment. That I'd needed to brace for the moment Nash returned. So I could tell myself none of it mattered.

But as he hauled me from the room, the brittle glue that had strained to hold my sanity together for the last three years snapped at last.

I want them back.

The truth collided with the brittle reality I'd clung to.

No.

You've done this before.

You can do it again.

But... before, there had never been grief. Before, I'd never had anyone I loved.

I'd never see them again.

I want them back. The second time the thought hit me, I cracked, throwing myself against Nash's grip. I screamed, losing control, trying to get back toward Viper.

The world went red.

VIPER

Half way out the door, Ice went feral.

I threw myself against the chains again, my aura sparking, scattering, desperate at the sight of his pain.

Demanding of me the last thing I'd never given it.

She was shimmering with the night rain as we danced. An echo of bliss. I didn't know at the time I would never feel that again.

It was at that moment that my pack bonds shuddered.

A threat on the perfect life I could see in her beautiful sapphire eyes. But I had to look away from those eyes right now in the dark and rain.

The cottage was through the trees. They were in there. I could see it through the moonlight shrouded trees and rain even as I felt the pack bonds tremor again.

Wrong.

That was wrong...

A strangled growl of terror tore through my chest as I launched toward them. But... it was too late. In that moment I couldn't reach my aura—I grappled for it, needing to get there before—

Threads snapped

One

By

One.

Jake. Vik. H—

NO! I choked, reaching for my aura. If I could just get to it, maybe I could—my feet pounded rain soaked grass toward them —there!

I seized it. Desperate.

But agony sliced the world in two, the stillness where my brothers had just been colliding with every atom of who I was.

I stumbled.

Mud and grass stuck to my face. I could hear everything, the faint creak of the gate at the back, my own wheezing breaths, the splashing footsteps of Onyx behind me. Bark tore at my palms as I dragged myself up and the world spun, a low, wounded howl echoing into the rain.

It was mine.

I strained for them within the walls. A footstep. A heartbeat. But the gaping mouth of this void slowly swallowing me up was its own promise of silence.

Shattered bonds left behind wounds unhealed. Mine was an aura that had been entwined with three others ripped away and left to bleed.

There were three choices an alpha faced when bonds were destroyed: Replace, cauterise, or follow them off that cliff.

I'd never bonded into another pack.

I'd never claimed silver status so that my aura was sealed off and I could live life as a lone alpha.

And I'd never followed them, even when I'd felt the pull before.

It would take one easy step.

Then there would be no containment, safety, or barriers. I could push it and push it and push it as far as I wanted to go. Like stretching old elastic, it would never return, its energy feeding from a place it never could before.

I'd never taken that step because of my one last anchor.

Her.

But tomorrow I would be gone, forced into another world to start a life I never wanted.

She was all I ever wanted.

They were.

And outside this door was her mate. One who could do a better job than I had with that chance.

So I let go and took one last step into the void my brothers left behind.

My aura untethered completely.

TWENTY-EIGHT

ICE

There was a thundering bang at the door behind me.

Nash froze, turning.

The aura that ripped through the air was poison. The other alphas who'd been waiting outside took a step away, eyes trained on the door, their auras hitting the air.

BANG!

I jumped as the door dented, my heart out of control.

"What the fuck?" Nash lifted his gun, holding up to the door as he backed up a few paces, grip still painful on my wrist.

BANG!

Another massive dent.

BANG!

The door exploded from its hinges and crashed into the far wall. My breath caught, my heart in my throat as I stared at the open doorway to the prison of my nightmares.

Silence.

No one moved for a long, long moment.

"Go!" Nash hissed at the closest alpha. The alpha glanced back at us, eyes wide. "You have a gun, don't you?"

The alpha swallowed, and then took a careful step toward the room.

One, two, three paces, and then he was standing in front of the doorway, gun pointed in. Despite his powerful aura, I could swear he was shaking.

The air was thick with auras right now, setting every hair on my body on edge. Only one brought me peace and didn't feel hostile. One that was protective, not aggressive. And that was the largest one of all.

The alpha took a few tentative steps forward, gun sweeping one way and then the next.

With a jolt, he was ripped forward and out of sight. I jumped violently.

A gun shot. A scream.

His aura vanished from the air.

The other alpha looked back at us, unsure. "Nash, I think we should—"

"Deal with him!" Nash was already dragging me away.

No.

I knew where my escape was.

Viper.

I needed to get to Viper.

I threw myself against Nash's grip, fighting to get away.

"Enough!" Nash didn't need to train his gun on me as he slammed me against the wall. Pain exploded across my back with the aggression of it, and I whimpered.

It was one flash of distraction, one sound from me, and I caught movement in the corner of my eyes. Blinded by the pain still shooting up my back, I didn't see what happened next.

There was another scream and a spray of red. A gunshot, then another, followed by a scream.

"*Stay!*" Nash's voice shook and then I felt the cold metal of a gun pressed to my head. It was too late. His grip was ripped away, the gun firing in a random direction. There was a crash and a grunt.

I steadied myself, staring up, processing the scene for the first time. The other alpha was dead. His heavyset body contorted at a strange angle, blood spilling from a massive gash on his neck. Viper was ahead of me, pinning Nash against the wall.

"Do you want him?" Viper's voice shook.

Nash's breathing was ragged. Nash's aura, which had once felt so huge and impossible, was barely discernible beside Viper's.

I stared at them. Viper shifted, almost looking back at me as Nash fought his grip. Despite the fact that Nash was a big man, he couldn't budge Viper's grip.

"Do you want him?"

I couldn't process much, but I could process that. I stumbled forward, grabbing the gun from where it had landed at Viper's feet.

Nash's gun.

But... No. This wasn't right. I reached out, fumbling at Nash's belt, drawing out the blade he always kept there.

"Ice!" Nash's voice was rough. Viper growled, slamming him harder against the wall, his fist closing tighter against Nash's corded throat. Nash's face was growing red as he struggled, choked sounds coming out.

"Don't.. " he begged.

I didn't care, though. I jammed the blade into Nash's stomach. He let out a grunt of pain, unable to do more with Viper crushing his windpipe. He managed a howl, though, as I twisted the knife. His hot blood leaked down onto my fist. I wanted him to suffer, but...

"Hannah. Where was she taken?"

Nash stared at me, a snarl on his face.

I twisted the knife further.

"I don't... know where they took them. They don't tell me."

"It was the Institute?" I demanded.

"Y-yes," he growled.

"You have to know something," I spat.

Nash coughed, blood trickling from his lips.

"TELL. ME!" I snarled.

"They mentioned a facility... once. That's all... That's all I know."

I stared at him. I'd already known about the facility. I already knew that the Institute worked with this place to secure alphas and omegas that wouldn't be missed. "Where is it!"

Nash just shook his head, face purple, whole body trembling with agony now.

Could it be true?

Was that all he knew?

But... We didn't have forever down here. Nash coughed again, low whines rising in his throat. Another few seconds stretched as I warred with myself. Then I dragged the knife from his stomach and jammed it through his eye.

He saw it only for a moment, terror flashing on his face right before I drove it in. I needed that. I would keep it forever.

It was harder than I'd imagined, which meant, for a moment, it got stuck in his socket. He let out a howl of agony before I threw my entire weight into it and the blade lodged into his skull. His howl cut off, his body going limp.

Viper released him, turning to me in a moment, shaking, bloody fingers reaching for my face as he... Well, what *was* he doing?

He... was checking me over, bright eyes wild as he searched my face.

"Are you hurt?" he asked.

I shook my head. My back ached, but it wouldn't slow me

down. His strained expression split with relief and, for a moment, it looked like he wanted to pull me into a hug. In a wild second, I wanted him to.

But... Now I was focusing on him, I realised his aura was wrong. Toxic. Like an oil spill still gushing out into the space.

"How did you do that?" I asked, voice weak.

"Don't worry about it. You know the way out?"

I nodded, glancing down the hallway.

I'd made this escape before, I could do it again.

VIPER

I could last long enough to get him out.

Now that I'd let go, I felt more peace than I had in years. Since those last happy moments.

This would be my last gift to her.

Ice's grip was tight on my arm, his fear keeping all of my senses on high alert. He directed, but I was first. Always. If bullets went flying it didn't matter if they hit me first.

This place was huge, though. I could hear distant footsteps, voices in different rooms. It helped us avoid people.

Once, I was able to drag us into an open room just before a group of alphas hurried by. It was large enough that if I pressed against the far wall with the door closed, they might not feel my aura. I couldn't rid myself of it now.

Ice was tense at my side as they passed. I heard the voices from here.

"—*Nash causing problems again?*"

"*They really need to rein him in—*"

The footsteps faded, and me and Ice moved more urgently now. They were onto us. There were traces of scents everywhere. Some fresh, some fading, but all strong enough that they had to be alphas or omegas. Many of the scents was marred with terror.

For one brief moment I thought I heard the faintest humming of a lullaby. There was a sadness to the song that drew me up.

"What?" Ice asked.

"Another omega..." I didn't know how I knew, but I did.

Only, in this maze of tunnels, the song was coming from a thousand directions. I turned, trying to pin it down. The further out I pushed my hearing, the more I was drowned with distractions. More footsteps. More talking.

"Where?"

"I don't... Fuck. I don't know." I tried again to locate the sound, but it was impossible. "We don't have time."

It went against every instinct I had, but I didn't know how long I would last. I didn't know the details of the detonation I had triggered, but I knew one thing: if my aura faded on us, Ice would be alone.

ICE

I had climbed this ladder before. It was cold and metal and stretched far up to a latched door above. Viper was first, slamming the door open with a burst of his aura.

"We... made it."

We were in a theatre, and I could see the streetlight through the double doors ahead. A few people walked by on the street.

The outside world. Out there, they couldn't touch us.

We had made it, and Nash was dead.

I had killed him.

I loosed a mad laugh, spinning to Viper only to freeze.

He'd buckled, his knees crashing to the wooden slats that made up the theatre floor. "Hey..." I made for him, kneeling at his side and holding him up as he sagged further.

The poisonous aura around him was waning, drawing inward, getting... sicker.

"What's going on?" My voice shook, something foreboding in the pit of my stomach.

"I think..." Viper croaked. "My uh... my time is up."

"What does that mean?"

"This wasn't going to last."

My grip was tighter and I grabbed his chin, forcing him to look at me. "What does that *mean*?" I demanded again.

"My aura isn't... isn't that strong, really."

"It is..." I trailed off, a part of my mind realising what he was saying before I allowed myself to think it.

"I might have..."

"No." *No no no.*

"Not much choice..."

This couldn't be happening. "You... saved me."

"I'd call that worth it, Little Omega," he croaked.

An alpha with severed bonds of dead packmates had an option no other alpha had. The open wounds of dead or cleaved brothers left their aura one small snip away from untethering completely.

And Viper had just done that for me.

It was why his aura was poisonous. Toxic. Why it was so powerful. Because it was drawing energy from the one place that it should never be able to draw from.

It was drawing it from him.

He was going to die for me.

That didn't make sense. Nothing made sense. No one saved me, not without needing something back. He knew saving me would kill him.

I stared into bright yellow eyes, every foreign instinct I'd tried to bury rising its head.

Mine.

He was mine. I wanted him. *Needed* him. And I'd never needed anyone, so he wasn't allowed to die.

"You need an anchor," I rasped.

"Bit late." His smile was weak. Anger flared in my chest.

"No..." My voice was faint. Then the realisation hit me like a truck. "I'm... an anchor. Bite in." He'd saved me and I could save him. And then... he'd be mine...

"I can't do that."

He was fading, his body getting heavy in my arms. I adjusted, resting his head down, leaning over him.

"No." He couldn't die. He'd protected me, given up everything for *my* freedom. Done what no one else in my life ever had.

"I-if you die, you'll never see her again." My voice caught. This was it. The first time I'd ever known beyond a shadow of a doubt, I *wanted* a bond. I wanted to be an omega if it meant being *his* omega.

Viper shook his head, a smile drawn across his lips. Tight, unhumorous. "I can never... be with her." Tears were tracking his cheeks.

"You can. She's ours, you idiot," I begged, my voice shaking. His breathing was ragged. "Please!"

I'd never claimed someone, but my instincts were like a torrent, and for the first time in my life, I wanted what they wanted. The universe had handed me something back.

Only to rip it away.

I pressed my neck to his mouth again, but he didn't bite.

"Don't do this." My voice was still trembling as I drew back, gripping his shoulders and shaking him. "You can't just come into my life like this and leave."

He's saved me.

Given everything for me.

I wouldn't... *couldn't* do this.

I lost myself in that moment and I pressed my teeth to his neck instead, claiming him. He seized beneath my teeth, and when I drew back he was staring at me with wide yellow eyes.

"I want y-you." The words shattered on the way out of my mouth. *Please don't take this away.* Even my pack... they didn't want me. It didn't matter if I loved them. I could never tell them that, because they didn't love me.

I'd made it impossible.

"Don't leave me." Tears blurred my vision. "P-Please don't leave me."

VIPER

"P-please don't leave me."

Ice had claimed me.

An ancient wound shifted, years and years of armour cracking away to reveal the foul infection beneath. The offer I'd made had been torn away. It went unreplaced, slowly killing me like the losses of my brothers.

"Take the princess bond."

Her smile had been dazzling.

"You know my answer."

But she'd waited, not wanting to give it until we were home with my brothers.

Only...

My thoughts jammed, an age of agony halting me.

We'd never... *She'd never...*

The offer I'd made had never been answered, ripped away with my brothers, then she was gone, too.

And silence.

For years and years. Immobilising silence.

I couldn't heal. I couldn't move. I couldn't release her from the offer I'd made that she could never accept.

I'd been left behind.

And now? A claim.

Panicked golden eyes stared down at me, tears splashing on

my face. Then he did it again, pressing his neck to my mouth. He was trembling, and his terror... I could feel it. It was for me. Not for him.

He wanted me.

He'd claimed me.

But if I bit him... then Onyx...

"Please!" His nails dug into my arms, and he drew back again, palm at my cheek. "Fuck! Come on! P-please!"

His eyes glittered, desperate, afraid.

Afraid for me...

I... wanted him, I realised. I wanted him as much as he wanted me.

Blasting my weary aura one last time, I leaned up, dragging him against me as I sunk my teeth into his neck.

TWENTY-NINE

ARSENAL

A bond lit.

An invitation.

A pack brother.

I drew up in the parking lot to the theatre we'd just arrived at. "What in the ever living *shit*?"

"What?" Malakai spun to me and the others halted.

"He just..." They wouldn't feel it. It was on me to accept or reject. "Someone just tried to join our pack."

"But... that could only happen if...?"

"Ice lets them." Onyx sounded confused, finishing the sentence.

It was true. Either I could initiate a bond as pack lead, or an alpha could be anchored in through our omega. Ice had a genesis bond, a normal bond, which meant—

"He would have had to *make* the offer." King finished my thought.

Malakai glanced between us. "Then you have to say yes."

"Just like that?" My voice was hoarse, but... he was right.

"He wouldn't fuck around with an offer like that."

I nodded, still reeling. No, Ice wouldn't make that offer lightly. If he had, it was life or death.

"Fine."

Throwing every goddamned rule of the universe out of the window, I said yes to a new alpha into our pack—without having even seen him. I trusted Ice, though. He wouldn't have done something like that without good reason.

This unknown fifth member collided with our pack bond like a firecracker. On a summer's day. In the middle of a drought.

Sickness rocked me, and Malakai had to place his hand on the jeep to steady himself. King drew up, his face suddenly pale.

"What?" Onyx glanced around at us.

"Holy shit." Malakai muttered.

"What?"

"He's... sick."

"The new alpha?" Onyx asked. I nodded. "Hurt? Physically."

"I don't know. Every way," King rasped.

I blinked, weathering the sickness that was seeping into every crack of the bond, setting me on edge.

I exchanged looks with the others. They seemed to be thinking the same thing, and I could feel the flicker of relief in the bond.

Whatever this meant, it was hope at the least.

But the fact was, no matter how the day ended, there would be no returning to normal. But without Ice, none of it mattered.

I felt more unstable than usual. A combination of my strained aura, losing my omega, having just come out of a rut, and this insane new bond in the pack. Onyx reached up, touch grazing my arm, and I could practically feel her aura soothing me. We weren't bonded though, which meant I was oozing instability.

We had to break the locks of the theatre to get in, but we hurried down into a large auditorium. It looked half under construction, and in the centre, down rows of seats, on the centre stage, was—

"Ice!" My chest loosened and I felt like I could breathe as I ran forward.

He was crouched over the body of a man, hands gripping a gun as he looked up at us.

"Fuck." The relief we all felt momentarily smothered the sickness from the newest pack member.

King tucked his gun away and began down the stairs. Malakai nodded to me, not lowering his gun. I didn't move mine, though I did begin down the steps in twos after King.

But seeing Ice holding a gun, a bloody mess as he stared up at us with terror etched onto his face, it was enough to send caution out the window. I lowered my gun, racing after King, who had almost reached them.

But no recognition crossed Ice's face as he stared at us, and as King hauled himself up onto the stage, Ice jumped. Then the gun was raised, pointing right at King.

"Wait!" My command shattered the calm. Ice flinched, fighting it, the gun dropping for the briefest moment before he'd raised it again, a choked growl sounding from him.

"S-stay back!"

King raised his hands, slowly getting to his feet on the stage. I was climbing after him.

"Ice…" King was confused, but I wasn't. I could feel it through the bond. From Ice, there wasn't a flicker of recognition.

"It's us, Ice," I growled. "Your pack."

Ice blinked, shaking his head as he turned the gun on me. "D-don't come closer."

My eyes dropped to the man beside him. He was a wreck, his breathing short and sharp. For a moment, a flash of anger burned in my chest. He was protecting this alpha?

I shoved it down, looking back at him and dropping low, setting my gun on the wooden panelled floor.

"Ice. Look at me." I edged in front of King and Ice's gun pointed right at me. He was shaking. "It's Arsenal, yeh? We've come to get you out. But you have to put the gun down."

"N-No." He shook the weapon, as if in warning. "N-no one's coming for me."

My heart cracked at the expression on his face, at the sickness that was flooding the bond. Sickness from him.

Cold and dark and alone.

And he'd felt this always. Hiding from us.

I took another step. "He'll die unless we get him to a hospital."

"I'll sh-shoot."

But I was one step away, and I couldn't let him spend one more second like this.

I'd failed him.

We all had.

I sank to my knees before him, reaching out, but he jammed the gun to my chest. I shut my eyes for one moment, and then steadied myself.

If my own omega pulled the trigger right now, then death was the least I'd deserved. I reached out, cupping his cheek. For a brief second, something shifted through the bond, and he leaned into that touch, eyes darting between mine. I had the barrel of the gun in my fist, and I dragged it from my chest. Once it pointed at the floor, I moved in a flash, ripping it from his grip and holding it behind me. I felt King take it in an instant.

I heard the click and my heart rate calmed. Then King knelt beside the body of the alpha. He reached out for a pulse, but Ice lost it.

"N-No!"

His expression cracked, panic crossing it, and before I could do a thing, his nail caught my cheek. I grabbed his wrist, but he threw himself at me.

Shit.

I had to seize both his arms, but he wasn't stopping. I caught him right before he went for my throat. I shoved him away, but even in the bond he was gone.

"Don't *touch* him!"

"ICE!" I shouted. "It's us. Your pack."

"N-no!" He sounded wild. "Y-you w-wouldn't come for me. You never w-wanted me. You h-have her."

I grabbed him by the chin, holding him down and forcing him to look right at me.

"We will *never* leave you behind."

MALAKAI

Arsenal had to slam Ice against the floor by his wrists, and even then he had a time avoiding his teeth. I reached out as Onyx took a step forward, catching her and shaking my head just slightly.

Ice was feral, his eyes wide as he threw himself against Arsenal's hold.

"Don't touch him!"

"ICE!" Arsenal shouted. "It's us. Your pack."

"NO!" Ice snarled. "Y-you w-wouldn't come for me. You never w-wanted me. You h-have her."

At my side, I heard the breathless sound from Onyx. From the corner of my eye I saw her hand jump to her mouth. I reached out to her, not taking my gaze from them.

I tugged her close.

This wasn't her fault.

This was on us.

Arsenal grabbed Ice by the chin, forcing him to look right into his eyes.

"We will *never* leave you behind!"

There was a long moment of silence where Ice stared up at Arsenal. All the energy died in his body. Tentatively, Arsenal let Ice go.

The moment he did, Ice launched himself at Arsenal. I tensed until I realised what it was.

A hug.

Arsenal shifted back until he was sitting on his heels, arms wrapped around Ice's neck as he held the trembling omega against his chest.

King was looking back at me, though, finally able to examine the alpha Ice had been defending. The look in his eye told me it wasn't good.

Shit.

Onyx broke my grip and hurried toward them, lifting herself onto the platform and approaching the alpha.

I glanced back around the auditorium, still on high alert for any noise. When I looked back at them, Onyx had recoiled. I was the only one who saw her expression of confusion. Her face was white as a sheet.

King was standing, hauling the alpha into his arms.

"We gotta go if he's going to make it."

THIRTY

ONYX

The alpha hadn't woken and Ice hadn't spoken a word in the ambulance. Now he was curled up on the same hospital bed, clutching the alpha's arm, a low purr rumbling in his chest. Anxiety rather than contentment, I thought.

We still didn't know who he was, but I knew the draw I felt to him. It was the same I felt toward everyone in pack St. James. That wasn't something I could allow myself to focus on.

I didn't know how I was supposed to feel. There was something wrong with the image of Ice curled up beside that alpha. I'd thought for a brief, guilty moment during Arsenal's rut, that there might be a place in this pack for me. Now I wasn't sure at all.

King sat beside me looking worn, his short blond hair was messy and there were bags beneath his eyes. Eyes which were dull, instead of their usual dazzling green.

At some point, King tried to tug me into a hug, but Ice shifted, eyes finally meeting mine. I couldn't read his expression, and couldn't tell if it was pain at seeing me with them.

Yet, right now it was strange, staring at him beside that alpha with an ache in my chest as he looked at me with King at my side.

Something was wrong. So, so wrong, but I couldn't place it.

"I'm okay," I whispered, shrugging King away.

After we had sat in a long silence, Arsenal spoke. "We have to talk about the obvious issue."

I stared at him, blinking. Obvious issue?

Malakai sighed, unfolding his arms as he glanced at Ice and then me.

"Oh…"

Right.

Ice had nearly died, and it was my fault.

I clenched my jaw to fight the burning of my eyes as I got to my feet. Holding my handbag tight to my chest was the only thing that kept my breathing steady. I nodded. "I'll—"

I cut off as King caught my arm. I dared a glance at him.

"What are you doing?" He looked wounded.

"I… put Ice in danger." My voice was weak.

"That's not—" Arsenal sounded shocked. "You aren't responsible for the years of crap our pack never managed."

"Then… What?"

What other issue was there to discuss?

King tugged me back down to my seat, shifting closer as if scared I would run.

"It's about him." Arsenal waved a hand to the alpha on the bed.

"What about him?"

"He dropped his bike off to the garage for repair yesterday," Malakai said. "Then, he followed Ice to the pawn shop in the middle of the night."

I stared at them. "What?" I didn't understand, glancing around. No one seemed to want to say it.

"He's been…" Malakai winced. "Watching us."

My lips parted. "You think…?"

"It adds up, Onyx."

I was on my feet in a moment. "No."

"Just think—"

"No!" My stalker had killed Devin. "Viper would *never*—" I cut off, silence ringing in my ears.

"Viper?" King asked, staring at me.

Yellow eyes.

I stared at the bed where the alpha slept. He hadn't woken, yet I knew what he looked like.

Piercing yellow eyes held mine in shimmering rain. "*Take the princess bond.*"

My nails dug into my handbag as those words echoed in my head. "He's uh… He was…" The words wouldn't come, my mind suddenly feeling as though it were on fire. "I…"

"Onyx." King was before me, trying to lead me back to the seat. He looked worried.

"We need to figure out if it was him."

But I was staring at the man in the bed. "I need…" I swallowed. "I need some space."

I was burning. Nothing… Nothing made sense.

"Okay. Um, this is a pack suite, right?" King asked, anxiety lacing his tone.

Malakai crossed the room in a moment, opening a door to a side room. Within was a small space, private and cosy with warmer light and a door to the hallway beyond. A round bed took up most of the floor. It was covered in pillows, and even had a soft duvet.

A nesting room.

"Is this alright?" King's brow was furrowed, concern etched across his face. I nodded, handbag still clutched at my side, my breathing coming easier.

King stood a little awkwardly. I glanced at him.

"I'll... leave you."

I just stared at him, my mind still scattering in a million directions.

I had to pull it back.

Rein it in.

King took a step back toward the door before turning to me. "Onyx..." He swallowed, and I was caught by the pain in his emerald eyes. "Please don't... leave us."

I swallowed, panic taking flight in my chest. But he went on. "I think I, uh... I fell in love with you the first time I saw you."

I couldn't speak, and he winced, cupping the back of his neck. "I'm sorry," he whispered. "I shouldn't have... I just need you to know... you're wanted here."

I nodded, mouth dry, but King backed toward the door and I was left in silence.

ARSENAL

A few hours passed before much happened. Nurses bustled in and out, changing fluid bags and checking vitals.

Ice was still curled up, sleeping on Viper's bed. I hadn't recovered from any of it. Not the rut. Not from the moment in which it had been possible I might never see Ice again. Not from the haunted look on Onyx's face, her golden skin ashen as she watched Ice and Viper.

I couldn't take my eyes off of either of them, and the early hours of the morning fatigue didn't touch me. It wasn't right that she wasn't in here with us.

King and Mal were the same as me. Exhausted, worn thin, and too in shock to even consider sleep.

We had almost lost him.

Years fighting for him, and we'd almost lost him in one night.

Finally, a woman in a white coat walked in, the tell-tale dry air scent around her that spoke of too many scent dampeners. Her hair was pure white, short, and cropped at her chin. One of her eyes was red, one blank white. She was a seer—someone who could visualise auras and bonds, which meant she was either an alpha or an omega. Betas couldn't be seers. "Dr. Rover, Arkologist."

"That's... aura shit, right?" King asked, blinking fatigue out of his eyes.

She nodded. "I'm going to ask you some questions. You've probably heard them before."

I nodded.

"Viper untethered his aura, then bonded your pack?"

"Yeh."

"How is the pack bond?"

Malakai snorted. "Like someone just jammed a bunch of knives in it and now they're being ripped out one by one."

Dr. Rover nodded her head sympathetically. "Would you describe the discomfort as progressively getting worse, staying the same, or getting better the more time passes?"

I glanced at my brothers. "Probably... better."

"And that experience is the same for all of you?"

The others nodded.

"Has your omega left his side?"

"No."

She scribbled something down on her notepad, then got to her feet. "Good, good."

"Is it?" I asked.

"What your pack just did is never guaranteed. I'm going to monitor for another few hours. As long as the bond continues trending this way, there should be no need for further treatment. Viper will be exhausted. He burned through much of his own body's energy, but it was only *just* reaching the point of organ damage when he bit in. Give it time, but there shouldn't be any lasting effects. And best he doesn't try to tap into his aura for a while, the experience may be... excruciating."

I nodded.

"I'll let his doctors finish with the fluids. That gives us a few more hours to make sure the bonds are stable, then you can take him back to the nest. Come back if anything changes in the bond, but so long as your omega stays with him for another day or so that shouldn't be an issue."

"The... nest?" I asked.

She glanced over at Ice. "His nest."

"Right. Of course," I said.

Well. Shit.

Dr. Rover departed and I was left looking awkwardly around at my brothers. Even if it was a good idea to put Viper into Ice's nest—which it wasn't—he was unlikely to fit.

"We'll ask Onyx when she comes back," King said, confidently. "Do you think...? I should check on—"

He cut off at a shout.

"Sir!" I heard another saying. "Please, it's a private room. You aren't supposed to—"

But the door burst open anyway. The man trying to enter was tall and well put together. Silver flecked hair was combed back neatly, and the black suit he wore was expensive. He was an alpha; I knew because his aura was out, something wild in his expression.

"Viper—"

I was on my feet, blocking the his way. "Who are you?" I asked.

"Me? Who are *you*?"

"This is *my* pack's room." I told him, my alpha instincts dragging up an unreasonable amount of defensiveness. I grabbed the door, shutting it and forcing us both out before he disturbed any of them.

"Bullshit," he spat. "That's my son! He doesn't have a—"

"He bit in."

"Bit in...?" The man took a step back. "But he... refused..."

"He untethered his aura. Our omega bonded him to save his life."

That drew the alpha up. His aura vanished from the space as he stared at me, every determined edge on his face cracking beneath something horrified. *"Untethered...?* No. He wouldn't. I was sure... if she was still..." He looked like he was going to throw up.

"He saved our omega. Our omega saved him."

"Saved... him?" Finally, he focused on me.

I nodded.

"I..." The man shook his head. "Alright. And he's safe?" he asked.

"Stable for now," I said.

"Pack..." The man's tone lowered. "What's your pack's name?"

"St. James. And we could do knowing his last name, too. They've been asking about registration."

"Oxford. Viper Oxford."

"Oxford?" My tired brain sparked to life. *You have got to be kidding me?* Did Ice just bite in a billionaire playboy?

"I'm Kenneth Oxford." The alpha held his hand out, a tremor in it. "Will there be any issues with integration?"

"Uh..." I rubbed my chin. "What?"

"Do you want him?" the man asked bluntly.

I opened my mouth, then shut it, stalled by that. He drew out a card and pressed it into my hand. "Anything— Anything at all your pack wants, I can make it happen. But don't tell him he wasn't wanted—"

"We want him," I said before I could catch myself. But it was true. Viper had saved Ice. I didn't care who he was. He was pack.

"Oh." Kenneth nodded. "Still, if you need anything, please reach out. And don't tell him I was here."

"You're leaving?"

His father's expression tightened. "Me and Viper... don't get on. He won't want me there when he wakes."

ICE

Mint and mist tangled with a dreamless sleep that faded in and out. My purr rumbled in my chest.

My alpha.

I'd never felt this before. Useful. Needed. And at the same time, guilty, because I felt the weight of their hurt.

I knew why. I knew the truth now, the truth I was so far from ready to face.

That they loved me. They had this whole time. And I... I clung to Viper, needing to see him through, not ready for anything else until that was done. The monsters on the other end of this, they had to wait.

When I woke at last, I realised there was something missing.

"Where is she?" I asked groggily, the purr in my chest stuttering out. The room was full of all scents but one. The lavender and brownies was missing.

"Sleeping in the next room." Arsenal looked exhausted. The raven hair that usually tumbled haphazardly into his eyes was pushed back as if he'd been running his fingers through it too much.

"No." That wasn't right. "She has to be here."

Nothing was right if she wasn't here.

Malakai and Arsenal glanced at each other. King was asleep in the corner.

"I don't think she feels welcome," Malakai said quietly. He usually wore his long hair up in a bun, but right now most of it was hanging loose, pitch black waves framing his lean face. I'd never seen him so tired.

"What did you tell her?" I asked, straightening.

"Nothing," Arsenal growled. "We told her we wanted her here. But she... We think she knows him."

"She does. He was her scent match."

Malakai looked uncertain. "When she saw him... it was like... I don't know, like she'd seen a ghost."

"Where is she?" My voice was strained. "She just watched me curled up with her mate, and you guys let her walk?"

"She's in the nest room. She wanted space."

I was getting to my feet in a moment, but Arsenal was at my side. "Doctor says you have to stay with him."

"Go and get her."

He scowled and, for a moment, I felt a flutter of relief at seeing that some of our communication was intact. What had just happened between us... I couldn't unpack it right now.

Arsenal nodded and crossed the room to the door.

I settled back on the edge of the bed. She'd left?

Dammit. There was room for both of us. She had to know that.

Silence.

Arsenal knocked again, and then cracked the door. "Duchess?" he asked.

There was a long pause, then he peered in.

"Fuck."

Malakai and King were on their feet in a moment.

"What?" I demanded.

"She's gone."

ARSENAL

I found Onyx alone on a roof garden under a gazebo. She was surrounded by windows looking into hospital rooms, huddled up in her black coat, emerald handbag clutched close as she smoked. The sky above was blood orange, the sun just cresting the horizon over the city. We were at a Westside hospital I'd never been to. I had tried to argue with the ambulance—pure instinct, since larger hospitals could cost—but Onyx had shut it down and told them to take us wherever he needed to go. She'd also upgraded us to the private pack room, which I'd never had before.

"Gave us a fucking heart attack, Duchess," I grumbled, sitting at her side, ignoring the goosebumps lighting on my bare arms. I tugged my phone out of my pocket and texted the others that she was okay. They were frantic. I had been too, my mind shaken images of her stalker finally stealing her away. Every instinct was in overdrive. The cold early morning air was probably what I needed to settle my frayed nerves.

She looked up at me, insecurity written all over her face. "I'm sorry."

"I'm just glad you're alright," I said, tugging her into a quick hug. She flinched at my touch and I withdrew. "Ice woke up."

She nodded, looking as if she was trying to sort out her expression. "That's good."

"He won't settle until you come back."

She glanced at me sharply. "I don't belong. You know it as well as I do."

I snorted. "I might be pack lead, but I'm not the authority on that. If Ice says you're pack, you're pack."

She swallowed, hugging herself as her eyes fell again on the pack inside the nearest window. Two men were fawning over a baby in a mother's arms.

"I can't…" I saw a flash of fear in her eyes as she glanced at me. I'd never seen her nervous like this before. "I can't give you that."

"Give us... what?" I followed her gaze once again. "A... *baby*?" Well, I hadn't meant it to sound so incredulous. She shrunk, though.

"I should have told you before I even turned up at your door."

"Uh... That's what this is about? You don't want kids?"

"I *can't* have kids." Her voice shook. "Never. I found out during the tests when I perfumed. Omega's curse."

"Okay?" I asked. But... shit. Omega's curse was a rare condition. The same part of an omega's aura that usually made them hyper fertile, instead did the opposite. I knew it could be detected by seers when they examined auras. "And you... want kids?"

She breathed a shaky laugh. "No, but it doesn't matter. I'm an omega."

I snorted. "Four other people in this pack—five if you add playboy-billionaire-charity case—why the fuck would it just be on you?"

"Because I'm—"

"*Ice* is an omega. Maybe blame one of us for not having a cunt."

She choked on a drag of the cigarette she'd been so desperately huffing.

"Why do you think we want something like that?" I asked.

"Why wouldn't you? I'm supposed to assume just because you've been in the system, you don't want normal things?"

"Christ, Onyx. Why do you think we never wanted an omega?" She stared at me, uncomprehending. "Because we can't do that." I waved at the window.

"What do you mean?" Her voice was low, her eyes darting between mine.

"I killed one of my pack fathers, not that it's a secret, but he was an awful man. Every goddamned day of my life, I worry I'm turning into him. Every time my aura isn't stable, every time I go into a rut too soon... It's bad enough worrying about it with the pack. I don't want to bring a kid into that. And neither do the others. Mal won't ever shake the Harpies—not really—and King won't shake what people see when they look at him. That—" I nodded toward the window once more. "That's not our dream, and we knew most omegas..." I rubbed the back of my neck. "That's their dream. One we can't deliver."

She didn't meet my eyes as she finished her cigarette, dropping it to the floor and staring at it where it smouldered. "Tell them for me?" she asked.

"What?"

"I don't want to say it again, but they need to know."

"I don't think—" I began, but she cut me off.

"When I went to the Institute," she added, "I requested packs who would be okay matching an omega like me, but that also didn't want another omega."

"Why?" Was she... *disappointed* we had Ice?

"I didn't want to risk... being the extra. The side piece, if what they really want is..." She nodded her head toward the hospital window. "That's... all I've ever been."

Oh. It all fell right into place.

She wasn't jealous. She just wanted to be sure she was valued for who she was. "Alright." I nodded. "I'll tell them. But Ice wants you to know you're wanted. We all do. None of this changes that."

Still, she said nothing, hugging her bag close. She was independent, and I knew if she truly decided to walk away right now, I couldn't stop her. "We... also have a problem the rest of us are unqualified to deal with, and we need your help with it."

"Oh?"

"He's going to be discharged. Doctor said he needs to be taken back to Ice's nest."

THIRTY-ONE

ARSENAL

I knew the moment I stepped foot through the door that something was wrong. I held out my hand to Onyx, who was just behind me.

"What?"

"Wait here."

Malakai was at my back in an instant.

The garage was destroyed.

Couches were ripped apart, their insides dragged everywhere. Chairs were knocked over and the wall hangings were torn down and smashed. Kitchenware was shattered across the space.

"Shit…" That was Onyx's whisper.

"Mal," I growled. "He could still be here."

Her stalker. I knew it to my bones.

Mal was at her side in a moment.

"Stay in the main room." I strode after King, who was already at our safe. He tossed me one of the remaining guns. The ones we'd taken with us to rescue Ice were still stashed in the car. We'd left in the theatre parking lot when the ambulance had picked us up.

Sure enough, forget-me-nots were scattered across the kitchen table. It was completely empty but for those. The stacks of paper that had resided there were scattered across the floor. I ignored them, making for the bedrooms.

My bedroom was clear. Same with Malakai's and King's.

"Check Ice's nest—" I began, but the hatch was open and King was already making his way down.

Onyx was following him down the ladder.

Then I felt King's aura hit the air, blasting across the whole apartment.

"What?" I was after him in a moment, dropping down into the space without regard for the ladder. What waited for me in Ice's nest sent a chill down my spine.

Along the wall, another message was written in lipstick.

He's not yours.

The nest had been deconstructed entirely. Every knife that had lived in the boards of wood had been torn out. They'd each been placed carefully into Ice's bed, blades jammed into the mattress.

The threat was crystal clear.

"Mal!" My voice shook as I shouted up. "Ice. *Now!*" I didn't give a shit how many alphas were in the car with him. It wasn't enough.

I'd thought that was the last of it.

But I did another last scan, the roof, the rafters, the garage. Every inch to make sure this fucker wasn't still here.

And that was when I saw it. More forget-me-nots were scattered across the motorbike Viper had brought in for repair. Around it, across the floor, were shattered white pieces of what looked like ceramic.

"It... doesn't make any sense..." Onyx's whisper cut through the silence as she knelt beside the bike, delicate fingers trembling as she examined the ceramic pieces on the floor. "Who could it be?"

"It does…" King's voice was a rasp. "You said this stalker was from your past. It can't be Viper, he's been with us the whole time, but we just bit him in. What if it's…?"

"Someone else from the pack?" I asked.

"Could they be stalking *both* of you?"

"I'll… leave. This is too much." Onyx's eyes were wide with horror.

"No." I turned on her too fast. "You aren't going anywhere."

"He got in here."

"While we weren't in. What does that tell you?"

"He…" Her chin quivered, mask shattering. "But Ice has a chance to heal."

"And what about you?"

"I brought this to your door."

"I'm not arguing, Onyx." I heard the anger rising in my voice, panic gripping me at the idea of her leaving. Of her being alone. Never.

It was the same panic I'd just felt in Ice's nest. We weren't leaving her to this creep's mercy. That was what he wanted. "You aren't going anywhere."

ICE

My nest was in pieces.

I stood staring at it.

Every knife had been ripped from the boards. They were driven into my bed. A violent statement, except… Onyx's fingers were tangled in mine. I'd wanted her to come in when I saw it, trusting her to keep me sane.

"I…" I swallowed. Out of nowhere at all, tears burned my eyes.

"Hey." She shifted closer, her touch brushing my cheek. I focused on the scent of lavender and brownies, letting it ground me.

"I..." But I couldn't say it. Instead, I stepped closer, as if I couldn't believe it. My palm pressed on the bed and I was sinking to my knees.

Shit.

I was crying in front of Onyx.

But she was at my side, winding fingers through my hair, holding me against her as I shook.

"I'm sorry," she whispered.

I shook my head, gripping her tight. "You don't... understand."

This nest was all I had been. It made me a victim, made of nothing but brittle bones. But I wanted more, I just didn't know how. Each knife had been lodged in a scar, the wound crusted over, impossible to remove. And now... they were all gone.

I drew back. Her beautiful face blurred. Her rich skin, faint freckles, cute nose, and caring sapphire eyes. A breath of a laugh slipped from my mouth as I took her face in my hands.

"I'm..." I had to take a shaky breath. "I'm free."

Her expression shifted, eyes darting to the bed before returning to me. And then a smile tugged on her lips, something genuine and relieved.

I drew her close and kissed her. She gave me strength I never thought I had. Everything had changed since she arrived.

She drew back with a smile, wiping the tears from my eyes. "We're going to make you a better one upstairs."

Nesting? I furrowed my brow. "Like... properly?"

She nodded. "He..." She swallowed. "He needs you, Ice. And... so do they."

I saw something shatter in her expression when she said that. "They need you too," I whispered.

She nodded, but she had a faraway look and her smile didn't reach her eyes. I almost told her how much Viper loved her, but I knew that part wasn't mine to tell.

Before we left the nest, I did one final check.

The small box I'd kept under my bed was still there.

I opened it, but it was empty.

"What was in it?"

"Almost nothing." Sometimes... Sometimes I would steal their mugs and stash them in here. Then I would panic and return them. It was the beginning of a nest I thought I maybe wanted." But there *had* been one thing in here. The mug I'd taken from the kitchen when we'd first met her.

I felt a slight tightness in my chest as I looked into the empty box, but then... Everything in this place felt toxic. Even that small claim—one which I'd hidden away—I didn't want it.

When we returned upstairs, Viper was settled into Malakai's room. I hadn't asked, but I knew why. His was the one I was most familiar with.

I stared at Viper resting in the bed.

My alpha. The one I'd claimed. I didn't know what would happen when he woke. I didn't even know him or what he'd want, but right now it didn't matter. For the first time in my life, I trusted my instincts, and fear didn't play a part in it at all. This was right. It was the only thing in my life that was. I was crossing toward him in a moment, eyes already shifting around the room anxiously.

It *was* wrong.

Too empty.

I needed... I looked back to see Onyx watching me with a much more genuine smile on her face. "What do you need? I can get you anything at all."

I stared at her, chewing on my lip. But... what if Viper woke up and the room was dull because I couldn't do this right?

"Um... Fairy lights?" The words were out before I realised it, and my cheeks burned. She'd think it was so childish.

"Warm or cool?" she asked, not even blinking.

"Warm," I said. "And... What if...? Would wool stuff be okay?"

I liked wool. Knitted stuff. I remembered little of my life before. My mum had died when I was five, but I think she knitted. I'd ended up on the streets until I perfumed, then I'd been snatched up and lived in the tunnels since. But wool always made me feel at home.

"I can do wool. Colour preference?"

I didn't know. Did I have to pick one? "As many as you can?"

Her smile widened. "Perfect."

KING

"What are you doing?" I asked as Onyx continued bustling around our rooms. "We'll have to go to the store for the rest of the materials, but we need the base scents to get it started."

I stared at her. "For Ice?"

"Yes." She looked up at me, tucking a lock of her wild brown waves behind her ear so she could fix me with a look that said *'obviously'*.

I hadn't lied in the hospital.

I did love this woman.

I wasn't an angry person, not like Arsenal—and even Mal, sometimes—who blew up pretty easily. I was a go with the flow kind of guy, always had been. So the simmering rage I was carrying around with me was a new experience.

I'd been afraid when Ice was taken, but when I'd found the garage ripped up and destroyed, and a threat on Ice's wall, all to scare her away from us, I'd been angry. It was like a fist, constricting my chest whenever I thought about it. It was the first time I'd felt—for myself—the fear she had been living with.

I wasn't a killer—despite the reputation I tried to escape–but if it came to it, I would kill the man who was doing this to Onyx. Without hesitation.

We'd been cleaning up the debris of his attack all day. Luckily the walls and floor were mostly concrete, which was easy enough to clean. Even in that, she hadn't stopped helping clean, and twice she'd ordered garbage pick up.

Right now she was dumping bundles of clothing on the ripped up couch.

"Those are our clothes," I said, curiously.

"Really?" She turned to me, an eyebrow cocked. "I hadn't noticed."

"For Ice's nest?" I asked. "He won't... uh..." I cupped the back of my neck, glancing at Arsenal and Mal for support. They both looked unsure, but Onyx got touchy if we started questioning omega stuff around her. "I just didn't think he'd want them."

She looked at me pityingly. "Is there a Nesting Needs near here?"

"Uh..." Shit. I'd never had to think about that. Plus Nesting Needs was expensive. My mum had used pawn stores and a lot of soap to wash off lingering scents. "I think so."

"Good. Does someone have time to take me?"

"I can," I told her. Getting nesting stuff for Ice?

Count. Me. In.

Nesting Needs was one of the few shops I'd entered in which most of the customers were alphas or omegas.

It was also insane.

It was a maze of a store, one that didn't look like a store at all.

Despite the fact it was indoor, we wandered through an artificial cobblestone street with vintage lamps lighting the way and the ceiling painted like the sky. The buildings we passed weren't buildings at all, but rooms fully decked out like a million different kinds of nests.

"I *love* seeing the theme of the week!" She dragged me over. "Oh..." She drew up when she saw what was inside. "That's... tasteful..." But her expression was dubious as she peered into a colourful room. Above it read: *Want a Saint Pack taste?*

Within, the walls were made of candy bars. There was a giant projector playing the second Hunting Falcons movie. That was a *great* franchise.

"Why would anyone want a waffle iron in a nest?" she asked. I tore my eyes from the particularly riveting action scene featuring Prey Nightingale to note that Onyx was absolutely right. On a counter beside the bed was a bright pink waffle iron with white graffiti across it that read: No Alphas Allowed.

I chuckled. "That screams of a pack war if I've ever heard one."

"I'm sure it's not accurate. How many of these are just based on rumour?"

We continued on, and it seemed to go for forever. There were shared nests, nests with dim lights and carpeted walls to simulate cosy 'tucked under the bed' feeling, and a nest made of white lace.

Onyx had picked up a little notepad and was jotting down items she wanted to buy, which seemed like an odd way to shop. Was she taking inventory so she could look them up online later? She didn't seem price conscious, though.

"So, how do you think you guys will do with a new pack member?" she asked, peering into a nest with bundles and bundles of cotton hanging from the ceiling like great, fluffy clouds.

Right.

Viper.

A new pack member. I had to fight a smile for a moment. It hadn't exactly been the best circumstances in which we'd got him, but... our family was bigger. Since Ice—and that hadn't exactly been planned—I hadn't really thought our pack would get more members. Not with me in it.

And now Viper and Onyx in a week—that thought snagged and I blinked, glancing over at her.

"What do *you* think, Duchess?"

"I think Ice's instincts shouldn't be doubted. I think he's going to be a bridge to you guys to heal."

I noticed she was fixated on the room full of cotton as she spoke, and there was something clipped and quick about her words.

"You already are that bridge." I said it before thinking, desperate that she know she was still important.

She leaned back from the ridiculous cotton cloud nest, looking up at me directly. "He's bitten in. It's much more important that you focus on him right now."

But... I wanted *her* bitten in.

"You are important, too."

"We—You can't afford to miss a beat here. This is it. Everything your pack has ever wanted."

"I told you how I felt—"

"You can't love me that fast King—"

"Don't fucking tell me what I feel!"

Her eyebrows shot up for a moment, but I didn't feel bad for once.

She didn't know. She didn't know how set apart she was from every other person on this planet.

"Alright. I'm sorry."

"Just tell me you believe me."

For a moment, I swore there was a glistening in her sapphire eyes

"I just don't know if it matters," she whispered.

A growl rose in my throat and I took her face in my hands. "It matters, Onyx. More than anything else in the world."

For a moment, she leaned into my touch, closing her eyes. There was the faintest smile on her lips as if she, too, let go of everything for just a second and felt it as well.

Then she drew back, smile falling away. "We should hurry. Ice won't be happy if Viper wakes up without a nest sorted out."

When we got to the checkout, I nearly fainted. The price... *Fuck*... "You can take this off the money you were going to pay me," I said. She turned on me. "But he's..." The words '*my omega*' dried up on my tongue at the look she gave me. "Your mate," I said. "Which means you're entitled to spend whatever you want on him."

"Speaking of, *could* you give me a place to send the money to?" she asked.

"Uh... Yeh." Truth was, I'd been too embarrassed to bring it up myself. "I'll text it to you when we get back."

The stockroom was an enormous warehouse of towering shelves. There were constant scent dampeners wafting through vents, and all the stock was preserved in plastic wrapping with the tag 'Your nesting needs untouched and ready for your pack's scent'.

She flagged down a few employees to help, and before long we were faced with a towering pile of fluff in plastic and boxes.

"I don't think that amount of pillows will fit in Mal's room."

"The pillows," she said with a tight little frown, "are for all of your *awful* beds."

"Ah."

Anything squishable had been suctioned and vacuum sealed, and still— "There's no way this'll fit in the car."

"It'll fit."

"Harder!" Onyx panted. "Fuck! Just... a bit *harder*!"

She was in our jeep, back pressed against the ceiling by the mount of nesting materials she was clutching, arms spread to keep it all in. My back was against the back doors of the jeep, my shoes scraping concrete as I heaved against the army of fluff determined not to be confined by our poor, old vehicle.

"It's not—"

"Are you an alpha or not?" she demanded, her voice high.

I blew out a breath, glancing around. There was no one nearby. I loosened my aura, and the doors smashed closed too quick. Damn. If I'd dented it, Arsenal would kill me.

I was just examining the doors when I heard a faint scrambling. I ducked down and peered through the back window to see Onyx was crushed, absolutely unable to move now the doors were closed. Her hair was wild, tumbling all over, her expression screwed up all cute as she struggled. She fought a little longer before giving up and looking to me.

"I'm stuck," she mouthed.

I crossed my arms with a grin, admiring the magnificent view of her cleavage bulging out of the low cut of her shirt.

I had to drag her by her heel one inch at a time to get her out. By the time she was free, her hair was a mane of chocolate static that had me cackling while she tried to tame it enough to tie it in a bun.

Finally, we were both in the front seats, strapped in with a wall of fluff behind us. "This is *so* illegal," I muttered. "Can't see a *thing* out the rearview."

Onyx waved a hand. "We'll be fine. It's only ten minutes."

THIRTY-TWO

ONYX

"I love watching you set up his nest." King's smooth voice caught me off guard. He leaned against the wall, staring at me.

It was evening, and I was cross-legged on the bed in his room, reading. I could only spend so much time on the roof, and when I puttered around the living room, trying to fix everything up, I was weighed down by their stares. Plus, I'd unpacked almost everything from our Nesting Needs trip—the normal amount of pillows crowding King's bed was evidence of that. It was soothing—as was my comfort read that I always kept in my handbag.

Out there, they kept telling me to relax, kept telling me I didn't owe them anything, but there was still proof out there of the stalker that had come for me.

The stalker that had threatened Ice because of me.

King tugged his shirt off and dropped down onto the bed.

"Oh. Do you want to sleep?" I asked, getting to my feet quickly. He was built like a fighter, without a soft spot on him. There was a cocky grin on his face as my eyes couldn't help following his every move.

He shifted over so that he was seated right before me, watching me with sparkling green eyes.

"Don't leave," he murmured.

"I don't know if I can sleep yet." I was too anxious. I'd already checked in on Ice and Viper in the last hour. I couldn't hover.

"Neither do I." King's words drew me up. Especially when paired with his hands coming to my hips, tugging me closer to him.

"I want you, beautiful," he murmured.

My thoughts stumbled over one another, a million reasons why that absolutely shouldn't happen right now all fighting for attention.

Ice and Viper for one.

Yet, in a guilty moment I knew my perfume hit the air.

"You haven't stopped once," he said, thumb caressing the skin between my shirt and waistband. "Let me help you relax."

I wanted that.

I wanted *him* so badly.

He tugged me closer still, a little smile curving his lips like he could see it in my eyes.

But we shouldn't be doing this. I was building connections I couldn't keep. Still, next thing my knees hit the bed on either side of his thighs and I'd pressed my lips to his. He groaned, seizing my hips and dragging me close. With each moment of the kiss, all my worries scattered.

What I'd cost them.

Ice.

Viper.

My stalker.

It was all getting smothered in apricots and champagne and his bright eyes that were so fucking sure that he wanted me.

And I let myself drown in it.

Even the guilt melted away as he tugged at my leggings, fingers slipping insistently beneath them to find my clit.

I let out a whine of pleasure as he pressed a finger into me.

"There's my perfect mate," he breathed, kissing up my neck as he began to pump into me with two fingers.

His.

I shut my eyes, wanting it to be real.

To be forever.

I gave in. "I want you," I whispered.

In an instant, we were a tangle of horny limbs trying to tug off stubborn items of clothing. Then I fell over him, panting, my lips an inch from his as I straddled him. One of his hands was on my hips, the other on his cock as he adjusted it to me. I sunk down over it—just a fraction—the moment I felt him.

His light brows bunched, his teeth digging into his bottom lip.

I knew there was a smile on my lips at the sight of it.

Slowly, I lowered myself further, feeling my own eyelids flutter as his huge width stretched me. I paused, feeling thoroughly stretched, only to peek down and see he was only halfway in.

The moan I let out was pure lust.

His fingers bit down on my hips. "Keep making sounds like that, Duchess, and I'll finish before you even take me."

With one palm planted on his chest and my fingers winding through his hair, I set the pace and let him match me. As I sped up, it was hot to see him lose his rhythm in lieu of mine. His expression tensed, low groans slipping from his chest with each of my movements.

I'd never made a man pant like he was before, one hand digging into my flesh, the other the sheets. His tanned cheeks were flushed.

The sight of it was enough to heat my veins even more.

"You feel so good..." he groaned. "Fuck."

I shifted closer, slowing down just a little and enjoying every change in his expression until I felt my climax rising in my stomach.

He groaned as I rolled my hips over his cock, pressing deeper and right up to his knot each time. I could feel him hitting that spot in my core.

I leaned closer, kissing him with each thrust, a moan sounding deep in my chest.

He shook beneath me, clearly so close to coming, so I drove my tongue down his throat. I rocked against him faster until I was holding my own orgasm just on the wings... The moment he tensed beneath me, I quickened until I couldn't hold my climax at bay anymore.

I broke the kiss with a moan. With one hand still planted on his chest, I pressed over his knot. He watched me as he came, eyes wide as I took him slowly, my lips parted. Every inch of him was bliss and the orgasm crashed into my system as I felt him spill within me.

"Mmmm..." I moaned as I took him and he locked me against him.

Fuck, he felt good stretching me out.

I kept my movements up, slowly rocking over him, drawing out his bliss and mine. With the last shudder of my orgasm, I sunk against his chest. He hauled us back so his head was propped up on one of the pillows I'd bought today. "Holy crap. You're so hot, Onyx," he breathed.

I felt a little purr rumble to life in my chest at that, another smile edging my face. I was determined not to think about anything but how good it felt in his arms until the hormones had died. His hands brushed my hips as he straightened more. When I looked up into his eyes, I saw worry in them.

"What?" I asked.

"I just want this with you... forever."

I stared at him, wanting to hold onto those words so badly.

"I told you I love you," he said.

"But Ice—"

"Wants you as much as I do. I'm not the only one who loves you, Onyx. The rest of them are just cowards and they won't say it."

I bit my lip, fingers digging into his chest where we lay.

"I'm the reason—" I cut off as King's grip tightened, and he ground my hips against him once more. I moaned, his knot shifting within me, sending bliss through my veins and wiping all thought from my brain.

"You're the reason he's letting us in," King murmured, tilting my chin up so I was stolen away by bright green irises. He lifted his hips again, pressing into me further and making me see stars. "Even when he hasn't since the day we met him."

I tried to catch my breath and rearrange my thoughts, but King wasn't finished.

"How about," he went on, "I give you my knot until you stop arguing about whether you belong with us."

He gripped me tighter and turned us both so he was caged over me. I gripped him as he ground against me, my pleasure peaking again. Then his finger found my clit and I moaned right as he pressed his lips to mine.

Finally, as I climaxed, he drew back, releasing our kiss, watching as I came again for him.

"You're so perfect, Onyx." The words were strained, the firm muscles along his neck, taut. I felt him spill within me again with a groan as my body clenched around him.

"Mal told me he thinks you're going to leave."

I said nothing, everything flooding back in.

"Please don't."

I curled up tighter, but he just tugged me closer. Still, it was too late. A thousand insecurities warred in my brain. I was taking the attention of Ice's alpha after nearly costing him everything, I was giving King hope—and all for what? So I could have a few minutes of relief?

I shrunk, hating how weak I was, when Ice deserved better. Hating how much King's warm arms made me feel so safe.

Later, when he'd released me and we'd washed up, I fell asleep surrounded by apricots, champagne and a guilt I couldn't shake.

THIRTY-THREE

ONYX

"You need to slow down, Duchess." Malakai's voice carried across the rooftop. It was noon, the day after we'd brought Ice and Viper home from the hospital. I turned as best I could, precariously balanced on their metal chair as I tried to hang the Edison string lights to their wooden structure. "How many deliveries have come in today?" he asked as he reached me.

Not enough.

Not for Ice.

"Well, I just thought—You said out here was his special place too, so we should do it up." I glanced at the boxes of string lights. The extension cord they needed had just arrived.

"I think your decor is much too fancy for our broken down shed." He eyed the creaking structure.

"I was actually browsing gazebos. The trouble is finding a company that will deliver it up here—" I cut off with a squeak as Malakai took me by the hips and dragged me right from the chair and into his arms. He turned, sitting on the chair I'd been standing on, holding me against him.

My breath caught for a moment as I was trapped by those intense eyes. He lifted a hand, thumb stroking my cheek. "You don't have anything to make up for, Onyx."

"I— I know."

"You're lying," he said.

"We're both lying," I told him. Of course I had shit to make up for. I'd nearly broken everything. Nearly taken Ice from them. And none of this even came close to me deserving his pack. And I'd still let King comfort me last night. "I need to—"

"Relax. And if you do, I'll help you put the rest up. No chair needed."

I narrowed my eyes with a sigh, but I sank into his arms, hands pressed against his rock-solid chest, inhaling his scent of riverside and clove. It was impossible not to find it relaxing.

"How are you guys doing? With Viper, I mean?" I asked. It had been hard to read Arsenal and Malakai since we arrived at the hospital. Even now, I was guiltily relieved that he still wanted to... to touch me. To hold me at all, after what I'd done.

Malakai nodded thoughtfully, frowning as he thought. He had lean features, a strong nose, and heavy eyebrows that complimented deep set eyes. "King is... Well, you know how King is doing. And he's fucking delighted we have another pack member. Arsenal... I think he's fucking traumatised all around." He snorted a rough laugh. "He keeps spiralling into panic. But I've got no resentment from him towards Viper through the bond."

"And you?" I asked. He didn't say anything for a long time. "Are you—"

"Jealous?" he asked. That wasn't what I had been going to say, but I stared at him, waiting. "Not like you'd think," he said at last. "He would have died to save him. To save *our* omega. Because we weren't enough."

"You would have gotten him back."

"At what cost?" he asked. "Would we have been too late?"

I hugged myself, and it had nothing to do with the cool February afternoon.

"What about you?" he asked.

"He's... my mate."

He stared at me. "I know he was part of your previous—"

"No. He's my mate now. In your pack." I'd known about it since the hospital. I was drawn to Viper just as I was drawn to the rest of the St. James pack.

Scent matches didn't work like that very often. Scent match happened between members of a pack and an omega. Those who joined after the scent match locked in were not often part of that particular bond.

Very rarely, though, a member could join and would also be a part of the scent match, feeling all of the magnetic attraction to the mated addition. Most people guessed it was about as chance as scent matches themselves—the likelihood of the additional member being so compatible that they became a part of the match.

And yet, that made sense in a way. Viper had been a part of a pack that matched me once. If he joined my scent matched pack now, it stood to reason that he was compatible.

"That's good, though. Right?" he asked.

I swallowed. "You've got a lot on your hands with a new pack member."

"Viper is pack and so are you. We aren't going to be choosing between you."

"I've caused too much—"

"Fuck that," he grunted.

I breathed a laugh, leaning back in the seat, but anxiety skittered through my veins.

Malakai sighed. "We're a fucking mess. You don't know if he'll want you, and we don't know if Ice will want us."

"You need to be honest with him. Tell him how you feel. He's ready to hear it."

VIPER

The scent of lavender and brownies drifted into my consciousness, directing my nightmares, reminding me of the mistake I had made.

I was in a hospital bed. My father was in the room, and Onyx's mother was seated in the corner, her face pale.

"She doesn't remember me?"

"I'm sorry, Son." My father's voice was unusually gentle.

"I've... I've asked they leave it to you to tell her," Onyx's mother said quietly.

"Tell her?" I croaked, staring at her.

Onyx had forgotten. She'd forgotten me. She'd forgotten the pack. She was free of an agony so deep that every waking moment of my life I felt I was burning.

"They want to be careful about it."

"Never tell her." This, I was sure of.

Her mother opened her mouth, her brows furrowed, and then shut it.

"What will it serve?" I asked, looking between them both.

"I assumed..." Her mother's face was pale. "You would—"

"I don't..." I choked. "I can't."

"These are unusual circumstances." That's what the doctor had said. "We don't know what will happen, when the psychosis will end, or even if it ever will."

"I don't want this for her." Not... Not if there was the slightest chance she might be free.

"But what about...?" Onyx's mother trailed off, her eyes full of pain.

What about me? For a moment, the question stalled me. I... would be alone.

Yet, if staying away gave her the slightest chance at a life better than the one stretching out ahead of me, that was a small price to pay.

"She can never see me."

ARSENAL

"Someone needs to take her phone off her again," I grunted as I answered another knock at the door to a delivery of plates. It was the early afternoon, and they'd been coming in all day.

King snorted as I began unpacking the stacks and rinsing them off in the sink to be put away.

"Fair, but how were we going to eat, otherwise?" King asked, grabbing a towel to dry them off.

He had a point. All of our kitchenware had been smashed to pieces.

"She's anxious. If it makes her feel better, let her do it."

Onyx was back on the roof for more rooftop decor—or a smoke. She kept flitting in and out of Ice's nest, checking on him like a mother hen. Then I'd caught her positioning all the new pillows throughout my bed, and King's too. I kept a log of what she was doing, trying for tips that might help me show our omega's affection in the future.

I hated the mechanical smiles she gave me anytime I looked at her, like she was holding me at arm's reach. Holding us all at arm's reach. But I didn't know what to do about it, not yet.

Ice, though, was another matter.

"I want to be honest," I said as Mal joined us in the kitchen, folding his arms and leaning against the fridge. He'd been popping his head out of the shop every time another delivery arrived. "We need to tell him about Riot," I said.

King and Mal looked at me with concern. I got it. I really did. Telling Ice was a risk.

We hadn't kept it from him because we liked to keep secrets. We'd withheld it because we were worried he'd have a meltdown.

But now?

Everything was different.

My mind flashed to that moment in the theatre. When I'd been clutching him in my arms. He'd been shaking, holding onto me as if maybe... And I'd felt it through the bond. But it was a truth my brain hadn't yet accepted.

That I was a place he felt safe.

"You think he'll take it alright?" King asked.

"I do," Mal said, surprising me. He was often the most cautious when it came to treading carefully around Ice. "Onyx... said we need to open up to him," he added at my look.

Of course she had. She was too good for all of us.

I got up and crossed toward Mal's room. "Hey," I said, peering around the corner of the new nest.

The room was a chaotic clutter of pillows and blankets and fairy lights that hung from the ceiling spilling warm light across the space.

"Yeah?" Ice was sitting up. His golden eyes seemed to glow in the dim light as he looked at me nervously. That was how he'd looked at me since... Well, since we'd found him again.

"I thought, if you were okay with it, we could talk—in here 'course..." I palmed my neck. "So you can stay with him." My eyes fell on the slender alpha curled up in the blankets of wool.

We'd felt a momentary flash of panic from him earlier, and then the bond had gone silent. King had peeked in, but Viper had been sleeping.

But it wasn't just Viper in here. Onyx had brought in clothes from our closet. I noticed that some of them were woven through the pillows and blankets on the bed.

Had that been Onyx?

Or maybe...?

Ice chewed on his lip, looking unsure. "Yeh... Sure."

I leaned back around the wall, nodding to my brother. Then I entered, ducking under some of the lower hanging fairy lights.

It was strangely calming in here. I leaned against the wall, folding my arms, taking in the space. "It's... nice in here."

Ice stared at me from where he was sitting up in the bed beside Viper.

They looked strangely perfect beside one another. Both had golden piercings up their ears. Ice's ashen blond waves, Viper's buzzed dark hair. Ice had pale skin, while Viper's was a light olive tan.

My stomach dropped as I saw Ice's fingers tangled in his. I shouldn't be upset. He'd found something that he cared about. That was the most important thing.

Mal and King arrived, both also staring around at the first thing any of us had seen from Ice that resembled a real nest.

Both of their gazes also lingered on our clothing tangled in the bed. I saw a brief flash of hope in King's eyes. Malakai, of course, was stoic, not a thing changing on his expression. But I felt something loosen from him in the bond.

"How's he doing?" I asked.

"Better," Ice said. "But... there's a problem."

"What?" I asked, brow coming down.

"He..." Ice winced. "He stalls out when Onyx is here."

"What?"

"It wasn't until her scent was gone entirely that he started stirring."

"It could be—"

"It's not a fluke. I've been paying attention every time her scent is around."

"Shit."

"Well, what are we going to do?" Ice asked desperately. "She belongs here."

I winced. Onyx already felt unwelcome. I glanced at Mal and King. Mal rubbed his face with his hands and King looked lost.

"I'll figure it out," I said. "Don't worry."

"So...?" Ice glanced about at us. "You wanted to talk about something?" For a moment, he looked trapped, as if he were making sure he had an escape. I swallowed, hating that our omega would ever feel like that.

"We need to tell you something."

Ice said nothing, but he tensed.

"We... want to be honest with you."

"Okay." He looked scared. For a moment I felt him through the bond. He was worse at hiding it now. He was standing on the edge of a cliff that was crumbling beneath him. Terrified. Like this was a dream and it was going to be ripped away.

"It's not bad." Well... it shouldn't be bad. But I also knew that Ice's view on the world wasn't normal.

"What?" His voice was a rasp.

I swallowed, suddenly regretting the suggestion that we do this now.

Stupid.

We should have given him more time.

If we pushed now, might we ruin how far we'd come? And we'd broken down more barriers in the last day than we had in years.

"We're trying to get you registered." Mal's words shattered the silence, doing what he did best.

I glanced at him, both relieved and pissed.

Fuck.

I looked back to Ice. He was staring at Mal, his lips parted. "What do you mean?" Ice asked, his voice weak.

"It's the job with Riot," I said, picking up Mal's statement. Trying to get back in control. Mal could be too cold sometimes. He was quick, calculated, and shit at emotions. And Ice was all emotions. "We're doing something for him when we go in for our check in. Then he'll put you in the system."

"But—"

"No application. The address is faked. There'll be no processing, no check in, no interview. You'll just be registered." Protected. Safe. On the other side of the wall Ice had been desperate to climb since the moment he'd perfumed.

Ice didn't blink as he stared between us with wide eyes, as if waiting for one of us to tell him we were joking.

"Why?" he asked.

"We want you safe. We can't... We aren't enough..." My eyes fell on Viper, my heart racing.

We hadn't been enough.

Without that alpha, Ice would be gone.

But there was panic through the bond and I could see him struggling with it, trying to shove it closed so we couldn't feel it.

He was shrinking back.

"Okay..." He swallowed. Then he shifted back to Viper, burrowing under the layers of pillows and wool. I watched as he almost disappeared completely. I could see his grip on Viper, curled against him, his breathing short and shallow as he buried his face into Viper's shoulder.

I looked back to Malakai and King.

King glanced to me, something wounded in his expression. Malakai was watching Ice intently though. No... He was watching Viper. There was something dark in his expression.

But that was it.

There wasn't anything else we could say.

I straightened, pulling the scowl from my face and crossed to leave, ducking again under the fairy lights. I clapped King on the shoulder as I passed. I could feel his pain through the bond.

Malakai went straight to the fridge and grabbed one of his special beers—some seasonal kind that were limited edition. He only drank those on particularly bad or particularly good days. There was no in between.

King didn't walk far from Mal's room, though. He looked lost.

"Give him time."

Malakai cracked his beer, returning to the couch and sipping it as he flicked through the channels, not saying a thing.

"It went well," I said again.

"Well?" Malakai snorted. He didn't even look away from the screen.

"Yeh," I said. "If that had happened last week it would have been a pack war."

VIPER

I woke to an omega's purr like the ones I felt in my dreams. But with it came a strange absence. Old wounds weren't aching. I hadn't thought it possible.

I shifted and felt a warm body pressed to my chest, and then he was uncurling, peering up at me in the warm fairy lights above. He had golden eyes and cheeks scattered with a night sky of freckles. His skin was pale, nose curved, the ash blond sweep of his hair messy over his eyes.

It wasn't Onyx.

It wasn't that I didn't love her still, but another part of my soul had unlocked. It was the warmth and safety of something new, something untainted from the pain of my past.

Ice.

My omega.

A gift.

He looked nervous, shifting back just slightly, unsure. I reached out, catching him by his shirt. "I... Are you okay?"

I frowned, not wanting him to leave. It was a feeling I'd never had before, as if, without him, I would be lost. I reached for him and he paused, fingers tangling in mine.

I drew him closer, touching his cheek.

It was connection I'd not felt in so long.

Everything had been cold and quiet. Any touch I could conjure was from ancient memories slowly wilting. I could see the blush creep onto his pale cheeks as he stared up into my eyes, his pink lips parted just slightly. Around us, fairy lights twinkled. I was in a room of massive woollen blankets and pillows. Had he brought me to his nest?

"You saved me." My voice was cracked and unused.

His eyes darted between mine.

I moved almost the same moment he did, and then my lips were crushing his. The kiss deepened the longer it went on, and despite my aching body, I shifted without thought, moving until I was over him, one hand through his hair, dragging him up against me. His touch wound around my neck, holding me against him. He smelled like roses and cookies, and I could swear there was that same sugar on his tongue as I kissed him. I needed more, and he was reacting to me as if he did too.

Finally, I drew back, something nagging at me. We were both breathing heavily, and his scent was thick in the air. I wanted it, but this omega... He was important. I had to do this right.

"What?" He looked hurt.

I shook my head, a faint smile on my lips. "Sweet Omega, you can't take all my attention. It's going to make my life very difficult."

"Why?" he asked. "I'm *your* omega," he said. "I can stay with you."

Comfort flooded my heart hearing those words, and a flush creeped up my cheeks.

"Can we stay a little longer?" he asked.

"Why?"

He stared at me, a flash of guilt in his golden eyes. "Because I haven't... fucked it up with you yet."

I stared at him, a small smile touching my lips. "You won't." I'd never been bonded to an omega like I was Ice, and it was new. But I trusted it.

The others in the bond... Finally, my mind lingered on them and it was like a shock to my system.

That part wasn't new to me at all.

"Hey..." Ice drew my eyes to him, and I realised my breathing had hitched. "Are you okay?"

The alphas on the other end of this bond weren't my brothers.

A low wounded sound ripped from my chest. They held the same tether to me, anchoring me down and into this world, but they were foreign.

Unfamiliar.

Ice saved me. I had let him. But in that act, I'd written over those old wounds. I shook. What was left of my brothers?

Vik... Jake... Hart?

"Viper!" Ice's voice was worried. My breathing was ragged, my eyes darting around the room in panic, my vision blurring with tears.

What was happening?

I'd never wept. People processed grief in different ways—that's what the therapists my father had forced me to visit all said. But crying had never been me. None of the normal ways to grieve had been me.

No one understood.

I couldn't breathe. Somewhere I could smell lavender and brownies...

Had I forsaken her?

Ice reached out, tugging me into his arms and a rumbling purr vibrated through my body. Thoughts jumbled together. I clung to him, tears tumbling down my cheeks.

This was wrong... I tried to fight it, but he was holding me too tight, not letting me go. I curled up in the warm nest, the likes of which I'd never had, and tumbled back into darkness.

MALAKAI

We had three problems: an omega who didn't feel welcome, a new pack member that couldn't be around her, and her stalker who had just come into our home.

"What are we going to do?" King asked, slumping down on a bar stool.

Onyx, it seemed, was out on the roof. Again.

This garage was too small.

"There's no way to bring it up without it sounding like she's the problem."

I knew now that she *belonged* here, even if she didn't believe it. "She's planning on leaving," I said quietly. Arsenal scowled, which meant he agreed.

"No," King said.

"The signs are there. She's getting Ice set up. Overcompensating. Things are still turning up at our door." The last had been a new couch, but I'd not let anyone bring it in. Me and King had. Ice and Viper were too unstable to let movers in right now. But Onyx had even organised the pickup of the one that had been torn to shreds.

"Then we stop her," King snarled. "This is where she belongs. You both know that."

"I know that," Arsenal replied. "But *she* doesn't. It wasn't just

Viper. When I found her on the roof she told me..." he trailed off, looking pained. "She can't have kids."

My eyebrows shot up. "She thinks we give a shit?"

Kids? That's what this was about. Absolutely fucking not.

"Okay..." King sounded hopeful. "But if she's telling us that, that means... she wants to be pack, right?"

He had a point there. Arsenal considered that.

"So, we don't let her leave."

"You know I can't do that. Not really," Arsenal sighed. "She's only really here because she wants to be."

"What are we going to do?"

"Assuming what Ice said is true—"

"This whole place is open. If her scent is impairing his healing, how are we going to—" I cut off at the sound of a latch clicking shut.

All of us turned in an instant to the door at the top of the staircase. The one leading to the deck.

"Shit," I muttered. "She heard us."

Arsenal was already striding toward the steps. "Fuck this."

"What are you doing?" I asked.

"I'm fixing this. All of it."

THIRTY-FOUR

ONYX

I had my phone in my hand about to dial my ride service when I heard the creak of the door to the roof.

I shut my eyes to blink away the tears, focusing on the late February air when I caught Arsenal's honeyed chestnut scent. His hand closed around my phone, tugging it down gently.

I was impairing Viper's healing. That's what I'd just heard.

It was too much.

I glanced up at him, trying again to keep my composure. He couldn't see me crack.

"We're going," he said simply.

"What?" I asked.

"Viper needs time to heal—"

"I know it's me—" I began.

"Me and you. We're going away for a night or two. Give them some space."

I stared at him, my heart thundering in my ears, something caught in my throat. "I've overstayed my welcome."

"Welcome?" Arsenal leaned onto the railing. "I never gave you a choice in the first place."

I had to bite my lip to keep it from quivering. From letting him know that even the slightest hint that maybe—just maybe—I wasn't about to venture back out into the world alone was enough to threaten tears.

"So. Your place or a hotel?" he asked.

A hotel?

He was serious about coming with me. I didn't realise how much I'd been afraid of what leaving would look like until this moment. I stared at him, suddenly and inappropriately distracted by how beautiful he was. His hair was buzzed at the sides, with a sweep of black that threatened his eyes. His rugged, pale features pulled off the scattering of tattoos that crept in from his hairline. My eyes lingered for a moment on the dagger that crept from his temple toward his eyebrow, wondering now if it had more meaning.

"Makes sense to do a hotel." I said, collecting myself. "See if I can shake him." I swallowed, that dread filling my heart at the thought of my stalker. "Even for a little bit."

He nodded. "Good. But I'm broke. You're paying."

I finally felt a smile pulling at the corner of my lips.

No matter what happened, I'd see them again, but I couldn't face Ice. I couldn't face any of them.

Arsenal packed me a bag and we slipped out quietly.

We were crossing the gravel to the jeep I'd called when Arsenal froze at my side, gripping my arm. I looked up at him, but he had his eyes trained across the street.

A man was crossing toward us. He was huge, wearing a massive trench-coat with thick boots and a hood that covered half his face.

Arsenal shifted in front of me, almost like he thought he might hide me from view.

"Get in the car." He pressed the keys into my hand.

"What?"

"Now."

His scent had shifted and I could swear there was fear in his voice. I was too slow, though. By the time I was fumbling the keys from his hand, the approaching man had closed the distance.

He was an alpha, the powerful scent of burned ebony and gunpowder much too strong. He had green eyes and golden skin. He tilted his head, adjusting his hood, but he wore a hat beneath so I didn't catch the colour of his hair.

"Arsenal."

"What are you doing here?" Arsenal's voice was tighter than I was used to. I was tense, just on merit of not having seen him off balance like this before.

"Told you," the alpha said. "Delivery."

"You didn't warn us you were coming."

The alpha grinned, pointed canines flashing as his gaze slid from Arsenal straight to me.

"Another omega?" the alpha asked, eyes drifting down to my neck, searching for a bite that wasn't there. I'd seen alpha gazes follow that route a thousand times before.

Arsenal shifted just the slightest bit, shielding me. I could see the clench to his jaw. He was afraid of this man knowing me.

"I didn't know the St. James pack had two omegas?"

"She's not with us," Arsenal ground out, but it was too late. The broadening grin on the alpha's face told him he absolutely didn't believe it. His eyes traced every inch of my face as if committing it to memory.

"I can't imagine why. She is beautiful."

A growl loosed from Arsenal's chest, his aura hitting the air. The alpha reacted in the same moment, but his aura was colossal. Overpowering.

"Touchy, Arsenal, when I don't see a claim."

They'd barely moved. Arsenal shifted in front of me another step, but that was it.

"It never fails to amuse how *idiotic* alphas become the moment you mention omegas." His eyes flashed with delight.

"She is *not* a part of this."

The alpha looked amused as his eyes slid down to me once again. He was enjoying this, I could see that.

I slipped my hand into Arsenal's, running my thumb along his palm. It was like I could feel his heart rate calming with each touch.

"We have somewhere to be. Did you need something?"

"He is the one who *needs* something," the alpha said, directing the statement at me and ignoring Arsenal completely. "I'm sure he'll ask nicely any minute now."

"You need us as much as we need you," Arsenal growled.

The alpha chuckled, taking a step back. He plucked a small black USB from his pocket, and suspended it between the tips of two fingers.

"You don't think there are other packs I could give this to?" he asked.

Arsenal looked ready to crack a tooth.

"Well?" the alpha asked.

I acted on instinct. Stepping between the two of them and turning to face Arsenal.

Alphas like this one—and Arsenal, if I was honest—hated one thing more than anything in the world, and that was having someone turning their back on them. Especially omegas. It was a subtle thing I'd learned as a duchess.

I could see it in Arsenal's eyes already as I reached up and took his face in my hands.

"Ask him for the USB. We have a night to enjoy."

I thought the tense muscles along his jaw relaxed as he met my eyes for a moment.

"Alright." He reached past me, presumably holding his hand out to the alpha. "Give us it then, so we can do your job for you."

I turned, peering back expectantly as if impatient.

The alpha chewed on his lip, a half smile on his face even if he was tense. He breathed a laugh, pressing the USB into Arsenal's hand.

"Lose that, Gray, and I'll put a bullet in her skull." His eyes were on me. "If you're lucky."

Every hair on my body stood on end. I'd learned how to keep a straight face through the most shocking circumstances in my job. Staying cool was my brand, but the way his emerald eyes were fixed on me? Bottomless. Depraved. It sent a shiver down my spine.

And the way he'd said it? It was a promise.

Then he was taking a step back, boots crunching on the gravel.

"Who was that?" I asked at last, when he was gone.

Arsenal was shaken. "The guy we were trying to hide you from the first time you came."

"Who does he think he is, making threats like that?"

"You heard of Riot?" he asked.

I froze. Staring at him. "You're doing a job for *the* Riot the Institute is hunting?"

The omega murderer. One of the most notorious criminals in New Oxford.

Arsenal was running his fingers through his dark hair. "You don't get it." He tugged the USB from his pocket again, showing it to me. *"This!* This is what we need if we want to fix things with Ice."

THIRTY-FIVE

KING

While Viper still slept, Ice was in and out bringing in basins with washcloths. Rearranging the nest—he kept switching out pillows, as if there were differences in them. If there were, it was beyond me.

I snorted as he arrived for the fifth time, pillow clutched in hand before the couch. Malakai sighed and sat up, tossing him the one that had just been beneath his head. Ice's grin was too much of a reward for Mal to be actually angry about it.

Soccer was on as I browsed on my phone, trying to keep myself occupied.

Mal was doing the same, popping between working on the bikes and catching the scores on the matches and complaining about how new couches were always too stiff.

I hated Arsenal and Onyx being away. It felt wrong. And not just because of Arsenal.

Onyx was pack.

I felt it to my bones. I wanted her here even if I knew that Arsenal was good enough to keep her safe.

And then there was the other thing. This morning Mal had checked. For the first time since she'd stayed, there wasn't a single forget-me-not on our front drive.

Finally, Ice appeared from the nest again and joined me on the couch.

"He still doing alright?" I asked.

Ice nodded.

I couldn't help but notice that he was sitting closer than usual. He tugged his knees up, hugging them to his chest as he watched. I could see that he wasn't focused though. He looked small. Like something in him had shattered and he was still struggling to figure out how it all went back together.

I had to fight the urge to lean over and tug him into a hug.

I would if it was Onyx.

It felt right.

What if... I tried it?

His scent had an edge of anxiety to it that I'd never caught before. He kept glancing at me. My cheeks heated. Finally, I lifted my arm, just at the same moment he dropped his legs, repositioning. I panicked, instead cupping the back of my neck and faking a yawn.

Malakai returned, eyes narrowed as he glanced between us as if he could feel the tension.

He dropped onto the couch on the other side of Ice. Closer than he usually would.

Good... Malakai was better with Ice. And if the edge to Ice's scent did mean something, he'd be the first to know.

Malakai leaned down and whispered something to Ice.

I stared, prepped for the kickback. I'd never seen anyone that intimate with Ice, not without massive fallout. Instead, Ice leaned back on the couch, a flush creeping up his neck. Occasionally, his eyes darted to me and the blush would intensify.

What the hell had Mal said?

A long time passed. Mal leaned back and was watching the soccer game as if there wasn't an anxious omega shifting at his side. I didn't know cookies could be anxious, but there was a wave of floral, sugary anxiety in the air right now—and Ice didn't do anxiety.

Then Ice moved closer to me, just a little. He didn't look at me when he did it, folding his arms and resting back as if it had been an accident.

I blinked, completely unsure.

Again, Ice shifted a little closer. One more shift and his thigh would be touching mine.

I was hot all of a sudden.

Way too hot. And the garage was not a warm place.

Ice made that last move, so he was pressed right up against me. Neither of us were looking at each other, but I felt a spark of deep amusement from Mal through the bond.

That, alone, was enough to push me over the edge.

I lifted my arm and put it around Ice's shoulders.

There was a moment of panic, very similar to the one I'd felt when I kissed Onyx, in which I thought I might have just ruined everything.

He wouldn't talk to me for weeks.

I flashed back to the time I'd dared ask him to go out to dinner with me. I hadn't even intended for it to be romantic. Three months after bonding him, and I'd hated what the pack had become. I'd been *so* sure that if we could just be a bit nicer to him, break down his walls, then everything would be better.

He'd vanished for a week. We'd resorted to dropping energy bars and water bottles into his nest in hopes he wasn't dying. It had soon been after that his first heat had come.

He'd chosen Malakai and never looked back.

With Ice now stiff in my arms, I wondered if I'd just done it again.

Fucked it up for how long?

And maybe this time Arsenal would repair his relationship with Ice when he convinced Onyx to stay. And it wasn't like Viper posed issues for Ice.

I would be the only one he hated.

My throat was closing up. I loved him. Not something I was allowed to say—with the potential to be so damaging I'd even been afraid to think it. But I love him so fucking much. I didn't know how I would survive that.

Then his fingers wound around my arm, holding it closer as he sank against my chest.

Relief flooded my system, washing all my panic away as I released my breath.

"You're shaking," he muttered, half looking at me.

"Cold." It was the only word I could manage, and still it was strangled. But I dared pull him closer, risked ruining all of this for what I needed to show him.

The quiet between us stretched, and the soccer game was incomprehensible to me. I couldn't focus on it at all.

There was nothing else in the world right now but Ice tucked into my arms.

He hadn't left. Hadn't moved. Hadn't argued.

He was tense, though, and I realised I was too, like at any moment he was going to crack and tell me this was another trick or joke. Not that he'd ever made jokes like that. He taunted us, but he *never* baited physical affection.

It took a long time before he looked up at me, and I could swear there was the faintest sheen to his golden eyes as if he'd been warring against tears.

God, he was beautiful. He had the kind of face and body that was just... fucking impossible not to dream about. But it was way more than that. Even when the largest range I'd seen from him was anger to viciousness, I'd thought he was beautiful.

"Ice." That was Malakai. The word a warning. Ice's eyes darted back toward where Mal was sitting. He chewed on his lip, eyes finding mine again. The blush had crept further up his neck.

"I..." He swallowed. Then reached up to me, palm brushing my cheek. His scent changed, that anxiety to it getting stronger.

"Your scent is giving you away, Little Omega," Mal murmured. "Tell him what you want."

"Kiss me." Ice was breathless as he said it.

I just stared at him, not understanding two of the most simple words in the English language.

What?

He drew closer, and his pupils dilated.

They did that in my dreams. Not in real life. Just like when Onyx came out in nothing but lace, I wondered if I was dreaming now.

Still, I stared at him, brain blank.

"King." Malakai sighed. "If you won't kiss him, I—"

My brain sputtered into life and I leaned down, drawing Ice into a kiss that ended up much more aggressive than I'd intended.

Ice didn't seem to notice, his hands coming up, gripping my hair, demanding even more aggression as his tongue pressed into my mouth. He groaned, a sound that set every hair on my body on end.

I didn't know how or when he got on my lap, but then he was straddling me, desperately kissing me as his hands roamed my chest, my hips.

Fuck.

Then he was fumbling with my belt, tugging it off.

Anxiety slammed into me, and I halted him. He broke the kiss, brow furrowed. "Should we take it slow?"

What if this was just hormones? What if he changed his mind tomorrow and hated me forever?

"Slow?" The word was a feral whine. "It's been *years*!"

"But what if—?"

"What?" he snapped. He rose before me and his hand closed around my throat, golden eyes blazing as his nose almost touched mine.

Every word died in my brain in lieu of the mass exodus of blood to my cock.

What.

The.

Fuck?

"Do whatever you want," I choked.

That really wasn't a sexy way to say that. But Ice *could* do whatever he wanted right now, I wouldn't stop him. Malakai spluttered a laugh, but I didn't care because Ice was unzipping my jeans and tugging my cock free.

Next thing I knew, he was sinking down to the ground between my legs. "You want to…?" I trailed off, unsure.

"You don't want him sucking your cock?" Mal asked, and I shot him a furious look. He had reclined on the couch. Raven hair, loose from his bun, swooped around his lean face, and the pupils of his dark eyes were blown as he watched us.

The fingers gripping Ice's hair dug in. What kind of fucking question was that? It was just.. "But I can… then you won't…"

"Isn't that what you offered Onyx?" Ice asked.

"But it's Onyx, she deserves…" She deserved that kind of treatment. Me, on the other hand…

"You're saying no?" Ice asked, his grip on my cock tightening.

I groaned. "No."

He didn't hesitate, tongue dragging all the way up the base of my shaft.

I might have imagined it a million times, but it was nothing to the reality. The ash blond waves scattered across his face as his lustful golden eyes held mine. He pressed his lips to my tip and worked it slowly with his tongue as he gripped my thighs.

"Fuuuck." I tilted my head back, gripping the couch arm, knowing my expression was strained with lust. "You're so goddamned hot."

His eyes sparked and his fingers circled my swelling knot as he began taking my length into his mouth.

Shit. It was a task to try and manage my orgasm already.

There was lust in his eyes as he looked up at me, and I reached out, brushing his cheek and nudging his ash blond hair out of the way. His fingers dug in at my touch, a low whine in his chest, and then he choked my cock all the way to the back of his tight throat, holding it there for a few seconds before drawing back for breath.

Goddamn.

He did me the favour of changing pace, slowing down a little so I could keep a hold of myself. I was grateful. I wasn't ready for this to be over.

Then Mal was there, kneeling behind him, fingers of one hand lacing into his hair and pressing him right over my length as his other hand reached down to Ice's crotch.

Ice's pupils were wide enough there was barely a trace of gold left as he stared up at me, the back of his throat squeezing the tip of my cock. He whined deep in his chest, seizing for breath as Malakai held him against me without reprieve.

Fuck, was he—But fuck, with each seize he tightened around my length.

Finally Mal released him and he drew back, chest heaving. He took one deep breath before his lips were back on my length, tongue running up the base of my shaft. Then he was taking me again, Malakai pressing him roughly over me. Malakai was still setting a pace that I wasn't going to be able to fight. Ice's fingers bit down on my thighs, and when he next took me all the way to my knot, I came.

Ice groaned, finishing with me as I shot my seed down his throat.

He squeezed my knot, while Mal pressed Ice's lips up against it, drawing the experience out.

He stood, chest heaving, as he did up his own jeans. Then he stared down at me, as if calculating what he thought of what just happened. Then he grinned, the tip of his tongue caught between his teeth. And those cute pointed canines and the slight dimples his smile drew out had never been so beautiful.

He looked... delighted.

I realised I'd never seen Ice delighted before. He turned, almost running into Malakai, then paused, glancing up at him. Malakai drew his chin up delicately and pressed his lips to Ice's.

I'd never—in all these years—seen them together.

Mal was cold and reserved, but there was a gentleness and care to the way he kissed Ice that surprised me. Ice's fists curled in Malakai's shirt, drawing himself closer.

I wasn't into Mal like that, but it was different seeing him with Ice. The view was hot enough that I felt blood make an attempt at my cock again, though it was a little too soon.

When Ice pulled away, Malakai looked dazed. Perhaps passion wasn't something he was used to.

"I should..." Ice sounded a little breathless. "I should go and check on him."

Mal nodded and we both watched as he crossed the room back to Malakai's room.

Finally, I met Mal's eyes, still a little stunned.

Despite the confidence he'd had with Ice, his expression mirrored mine.

THIRTY-SIX

VIPER

Vik and Jake were curled up on the couch, holding each other peacefully. My eyes slid to the other in the room.

Hart was there, too, still and silent and peaceful. Then the memory shuddered and there was a gun on the coffee table. Blood was everywhere. Another shudder and it was a knife stained with red. Another shudder of the dream and there was a glass bottle and three glasses. Within was a clear liquid.

I'd had this dream enough times.

Poison.

I blinked, and three glasses turned to two.

When I dragged my eyes back up, the ratty patched up couch was empty.

Hart was gone.

When I woke, the panic had settled.

I'd drifted in and out, but sometimes when I'd blinked my

bleary eyes open Ice hadn't been there. I'd shut my eyes again until sleep swept me away.

Finally, I woke with his contented purr and arms wrapped around his waist. I caught the other scents on him. Apricots and champagne. Clove and riverside.

My pack.

My *new* pack.

The blow was duller this time, not something that sent me into a panic. A part of me wanted to shut my eyes again and vanish into sleep for longer. But I knew that wasn't going to help.

Ice scrambled up as I stirred, eyes worried.

"Are you... feeling a bit better?"

I nodded, trying to loosen the grip I had on the pack bond. Trying to let him in. It was just... if I let him in, I was letting them in too.

I could do it.

"Maybe... Need a shower." I was sticky with sweat, and my mouth was parched. I realised I was starving as well. How long had I been drifting in and out of sleep?

"Right." Ice nodded his head to the door entrance. "Just round the corner. I'll show you. And I got some clothes I thought would fit."

"Thanks." I hauled myself to the edge of the bed as Ice grabbed the pile of clothes on the side table.

The riverside and clove scent was heavy.

"This isn't your nest?" I asked. I'd assumed, but now that I focused, I realised the scents didn't add up.

"It's Mal's. I'm... between nests."

A part of me shrank, uncertain. I was in another alpha's territory. With *his* omega.

Would he be pissed?

He should be, pack or not.

That wasn't a good start. A start to the thing I wasn't prepared for... I blinked that thought away, focusing on Ice.

"Where's Onyx?" Her scent was faintest of all. She'd been here, I could have sworn it. But maybe... Maybe I'd dreamed it.

"She's... out with Arsenal. They're going to be away for a few days."

"Oh." Sorrow struck my heart at the same time I felt a guilty relief.

It hit me again.

I'd claimed her pack.

Her mates.

I shook it away, getting to unsteady feet and letting Ice direct me to the bathroom. I kept my eyes down, not ready to risk looking up to see anyone else yet.

MALAKAI

"He's up?" King was staring over at the bathroom door through which Viper had just vanished. It was early afternoon; Arsenal and Onyx had left last night.

Ice was taking a seat in the kitchen as King got to his feet and hurried over.

"He's gotta be hungry, right?" he asked, opening the freezer.

King was excited we had another packmate. Arsenal was grateful to Viper for saving Ice. Sure, I was a bit of both, but I was struggling. I had a hard time trusting, always had. And this alpha had just appeared in our pack, stolen our omega's heart, and neither of the others were blinking.

I was.

Even if it made me feel like absolute shit.

I'd looked him up. His reputation was about right. He was rich, obnoxious to press that tried to talk to him, and a troublemaker. For the kinds of things that would get me and my brothers sent to jail, Viper Oxford walked away with nothing but a slap on the wrist. Most often thanks to his father.

He was in the shower right now, and King was in the kitchen while Ice played on his phone.

They were both nervous. King was currently making a grand meal while Ice's anxiety was clear through the bond. We were better. Well, more than better after what had happened between us, but I knew he wanted us to get on with Viper.

The biggest problem I had, however, was that nothing that I had felt so far from Viper through the bond matched a thing I read up on him. He wasn't hostile, defensive, angry, or anything at all I might expect from a rich kid who just got landed with a pack of poor criminals.

He was more nervous than even Ice and King. I could feel him trying to shut down his side of the bond, and he was failing miserably. His aura was too sick. He didn't have much control at all. And it was leaving him wide open to all of us. And he was a mess. I didn't want to feel sorry for him, but dammit, I did.

I sighed, getting to my feet and joining Ice at the table. King—who clearly hadn't been sure what kind of shit food Viper would want—had made it all.

On the island there were a few different flavours of pot noodles steaming, a plate of pizza pops, a bowl of chips and dip, toasted Pop-tarts, and another plate of Jamaican patties. By the time I entered the kitchen, he was grabbing all the condiments out of the fridge.

"I'm sure he'll survive without expired ranch," I noted. King shot me a glare as he laid it all out on the table carefully. I reached for a Jamaican patty, but King slapped my hand away.

VIPER

I showered and dressed, then found myself stuck.

I stared at myself in the mirror. I was still tired of the man staring back at me. Golden piercings lined my ears, tattoos scattered to my knuckles. Remnants of my past life. That was all I was made of. Fragments of a life that no longer existed.

Idiot rich kid.

Shoved your way into their pack.

Nothing to offer.

And what if I complicated things with Onyx?

She was falling for them.

Ice had... He'd begged me. And selfishly, I'd clung to the first flicker of hope I'd felt in years.

Now I might have stolen away another thing from her.

I straightened, fist clapping my palm as I took a breath. They were out there. I couldn't avoid them forever.

ICE

Viper came out wearing a pair of Malakai's baggy pants and an oversized shirt. They were about the same height, though he was more slender. I couldn't stop staring at him. He did kind of look like a model, with dark brows, and the chiselled lines of his face were pronounced. He was wearing a golden necklace that I'd wiped blood from back in the hospital. He had pale skin and the tattoos that wove around his arms and down to his knuckles suited him. I was kind of a sucker for tattoos, not that I'd ever admit that to Arsenal.

Well... Maybe now I could?

I was anxious for when Viper came out, desperate for this to work. I'd tried to help King with the food, but he'd shooed me away.

I didn't have to worry about King, but Malakai was tense as Viper entered. Viper's eyes fell on the table of food that King had set out. He palmed the back of his neck, an awkward look on his face. He was hungry, clearly.

King—who had his head in the fridge—noticed Viper. He shut it quickly.

"Hey…" He held out his hand. Viper took it. "King. Thought, uh… Thought you might be hungry. Didn't know what you'd like…"

Viper nodded, eyes darting to the table again as he took a seat.

Should I go and sit next to him? Would it make him feel less anxious? Or more? He didn't know me. Not really. I thought I could try.

I slipped from my seat, as he gathered some of the food onto his plate, and took the seat beside him. I felt his anxiety through the bond wane as his eyes darted to me for just a moment.

"You probably eat way better stuff where you come from," King said. "We can get some more stuff in."

Viper snorted. "I uh, pretty much live off of Pop-Tarts and noodles."

"Oh." King visibly relaxed, as if all his worries about Viper had just been wiped away in that one statement. He grabbed his own plate and began filling it up.

Malakai still hadn't said anything. Nor did he take anything to eat.

THIRTY-SEVEN

ARSENAL

The first night with Onyx had been quiet.

We'd arrived in a hotel room and both crashed, then slept well into noon. I hadn't realised how tired I was until my head hit the pillow. The same, apparently, went for her.

She looked more relaxed than she had before today, and I thought maybe this was the right choice. She needed space—she'd been driving herself crazy checking in on Ice. To be honest, I might have been, too.

I let Onyx pick what we did for the day, so we spent the next few hours wandering around Pineford Mall on the Westside, which I'd never previously been to.

It was strange to be walking about a mall with a woman like Onyx. Today she was wearing a beige jacket with a low cut silken top and high-waisted leggings that hugged her hips beautifully. I didn't feel like I looked right with her, hearing the click of her heels as she walked at my side. My eyes kept catching on her beautiful mane of chocolate hair that was down still. She'd worn it down since the night she'd been with Mal in that lingerie.

I halted that thought. My dignity couldn't afford to think about that in public.

We were shopping for... fun? I thought, anyway. Which—if you'd told me ahead of time—would have seemed extremely boring, but it wasn't. Not that I'd admit that to any of my brothers. I had to admit it to Onyx, though, when she caught me snapping a picture of a superhero mug.

"For Ice," I said, quickly. If he thought he could hide the fact he was mug-obsessed, he was sorely wrong.

I could sense her energy change when we entered the home decor section of the store we were in. Yup, there were definitely stars in her eyes as she looked around.

"You like interior design?"

"Not usually," she said. "But think what the garage could *be* like."

I grunted. Not with those price tags, it couldn't. Except... we *did* just bond a billionaire. I slapped the thought away.

"Well, I mean..." She sounded tentative. "It's your place. Obviously. But it's such a big space..."

I side-eyed her stifled excitement

"Probably needs an update," I said. "What would you suggest?"

She chewed on her lip anxiously and it took everything in my self-control not to take her chin and kiss her right there.

I blinked the thought away, a little taken aback.

"Well... You're going to need another room for Viper. It does look like there was another floor. We could put in a loft..." She trailed off and I saw the flush creep up her neck. "You guys could, I mean."

"Who would we put in charge of that?" I chuckled.

"Ice."

"He's hopeless. He's going to need a little help."

"I'm sure Malakai or King could—"

"Show me right now," I said. "You know, so I can impress him. What would *you* do to the place?"

She still hugged her bag close, but there was a guilty flash in her eyes as she glanced back at the sea of beds, and desks, and couches scattered across the shop around us.

"Okay, well…"

Once she got started, she couldn't seem to stop. She even fumbled in her handbag to get out a notepad and pen so she could sketch out her idea for me.

We chose a display to settle on, and I put my feet up on the ottoman as we lounged back on an abhorrent couch with cow-print pattern.

"What are those?" I asked, peering at what she had just penned in.

"You need doors on your bedrooms."

"We do not," I scoffed.

At one point, an employee headed our way as if to tell us to get out, but she took one look at my tattoos and took a sharp left turn. I snorted, returning my attention to Onyx.

"Lot of space up in that loft," I noted, peering at her design. "Could put a couple extra rooms in there," I pointed out.

"Oh. Well, I was actually thinking Ice deserves a big nest, right?"

"Sure." I lowered my hand and brushed hers. Out of the corner of my eye, I saw the shift of her throat as she swallowed. "But it's huge," I went on. "Could probably fit another room and a big nest. Or a double nest."

I was suddenly very hot.

She froze.

Maybe I hadn't eased her in enough to drop that. Slowly, she drew her hand away, sliding her touch from mine. When I darted a glance at her, her expression was tense. I could swear, for a moment, there was a glassy shine in her sapphire eyes.

Then she blinked and it was gone. "I think that couch over there is perfect for Ice. Big enough for a pack to spend time in his room—and we'll have to see if they have any pack beds here. Those will be worth checking out."

I nodded, eyes still fixed on her drawing. "It looks great," I forced out. "I'll uh... have to tell Viper there was actually a pack buy in if I want to afford it."

Her laugh sounded genuine and delighted.

"Shall we head back to the hotel?" I asked.

"We could. Did you want to eat first? We could do a restaurant. Or would you prefer room service?"

"Definitely room service." I still didn't feel completely recovered if I was being honest, and this mall was bustling with people.

We returned to the grand hotel. Today, a bit more rested, I was paying attention to it. It looked and felt far too high end for me. The room was crazy, with round beds and grand red curtains that could be pulled around them. The whole room was creams and reds, with dozens of pillows. Perhaps that's why she'd chosen this place.

She sat on the edge of the bed, a faraway look on her face as she set her handbag down.

"You were trying to... make me a part of the planning," she said quietly.

I leaned against the wall, folding my arms. "Yes."

There was no point in denying it.

"You need to let me go." Her brilliant, sapphire blue eyes found mine, and she looked so sure and so broken.

"And then what happens? He comes for you one day and there's no one there to stop him?"

"I can find another pack. Be up front—"

"You're lying, Onyx. You won't take this to anyone else's doorstep and we both know it."

"I never should have brought it to yours—"

"I wouldn't have it any other way." The words came from my lips before I had thought them through.

But it was the truth. No matter what had gone wrong, no matter the change and upheaval, she was one thing I would never change.

"But they're not going to," she whispered.

"What?"

"Whoever they are, they won't... *do* anything. They won't take the next step." Her fingers ran wildly through her hair. "They won't hurt me, or... take me, or tell me what they want. They're in my house, in my head, and I feel like it's never going to end! I have no control and I'm stuck! I can't get close to anyone. I can't move. Sometimes it feels like that's what they want."

I stared at her, brows furrowed. "What if... it is?"

"Is what?"

"What if that *is* all they want?" I asked.

"To frighten away anyone I could possibly love?"

For a moment, I got tripped up over that. Love? Onyx thought she could love us?

I shook it away, focusing on what she was saying. "They've never done anything else. They could have, a thousand times they could have hurt you. What was that message they left in your apartment the first time?" I wracked my brain.

"You will never escape me," she whispered.

"We thought they were making a claim. What if they weren't? What if they never intend to come. What if they're just trying to keep you alone?"

"Like... vengeance?"

I nodded, mind still working a million miles an hour. "It would explain why they've never touched you. Even when they were in your house."

"But who...? Why would they?"

I winced. "Could it be... someone from the pack you rejected?" If the pack had shattered, if there were deaths... "You saw what happened to Viper." I could feel it through the bond even now. "That pack was broken, and whatever did it was enough to drive him to that. What if Viper got off easy compared to the others?"

Onyx's face was ashen, a million unspoken words hanging in the air between us. There were horror stories of packs left behind by duchesses like Onyx. Infighting could become violent and deaths could follow. "But I don't remember..."

I was pulling out my phone, sending a text to the pack. Viper wasn't in it yet.

> Me: We need to know what happened to Viper's pack if we're going to figure this out.

When I looked back up at her, she looked so lost. "I took away their pack," she whispered. "And now..." She didn't finish. She didn't have to.

Now they wanted to take away hers.

It fit.

It fit for the last message too. We'd claimed Viper. If I was right and he tied into this just like Onyx did, this guy would be just as attached to Viper.

"Okay. So what happens when they figure out—" I cut off, taking a breath, running my fingers through my hair.

"What?" She was looking at me sharply.

Shit.

I sat down on the bed, staring at her, wondering if I should say what just went through my head. But she had to know by now. "What happens when they realise they can't scare us away?"

Her lips parted for a moment, and then she closed her mouth. Ever so slightly, she shook her head. "That's not how this goes."

I let out a breath of a laugh. "You can't take back the last week."

"You have *everything*." Her voice shook. "Ice is better. You have another packmate to take care of. You don't need—"

"Need?" I demanded. "That's not what this is about."

"Then *undo* any magic you've got tangled on in your head and make it about that."

"I can't. None of us can. It's not how we're wired and you know that."

"Then how are you wired?" she asked.

"We don't leave anyone behind."

"I'm not pack."

I was on my feet before I could catch myself. "You are fucking pack, Onyx. As much as Ice, or King, or Mal, or Viper."

She stared up at me, trembling fingers fumbling for her handbag again. "I've..." She swallowed, composing herself as she stood, and the full duchess returned to her eyes. "I've known you for a week," she said coldly. *"This* is hormones—"

"Oh, for fuck's sake."

"You are getting too attached. Soon I won't be able to tell you from this stalker—"

She cut off at the snarl on my face as I challenged that. "Say it then. Say we mean nothing to you."

She stared up at me, chest heaving, sapphire eyes furious as I challenged her.

"Tell me you don't want us, and I'm gone. Right now." Why had I said that? Was I willing to follow through? I'd meant to push her, not give her an ultimatum, but unexpected anger stirred in me at the words she'd so brazenly spoken.

After everything.

She drew herself up. "This wasn't a mutual arrangement, Arsenal. I didn't want—"

"Say you don't want us."

Her eyes darted between mine. "*I* put Ice in danger."

She was baiting me. And sure, there was a faint rustle of panic at the words she'd just spoken, but not nearly as much at the idea of leaving her in this place alone at the mercy of this stalker.

"We will protect you both," I snarled.

She was avoiding it. I needed to know the truth. Silence fell between us as she gathered herself again.

"I don't want you." Her teeth were gritted. "Not you. Not King, or Malakai, or Ice."

The words stung, catching me off guard.

"So *leave!*" There was fury in her eyes as she shoved me a step back. "Get *out*."

"You'd rather be alone?"

"Yes." But the word caught in her throat, shattering on the way up. She took a steadying breath, shifting to the side just slightly as if she thought she had to defend herself from me. She pointed at the door. "Yes."

This time, it was crisp and cutting.

ONYX

"Okay. Then..." Arsenal's voice was broken. "I'll go."

I nodded, shock spiking my system. I wanted it from him. Needed it.

But I hadn't expected it.

I couldn't move as he took a step toward me.

"I'll go," he repeated.

I nodded, eyes darting between his as his movement violated that statement.

He cupped my cheeks, tilting my head up to look at him. "But just tell me once, in your own words, that you'd rather be alone."

My chest felt too tight, my voice barely a whisper. "I already did."

"Say it for me, and you won't hear from us ever again."

I had to.

This person stalking me, they'd cost me over and over again. But never had they cost me more than they were right now.

And knowing that changed nothing. I was so... angry. Angry that this was taken from me, more so because now I'd had a taste of what it might be like not to be alone.

"I..." My heart felt like it would shatter my rib cage and my throat was closing up. "I..."

A thousand moments from my life before shattered the buzzing anxiety of my mind. Every minute stretching with a glass of wine in my hand, the room slowly getting darker around me as night fell.

Silence.

True silence that the TV or radio couldn't shatter. Not really. A home that could never be a home, for the fear I felt every time I entered.

My nest... I shut my eyes, fighting the tremors, trying not to think of Ice right now, in the bundle of wool and fairy lights with Viper. Taking the step I was too scared to take.

"I would rather..." I had to steady my voice. My lip trembled and I shut my eyes, but it was too late to stop the hot tears that leaked down my cheeks.

I felt Arsenal press his forehead to mine.

It was enough to break me, my fingers closing around his wrists as I shook.

"We don't leave anyone behind," he whispered softly, but with resoluteness.

Those words were destruction as much as they were salvation. I could feel the chaos they left in their wake, burning down expectations, and plans, and everything I'd thought my life was.

Or would ever be.

I don't know how it happened, but in the next moment he'd drawn me against him and I was trembling in his arms, tears flooding my cheeks at last.

"What are we going to do?"

"I don't know. But we'll do it together."

ARSENAL

I held her in my arms, heart pounding and heavy in my chest.

For a moment, I'd been afraid she was telling the truth: that she didn't want us.

But it wasn't the truth. And I wanted her as much as she wanted us.

At last, she looked up at me with glowing, sapphire eyes, and there was hope in them. Real hope like I'd never seen in her before.

Then her fingers curled around my shirt, and the tone shifted in a flash.

We both moved at the same time, and she all but threw herself at me. Her lips were crushing mine, her hands winding around my head and neck, and her legs wrapped around my waist as I staggered one pace back, grabbing at her clothing wildly as if I might just tear it right off.

When my back hit the wall, she shifted up so she was looking down at me and her wild waves were curtaining our faces; a little pocket of bliss, in which the wet diamonds glittering in her eyes meant nothing at all, and there was nothing to fear beyond this room.

Her chest heaved, her curved nose brushed mine, and she smiled. I squeezed the perfect flesh of her ass and she let out a breathy noise before dragging her lips to mine again.

This was it. The thing a part of me had been waiting for since the first time she turned up at my door, all hard edges and perfectly tied up hair.

She was feral inside, more even than Ice.

Ice was something soft, covered in blades. She was something wild, tamped down by the world she was forced to please.

But not here. Not in this room with me. Never with any of our pack.

I don't know how we got there, but I was pinning her to the bed, not a care for the buttons of her shirt as I ripped them free. She was captivating, the silken skin of her breasts pressed against the black lace bra she was wearing. It was the same lace she'd worn when she'd been with me during my rut.

She had saved me from that. Just like she had saved us all.

I needed more. She was fighting for the clasp, but instincts were gripping me. For the first time they weren't pure violence and aggression, they were made of lust and desire.

I needed to have her. To claim her.

I leaned down, catching the dark tip of her nipple in my mouth. She loosed a whine, the fingers fighting her bra dropping away. I didn't care, taking it and snapping it away with ease, enraptured as her breasts came free. I groaned, dragging her against me as I took her nipple in my mouth again, the palm of my other hand squeezing her other breast.

She was perfect.

As perfect as Ice was. For a moment, I was stolen by the image of them together. Of King behind them.

I imagined being the one behind her, gripping her hips as I pressed her over Ice's hard cock.

Shit.

She gasped, and I realised my aura had hit the air. Still, it was lust and no aggression. I drew away, brows furrowed, checking myself. "Sorry."

She reached up, nails digging into my chin as she drew me close. "Ruin me, Arsenal. Make me forget."

A growl rose in my throat, though I did force my aura back. It was too dangerous to be holding her with it out. Even for the most controlled of alphas, things could go wrong. And I was far from the most controlled alpha. Usually, that thought would wound me, but right now I could see in her eyes that it was exactly why she wanted me.

I tugged on her panties, dragging them over her smooth legs before leaning back to rip my shirt off. I was snagged by her beauty. She was panting, fingers digging into sheets, her whole body bare but for the delicate golden necklace that hung on her neck. Her hair was wild, tangled across the bed behind her. A mane of chocolate waves that tumbled down to her hips. I liked it better like that than the straight hair and buns I'd first seen her in.

The room was suddenly filled with the heated scent of lavender and brownies. There was an edge of need to it as she lay before me. Smooth, golden skin, full breasts, her knees bent and legs parted. From here, I could see she was wet for me, and even more blood rushed to my cock.

I realised I'd just been staring at her, my brain short circuiting like it couldn't figure out if we were dreaming or not.

Before I made it weird, I forced myself back to action, tearing off my jeans and freeing my erection. Her eyes slid to it, her pretty pink lips parted slightly, and I paused, holding my swelling knot for a moment and enjoying the flash of want in her eyes.

The rise and fall of her chest intensified as she looked at it, and then her gaze darted back to me, her brow pinching.

In those sapphire eyes right now was her need for me.

I wanted to see that forever.

THIRTY-EIGHT

ONYX

Arsenal was handsome; that was undeniable. But the sheer godliness of what he was hiding beneath his clothing was—simply put—unfair. His tattoos tangled down his chest with perfect emphasis on all of his muscle. And fuck, did he have muscles. I was riveted by him, by every chiselled edge, the tattoos that tapered off just at the top of the V that dipped to his hips.

And holy hell, his cock was massive.

He was gripping it right now, palm stroking it slowly as he stared at me. Why was he waiting? I whined.

I needed him.

My scent had to be smothering. It was so strong I swear I could practically drown in it.

His scent was different too, tangled with lust, and for the first time there was no charred edge to the chestnuts and honey.

I licked my lips as his eyes continued to roam my body. "Don't you dare pull a Malakai on me now," I breathed, trying not to let on how fucking desperate I was.

"Mal didn't fuck you?"

"No." Shit. The spark in his eyes told me that might have been the wrong thing to say.

"But he punished you?"

I bit my lip as he chuckled, finally dropping down on the bed and caging me in. "We all heard that, Sweetheart," he breathed in my ear.

I wound my fingers around his neck, dragging him into a kiss.

"Fuck me," I whispered.

"So desperate, Duchess."

But I was. Another whine slipped from my lips. Mal was one thing, but Arsenal was one step away from feral. I'd just been witness to that. "I need you," I moaned.

Arsenal tensed and his pupils blew wide, a growl rising up his throat. Then his fingers bit down on my thigh, pushing my legs open, and I felt his tip against my entrance.

The moan that slipped out was not intentional. I lifted my hips toward him. I didn't want to wait. I wanted him right now.

I held his gaze as my chest heaved and he slowly pressed his tip into me. He was so wide I groaned, desperate.

"Fuck. Me!" I demanded. I was soaked.

He snarled and then drove his cock into me without hesitation. I let out a moan of pleasure as his fingers dug into my hips and he began slamming into me at a ruthless pace, his massive cock stretching me tight.

"Yes," I moaned, fingers closing around the sheets as pleasure rocketed through my body. Every time he thrust in, I could feel his knot. I was out of breath, my lips parted, my faculties entirely gone as I stared up at him completely dazed.

There was a cocky grin on his face as he saw my expression, and he hooked my knees under his arms and shifted them closer to my chest. The sound I made as he drove into me was feral, my back arching toward him as he slammed into my core, sending lightning through my veins.

His fingers curled through my hair, tilting my chin up. "Look at me while I ruin you, Duchess," he growled.

My eyes snapped to his as he drove in again. This time I let out a whimper at the pleasure of it, but he didn't draw out straight away, resting his knot against my entrance and pressing against me just slightly.

My nails dug into his arms as I stared up at him, unable to find words or form cohesive thoughts as lava burst through my veins.

"Say you're ours, Onyx."

"I'm..." I gasped. "I'm yours." It was the truth. I realised, in that moment, that I wanted them. I wanted them forever, even though right now I didn't know how we would make that happen.

So slowly, he drew out before slamming back in. I moaned again at the feeling of his knot connecting with my flesh.

"Please knot me," I whimpered in a breathy tone.

He grinned, drawing his cock back, and each inch in which his length slid against my flesh was dizzying. Then he leaned close, driving back in. "You aren't nearly ruined enough for that."

Next thing I knew, he'd released my legs, his cock still buried in me. But then he dragged me off it as he spun me on my front, pressing me against the sheets but for my hips as he slammed into me again. I was soaked and moaning with each thrust, the trembling sounds I was making unrecognisable. I tried to push myself up, but my arms were shaking. His hand found my breasts, squeezing them roughly.

I was panting, his fingers twisting my nipple as my breast jolted at the thrusts of his cock, each tug sending a shock of pleasure through me.

I came without warning, my whole body seizing as wetness spilled from me and I cried out, buckling. He groaned, slowing his pace as if it were the only thing keeping him from finishing, but his fingers found my clit and he began working it rapidly. I shuddered, a feral whine spilling from my lips as I was seized by a shock of pleasure.

"Again, Duchess. You feel so good when you come for me."

I cried out, clenching down on his cock for the second time as another rolling orgasm seized my body. I was panting by the time it was over, my chest pressed against the sheets I clutched, low moans rising in my chest with each of his slow thrusts.

His touch ran down my back, squeezing the flesh of my ass. I heard a low, contented rumble in his chest as he squeezed the flesh there still sore from Malakai's bite. I shuddered at the vibration that travelled through his cock and right into my core, a thrill at the claim.

He kept up that rhythm, dragging my hips back against him for a while while I caught my breath. By the time I had, there was another threat of pleasure shivering through my body. I felt it grow each time his swollen knot touched me. Occasionally he would linger, nudging my entrance with it, as if enjoying the feeling of my pussy stretching just the slightest bit for him.

"Knot me," I breathed. "Please, Alpha."

ARSENAL

Her body trembled beneath me, her cheek pressed to the sheets so one sapphire blue eye held mine as I rocked inside of her. She was recovering from the shuddering orgasm still.

Once more I nestled my knot against her, biting my lip at the momentary soaring pleasure of feeling her pussy stretch for it.

"Please knot me," she whined.

I had to fight the primal urge to press it in immediately. Another shuddering growl rose up my throat and she shook. I just needed one more thing. I drew out, and then gently turned her on her back.

I wanted to see the ruin on her beautiful face as I forced her tight walls wide around me and held her there, milking me while I spilled inside of her.

Seeing her looking up at me sent me over that edge. I pressed into her, coming apart as I felt her tight walls trying to accommodate my knot. Her fingers tore at the sheets as she gasped. My hand came down on the bed, a great shuddering orgasm squeezing my knot in a vice, dragging me through another and another wave. I finally stopped when she was panting and shaking, absolutely spent.

Then I drew her up against me to little shudders as my knot shifted within her, and I lay against the headboard with her against my chest, our bodies connected.

She panted, resting her head against the crook of my neck, her wild hair tickling my arm and chest.

We sat like that for a while, the rise and fall of her chest calming as I held us together while I was locked within her.

"You're perfect, Onyx," I murmured in her ear. "I want you."

She looked up at me, eyes wide. I pressed a kiss to her forehead.

Her brows bunched as she considered what I might mean by that.

"I want you in our pack," I said, brushing her cheek, thumb lingering on her lips. "I want to see you come apart for them, too. I want to see you with Ice again. I want to keep you safe and make you happy for the rest of your life."

She stared at me and for a moment, then tried tugging her chin from my grip, something anxious in her eyes, but I didn't let her.

"Do you want us?"

"Of course..." She swallowed. "Of course I do."

My heart skipped a beat. I'd asked. Hoped. And yet, to hear it from her...

"Bond with us."

Fear flashed in her eyes. "You can't... so soon. What about Viper?"

"We can manage. We'll be a pack. We'll figure it out, just like we'll figure out everything else."

Still, she looked so worried.

My voice was rough. "Take a bond with us."

She couldn't see it, but she was *it*. Our solution.

Our missing piece.

She stared at me, eyes darting back and forth desperately as if not sure what she'd just heard.

"Let me make it official. I don't want anyone—not the world, not this fucker stalking you—to think for a second you don't have a pack at your back."

She was staring at me like I was mad. "I *can't*."

"Why? What difference does it make? We are going to protect you, but the bond will make it easier."

She was shaking her head. "Viper isn't fully healed. There's still so much to figure out. I can't be bonded with him until we're sure it won't hurt him."

I swallowed, hating how her words made sense.

Viper was broken. I got that—we really, really didn't have room for another broken pack member—but here we were. I wanted to respect that. And no matter how it grated—having an alpha flung into our pack with no hierarchy established—he had saved Ice.

Our omega would be dead, or worse, without him.

For that, we owed him.

"We need more information," she said quietly. "If we get it, if he is better, then I will... consider it."

"You'll *consider* it?" I asked, dragging her closer, my voice a low growl.

"I'll take it." Her voice was shaky. But she nodded, as if trying to steel herself. "I'll take your offer of a bond."

I felt the broad grin on my face.

"And you better be thankful Ice found Viper. The three of you wouldn't be able to handle two omegas."

I snorted.

She was probably not wrong on that.

"And if this fucker keeps it up once you're bonded, we can move across the country if that's what it takes to get your happily ever after."

I'd offer to move countries with her if that's what it took, but the prospect of us moving out of the country at all was poor, given our history.

Would that put her in danger? What if the only solution to this fucker *was* to leave the country? If I bit her, I'd steal her chance at that—

"I don't want to move," she said. "I swore I wouldn't."

"Oh."

"This city is my home. I love it. I'm *not* letting him take that from me as well."

"Okay. New Oxford, our last stand."

THIRTY-NINE

MALAKAI

"You're all grouchy shits," Ice declared after Viper had vanished to his car and returned. "We're going to the roof."

"We are?" I asked.

"It's fucking cold," King grumbled, rubbing his hands together.

"I don't care. You have to bond," Ice said.

"Bond?" I asked. For fuck's sake. I side-eyed Viper, who had his hands in his pockets.

What had he and Ice been planning? Still, I followed them up, unable to deny Ice.

Ice happily plugged in some Edison lights that hung from the precarious wooden structure covered with a tarp. Then he comfortably tucked himself beneath a thick woollen blanket in the chair at Viper's side. It seemed as though he were trying to make up for missed time with us all right now, but with Viper... Well, with Viper it was like he had a crush. There was just no other way to put it.

Viper dug in his pocket and pulled out a lighter and blunt.

Oh.

That was the plan.

Not actually a bad idea. I needed to fucking decompress, and King definitely did.

I huffed a laugh, but took a drag when Viper handed it to me.

It was oddly silent for a while as we passed the blunt around. I leaned back in my seat, watching the clouds pass over stars up ahead as the drug hit my system.

"So, what do you do for fun?" Viper asked, glancing around at us.

"Mal and Arsenal have the shop," King said. I nodded. It was work, but we both enjoyed it. "And I..." King trailed off. "Not much, really."

It wasn't totally true. He liked going to the gym down the street. But I knew how insecure he was about going out. He spent a lot of time with us, or watching whatever sport was on.

Viper glanced at Ice, who shrugged.

"Only thing I've ever seen Ice enjoy is piercing people."

"Piercings?" Viper asked.

"Yeh. Does it sometimes in the garage. Just locals."

The piercing kit was the only gift Ice had ever seemed happy to receive from us, which checked out since the result was that he got to stick us with needles. Literally.

"For fun mostly," Ice said. "Don't charge or anything." And he'd never wanted to make anything of it, since he was too scared to draw attention to himself.

"He pierced Mal," King added.

"Where?" Viper peered at me.

I just leaned back on my seat, taking a longer drag of my blunt to hide my grin.

Viper snorted. "Shit, dude..." His gaze drifted down to my crotch. He got his confirmation by the smirk on Ice's face. "More balls than I have."

"You don't look like I'd think a rich kid looks," King noted. I noted the line of golden piercings along his ear and black gauges in his lobes, and beyond the piercings, there were tattoos creeping down even to his hands.

"Well, anything to piss off my old man."

"How does bonding with a pack of criminals rank?"

"Surprisingly low, considering," Viper snorted. "He just wanted me to get a bond. At this point, I don't think he cares how it happened."

"Do you?" I asked, curiously.

"Do I what?" Viper asked. "Care who you are?" He shook his head with a shrug. "Not really. You know I saw you in a few magazines—"

The weed wasn't enough to stifle the anxiety that suddenly rocketed through King's side of the bond. Viper caught that, cutting off.

A long, awkward silence passed. It wasn't like with Onyx. I didn't know why silence between me and her was okay, but it was.

"You know about it," King said, finally.

Viper looked uncomfortable. "I'm not... It's not my business—"

I cut him off. "If we're going to get that through the bond from you every time, it's everyone's business."

Viper winced. "Sorry."

I gave King a look. I knew King hated talking about why he had ended up in juvie, but this dude was stuck with us.

"You really don't have to," Viper said. King wrinkled his nose and shrugged, though it looked a little forced.

I ran my tongue along my teeth, thinking for a moment. "His mom had a history of negligence," I said, knowing it was better to get it over with. "She was on her last chance. His sister fell down the stairs and died—an accident," I added. "But King told them he lost control of his aura so the rest of the kids weren't taken away."

When I was done, King was ashen. Viper still looked guilty, but the discomfort we'd felt down the bond had vanished.

"She..." King's voice was weak. "She wasn't a bad mom. When I was young, there were... dark times. But then she'd got clean for me and Sarah." I hated how shaky he got through the bond when this came up.

Part of the condition for King's release when he was 18 was proving his aura was stable. Not an issue, since it had never been unstable. Arsenal's had been more of a challenge, but then his charge wasn't as bad. In fact, if he hadn't been an alpha, he'd probably have never been locked up at all. His dad had been strangling him by the time his aura surfaced. But the Institute had to make sacrifices, and not locking up someone who'd left a body as mangled as that to roam free? It just wouldn't fly. King, though? He didn't belong here. He'd never hurt so much as a fly in his life.

"And you?" Viper seemed happy to shift the topic as he glanced at me.

"I don't want to talk about it," I grunted. Ice snorted and King had to stifle a grin.

"Uh..." Viper glanced between us.

"Look. I'm not saying there's anything funny about armed robbery—" Ice began.

"But when big, ol' Mal got caught because of an old lady's pet, then you have a story."

"What?" Viper perked up.

"He was on a robbery and her bird attacked him," King chuckled. "His mask came off, he was caught on camera."

"It came at me like a wild animal," I muttered. "And I hate birds."

"A bird?" Viper asked, incredulous. "At least say it was big."

"It was huge and fucking rabid."

I was honest with my pack. *Always*. But until the day I kicked the bucket, I would never confess to my brothers that I spent four years incarcerated all because of a little yellow budgerigar.

"Look," I said, before they pushed. "I was young and stupid and getting caught was the best thing that ever happened to me, alright?"

Juvie had given me distance from the Harpies, and I'd met my brothers there. Viper looked like he had more questions, though, so I changed the topic again.

"So," I said. "You bike?" That bike he'd brought in for fixing was nice. Arsenal was obsessed with it. I'd caught him polishing the rims—not something we did for clients.

"Oh. No... I just got it from a shop for an excuse to scout you."

"Would you?" I prodded.

"What?" he asked.

"Learn." At my side, King and Ice both turned on Viper hopefully. Arsenal would never stop grumbling about how none of us wanted to learn.

"Fuck, no," Viper snorted. "Scares the crap out of me."

Damn.

"They sold it broken?" King asked.

"Uh... no." For a moment, he looked quite proud of himself.

I stared at him, my eyebrows going up. "You... broke it?" A Hound?

"Yes..." He trailed off.

"If I were you, I'd make sure Arsenal never found out," I chuckled.

"Okay." Viper's face was ashen. "Right. Noted."

"How much was it?" King asked.

"Couple of hundred."

"Thousand?" King groaned.

"They said it would make me look good." Viper sounded defensive.

I snorted, leaning back in my chair.

My phone buzzed and I checked it.

> Arsenal: We need to know what happened to Viper's pack if we're going to figure this out.

I stared for a while, my sluggish brain trying to catch up. Reality crashed back in, and I looked back to Viper.

The topic had changed to something else light, and I pondered for a while, glancing out over the city.

I hadn't sensed this kind of peace through the bond in a while. Even King was more relaxed than usual. And Ice... I kept catching him eyeing Viper with... Okay, well, lust.

He was fucking smitten.

I grinned, the thought surprisingly cheerful.

Things were changing. I wasn't alone anymore. And it wasn't just Ice. Onyx was into them all.

We had Riot's job in two days, and Onyx's stalker to deal with with no end in sight.

We *could* have it all, if only we could deal with this fucker.

After the talk lulled and the quiet stretched, I finally asked.

"I'm sorry," I said, my voice dry. "But I need to ask. Your old pack...?"

The peace in the bond shattered for Viper's anxiety. "Gone."

I nodded, handing him back the joint. "All of them?"

"I..." He was staring at me with wide eyes. He blinked. "Y-yes."

That hadn't sounded certain. I frowned, but King shot me a look before I could prod. Poison oozed from Viper's side of the bond, and his expression was stiff.

Ice slipped his fingers into Viper's, but when I looked to him, there was a thoughtful frown on his face and he caught my eyes.

I didn't push anymore, but I saw Ice tapping on his phone. A few moments later, mine buzzed.

> Ice: We need to figure out what happened with their pack.

> Ice: He's too unstable. Arsenal said his dad visited. Think we can go and talk to him?

I looked at him and nodded.

> Me: Tomorrow.

Luckily, King had seized another topic and Viper's anxiety was rapidly fading.

He was rich, spoiled, and came from another world, but he was also anxious. He was trying, and his sacrifice for Ice, it had been real.

I was starting to realise there was nothing at all that set him apart from my brothers.

FORTY

ONYX

"You think you're ready, Duchess?" Arsenal asked.

"It's take out."

He gave me a look that said he wasn't buying it—and he was right. But I'd agreed, and now we were doing it. We'd only been gone two nights, but Ice and Viper had apparently both insisted that I return now that Viper was awake.

When I entered the garage it was... different. Clean. Well, as clean as a great, industrial, concrete building could be. But the kitchen was empty of the old pots that had been a permanent fixture.

"You... cleaned?" Arsenal sounded disbelieving.

"All of us. Ice suddenly needed the place spotless. Won't leave us be."

"Turns out." Malakai popped his head up from the shop. "He's *more* annoying as a normal omega."

Arsenal snorted. We walked over to the kitchen table. I set my handbag down, peering about.

"Where are they?" I asked.

"Viper's napping. Still doing that a lot. Ice is with him." King shrugged.

"Does he still have to stay with him all the time?" I asked. I hadn't realised I'd missed the scents of the place. Of them. But there was something so comforting about Malakai's riverside and clove, King's apricot and champagne, and Ice's roses and cookies.

"Nah, it's better now," Malakai said, crossing toward us wiping his hands on a rag he tossed to the pile that usually amassed outside the laundry cupboard. He frowned, seeing the lone rag on a now laundry free floor, then crossed to it, opened the cupboard, and put it into the machine. "But I think he likes to," he added as he reached the sink, glancing back at us. "They're getting on well."

"You look cheery about it," Arsenal said.

I'd noticed, too. Malakai had been tense before. It had been hard to pinpoint about what, but I had caught him giving Viper some lingering, cold looks in the hospital room.

"Yeh. We're good." He dried his hands off. "You want me to get them? Food'll be here soon."

"Sure." That was Arsenal. My mouth had suddenly gone dry. My eyes flickered to the corner around which Viper and Ice were sleeping. I could see the warm light of the fairy lights spilling out.

He was just in there.

I didn't know why that made me nervous. I'd seen him. Yet, knowing he would come out, awake, and would see me... I tried to tug my handbag closer without being too obvious about it.

I knew Ice had been right about it being my nest. I knew the others had picked up on it. I *was* too obvious about it, because Arsenal's hand dropped to my thigh comfortingly.

Then Malakai was returning, Ice at his side.

"He'll be out in a minute."

Ice was wearing a white button-up with light wash jeans. I'd... Fuck, I'd missed him even just these few days. He grinned as he saw me, crossing over instantly and then I was being pulled into a tight hug. I clutched him, inhaling roses and cookies and traces of mint and mist. I tried to shove away the anxiety.

"I told them you'd come back," Ice whispered in my ear.

Was that what this was?

Me coming back?

Or me saying goodbye?

I didn't know why that thought went through my head. But I'd told Arsenal we could try. It held no guarantee.

"You alright?" Arsenal asked, clapping Ice on the shoulder when he released me. He darted Ice a look out of the corner of his eye and I noticed the slight hunch in his demeanour, as if he were just as anxious as I was.

"Yeh." Ice bit his lip, shrinking a little. "We should, uh… talk later."

Arsenal turned a little more, as if trying to read Ice's expression. "Whatever you need."

I spotted Ice shoot King a look, and King gave him a reassuring nod. That was all I saw, though, because then Viper was stepping into the room.

It was one thing seeing him ashen, on a hospital bed. Quite another to see him well and walking around. My heart rate picked up.

He was… beautiful. He was lean and tall, wearing a simple black t-shirt and matching joggers. I'd stared at him for so long at the hospital, but it was different now he was awake and out of a hospital gown. He had golden earrings along his ears just like Ice, and black gauges in his lobes, and there were scattered tattoos along his arms trailing to his knuckles. He had olive skin, dark brows, sharp cheekbones, and full lips. He was everything.

My whole world once upon a time.

I felt that, even if I didn't know how or why. His eyes found mine. Bright and yellow and nervous, just like me.

There was a long pause in which we stared at one another, and he palmed the back of his neck. No one said anything.

Then Arsenal's chair scraped and he got to his feet. Viper glanced at him, seeming to come to himself, taking a few steps forward as Arsenal drew up before him.

"Hey, uh…" He held his hand out awkwardly, nerves written all over his face. There was a long second in which Arsenal glanced down at his hand. And then without warning, he drew Viper into a hug.

Viper froze.

"Thank you." Arsenal's voice was low and gruff and I barely heard it.

Slowly, Viper's arms came around Arsenal's back in a movement more tender than I had expected.

When Arsenal let him go, Viper ran his fingers through his buzzed black hair, a little less nervousness showing on his face as he looked around at us as if he hadn't expected that.

"How much uh…" His smile was odd. "How much did my dad pay you to do that?"

Arsenal was already sliding back into his chair at my side. "I told him it wasn't necessary."

That caught me off guard. Viper snorted a laugh, as if he'd only half expected it to be true after all. Then there was a knock at the door.

"Food," Viper croaked. "I'll… get it."

He hurried to the door and then returned with armfuls of white bags that smelled amazing.

"Kirriman's Noodle House? Never seen it in our delivery range," Malakai noted as he helped us lay it all out. King was handing us all plates. By the time they were done, the island was sprawling with Chinese. There were boxes of rice, noodles, a massive array of meats and veggies, and a huge bowl of prawn crackers.

"Best food in New Oxford."

"There's one on the Westside, isn't there?" I asked.

"That's the only one," Viper said.

"Then how—?"

"I paid one of my dad's chauffeurs. He gets real pissed when I do that."

Ice snorted.

I opted to watch as the others began to chat, still working hard not to end up staring at Viper too much. He relaxed as the meal went on. He was clearly comfortable with Ice, but jumped into conversations with King and Malakai with no problem either.

It was good. He fit in here. That's what they deserved.

But occasionally, I would catch him shoot a guilty glance at me and our eyes would meet and my heart would suddenly leap to my throat.

I... loved him.

That's what this was, I realised. I loved him more than words could describe.

I didn't remember him, but I loved him.

Yet, looking at him was making something ancient in me ache, and I had to fight the tears burning my eyes and duck my head so no one would see.

I thought maybe Arsenal did, because of the occasional touch on my leg.

"Where should I sleep tonight?" I asked him under my breath when Ice and Viper were in the middle of a conversation about where Ice should give him another piercing.

I needed an escape route.

"It's up to you, Duchess."

"You could, with me. If you wanted to?" That was King. I glance to him to see that warm light in his emerald eyes. "I missed you."

I bit my lip. What had happened between us the last time I'd been in that room... Thinking about that threatened more tears.

But I wanted it. I wanted his warmth and comfort, because I didn't know if I would be able to stay with this pack after all.

I nodded, making myself smile. "Okay."

I didn't leave, but it made me feel better to know where I could go if it became too much.

"Viper, how long you been riding?" Arsenal asked, setting his fork down.

"Riding?" Viper asked, chopsticks full of noodles halfway to his mouth.

"The bike." Arsenal nodded toward the garage.

"Oh... I don't... I just—"

"Scouting us," King cut in.

"Where did you find a broken Hound?" Arsenal looked a little taken aback. "Those are rare. People take care of them."

I swear Viper's face paled, and his eyes darted to Malakai briefly. "Yeh..." He cleared his throat. "Just bad luck, I guess."

Arsenal frowned. "What you planning on doing with it when I get it fixed?"

"Hadn't really thought about it."

"I could teach you to ride?" Arsenal asked, his voice uncharacteristically hopeful. I peered up at him. This was the other side to him I didn't see as often, but I realised it had always been there. The Arsenal that took care of the others. And he didn't just want to keep them safe, he wanted more.

Viper stared at him for a long moment. Out of the corner of my eye I saw King and Malakai exchange a look. There was a faint smile on Malakai's face.

"I'd uh... really like that." Viper's voice was faint.

Arsenal grinned, leaning back in his chair having missed everything I'd just spotted. "Excellent. These babies won't get on one."

There was a bit more chatter, mostly about inconsequential stuff. I ate slowly, and not because it wasn't good, but because it felt like there was a pit in my stomach.

Sitting here with them all, I realised it was all perfect. A rumble of a purr almost began in my chest.

My mates.

King and Viper getting on, even Mal with a warmth in his eyes as he looked at Ice's smile. And Arsenal was watching the others with relief in his eyes.

It was all perfect but for one thing... Something deep within me, buried and whispering of darkness, trembled.

As the seconds ticked by, dread began to seep up my throat.

Something was wrong.

"Ice said you were doing something important in few days. What's up with that?" Viper's question drew me up as, at my side Arsenal shifted uncomfortably.

"Our last check in at the Institute."

Viper nodded. "Cool."

"But uh, we're also doing a job for someone," King added.

"King." Arsenal's voice was warning.

"What?" King asked. "He's pack. He should know."

Viper narrowed his eyes, looking around. "What?"

"Yeah. I'm not..." Ice swallowed, but cut off as he caught Arsenal's tense expression.

"Fuck me," Arsenal sighed, working his jaw, eyes lingering on Malakai as if debating. Then he sighed. "We're in the process of registering Ice."

"Wait. Not registered?" Viper asked, clearly shocked.

"That place you both just got caught up in, the Institute knows about it. They hand omegas over to them. Why do you think he might not want to go through the process?" Malakai asked. "He won't get past the first step before they come for him."

"Shit." Viper considered that. "What if I could get it done, but no red tape, no process. Just... he's registered and done."

"What do you think we're trying to do?" Arsenal asked.

"No... No, wait. I can..." Viper was fumbling for his phone. "Look. I can sort it. Just give me a minute."

Arsenal opened his mouth, but Viper was already dialling.

I heard a male voice on the other end of the phone. "It's late."

"I'm doing great, Dad, thanks for asking."

I stifled a smile at that, hit with something nostalgic: Viper and that attitude he kept up with his dad. They didn't always like each other, but I'd always known his dad cared, even if he didn't know how to show it.

I drew up at that thought, scrambling for the memories that had to come with it, but the moment I tried it all vanished.

There was a sigh on the phone. "What do you want?"

I forced myself to keep listening.

"Yeh. Bit of a situation. Trying to register with the new pack. You know, so you can sleep easy and all. But I have a *bit* of a problem."

"What?"

"Ice isn't registered. I don't want to finish the process without him."

"Your omega isn't *registered*?" He sounded affronted.

"Nope. Can't start the application—He'll get in trouble, caught up in some shady—"

"It won't do." I heard a sigh on the other end. "Could I just have him put in the system?"

"Uh..." Viper grinned, nodding around the table as he pretended to think about that. "Could you do that? He's worried about his address—"

"Paul Peterson owes me a favour. Send me the details. I don't care if the address is fake. He'll be in the system by tomorrow."

"Alright. Great. Thanks."

"How are you doing—?" his dad began, but Viper cut the call off before the question was answered and tossed the phone down. "There. Easy."

The table was silent for a long moment. Arsenal stared, and the tattooed muscles on his neck were strained. He glanced to King and Malakai. Even my lips had parted slightly.

Ice looked dumbstruck. "That's it?" His voice was weak.

Viper waved a hand, digging his chopsticks back into his noodles. "He's got more connections and favours than he knows what to do with."

"Shit." King muttered. "Well… What the fuck are we going to do about Riot, now?"

"Tell him the deal's off?" Malakai asked.

"It's Riot," King said.

"Riot?" Viper asked, voice a little high. "Like you had a job with *The* Riot?"

Arsenal blew out a breath, still looking a little stunned, his eyes on Viper.

"Fuck," Viper muttered. "Isn't the GPRE hunting him?"

"Sure fucking is, but we won't be taking the risk of calling on him," Malakai said.

"And now…?" Viper asked.

Arsenal answered. "I'm not putting our pack at risk for him if I don't need what he's offering."

"So, what are you going to do?"

Arsenal sighed, rubbing his face. "I don't know. We got a day before our check in. I'll deal with it."

Finally, when the chatter had died down and the plates were finished, I felt I could finally get up and leave without it looking too awkward.

VIPER

Onyx left.

The whole world was in orbit around her. I'd forgotten that feeling. I'd forgotten what it was like to be held in place by those sapphire eyes.

Except when she looked at me, it was with sorrow, not the warmth I remembered from before.

I couldn't move, staring at the place where she'd turned the corner into King's room.

I hurt her.

It all came crashing back in.

I hurt her. I followed her here, bonded the pack she was destined for, and made her an outsider. Ice's touch was on my arm: soothing and caring, and I managed to drag my gaze to his golden eyes.

The table was silent, I realised. My side of the bond was wide open and leeching turmoil like poison. I tried to slam it closed, but it was hard. As was any control I had over my aura. I was healing, I could feel that, but until then I was vulnerable.

They were all doing their best not to make me feel uncomfortable about that, and I appreciated that. Sleeping was the only time I could close it down. At least... I hoped I closed it down.

But now, here I was, sitting with her pack while she was alone.

I was on my feet before I caught myself, striding toward the room.

She'd taken a seat on the bed, handbag at her side, wrapped in that fluffy cream nightgown she'd always loved. It was never far; the only fixture in her life that was still hers. It broke me every time I saw it.

She deserved so much more.

Her eyes lifted to mine as I stepped around the corner, and I watched as she tried to straighten the shattered expression on her face.

"Can we talk?"

She gazed at me for too long, then nodded.

I took a seat at her other side, all my nerves on edge.

"I never wanted to take this pack away from you."

"I am the reason Ice was in danger," she whispered. "You saved him. You deserve this—"

"No."

She didn't know what she deserved. The world, with the moon and the stars on top, and I would have given it all to her.

We would have given it all to her. She saw the agony in my eyes.

"I don't remember you, Viper."

It was both terrible and a cold wash of relief.

"Nothing?" I asked.

She shook her head, yet it gave me a strange spark of hope. She could look me in the eye and she wasn't shattering. She didn't remember. Could she heal like I was beginning to?

"What... if we start over?" I asked.

She stared at me, and then she reached up, her palm pressing against my cheek. Everything in the universe melted away as she offered me that touch. The touch I hadn't had for years. The one I had dreamed of every day.

I saw a flash of something in her eyes. Hope and sorrow all at once, as if she wanted what I was offering, but didn't know if she could have it.

"You didn't heal when I was here," she whispered.

"Not because..." I swallowed a lump in my throat as I leaned into her touch. The nightmares had been horrible. "Not because you hurt me, Onyx. It's because I was afraid... I was afraid of what I might do to you."

Guilt slammed into me again.

But she was still here. Still strong.

Her brows furrowed as if she was trying to process that.

"You cannot hurt me, Onyx. I swear it," I whispered. "And they want you, too. I can feel it through the bond."

She dropped her hand, staring down at her fingers.

"Do you want them?" I asked.

"I don't want to take anything away from their happiness," she said brokenly.

"You won't. You can't." Never. I moved, kneeling on the floor before her and taking her hand in one of mine. I reached up, cupping her cheek. "Let me try," I whispered. "You gave me your heart once, Onyx. Let me try for it again."

"You... were my scent match before?" she asked.

I nodded, but something tightened in my chest. Could I tell her? But this part, it had nothing to do with the memories that might hurt her. "I loved you before we ever matched. Finding out you were my mate was the best day of my life."

My chest tightened further.

She swallowed, tooth pinching her bottom lip. "I don't remember any of it. There are gaps, even before. Do you know...?" She lifted her arm and I saw the tattoo and the scar across it.

I shut my eyes.

"Why are you lying to me, Viper?"

I heard the sound of my own blood dripping on linoleum. Each beep of the machine pounded against my skull. "HELP!"

"It's not your fault you don't remember," I told her, forcing the flash away. Her mind wiped me from every waking memory.

Protection, the doctor had said, and just like that, we were gone.

All of us.

Vik. Jake. Hart.

She opened her mouth like she was going to ask, but closed it, something wary flashing in her eyes. "I want to try," she whispered.

I knew there was a smile creeping onto my lips. "I—" I cut off.

I love you.

Not yet.

"Okay."

"Tomorrow?" she asked.

I nodded, the tightness in my chest finally loosening as I stood, fingers lingering on her cheek as I did. "Goodnight, Onyx."

FORTY-ONE

ICE

Onyx was going to talk to Viper. He was okay for a while, and that meant I needed to deal with the shit I'd been running from.

I crossed the room, unable to meet King's eyes as I passed him at the dining table. I knocked on the wall beside Arsenal's room. He'd left not long after Onyx, though there was more fatigue through the bond than anything else.

"Yeh," he grunted.

I stepped around the corner tentatively, heart hammering in my chest. Arsenal was propped up in his bed, tea in hand, looking distant. He focused as he saw me, though, brows furrowing.

"Not your usual mug?" I said, glancing at the brown mug in his hand.

I kept track of the mugs in the house. Arsenal's current favourite was a cherry red one.

I then realised how absolutely stupid that opening line was. He was looking at me like I was mad.

"Yeh, I uh… don't know where it went."

I nodded, glancing around the empty room.

For a moment, I flashed back to the last time I was here, when Arsenal's face contorted with rage as he tried to lunge at me.

I wasn't wanted.

I never had been.

I almost ran, but closing my eyes, I tried to ground myself. I'd felt him through the bond. I'd felt who he was, truly, when he'd found me.

Slowly I stepped into the room. "Can we talk?"

He nodded, a frown creasing his expression, as if he wasn't sure what to make of me. He shuffled to the edge of the bed, planting his feet on the floor and setting down the tea. I crossed toward him and sat at his side before I could change my mind. But then I couldn't look up and meet his eyes.

Guilt twisted me up.

Onyx had barely pulled him from the rut when I'd gone. I could feel it now, the jittering instability of his aura, as if it hadn't quite settled.

I'd done that.

I was the reason his aura was always so unstable.

Then I'd left and got myself caught by Nash—putting them all in danger. Onyx included. I opened my mouth to speak, but the words were stuck. Completely and totally stuck. Where could I start? Years of neglecting them.

"I'm..." I swallowed. The word wasn't enough. It wasn't even close to enough. "I'm—"

"Don't," Arsenal rasped. "I don't want an apology from you."

"But I—"

"I wasn't angry at you," Arsenal said quietly. "The other day..."

I glanced over at him, and saw he looked about as unsure as I felt.

"When... When I was in the rut and I saw you. I didn't... It wasn't what it sounded like. I didn't want you gone because I was angry at you. I was never angry at you."

"You should be."

He shook his head. "Seeing you is seeing how much I've fucked up."

"You didn't—"

"We failed you, Ice. We bonded you. We took everything, and then we couldn't give anything back."

"No." He didn't understand.

I'd been angry about that at the start when I didn't realise. When I didn't realise how terrifying the world would be.

Sometimes, before I slept, I would dream of the life I would have if they hadn't bonded me. It would start wild and wonderful and free. Only, that was never enough. I would dream of a family, but I could never conjure faces. A pack? A wife? A child?

Nothing would come because I was too broken for that.

And I would never have survived.

Dark bonded.

Caught.

Sold.

Alone.

And it wasn't until today that I realised the truth. The sick, twisted truth I'd been running from. What I'd been dreaming of, they were right here in front of me. The same people I'd been cursing for stealing it away.

I had a family, and they loved me. They loved me more than I could ever have dreamed anyone could love me.

It's why I'd been afraid to leave that nest with Viper.

Now, I had to face the truth. That I had everything I dreamed of, and I'd been slowly poisoning it since the moment I'd found it.

Arsenal, sitting at my side right now, refusing an apology while his frayed aura hurt him. Malakai, who always wanted me to be a bigger part of his relationship with the others. King, who

I'd pushed away for trying to show me affection, who just wanted to be able to talk to me.

I cracked as it all hit me in that moment. Tears flooded my eyes as I curled in on myself. His arms were around me, and before I knew it, he'd pulled me into a hug, curling up on the bed and holding me as I shook.

"I'm sorry." My voice was thick with tears.

"No."

He didn't understand. "I'm sorry for everything."

Arsenal's embrace became tighter and when he spoke, his voice shook. "Please stop saying that."

"I didn't know... Onyx helped you without..." I'd been so scared that if I went near him while he was in a rut... I squeezed my eyes tight shut.

But I had seen Onyx with him. She'd just been holding him. Nothing else. All this time... Could I have done that? Asked for that? And it would have been safe to do so. To tell them I only wanted them holding me because it was my job as their omega.

Even the broken, twisted up shadow of myself that had been running my life for years, could have justified it. And maybe... Maybe I wouldn't have felt so alone.

Arsenal's voice was rough. "Of course you didn't know."

"S-she knew." Onyx had known what to do. She had brought him out of the rut with so much grace. He hadn't hurt her. If I was better... he wouldn't have suffered all those times—

"And while she was in school, learning how to be an omega, you were fighting to survive."

I could barely breathe. "I *should* have—"

"All we wanted was for you to feel safe with us."

"I don't understand..." I couldn't stop shaking, and my breaths were coming in sharp pants. I'd never been held like this. A week ago, I'd never have considered it. It was too weak, too vulnerable. But the chained up part of me ached as his aura touched mine, offering something I had always been too scared to accept.

He was my alpha.

I squeezed my eyes shut.

The alpha I'd hurt. "Y-you shouldn't want me at all."

Arsenal loosed a low growl and drew my chin up to face him, his hazel eyes holding mine. "I love you, Ice."

I stared at him, breath caught completely for the longest moment. I tried to deny it, but his side of the bond was wide open and utterly irrefutable.

In that moment, I shattered. My grip became vice-like on his arm, my airway closing completely. Before I could descend into a total panic attack, he shifted forward and pressed his lips to mine.

My mind went completely blank, my chest loosening as I reached up on instinct, gripping his face as I held him against me.

"You're ours. We will *never* let anything happen to you again."

ONYX

Start over.

A second chance.

Could Viper do that? Might it be possible?

Viper was gone, but there were butterflies in my tummy. My nerves were alight from his touch.

This was love. I knew it like an old friend. I didn't know its name or face, but I knew it like I knew the tattoo across my forearm.

I got ready for bed and curled up under the blankets until King arrived. He tried to be quiet until I rolled over. Still dazed by this feeling that was loosening my spirit, I couldn't not stare at his chiselled, tan chest.

He got into the bed, leaving a respectable distance, which set me on edge. I shifted closer. I wanted him to hold me.

I felt... different since Viper had left. As if something was freed within me. I'd been here once before, dreaming of more, dreaming of a pack, and letting myself sink into these desires. Like the one I felt right now, that he'd just draw me into his arms and never let me go. I'd pushed those feelings away for so long.

He raised his eyebrows from where he lay, head propped on his palms as he looked at the space between us. "Are you sulking?"

I blinked. "I don't sulk."

He shifted closer and all I could smell was that fine apricot and champagne scent and— "Why does it smell like Mal in here?" I asked, peering around. There was definitely a lingering scent of clove and riverside.

"He kipped here last night. Thought the couch was a little miserable."

"Does he want to tonight?"

King considered me. "Do *you* want him to?"

A little thrill skittered through my veins. "I wouldn't mind."

A smirk appeared on King's mouth as if he saw right through that. Then he grabbed his phone and sent a quick text. "Now. Back to what you were sulking about?"

"I'm not sulking," I muttered, shifting closer.

"Are you sulking because I'm not cuddling you?" he asked.

I worked not to pout, but my instincts were on overdrive. I'd gotten much too used to being in their beds—it had gone to my head. Or my hormones.

"If you let me put my hands on you, Duchess, I'm not going to want to let go."

"That's okay." I said the words before catching myself.

King rolled on his side and tugged me into his arms before I could say another thing.

I was warm, with my back firmly pressed against his chest when Mal walked in. A little purr rumbled to life in my chest as I saw him. Topless, with skin that was rich even in the dim light. Dark hair tied in a bun, with the soothing scent of riverside on a sunny day. They were both much too fucking hot. It wasn't really fair.

"He said you asked for me," Malakai said, dropping down onto the bed.

"I was just being polite."

"Of course." He dug under the covers and lay on his side, facing me and King, a smile curving his lips.

"Does this mean your conversation with Viper went well?" he asked. My purr stuttered out, which made my cheeks heat. I felt King tense around me as if worried.

"We're..." I swallowed. "We're going to try and make it work."

"Good," King breathed, his breath tickling my neck as he held me closer.

Malakai reached out, curving his fingers beneath my chin, his thumb brushing my cheek. "We're going to fix this, Duchess. You belong with us."

I shut my eyes for a moment. When I opened them, he was still there, still reaching out and touching me.

Skin pale as death with jet black hair, his full lips were curved in a smile with the cutest dimples. Ocean blue eyes like mine were crinkled in crescents as he looked at me like he never wanted to look away. His scent tangled in the air.

Sugar and spice.

I blinked again and Malakai's dark eyes held mine. The sweet scent gone, replaced with riverside and clove.

That was... I stared, my heart rate elevating for just a moment before settling back down, before I sank further against King and reached up, taking Malakai's hand in mine.

This was right. He was mine.

My purr rose again as I shut my eyes again and drifted off between them both.

FORTY-TWO

ICE

The Oxford house was massive.

It was the next day, and Malakai and I were following up on our plan to visit Viper's dad. We were at a mansion in the middle of the city, yet the perimeters of the property were acres wide, which meant it must have cost a fortune.

Then again, he was an Oxford, so it's possible the family owned the house long before the cityscape grew the way it did.

We pulled up in our beaten up jeep at the front of a set of tall gates.

There was a little drive up button thing, and Malakai drove near it to hit the comms.

A voice appeared on the radio. "Who is this?"

"Um…" Malakai cleared his throat. "We're here to see Kenneth Oxford."

"Do you have an appointment?"

"Appointment?"

I snorted. It was 5pm, and this was supposed to be his home.

"I'm sorry sir, but you can't see the family without—"

"We're from the St. James pack. Viper's pack. Tell him that."

There was a long pause, a buzz, then it cut off.

Viper was sick. Pressing him on it would just make him worse. And we needed Onyx to feel safe.

This was it. We had to get information. Onyx had fallen asleep in King and Malakai's arms. I had fallen asleep in Arsenal's. I hadn't planned it, but Viper had been left alone.

I couldn't miss how wounded he felt in the morning, still unable to close off the bond—and then feeling guilty about that, too. He'd put on a cheery smile and ordered us all breakfast in so we didn't have to cook.

We needed to fix it. No one needed to be left out.

For a moment I daydreamed of a pack bed where I could keep them all in one place and no one felt left out. And then I could cuddle Onyx too. All night.

I blinked, taken aback. I didn't have basic bitch omega dreams like that—

The intercom buzzed to life again, cutting off my thoughts. "Mr. Oxford will see you. Please drive up to the visitor's parking."

We entered the vast property, and I stared at the stupidly clean cut lawns with little pathways and benches. What the fuck was this? I didn't believe anyone wanted a nice garden stroll when they could hear the city of New Oxford blaring around them.

We pulled into what was our best guess of 'visitor's parking' and hopped out of the car. I noticed Malakai positioned himself just a little ahead of me as we walked up the drive.

We were met by two towering doors with large knockers that Malakai banged a few times. There was a long pause.

I was surprised, given the rest of the place, that it was Kenneth Oxford himself who opened the doors. A maid or a butler would have been more fitting, but perhaps the mention of his son's pack was enough to draw him out in person.

"What are you here for?" he asked coldly. He had a neat strap of a beard, his attire was rich-man-casual—as in golf shirt instead of suit—but despite all of that, he did remind me of Viper. He was tall and slender, and his eyes were bright yellow.

He smelled like licorice and rum. Why did older alphas always smell like some sort of alcohol?

"We need information about O—Viper's old pack," Malakai said.

Kenneth's eyes flicked from Malakai to me. "Is there any reason you can't ask him yourself?"

"He's not well enough, yet."

"And you're in such a hurry, because...?"

"Our pack is being threatened," Malakai said.

He considered us for a long moment. "Her stalker."

"You know?"

"I make an effort to stay current with my son's business. He does tend to cause trouble if I don't."

I opened my mouth, but Kenneth Oxford held up his hand. "Before you ask, no, I don't know who is harassing Onyx Madison." He said her name like it was poison on his tongue, and I heard the faintest rumble of a growl from Malakai.

Kenneth sighed. "I *have* tried to find out."

My brow furrowed. Kenneth Oxford was one of the richest people in New Oxford. I'd be willing to bet he was one of the richest men in the country. He'd looked into Onyx's stalker and found nothing?

"We just want to—"

"I am aware of what you are here for." But his eyes were weary all of a sudden. He sighed. "Come in. But I warn you, you might not like the answers I have."

ONYX

The rain tumbled down around the wooden gazebo, landing on the tiles and shattering into a million glittering flecks. Viper handed me a mug of hot cocoa as he sat on one of the metal chairs at my side.

This was it. Our time to try and figure out a middle ground.

"You're... okay?" he asked.

"I'm..." I considered that, swept away by the piercing yellow of his eyes. "I don't know. Where do we start?"

"Right out here. The rain was always our thing."

I smiled, something about that feeling right. "Why are you so afraid?" I asked.

"Because there is nothing worse in this world than seeing you hurt."

I held the warm mug close. "Whatever it is, I'll have to face it some day."

"I hope you're wrong," he whispered.

I smiled faintly at that, getting to my feet. His scent, mint and mist, drew me to the rain. It made me want to step out into it and feel it on my skin.

I set my mug on my chair, stepping out into the rain before looking back at him. His brow was pinched as he watched me, but his scent changed. Shifting to something wanting.

He followed, his hand tangling in mine. "I don't know the right way to do this, Onyx. If I fuck this up, I could hurt you again."

"If you don't try, you hurt me, too," I replied.

How silent my life would be, returning home after getting a taste of what it might be like to love. Going on dates with packs of alphas who didn't value me for anything but my looks. Spending my evenings alone, afraid...

Viper looked pained, glancing away and out over the city. "I know." Mint and mist tangled with rain, rising in the air around us and I took his hand without thought.

"We danced," he blurted. "Like this. In the rain. We did it all the time."

"Show me."

ARSENAL

Riot was at the door.

I had called him, knowing I had to bite this bullet sooner rather than later. Ice and Mal were out. Onyx was upstairs with Viper. It was just me and King.

I blocked the way as he made to step in. "I'm not welcome?" he asked, a thick, dark brow raised. His dark hood was wet with rain, but his coat was open. Enough that I could see the gun at his belt. I had mine tucked away, too. I'd been carrying it since the moment I'd told him I needed to meet him.

"This won't take long," I said, then steeled myself. "We won't be doing the job."

"You won't?" Riot asked, a crooked grin on his face as he cocked his head, emerald eyes flashing.

My heart smashed into my ribs, my mind spinning the thousand tales I'd heard of him. But he was just a person. Another alpha just like me. "Find another pack. We found another way to get what we want. I can't risk our pack on a job I don't need."

Riot cocked his head. "You're backing out."

People were terrified of him—and for good reason—but acting like I was too wouldn't get me anywhere.

"We have nothing to discuss. I won't do a job for free and I don't need what you're offering."

Riot's eyes were narrowed, and I was afraid, for a moment, of what he would do. Then slowly, he held his hand out, palm up.

Right.

His USB.

I almost released a breath of relief. I dug in the inside pocket of my jacket—the one I'd barely taken off since Riot had come last.

I frowned, rooting around. Could it have slipped through a hole? But my fingers closed around something. Something that didn't feel right at all. I tugged it out and stared at the brittle thing.

My blood turned to ice.

In my palm was a single dead forget-me-not.

FORTY-THREE

VIPER

My hands gently touched Onyx's waist, drawing her closer. She reached up, as if on instinct, wrapping her arms around my neck. Cool rain trickled down my face and neck and into my clothes as we swayed.

"You remembered me?" she asked. "All this time?"

"Always," I whispered. I reached up, brushing her cheek with my knuckle. For a moment her eyes closed and she leaned into my touch.

We remained like that, taking slow steps in the rain until she bumped into the railing of the roof. I glanced out, eyes finding the Gritch District in the dark and rain, gaze sliding down to the street beyond, and then to the gravel and doorstep below us.

There was not another soul in sight.

Just me and her in the rain, like in my dreams.

She reached up, her hands cupping my cheeks, her eyes holding mine. Her hair was damp with rain, her sapphire eyes everything I'd ever remembered. There was the smallest hesitation, and then she seized me, drawing me closer in a kiss like I'd never felt before.

A warning sounded in my head.

Danger.

I woke in the hospital, knowing there was something wrong. There was nothing else in the world but her. Nothing left for me to live for.

And she was in pain. I didn't know how I knew.

Blood dripped down my fingers. I'd ripped out... something from my arm. Machines beeped, each noise pounding against my skull. I staggered toward the room beside mine, needing the wall to hold me up until I saw her.

Then my heart sank.

She was alone and there was a metal nail file gripped in her hand.

"Onyx!" I staggered toward her. She shied away, sharp edge coming closer to her skin.

"Don't!" I froze, hands up, hearing nothing but the horrible beeping and the faint sound of my own dripping blood on the linoleum floors.

"They keep telling me they're gone," she whispered. "Why, Viper?" The shake in her voice split my heart in two. "Tell me they aren't..."

"No... They're..." I tried so hard because she needed it, but the words wouldn't come.

"T-tell m-me..." Her breath caught, a wild look in her eyes. She shook her head. I took another step toward her, slowly.

"You're all lying! Why are you lying to me, Viper?"

"P-please, Onyx. Give it to me."

"I n-need it gone," she sobbed, tears in her eyes as she stared at me. The sharp edge of the file was hovering over the tattoo of a forget-me-not. Each flower was a member of our pack.

"I don't... I c-can't..." She shook her head again. "I need it gone."

I lunged for her, going straight for the nail file. She panicked, dragging it down to her skin. I was a second too late. It tore down her arm just as I seized her wrist.

"HELP!" I shouted, ripping her arm back.

"I don't want it!" she screamed, fighting me with wild eyes. "GET IT OFF ME!"

I was trembling from head to toe while I clutched her writhing body as she tried to claw at her own skin.

"GET IT OFF! GET IT OFF!"

I trembled, sobs tearing from my throat as I held her, staring at the nail file upon the ground, smeared in her blood.

ONYX

It was years of distance and need and grief, closed in one.

My world shuddered, other kisses just like this flickering through my mind. And when he drew away, they were gone.

I was breathless and he looked panicked, eyes darting between mine as if he expected something terrible to happen.

But it didn't.

There was nothing terrible about that kiss.

I smiled, and in that moment it felt like everything clicked into place.

"I'll take the bond," I whispered.

He stared at me, his mouth working for a moment. I traced my thumb along the ridge of his high cheekbones, committing every inch of his face to memory.

I'd forgotten it.

How had I ever forgotten it?

"You will?" His voice was hoarse.

"Yes."

Finally, a smile lit his face, a guilty excitement brightening his features.

"We should go and tell them," I squeezed his hand, dragging him toward the door.

"Mal and Ice are still out."

My grip was on the door handle as I glanced back to him with a smile. "I'm not keeping him waiting. You know he told me he loved me back in the hospital?"

"Who?" Viper asked, startled.

"Jake."

Viper halted as I pushed the door open. I blinked.

My heart smashed against my ribcage.

What just...?

I shook my head, daring a glance back at him. He was staring, all peace gone from his face. His yellow eyes were wide. "Who?" he asked, voice a croak.

I frowned. "King."

I'd said that, hadn't I?

"He... said he loved me the first time he laid eyes on me."

Viper said nothing, still frozen.

But... Why were we waiting?

I tugged my fingers from his grip and went to hug my handbag to my side, only to find it wasn't there. My eyes snapped to it in the room below. On the kitchen counter.

I hurried down the steps toward it, fixated, but when I stepped onto the main floor, I drew up.

There was something wrong. The *air* was wrong.

In it was a scent that wasn't supposed to be.

Then my eyes fell upon the first body in the garage below and my mind shattered into a million pieces.

FORTY-FOUR

ICE

We followed Kenneth Oxford across a grand entryway. I couldn't help staring around. Had Viper grown up here?

How... completely opposite that was to us. It didn't upset me, but it made me curious. How different was he from the rest of the pack? We needed different.

Kenneth ushered us into an office and I took a seat as he slid behind a desk, leaning on his elbows and arching his fingers.

"What has Viper said?" he asked.

"Barely anything," Malakai said. "He's still healing. It's difficult for him to speak about it. But we know his pack were Onyx's mates.

"She wasn't a good suitor for my son," Kenneth said quietly. "She's a good woman. I've kept tabs on her over the years. She gives—and not just where it's easy like many wealthy young people. I did not warn my son away from her lightly."

"What?" I asked, shocked. "How is she not a good suitor?"

"Well, her... condition, of course. It might have been alright—"

"Condition?" Malakai's voice was low, and his riverside and clove scent went bitter in the air.

"What?" I asked.

"She can't bear children," Kenneth said, much too mildly.

Wait.

What?

Kenneth Oxford continued on, but I barely heard him, mind reeling. "I had her records all unsealed when the match happened, of course. And like I said, it might have been fine, but then I was a fool and I told my son he wasn't to offer her anything but a normal bond. So, of course, what did he do?"

"She was his match," Malakai said, shocked. "If he wanted her to have the princess bond, it was his right."

Kenneth sighed. "Yes. I should have had the foresight to realise he would absolutely claim that right simply because I forbade it."

It took me a second to catch up.

Princess bonds could only be offered to mates, and—like dark bonds—packs with princess bonded omegas could never have another. If Viper had offered Onyx a princess bond, it would have been reasonable to assume they would never look for another omega.

To Kenneth Oxford, a princess bond meant... "You were worried about lineage?" I asked, disgusted.

"Of course I was. I thought, at first, that was all there was to it, but even after everything, he was still in love with her. It took too much to keep him away from her."

"Keep him away from her?"

Kenneth sighed. "If he hasn't told you yet, it's only a matter of time. My son and I don't get along—we never have, but I do love him. His circumstances, over the last few years, have worsened. I have been pushed to further extremes in order to try to keep him well."

"You tried to force him into another pack?" Malakai asked. I knew about that. My stomach turned. Malakai had sent me the article to read on the way here.

Last month Viper had been bought a place in a pack. Because dark bonding gold pack omegas was legal, packs could be formed around them. Before he bit in, however, the pack had fallen apart almost before it had begun, and the Oxford mansion had burned down. I suspected Viper had something to do with it.

"I did." Kenneth didn't even blink. "And I lost a rather invaluable family property for my trouble."

"You tried to make him dark bond a gold pack omega," I said quietly. "Though that wouldn't bode well for grandchildren, either, would it?"

Gold packs like me weren't allowed to have kids. Our children would be born rogue, outside of the Institute's laws that kept society safe.

Kenneth sighed, gaze lingering on my eyes for a long moment. "I am beyond the grandchild concern at this point. Viper is—was sick. He was not capable of going through the process of a traditional pack formation again. It was my belief that biting into a pack—like he has yours—was the best option. A dark bond requires little attachment. I believed it would not seem a replacement of his old pack and the bond he lost."

Malakai leaned back in his seat, wrinkling his nose in disgust. "Because Onyx wasn't gold pack?"

"Because he offered Onyx a princess bond," Kenneth corrected. "The dark bond is as different an experience as he could find within a pack."

"Why did you think he would do it?" I asked.

"Because I told him that if he didn't sort himself out and move on from Onyx, then I would instead drive her away. I didn't wish to, but it's not beneath me. Viper knows she loves this city. I thought he would give in. I underestimated, however, that noble streak of his."

"Noble streak?"

"Something you should know about Viper; he cannot watch injustice," Kenneth said.

I knew that already from what he'd done when Nash had taken me...

"So," Kenneth continued. "Fully aware he was on his last chance, he blew it up in an attempt to save her."

"Her?"

"Havoc Saint," Kenneth said mildly. "The gold pack omega he was destined to dark bond."

Still, it sent a shiver down my spine to hear him talk about it so casually.

"So, did you go after Onyx?" Malakai asked.

"I never had to. He agreed, afterward, to get on the plane to England. Only then, he ended up in your pack. Not the outcome I expected, but I *am* relieved. He has a chance to heal. And he *perhaps* won't resent me forever. Though," he chuckled. "I don't hold out much hope."

I stared at him.

"But, you're here—I assume—about Onyx?"

"Her stalker is after our pack," I said.

"I'm afraid I might not offer you much there."

"We just want to know what happened. Viper can't talk about it."

Kenneth nodded. "What happened to Onyx was—possibly—worse than what happened to my son."

"How?"

"After he lost his pack, my son could have closed off his bonds at anytime—chosen silver status and committed to no future pack bonds. He could have chosen another pack. But for Onyx... it was worse. Princess bonds are artificial, you understand, just like dark bonds. Unlike normal bonds—" His gaze dropped to the bite on my neck. "—They are unnatural. They don't have the backing of centuries of evolution. When the bond my son offered was ripped from Onyx, it was still open. She had never accepted or declined it. She was driven to madness, left in limbo until the moment her memories fled her."

ONYX

Wooden floorboards, once comforting in their noise, creaked ominously.

This was our cottage. The place my mates were building for our future.

My heart was thundering in my ribcage, every hair on my body standing on end. My mates' scent hung in the air; the entire pack saturated the house just as it should be, except... It was wrong.

Sour, somehow.

Burned sugar, soured grapes, and ocean breeze marred by pollution. I blinked, recoiling slightly, unsure why it was all so wrong.

Viper was ahead of me in a moment, his aura still heavy in the air around us. His eyes darted from room to room, alert for danger when he drew up, his eyes fixed on a spot beyond what I could see.

He didn't move, everything down to his expression frozen in place. I'd never felt a chill like I did seeing his rigid, ashen expression.

Then I saw them.

My heart stopped. For a fleeting moment, I was swept away by dread.

Then it drained away, and a smile tugged on the corners of my mouth. They were all here. My pack; all sleeping.

Hart was curled up on the far couch, the one with all of the patches he'd refused to throw out because it had been his grandma's favourite. I'd been texted pictures of every inch of this room. Jake and Vik were curled up on the other couch, holding one another as they rested.

It was so peaceful in here, and for a moment the only sound was the pitter patter of rain on the roof above.

I smiled.

All the prestigious pack offers in the world couldn't compare to this.

Home.

VIPER

The first body I saw was King's.

He'd fallen to the floor just beside the kitchen. Arsenal was slumped on the couch. Onyx was knelt beside King's body, fingers clutching his shirt, her body trembling.

No... I'd seen this before.

Terror struck my heart, drawing everything else as I braced for the agony that should be here. But... my bonds were intact.

I was halfway down the steps toward her when I saw movement. An alpha was resting against the kitchen wall, watching me. He was huge, wearing a trench coat and black boots.

"Onyx!" I reached for my aura and hit a wall. It wasn't well enough yet, my wounds were too recent.

She didn't look up at me.

I had to get her out. I took the stairs by twos to get to her, but the alpha never moved. Still, he watched me. Unhurried.

I reached her, grabbing her shoulder, not looking away from the man who fixed me with piercing emerald eyes.

She fought my grip, tearing away to clutch King.

That was when I noticed what was wrong. There was a strange, bitter scent in the air.

"Onyx! We have to go. It's not safe."

FORTY-FIVE

ONYX

"Onyx! We have to go. It's not safe."

I didn't turn back to Viper. I didn't take my eyes off my mates. Not once.

Unsafe? This was the place our pack was going to make a home.

I crossed the room to sit beside Hart, running my fingers through his pitch black hair.

"Onyx..." That was Viper behind me.

"I just got in," I whispered. "I'm not leaving. You..." I trailed off. "You offered me the bond. I said I'd take it when we got back."

I looked back to Hart, then over at Jake and Vik. Vik was curled up in Jake's arms. They were both resting peacefully. Their scents were better now. So was Hart's, his sugar and spice scent was perfect. I don't know what I'd been thinking when I thought it was off. I glanced back to Viper. "I want to take it now."

The bond. Where was it?

I frowned.

I didn't understand. It couldn't be taken back.

Viper hadn't moved. His eyes were fixed on me now.

"Hart? Hart baby, wake up." I crouched before the couch, running my palm along his snow white cheek. "I'm back. Graduation is all done." I took his shoulder and shook it.

He didn't move.

"You can show me my room." I smiled, hot tears now tumbling down my cheeks.

Why?

Why was I crying?

My grip fumbled, my fingers trembling, but I didn't know why. He was the builder—the mastermind behind this house. Our perfect cottage in the middle of the woods. He promised me the best room. He'd been stocking up on everything I loved for nesting too, but he'd never shown me a single picture. "I can't wait to see it." I stroked his cheek gently. He was pale. More pale than usual.

Was it too cold in here? I should get him a blanket.

"They're... gone." Viper's voice was the lowest whisper.

His aura still shivered in the air, much too unstable. Mint and mist drowned the room. It was smothering their scents. He shouldn't do that. If he got rid of them, they'd never—

I shook my head, brows pinching as I turned back to him.

"They're right here." Something hot was on my cheek. I lifted my hand and wiped away another tear. I stared at it, unsure, before looking back at Viper. "We just have to wake them up to tell them."

"It's not safe," Viper said again. "We have to go."

ICE

Kenneth Oxford clasped his fingers, leaning back on his desk.

"There was no expert in the city that could predict what would happen to Onyx if she got her memories back. Viper did the only thing he could. He had her transferred to another hospital. I saw to it her records were wiped completely. There was no trace of what had happened to her. No pack. No bond. Nothing. It wasn't hard to hide the pack. Viper had known I would disapprove of the alphas he'd chosen. The bonds were formed quietly."

"Onyx then, how is she a duchess—she never rejected them?" I asked.

"Viper offered Onyx the princess bond within minutes of his pack's death. It was open and alive when they passed. A rather unlikely phenomenon, but her aura became the same as an omega who rejected her pack. I didn't interfere. I tried to ensure she did well, in hopes that he might move on. I used my connections so her job went as well as it could, and even jumped her on the list for the omega apartments on the Westside that she lives in now. It never mattered, Viper wouldn't let her go. I'm not proud of the methods I've used to try and push him onwards, but he's been in stasis for years."

"You said his old pack all died, but this stalker has shown signs that they had a previous link to her," Malakai said. "Did any survive other than Viper?" It was possible that, if enough members of the pack died, that the rest of the bonds still dissolved along with them.

"We asked him, but he didn't seem—" I began.

"They're dead." Kenneth Oxford's voice was firm. "Viper has had a million visions of that day. Conspiracies, wishes, bloody deaths, and plots that they were murdered for her; that I poisoned them. But the one he had the hardest time accepting was Hart."

"Why?"

"They were inseparable from the moment they met, as close as brothers. I might have had my opinions on the other two, but I always knew Hart and Viper would be pack brothers. His visions where Hart is not on that couch is a result of his unprocessed grief. Grief, I hope he can begin processing now."

"So... what happened?" I asked.

Kenneth gave me a strange look.

"What killed them?" I asked again.

He arched his fingers. "Something much more impossible for either of them to process than if it had been a shooting, or a poisoning, a murder, or a fight. It was preventable, invisible, simple, and utterly incomprehensible." He took a breath, pain on his expression as he spoke next. "It was a carbon monoxide leak."

"A... gas leak killed his pack?" Malakai asked, clearly shaken.

"The house was old, the rooms enclosed. His pack became tired, closed their eyes to sleep and... never woke up. They were never frightened, never suffered or even worried. The deadliest kind of poison for a pack, because by the time Viper knew anything was wrong through the bond, he was too late."

VIPER

In the garage of my new pack—my new family—I crashed to my knees, grabbing Onyx. She turned on me, her eyes glassy and unseeing.

This had happened before.

I had been here before.

I shoved back the memories that threatened. I had to keep reminding myself of the truth: my bond was still intact.

They were alive.

The alpha ahead of me still watched on with emerald eyes, not a care in the world as I tried to grab her. The world was spinning. My vision was blurry.

There was something on the kitchen table, next to takeout boxes from last night's Chinese... A device... There was the faintest trail of smoke coming from it.

"Enough to knock out even the cockiest alpha," the man's voice was low. He was striding toward me, almost casually. I blinked, trying to keep my vision steady.

But... *he* was an alpha too...? I knew that. I caught his scent of gunpowder in the air.

"We... have to go..." My words were slurred. Trying to reach for her.

She was in danger.

The alpha reached us as I crashed to my knees.

"Not the omega I was expecting," he murmured. I tried again for my aura, knowing I had to get her out. "...But she'll do."

I choked, the world spinning.

"No..." I made one more desperate attempt to reach my aura.

Pain split my mind and the world went black.

FORTY-SIX

ONYX

The world was flickering.

I was in the cottage.

Vik and Jake and Hart were here, and then...

A firm hand had me by the arm. The room shook, colours filtering into one another.

I was in the garage.

King lay on the floor below me... I sobbed, my breathing coming heavy.

"Not the omega I was expecting..." That voice was... familiar... faintly... "But she'll do."

Someone had me by the arm. They were dragging me up. I couldn't process anything.

The room in the cottage flickered with the garage. I was having trouble breathing.

My... My emerald bag... It was just there...

Something high pitched sounded. There was a bruising pain in my arm.

It was me. *I* was screaming, throwing my whole weight against an alpha. His scent was familiar... burned ebony and gunpowder.

Riot.

Danger.

My teeth bit down on flesh and I heard a curse. But I was halfway there... staggering toward my—

"NO!" My fingers grasped thin air, a weight halting me.

My bag.

I sobbed, fighting again, trying to reach it—my bag. *I needed it.*

It was in my arms just as firm hands seized me again.

My breathing was rapid. But I had it clutched in my grip. I let out a breath of relief, the world coming back into focus just in time to feel his hand closing around my hair.

A huge weight was pinning me against the kitchen counter and hands tried to rip the bag away. I wailed. Nothing in the world made sense but this. Nothing but the handbag clutched in my arms. Then I felt the cold metal against my chin and I froze.

A gun.

His voice was a growl in my ear. "Behave, you crazy fucking omega, and I won't need it."

He tried to tug it away again, but I couldn't loosen my grip on it. A terrified gasp choked out.

Was he going to kill me?

"What's in the bag?" he demanded.

"N-nothing," I choked out.

He scowled. "Put it down."

"I... n-need it."

"Put. It. Down."

Slowly I set it down on the table, but I didn't release it.

"Empty it."

My breathing hitched, trying to process that question.

Empty it?

"Now!"

With trembling fingers I reached in, trying to find something that would hurt least. I drew out my smokes and cigarettes and set them down. Those were okay. They were safe to take out. *What... What could I take out next?* I reached back in, desperately rooting around.

Riot let out an impatient growl. He dug the gun harder into my neck as he shoved my hand away and began grabbing items from within.

I choked out a sob, tears flowing down my face as he ripped out item after item, each tearing away a piece of my soul.

The handmade bracelet I'd made. It... It was for Hart.

A Green Arrows Soccer pack keyring—That was Vik's.

A fountain pen with hand painted edges that Jake had bought me.

Then there was a small figurine I'd taken from Malakai's desk.

Arsenal's favourite cherry mug.

One of the necklaces from King's bedside table.

Devin's earring.

My favourite book, A Court of—

"What the fuck?" Riot snorted.

I couldn't look at him, but with a click, the gun was gone.

"Keep the damn bag," he grunted. "You're coming with me. Try anything, I'll fucking burn it."

KING

I woke first.

"Fuck..." I blinked, trying to remember what had happened.

I sat up on the concrete kitchen floor and the world spun, reality crashing in.

. . .

Riot stepped into our house, a with staggering Arsenal's shirt in his fist and a deadly snarl on his face. The scent of bitter gunpowder followed him in. Arsenal was weak, his eyes falling shut.

"What did you do?" I'd demanded, my aura splitting the air— and not even close to a match with Riot's.

I crossed toward them as he shoved Arsenal onto the couch. I hadn't seen what he clutched in his other fist—the object faintly trailing smoke.

Riot had ignored me, stepping further into our home and peering around. I'd glanced between Arsenal and him, afraid and about to check on my brother when he spoke.

"Here for Ice."

No.

My aura hit the air—at least... I thought it did. The power it usually leant me wasn't there.. The world spun as I tried to follow Riot. My mind sluggishly grabbed for a dozen things.

The guns in the safe... No, Arsenal had one, too.

But my phone... I had to text the others... tell them not to bring Ice home.

And Onyx...

She was on the roof.

Viper was with her...

It was the last thought I had before my knees hit the floor and I passed out.

When I got to unsteady feet, I saw Viper and Arsenal passed out.

I had a moment of icy dread. They would never wake up—just like Sarah hadn't. But... I blinked again, searching my bond. No... they weren't gone.

Just asleep.

I shook them awake, shouting for Onyx, fumbling for my

phone to call Ice and Malakai. Once I had been sure Viper and Arsenal were alive, I searched the whole place for her.

With every room I searched, foreboding clamped an iron grip tighter around my heart.

She was gone.

Not in my room or Arsenal's or Mal's. Not Ice's old nest.

Riot had taken her. A thousand tales of what he did to omegas ripped apart my mind. But... we'd brought her here to *protect* her, not be the reason she was taken.

Finally, I slammed the door open to the roof, only to find it empty.

My mind reeled. She'd be terrified right now.

Because of us.

Again, I dialled Malakai, rushing back down the stairs. None of the others were awake. I *needed* to hear his voice. He would know how to fix this better than I would.

It was as the phone began to ring that I spotted the note on the table. I barely collected myself enough to read it, my fingers trembled so badly.

My blood chilled.

"Bring the USB or Gritch's Tower will take her at sunrise."

ICE

We sat in the jeep for a while in silence.

"He said that if she gets her memories back she might get sick again." Malakai sounded unsure. "Was Viper right? Are we putting her in danger?"

She'd gone mad?

What did that mean?

We'd visited Viper's father in hopes we might get a clue about the stalker, but instead we were further away than ever.

The whole pack was dead.

I'd been holding out on that.

"I want to look at her apartment again," Malakai said. "I've found nothing at ours. But maybe he slipped up."

I wasn't really sure what he thought he was going to find, but I nodded anyway. They'd repaired the locks, and Malakai had asked Onyx if he could keep a key to do exactly this.

Something else nagged at me as we drove down to her apartment block on the Westside. Neither of us spoke, both running through the dump of information we'd just heard.

We found the apartment exactly as it had been left. The bathroom was still in shambles, the rest of the place almost clinically clean.

Now I knew her better, this house sent cracks down my heart. There was nothing cosy or safe or comforting. A few books were stacked by her bed, a few quilts on her couch, but that was about it. No pictures on the wall. It almost looked empty enough to be sold.

I sat down on her bed, staring around at the bedroom.

She'd set up the cameras at her windows and doors. Those were the ones she said had caught nothing at all. Viper's guy had checked the footage to see if it had been looped. He'd got the text last night that there was no sign of any tampering.

Malakai was still rooting around in her bathroom, but something nagged at me. This was a what kind of building had Kenneth Oxford said?

Omega apartments?

I frowned, checking the space again. I'd seen advertisements for shit like that on TV. Usually, one of the selling points was a nest.

Safe.

Secure.

Tucked away.

And what was it Mal had said when we were last here?

"This prick's trying to get in her head. Nest would be the perfect place to target."

I got up, staring around again. It should be near the bedroom... I crossed to the huge walk-in wardrobe, which was still scattered with clothes from our abrupt departure. I rifled around, sweeping hangers away until—*there!*

I froze, staring at the door in the back of the closet, deliberately hidden just like I'd needed the rug above my trapdoor. I knew the need for that safety. I reached forward, turning the handle and opening it to find a small room within.

My phone buzzed, but I ignored it.

Staring around at the space, every hair on my body stood on end. My phone vibrated again, this time longer. A call.

But I couldn't move with what was within.

"ICE!" That was Mal. He sounded urgent.

But I couldn't rip my eyes away, staring at what might once have been a place of safety for Onyx.

I knew. I knew, without a shadow of a doubt. I spun quickly as Mal burst into the closet—eyes wide with fear, phone at his ear—still reeling.

I spoke before he could.

"I know who the stalker is."

FORTY-SEVEN

ONYX

The world was steadying and, as it did, my terror crept in.

Where was I?

Was I going to die?

It was late. The night was obstructed with clouds, the rain still sprinkling down.

The rain...

I'd been in this same rain not long ago... in his arms. Tears still wet my cheeks.

As I managed to focus, I realised we were on a downtown street and there was no one around. It looked abandoned. The buildings were boarded up, and before us was a huge tower.

"Are... they dead?" I whispered at last. That question had been clattering around in my mind since we'd left, but I finally felt strong enough to ask. I squeezed my handbag against my chest. It was the only thing keeping me sane right now. There were cracks in my mind; another time, another reality trying to spill into mine.

I was warring with it, doing everything I could to keep it at bay.

"They'd be useless to me dead, Duchess," Riot murmured, still gripping me as he strode toward an old wooden door in the side of a massive stone tower. I stumbled to keep up, but his words repaired something within me. My breathing came easier, my surroundings became clearer.

He drew out a set of keys, unlocking the door, and then he was dragging me with ease up a spiral staircase that seemed to last forever.

Finally, it ended. Cold air slammed into me as he opened a door and dragged me through. We were at the top of a tower in the Gritch District. The freezing air chilled me to the bones. There were arches around us, open to the night. It was the middle of the night. In between every arch, great mirrors stretched across the stone. They were cracked and tinted with age, all facing the centre of the room.

When I saw what was in the middle, my breath caught. I tried to turn away, but Riot seized me by the hair.

"You are just like the rest of them," he growled as he forced me to face the platform in the centre. I squeezed my eyes tight shut. "Anything so you don't have to see what is right in front of you."

A panicked whimper slipped from my chest.

"Look at it," he growled.

I tried to steady my breathing, forcing my eyes open.

In the middle of the room was a cage, bars stretching to the stone above. Within, upon a platform, was a large stone chair draped with shackles.

An ancient executioner's chair. It was made for alphas and omegas.

"A piece of our history we left behind long ago," Riot said as he dragged me to the cage.

"No!" I threw my weight against his grip. "Don't—"

The door screeched as it opened, and I jumped as it clanged shut, hearing the lock click. Riot let me go, standing in the cage with me.

"W-what are you doing?" I asked, trying to keep my voice steady as I turned to him.

"Sit." It was all he said.

I shook my head, fighting the urge to take a step back. Instead, I forced myself to look up into his glittering emerald eyes. I had to pull myself together. I didn't know what was happening to me, but my pack wasn't dead.

They were alive, and they needed me to survive. "We don't need to do it like this," I whispered.

His eyes were locked on mine, his brow furrowed as he analysed me. I dared reach out, hand brushing his wrist above his gloves. "They're coming. They'll get you what you want."

He didn't say anything, still calculating.

I brushed my thumb along his skin, knowing my scent was giving away my fear, hoping it might work to my advantage.

He leaned closer, cocking his head slightly, his mouth drawn in a line. A purr stuttered to life in my chest. I always hated that it was one of my fear responses—hated how vulnerable it made me look. But right now I prayed it did its evolutionary job.

"You're scared," he murmured.

"Y-yes," I whispered. "B-but no one has to get hurt."

He leaned back, eyes calculating, a smile edging his lips. "There is so much right before your eyes that you cannot see. Isn't that right, Onyx Madison?"

I flinched back, my words deathly quiet. "I don't know what you mean."

"Did they stop using us and killing us?" He leaned closer, his voice a breath. "Or did we just stop looking?"

He was mad, I realised, my heart sinking in my chest as he went on.

"The very system that holds you up isn't there to protect you. It's there to use you."

"And you?" I dared ask. "What is this to you?"

He took a step back, spreading an arm and glancing around at the surrounding arches, a smile on his face. "A fair game." His eyes fell back on me.

"A *game*?" He was insane.

"They can't claim you, but can they save you before the sun rises?"

I stared at him, bile rising in my throat. I couldn't help but glance again around the space; the stone arches around me, the glowing orange lights of the city beyond, and the mirrors all showing worn reflections of me and this mad man in a cage.

Freezing wind chilled me to the bone.

Was this where I would die?

"Let's be civil, Duchess." Riot gestured toward the executioner's chair. "Why don't you *sit?*"

MALAKAI

Something primal rose within me when I saw her with a metal collar around her neck. The beautiful, fierce, protective woman who we'd fallen for, chained like nothing more than an animal. It held her in place, trapping against a chair grand enough it might have been a throne, had I not known its purpose. The storm outside whipped rain through the arches and into the space.

She was my omega, and we had let him take her. It had opened a wound that was still gaping wide, a seething, screeching panic in me like I had only felt when Ice had gone missing.

Riot was waiting for us as we approached the massive iron cage, his elbow propped on the edge of the chair at her back. He watched us as we entered, taking in each of our reactions to what he had done to her. As we approached, he tugged a lighter from his pocket and flicked it on, lighting the cigarette between his teeth.

"Onyx!" King flung himself against the metal bars, loosing a snarl. I understood. Every instinct was alight with the need to reach her, to take her in my arms and keep her safe. There was a tremble to her lips and her hand lifted slightly as if she wanted to reach for me—King. But these bars were made to resist the strength of the strongest alphas.

"We're getting you out," I told her.

VIPER

Terror seeped through every vein in my body when I saw her, a growl tearing from my throat. It was fuelled by the echo of the same fury from every other person I was bonded to.

Riot didn't flinch when Arsenal raised his gun, though a little smile appeared on his lips.

"Let her go," Arsenal snarled.

"Kill me, and you get to watch her die, slowly and horribly, the moment the sun rises."

That's what the collar was. It was an ancient thing, rigged to choke her inch by inch with the rising of the sun.

"This is not *fucking* necessary!" Arsenal spat.

"Onyx!" Ice reached the cage first, pressing against the bars. "It's going to be okay."

I noticed Riot's gaze on him, eyes narrowed. Malakai and King caught up. Malakai's fists closed around the bars, and King hung back a step, absolute panic through the bond. I approached slower, unable to tear my gaze from her until Riot spoke again.

"Give me what's mine." I could swear his pupils blew, a quiet fury in his voice as he said it. Smoke coiled around his cheeks as he burned through his cigarette slowly.

I looked back to Onyx though, and her eyes locked with mine.

How long had she been there alone?

She was composed. Seated like a queen. As if Riot wasn't at her back with a gun. As if she wasn't chained there by her neck. Somehow, she still had her handbag on the crook of her arm, holding it carefully against her body.

There were cracks, though. It was rare for her makeup to track her face, but there were streaks of black on her cheeks even if her tears were dry now. She was shaking with the cold as her eyes drifted to each of us before returning to me.

"Let me in," I said, looking back at Riot.

He cocked his head, raising an eyebrow. "And *why* would I do that?"

We'd made a plan on the way here. It was the only thing that might save her. And now it was up to me to do the thing I swore I never would. I had to return to her the memories that might reap her own destruction. Because without them, she would die.

I took a steadying breath.

She was strong. She could survive it, and I would be waiting on the other side.

"I can get you what you want," I replied. "But you have to let me in."

ONYX

Viper knelt before me.

Mint and mist settled my heart.

"Eyes on me," he murmured, reaching up and cupping my cheek. For a moment, it was just us.

There was no tower. No Riot. No memories trying to tear my mind apart.

"Take the bond," he said.

An offer lit between us for the second time in our lives. I stared at him, lips parted, everything else in the world rushing away for one beautiful second.

A bond?

Viper's bond?

Something desperate, ancient, and wounded creaked in my soul, begging for release. And I didn't care that it wasn't a princess bond.

"Arsenal." Riot's irritated voice made me jump, ripping me from the moment. "What fucking game is your pack playing?"

"Just wait." That was Arsenal, but Viper's touch brushed my cheek.

"Eyes on me," he told me again. I forced myself to focus on him. He was waiting. Waiting for my answer.

"Yes," I whispered, my voice thick.

He leaned up toward me, gentle in how he drew my chin out of the way. Beneath the heavy metal collar around my neck, above my collarbone, he pressed his teeth to my flesh.

Our souls collided.

The ancient, open wound snapped shut.

The final missing pieces of the puzzle came crashing back as the final memories swept me away.

FORTY-EIGHT

ONYX

Two months before

It was icy outside, but Devin had been gone long enough I was ready.

The deafening music from the bar spilled out onto the street as I slipped out, looking around. He'd taken a break—which was unusual for him, but he'd needed it. He was under so much stress right now. I wished I could do more to help him.

There were a few passersby, all bundled up well in the icy air. I hugged myself, my coat only hanging around my shoulders as I gazed around.

Where was he?

He wouldn't have gone far.

My heels clicked on the concrete as I hurried down the steps of the bar, peering around until I walked by the slim alley at the edge of the building.

I paused.

A man was sitting against the wall, only—that was Devin's jade suit he'd chosen to match my handbag. *His* cropped haircut.

"Devin?" I hurried toward him. "Are you…?"

I trailed off, the air leaving my lungs as I spotted the blood on the concrete around him. The trickle down his chin. The paleness of his face.

My hand jumped to my mouth as I took another uncertain step.

"Devin?" My voice shook.

Next thing my tights were scraping the concrete as I knelt by his side, trembling fingers gripping his collar as I shook him.

The scent.

It was off.

Cherry crumble. I always laughed that he smelled much too sweet for a guy his size. It was bitter. Stale. Sickening.

Poison.

Three bodies slumped on couches in a paradise cottage. Their scent in the air was wrong. It was poison. What once was sweet now twisted my stomach…

I blinked, back in the present. "Hey…" I shook Devin. My throat was tight. I reached for my phone, but my mind was cracking in two.

"Hart? Baby, wake up…" I ran my fingers along his cheek…

… I was in the hospital… They were gone… The bond was unfinished, a wound forever bleeding out; a princess bond scarred across my soul from where it was ripped away, forever open…

I choked a sob, standing in the alley before Devin's body.

I had to leave. I had to find a way to undo this. I took a step away from Devin, then another.

This was wrong… but he was my friend. I couldn't leave him to be found by a stranger—No. No. I had to go.

Now there were whispers of danger in my mind. A looming monster ready to tear what remained of me to pieces.

I stumbled forward, hand still trembling as I touched his cheek one last time.

"I'm sorry," I whispered.

I was never going to see him again. There had been times, in the last few years, when he had been the only company I'd had. Tears leaked down my cheeks and my eyes caught on the golden stud earring in his ear. The one I'd given him.

I reached for it, needing something.

With it clutched in my fist I drew back, moving to stand, then paused.

My handbag. I'd almost forgotten it.

Snatching it up, I fled.

The next morning, when I woke, I remembered nothing at all. But that was the first crack.

Onyx
One month before

Sometimes I woke.

I existed in a world that burned white hot. She lived in a world of ice.

Cold.

Uncaring.

Empty.

And all the while she forgot. Forgot that they were gone.

She spent her evenings with packs that paid for her time while the men who loved her rotted in the earth.

I hated it.

I hated more that she didn't know; that I was silenced. The few times I woke up, I fought for my voice while our other half warred to protect her from the poison that I was.

So instead, I woke in the night and tried to tell her the truth she was ignoring.

She violated everything we had ever loved; going on dates with alphas, accepting gifts from them as if they deserved her.

I couldn't speak, so I smashed them all.

9 days before

She was going to match a pack.

Another pack.

Bloodcurdling rage consumed me. My makeup box was in my hands and I flung it at the mirror. It shattered, but it wasn't enough.

This was it. If she found another pack, she would erase them completely. It would be like they never existed.

I ripped the drawers open, smashing everything I could.

I hated her.

She was leaving us behind.

Jake.

Vik.

Hart.

Viper.

She was going to leave us behind.

9 days before, evening

She'd matched a pack.

She'd gone to their house and now she was waiting at their doorstep protecting an omega that wasn't hers.

A vault? Who cared what happened in a pack that wasn't ours?

I hated it.

I could feel Viper here, as if he were sitting beside me.

My love.

My heart.

The only piece left.

We were about to forsake him. Forget him again. Again.

Again.

I grabbed my purse and reached for the pocket I so rarely touched. I opened it and drew out one of the wilting flowers.

A forget-me-knot. The greatest taunt of my life. Slowly I ripped off petal after petal, whispering to myself.

"He loves me. He loves me not. He loves me. He loves me not..."

8 days before

The world shuttered and I lost myself.

I'd just returned from my date. King had been my bodyguard and I'd let him in. Let him close. He'd kissed me. Touched me. Claimed me.

This was a betrayal. I was dying—slowly getting smothered.

My fingers shook as I reached into the purse clutched in my arms as I leaned against the railings on the deck. I unzipped the pocket of my handbag.

I clicked it open and looked inside.

Dead flowers stared back at me. Some were wilting and dying. I took a breath so the panic didn't choke me. I reached in and withdrew the ones with the most brittle, dull leaves. They were dead because of her. Because she was trying to kill me. Trying to leave me behind.

I had to make it impossible.

I held the dead forget-me-nots over the railing and let them drop. I watched them descend until they landed on the steps of the patio below.

I was dying. I had no voice.

But *this* I could do: leave a warning on the doorstep of the men who were killing mine.

5 days before, early morning

We'd matched a pack.

It had been the worst thing I could imagine. Until... Viper had bitten in. He was *here*, lying in a hospital bed.

The rest of them had tried to comfort me, and I'd told them I needed space. I left the hospital and went home first. My nest was low.

I stopped on the way, buying bunches of blue flowers. Then I entered my apartment and crossed to my walk-in wardrobe. Behind a rack of clothes was the handle. I turned it and pushed the door open to reveal my nest beyond.

The space ahead glowed with sunlight spilling from a small window, a desperate attempt to keep the flowers alive.

Still, they died.

There was no bed. No pillows. Nothing that would mark it a nest. Instead, a single vase sat upon a table in the middle of the room.

The forget-me-nots within were wilting.

I shut my eyes, taking a deep breath.

This was always the worst part.

It felt like I was ripping my soul in two, pulling out those flowers. But before I could break, I'd replaced them.

The world steadied. Before me, a fresh vase of forget-me-nots stared back at me.

Bright.

Alive.

I knelt on the floor of the nest, plucking the dead flowers that were still intact.

Once there was a collection on the floor before me, I picked them up with shaking fingers. Carefully, I tucked them into the small pocket in the zipper of my handbag.

I carried them everywhere with me.

They were my only voice.

Next, I went to their home, walking slowly through the garage, a tremor in my soul.

Things had changed. Could I keep up? I was never here for long...

I hugged myself, avoiding the tattoo on my forearm.

Viper was bitten in. My love. My rock.

Only... I stared around at the space. Before, they'd been traitors, but what if...? Bracing myself, I looked down to the flower tattooed on my forearm.

Four.

I traced Viper.

The one who had stolen my heart. Then the other three. Their names... I shook. Four of them in that bond.

I *could* remember them.

I choked as I realised my mistake. All this time, I'd been wrong.

They weren't gone at all, they had just changed. Grown. Become something new, just like I had.

As my finger moved across the flowers on my arm, I could picture them clearly in a pack. Viper's arm was draped around Malakai. At his side, Arsenal was there, and King too.

This was their home and I was their omega.

But panic surged as I stared at the tattoo. Something was wrong.

I blinked furiously. Something was in the way.

A threat.

I was supposed to be their omega.

But they had one? Another one? I choked on a sob.

No.

I lowered my arm, staring around at the space.

Something didn't fit.

And everything had to fit. It couldn't be any other way, or they... or they... *Their pale faces flashed in my vision. Still and dead.*

"No." My voice was thick. "No, no, no..."

My tattoo was burning.

Tears stung my eyes as I made for the part that didn't make sense. I was down the ladder and into the poisoned place in seconds.

A nest.

His nest.

The piece that didn't fit.

I searched it first, finding the box beneath his bed, finding a mug in it. I couldn't tell whose scent was on it—it might be old, but I knew what it was.

A claim. On *my* alphas. On... Viper? And he was curled up with Viper right now in the hospital... I sobbed, taking it with me as I climbed out of the nest, finding the bike. The only thing in here that was Viper's...

Mine... He was... mine.

My vision blurred as I let the mug drop to floor, watching it shatter. Then I stepped toward the bike, toward the mint and mist, scattering my own claim of wilted flowers.

Then I returned to his nest. The omega who shouldn't be here.

I ripped out each blade, breaking down the nest, needing it gone—needing it to have never been here. The mistake.

Each blade I drove into the mattress, a threat.

He *couldn't* be here. Not if I was.

I took the lipstick in trembling fingers and wrote the message on the wall.

I needed to write more. To say more. But I couldn't...

Why did we keep forgetting? I kept dying over and over. It wasn't fair that she lived and I burned, bundled away in the back of her mind.

That... wouldn't be enough...

"He's not yours."

I'm yours.

How could they not realise that? But after this, everything would be fine. I would have them back.

It would be perfect.

With the message written, my lipstick snapped and fell to the bed of knives beneath me.

2 days before

I was finally getting closer to the pack, but the omega was still here.

Nothing had worked to get rid of him. I was in a hotel right now, while the omega was curled up with Viper. I hadn't done enough.

But today, Arsenal's words had been clear as day as he showed me the USB. *"This is what we need if we want to fix things with Ice."*

Ice was the piece that didn't fit. The omega who had claimed my pack.

So, in the hotel room where Arsenal had shrugged off his jacket, I reached into his pocket and slipped it out.

The USB.

In its place I left a single wilted forget-me-not.

FORTY-NINE

VIPER

"I... remember," Onyx whispered. Tears flooded her cheeks and my heart shattered. "It..." Her voice broke, her fingers squeezing all the blood from mine. "It h-hurts."

"I know, My Love." I didn't move, holding her terrified gaze. "You took it from Arsenal's jacket. I need to know where it is."

"*She* took it?" Riot growled.

Onyx stared at me, glittering eyes unsure, but they went wide as I felt the metal of a gun pressed against my skull. I almost looked away from her, almost closed my eyes, but I'd faced death before. I'd faced it for her.

"W-wait," she choked. "Don't... I..." Her expression was desperate for a moment as she tried to remember.

Then her expression crumbled. She released my hands, her fingers drawing open her handbag. She fumbled until she found a zip for a little pocket in the silken lining.

She unzipped it, staring at what was inside.

It was full of wilted, dry forget-me-nots. Shaking fingers

pulled them out, and her breathing was coming short and sharp until I saw the glint of silver.

The USB.

The hard edge of the gun vanished, and I saw the dull glow of a cigarette stub tumble to the ground at my side. Riot ripped the USB from her grasp, but Onyx barely seemed to notice. Her hand jumped to her mouth, a choked sob slipping out.

MALAKAI

The moment Onyx entered our pack, her wound, her pain, ripped our bond open completely, exposing everything we had ever tried to hide or run from.

I buckled, grabbing the iron bars before me to steady the world that was spinning around me. I felt them all.

Viper and Onyx. Wrecked by grief that had festered for so long it had hollowed them out leaving them isolated. Trapped by silence, unable to find connection.

King. Unworthy, tearing himself apart trying to make up for what everyone else gave him. Never enough, no matter what he did for the pack he loved so much.

Arsenal. A failed leader, killing himself to do better, fuelled by self loathing when he couldn't fix us.

Ice. Shattered and put back together so many times that he didn't know where the pieces went anymore, yet so desperate to find a way to make them fit.

And I knew they could feel me, too. Isolated. Unable to connect the way I needed. Unable to connect like we were right now, the wide open bond giving me a breath of reprieve.

But despite the pain, there was hope, because it also smashed apart the barriers we'd been clinging to. We'd been terrified of our own poison, afraid that if we spoke our pain out loud, we might give it to each other. But silence had festered wounds worse than any of that.

And of course, it was her.

She was our answer.

ARSENAL

The world rocked as Onyx collided with our bond. I could feel *everything*. But she was still chained, so when Riot opened the cage, stopping in front of me, I gripped my gun in shaking fingers.

"Let her free," I hissed.

I could still hear Onyx as she wept, still chained to that chair by her neck. The much less stable part of me—the part that could feel her terror through the new bond—wanted to put a bullet in his skull right now.

"It takes a lot to surprise me these days, Arsenal. But this—" He glanced back to Onyx. "—Was thrilling."

He began toward the door.

"Riot!" I started after him, but he just raised his keys and shook them loudly. "She'll be free when I'm out."

I was torn between following him to make sure, and returning back to the others. Ice was in the cage now, clutching Onyx's hand as she wept.

I waited, breath stuck in my chest. For too long, the only sounds were the billowing wind and rain and Onyx's pain.

Finally, there was a click of metal and the collar came free. She collapsed into Viper's arms, her sobbing devolving into wails.

I felt her pain.

We all did.

Ice was kneeling at their side, shaking fingers brushing her tangled chocolate locks. King had taken a few steps toward them, but stopped. Malakai was staring, unmoving, his face ashen, knuckles white where he gripped the iron bars.

"It's... gone..." Onyx's choked whisper carried across the space as she finally found the strength to draw away from Viper's embrace. Her hand traced the bite on her neck. "They're gone. Did we..." Her voice cracked. "Did we leave them behind?"

"Never," Viper whispered, cupping her cheeks and wiping her tears away. "We never leave anyone behind."

FIFTY

VIPER

Traumatised and trembling, Onyx stayed curled up in my arms in the car. She hugged her knees to her chest and her head was bowed so her tangle of brown hair obscured her face.

When we got in, she didn't settle.

"I can't be here." It was the first thing she said as I led her to the nest in Malakai's room.

I had the bond I had dreamed of since the moment my aura had come out. A connection with her. So now I felt her pain. Her fear.

More than anything else, I felt the choking weight of her guilt.

I could sense the rest of the pack too. We were all in shock, and there were a lot of wounds to unpack. But I could see they were willing to give her space. Never once did I feel a single bit of compassion waver within the bond.

"I can't be... in his nest," she croaked.

I frowned. If she wanted to leave, I wouldn't stop her. I would take her anywhere she needed to be. But the idea of her not being here—not being home... It made my chest ache.

This, I realised, was home. And she was pack.

ONYX

The warmth and love that filled Ice's nest was like daggers in my soul; the twinkling warm lights that hung across the ceiling, the piles of woollen blankets draped across the bed, the small—but slowly growing—collection of mugs upon the coffee table.

More than any of that, it was their scents.

Roses and cookies, riverside and clove, apricot and champagne, honey and chestnuts.

Mint and mist—that was, perhaps, the only safe one.

It was everything I couldn't have. So I pulled from Viper's arms and left.

I couldn't run from them. Not completely. I didn't know why—because a part of me knew I should—but the selfish, wounded piece just couldn't walk out of this place. Despite everything, this run down garage in the middle of the Gritch District *was* the safest place in the entire world.

And I wasn't strong enough to leave.

So I followed my instincts, tugging from Viper's arms and going to the only place that felt right.

The old nest was emptied of knives. There were no linens on the bed, and all that remained was an empty mattress in a tiny cellar. That... was right. For a moment, I felt I could breathe as I climbed onto it and curled up.

Everything empty about this place reflected what I'd taken. What I'd done to this pack that was now trapped with me. To Ice.

This place was right for my soul.

Nails bit into the tattoo on my forearm, palm brushing the scar.

I knew now it was a scar I'd given myself.

I felt like I had been ripped open, all my wounds exposed, and

I was made of nothing but grief and guilt. Guilt for what I'd done to Ice.

Grief for love, for old wounds that still felt angry and fresh and open—never given the chance to heal.

And it was a cruel, cruel thing that I could only face them now I'd made the choice to leave them behind.

VIPER

She didn't drink.

She didn't eat.

I took blankets down, but she would tug them off, leaving the bed bare. She let me hold her, but her scent shifted to terror every time I asked if she wanted to go upstairs or let one of them visit.

For too long she was silent. She hadn't shed a tear since I'd carried her from the tower.

"Talk to me," I whispered.

She curled up tighter.

I stroked her hair, tugging her closer still. "Please, My Love."

I felt her fingers ball in my shirt. "I didn't know..." she said, at last. "When I said yes..." She couldn't finish.

But I knew.

When she'd taken the bond, she hadn't known what she'd done. And now she didn't feel she deserved to have it at all. Yet, she was stuck with it. It couldn't be undone. And that was, I thought, what that seething ball of guilt was made of.

"It wasn't your fault," I whispered.

"*I* still did it."

ARSENAL

After arriving back from the tower in the early hours of the morning, we barely slept a wink. Mal just sat at the kitchen island, open beer in hand. When Ice finally tried to force him off the seat to grab a nap, he just said, "We missed it."

"Can't blame yourself, mate," I told him.

We'd all missed it.

After everything, we'd all tried and failed to get sleep, but in the end Viper insisted on getting us a ride to the Institute, not trusting us to drive.

I was completely numb during our pack check in. We all were.

I'd never witnessed Mal in shock. Yet, as we went through the screening—as seers examined our auras and as we were barraged by a million questions—Mal said barely a thing, letting us answer for him when we could.

Everything went through without a hitch.

And that was it.

We were completely clean, our records sealed permanently, with no more restrictions.

I'd dreamed of this day for years, and none of it was right. I'd only wanted it for what it meant for our pack. A chance to offer something more to Ice, a chance to do better, to make more of ourselves and leave the past behind. Now Ice's registration was in process, and everything was on track. Except her.

And we could all feel her agony. Her grief wasn't the part that hurt the most. I knew she wasn't alone in that. Viper was with her every moment.

It was the guilt. The self blame.

The feeling that she wasn't deserving of us.

Yet, none of us blamed her. I could feel it from them all, every instinct on overdrive.

We just wanted to haul her out of that hole and make her see how much she was wanted. To tell her she could lean on us for anything.

And we couldn't. Not yet. But it wasn't in our nature to coexist with that and not fix it.

When we returned from our check in, Ice hurried over.

"How'd it go?" he asked, anxiousness bubbling through his side of the bond.

"Fine." I tried to force a bit more energy into my answer for his sake. "Good. We're all clear."

He nodded, clearly relieved.

"Has she come up?" King asked as we took the few steps to the main living area. Ice shook his head, another sharp pang of anxiety shooting through the bond again.

I glanced over to see there was another large stack of takeout on the kitchen counter.

Viper had been ordering us food nonstop, wracking his brain for all of Onyx's favourite places in hopes she would eat.

The truth was unravelling in pieces, and Ice updated us.

"Her bodyguard—Devin–died a few months ago."

"Yeh," Mal rasped, his attention finally present. "That's the one the police said wasn't targeted."

"Onyx found him. Seems like that's what triggered her other memories returning. Makes sense, her pack and Devin were both unexpected and random. She uh... blocked it out, but took his earring. That's what made her think it was a stalker."

"Why did she take the earring?" I asked.

Ice furrowed his brow. "Probably because she cared about him," he said, as he shovelled sushi onto a few plates for us. I blinked, but it seemed none of us were processing.

"Uh. Okay. Omega thing, apparently. She probably just... needed something of his."

The other stuff—the forget-me-nots on the driveway, they made sense for all that time Onyx spent on the roof. There was that stretch of hours she was on her own in the hospital when our apartment had been ruined. We'd thought she'd been napping and then I found her in the hospital garden.

Right after Viper had been bonded in.

I felt hollow for having missed it.

Ice was shoving a plate of sushi into my hand when I heard the creak of the trapdoor, and my gaze snapped to it to see Viper climbing out.

"What can we do?" King asked, lifting his head from where he rested on his arms, his plate of sushi untouched at his side.

"Will she see us?" Ice approached Viper, looking up at him with an anxious gaze. Viper just shook his head, and I saw he slipped his hand into Ice's.

"She's not ready."

I could feel Ice through the bond, more unsettled than the rest of us as he carried a deep wounded desperation to fix this. Their connection was different. I hadn't really understood that until now.

I wanted Onyx in my arms because I wanted to know she was safe. I needed her to know she belonged. That she was loved.

Ice's need was different. He was protective, but it wasn't the same. His experience was of the pack, of the part of it that wasn't well. He needed it fixed. He needed her to know she was welcome.

This was his pack. And now hers.

"She just needs time," Viper said.

"But she's hurting now," King said.

I got to my feet, an idea hitting me. I searched kitchen drawers for a piece of paper and pen.

"What are you doing?" Mal asked.

I didn't answer, my mind trying to conjure up a memory.

Onyx had told me exactly what she wanted. "If time is what she needs," I said, beginning to sketch, "then we're going to have the world waiting for her when she comes out."

ONYX

I didn't know how many days I'd been down here.

The room was quite sound proof, but I still heard faint bangs from upstairs, as if they were building something. I couldn't consider it, or what it might mean. My sleep was random and sporadic, though Viper was at my side the whole time.

He was patient, and so far he hadn't pushed me.

Today, however, he carried me to the shower in the little bathroom attached to the nest, and told me he wouldn't leave until I was done.

I stood under the hot water numbly for a long time, as if hoping it might wash away my very mind. Now he was brushing my damp hair as I sat between his legs, my back against his chest.

He had been right. After the shower, I felt more clear. Still, I didn't know if I was ready to talk. The last few days had been a blur of grief. I hadn't been able to move.

"What do you think?" Viper asked. "Would your dream nest be the same as it was then?"

I stilled at that question, my mind scattering off in a million directions, none of them comfortable.

"You told us no real flowers just—"

"Paintings." The word came from my mouth before I caught it, the ghost of the memory tumbling back.

Vik's long blond hair was down as we walked along a busy city street. "We're going to have a whole garden of every flower you can think of. Then you'll have to let us put some in your nest."

"I wanted paintings because I didn't think I could keep real flowers alive..." I trailed off, the statement crashing into me like a truck. Viper's fingers tightened in mine.

"I've never been more embarrassed in my life," Viper snorted, still tugging the brush gently down my hair. "You said you wanted those damn paintings and next thing he's dragged us shopping.

He raided every single painting that had so much as a petal. The shopping cart didn't fit it all, so he made us carry them all around."

There was the faintest stirring of something warm in my chest as I tried to picture it. "Was the nest even big enough?" I whispered.

"No," Viper snorted. "Hart started nailing them to the ceiling."

A weak smile crept onto my lips, followed by another stab of pain, but this time it was... different. Safer. He talked about them as if it was normal to do so.

They had been real, and now they were gone, and he could just... say all that like he was talking about anyone else in the world.

"You never... grieved them?" he asked quietly.

"I don't know..." My voice was thick. "Sometimes it feels like it just happened. Sometimes not. Like I was grieving them somewhere?"

It was jarring.

"I never had anyone to talk to about them." His words caught me off guard, and I peered up at him, realising that maybe this wasn't just all for me.

I traced the carved lines of his face, taut in something sorrowful right now. I was stolen away by his piercing yellow eyes, more vulnerable than I ever remembered, the furrow to his sharp brow with the glint of his piercing and the slight rosy colour to the tip of his nose—as if he were a few steps from crying.

"Then keep going," I breathed.

He held me tight as he spoke more about the things I'd missed. All the things they'd done to build our future together. A surprise I'd never seen.

Hart obsessed over the kitchen wallpaper. Vik and Jake would bicker over the stupidest things, like if I'd prefer the see through kind of honey or the 'proper stuff'. About how much they wanted it to feel like a real home, knowing I'd been scared that I wasn't enough.

I don't know why, but sometimes, when a little tremor would go through him, and his fingers would tighten around me, it grounded me.

He had been just as alone as I had...

"They would want this pack for you. You know that, right?" Viper asked, at last.

I couldn't answer that straight away. Not because I didn't know the truth, but because for one wild moment, I rejected it. It didn't matter what they wanted.

It was wrong.

But that... *that* was what I'd been carrying around all this time.

"They want to build you a nest," he whispered, dropping the brush and holding me tight. "They want to give you everything else we wanted to give you."

I nodded. "I know." But my voice was a wisp, something lodged in my throat.

"Do you want that?"

Again, I nodded. "I..." I swallowed. "I love them, too."

The shock of that truth was dizzying, and once more I was left to war with the guilt. The pain. The *everything*—

"They want to talk to you," Viper's soothing voice cut off that spiralling thought. "Will you let Ice visit?"

Ice...

I wanted him here like Viper was, and yet still my stomach turned at the thought. At long last, I nodded. "Can I have one more day?"

I thought maybe then I could face them.

FIFTY-ONE

ICE

I ached knowing Onyx was down there.

Knowing she was in pain, and I could do nothing about it.

I nearly fell down the ladder in my haste when Viper said she was ready to see me, the letter I'd refused to open clutched in my hand.

Then my heart broke all over again.

She was huddled in my old bed, pressed up against the wall. The bed was bare and all the sheets that Viper had brought covered the small floor space. Her perfect mask was finally cracked. Usually sparkling sapphire eyes were dull and sunken, and there were bags beneath them. Her skin was ashen, and she hugged her knees to her chest, damp hair tumbling about her shoulders.

She looked too small for Onyx.

I crossed toward her, inhaling the brownies and lavender I'd missed, trying to ignore the anxious edge to it.

She didn't resist as I tugged her into my arms, not knowing

anything but the fact that I wanted to hold her right now. Slowly she reached up, fingers gripping my shoulder as she held me too.

"I missed you," I whispered.

She shook her head. "Don't say that."

"It's the truth. We're all going crazy without you."

She didn't say anything, though.

"I'm going to scent mark every inch of this place. Then I'm going to start dropping their nasty old socks in until you can't stand it anymore—"

I cut off as she giggled, but then she ducked her head further into my arms as if guilty she had.

I pressed a kiss to her head. "No one is going to rush you, Onyx, but they're desperate to see you and show you how much they want you here."

"Why?"

"Because I love you." I had known since the moment I'd woken in the hospital and she wasn't there. "We all love you."

She drew back for a moment, staring up at me with those mesmerising sapphire eyes, brows pinched as if she wasn't able to comprehend what I'd just said. Then she returned to burying her face in my shoulder.

"You shouldn't."

"I don't care." I tangled my fingers in her hair, dragging her closer. "Seeing you trapped down here like I used to be is killing me."

"It shouldn't... after what I did."

"You were sick. I get that more than anything," I told her. "I literally walked my own ass into Nash's shop a week ago, so *technically*, I win."

She let out a little choked wail that I wasn't sure was laugh or sob.

"Come on, Onyx." I straightened, trying to coax her to face me again. She tilted her head up just slightly, so I was looking down into her eyes. "You can't stay down here forever. Viper says you've barely eaten or drank anything."

"I just... feel stuck," she whispered.

"Let me help you un-stick."

Again, there was a quiver of a smile on her lips. Then her eyes fell on the letter I'd dropped on the bed.

"What is that?"

"It's a letter from the Institute," I said, my heart in my throat. She reached out and read it.

"For you?" she asked, her tone shifting for the first time, becoming more businesslike—much more Onyx.

"Yeah. I haven't opened it."

"When did it come in?"

"A few days ago."

Her eyes widened. "But it's probably—"

"I know."

"Then you have to—" She'd begun fumbling with the edges, but I put my hand on hers, halting her.

"I'm not opening it without everyone there."

Her lip trembled as she stared at it, her brows bunching again. "Don't, Ice. Not for me."

"You're pack. I *won't* do it without everyone," I said again.

"I don't deserve—" Her voice broke, but I cut her off.

"You deserve it as much as anyone up there. Us—this pack. It's ours."

"B-but I don't even know what we're supposed to do, even if I did," she whispered. "There's not enough rooms in the garage—"

I cut her off, pressing a finger to her lips. "Come upstairs with me."

ONYX

"A blindfold?" I asked. "What for?"

"Just trust me?" Ice's eyes were sparkling with excitement.

I still felt brittle, but I was getting weary of it, and Ice's warmth and forgiveness gave me life I'd forgotten I was missing. Was he telling the truth?

Were they waiting for me up there, wanting to do the same as he had?

For a moment I felt that spearing guilt again, and then it calmed.

"They would want this pack for you."

I knew Viper was right.

I was the one holding back.

I nodded, and Ice tied the piece of fabric around my eyes before leading me up the steps.

Something settled my soul as I climbed up into the garage, the scents of the St. James pack tangling in the air. Mint and mist was strongest as I reached the top, and I felt Viper's touch on my arm, helping me steady as I climbed out.

They led me up to the roof, my slippers making the familiar dull, clanging thud with each tread on the metal steps.

They'd been doing construction. That much I'd guessed from the noises above, though wondering about it had just given me anxiety, so I'd buried it deep. When the blindfold came off, however, I got a glimpse of what might have been going on.

"Oh."

It was night, but even so, I could see how different the roof was. It was paved with new tiles, and along the edges were long planters full of soil, though with no plants in sight. Across from us was a broad, ebony gazebo, under which was an outdoor sectional set. In the centre was a blazing fire pit, and Edison bulbs were strung along the gazebo railings and the wall behind me, brightening the night.

Everything out here was beautiful—down to the alphas seated on the sectional, waiting for us.

I swallowed, but Ice's fingers squeezed mine tight. There was a lump in my throat as Ice tugged us through the light rain toward them. Once under the gazebo, I felt the warmth of the fire, though I couldn't bring myself to look up at them.

A weight that had been piling on for days and days suddenly felt crushing, like a fist squeezing my heart. Viper's hand was at the small of my back, and he rubbed up and down comfortingly. Ice drew near.

"I'm..." I swallowed. My voice was hoarse. I forced myself to look up, no matter how much it hurt. "Sorry for everything."

"Onyx." King's voice calmed me. He was the closest, and I could see the worry on his face. "Anything you did is forgiven. No one holds it against you."

For a moment, I did what I'd been too afraid to do. I opened myself to the bond to check what emotion he was feeling. I was flooded by a warmth and compassion that brought tears to my eyes. He... was telling the truth.

I was a coward and didn't reach out to the others.

They all wore the same expressions as King, though.

"King said it, Duchess," Mal said. "Take the time you need, but we're here waiting for you on the other end."

I couldn't find a reply. Arsenal said nothing, but when I found the courage to meet his eyes he just nodded, expression resolute.

At my side, Ice got to his feet.

"You want a drink?" He didn't wait for an answer before hurrying over to the bar built into the gazebo. He was hauling out a pack of beers, a bottle of wine, a club size packet of chips, bottled water, and a few other boxes of snacks. "I mean... if you wanted to hang out for a bit... Didn't want to overwhelm you..."

I couldn't help the smile on my lips as I stared at him, his golden eyes dancing in the firelight.

He was beautiful... Too beautiful with the warm glow on his pale cheeks, and the scattering of freckles. Trying to host for me just like the day we met.

"Yes," I said as a little flutter of anxiety came from his end of the bond. Now I'd reached out to King, the others were seeping in.

I realised I'd been staring at him for a long time. "I'll have a glass of wine."

Viper was on his feet too, crossing to help Ice get the snacks ready. I watched them for a moment before feeling my attention drawn in the other direction.

The other three were still. King was picking at his nails furiously, but his eyes darted to me as I looked over. Malakai *looked* relaxed, but his dark gaze was fixed maybe a little too intently on Ice and Viper. There was a clench to his lean jaw. Prodding the bond again, I was surprised to feel even more anxiety from him than I had from King. I didn't feel nerves from Arsenal. I felt... desperation. Frustration. Not at me, but around me. As if he was banging on the glass walls of a box, but couldn't get in. When I glanced at him again, I found him still watching me, perfect patience in his eyes no matter what the bond might say.

I got to my feet and dared cross toward them.

King watched me approach, averting his eyes, then shuffled on his seat as if unsure if I wanted to join him.

First, I took a seat beside Arsenal, then took a breath. "Thank you for coming for me," I whispered. "Even when you knew."

"You're pack," he said gruffly.

I leaned up and pressed my cheek beneath his chin, settling against him for just a moment, following an instinct I'd never followed before. His arms came around me before I drew away.

When I looked back up at him, I swore he was blushing. His

hand jumped to the spot on his tattooed neck where I'd scent marked him. Then I leaned close. "I'm going to go sit next to King, though," I whispered. "Or he might have a heart attack."

Arsenal chuckled, tugging me against him for another quick hug before I moved to sit between King and Malakai.

King sat, frozen for the longest moment, but Malakai dropped his arm around me, pulling me close briefly as he pressed a kiss to my head. "Missed you, Duchess."

As soon as he let go, King shifted to my side, drawing me into his arms like he never wanted to let go. I let him pull me close until I was settled between his legs with his arms wrapped around my waist.

He didn't say anything. He didn't need to. The relief and love that flooded the bond was everything. The low, rumbling purr that vibrated against my chest soothed my soul.

Ice and Viper brought everyone drinks, and I didn't fail to spot the spark of hope in Ice's eyes as his gaze lingered on me and King.

"We came out for Ice, though," I said, turning my attention to him and taking a sip of my wine. Still, I had to settle my nerves. This contentment was still unsettling to me.

"We did?" Malakai asked.

Viper and Ice had settled back in their seats. Ice chewed on his lip, eyes fixed on me with his own glass of wine in his grip.

"Oh... Was I not supposed to—"

"No. It's okay. I just, uh..." He glanced around at everyone else, suddenly flighty. Then he dug in his pocket and pulled out the letter he'd shown me. "It's from the Institute. Came in not long ago..."

I felt the shift in the bond.

Every alpha reacted. Relief, hope, joy—it all came barrelling in at once. But Ice shrank, his eyes fixed on the letter in his hand.

Viper brushed his arm, the touch comforting. Ice fumbled for it, seizing Viper's hand.

"You know, I, uh... thought I could..." Ice swallowed. Then he glanced to Viper nervously. "Do you think... Could you?"

Viper took the letter from him gently. He opened it, eyes scanning it quickly, a smile crossing his lips.

"Is it...?" Ice asked. But Viper was tugging out a card. It was a blue Institute registration card. I had one. I knew the alphas here would all have green ones in their wallet too.

Ice stared for a long moment, and it was like each one of us was holding our breath. He reached out and took it.

Hope.

From him came a brilliant, powerful moment of hope. And following it was an explosion of emotions. Panic. Fear. Disbelief. The bond slammed shut as Ice set the card down, his body trembling.

"Hey..." Viper had his arm around him in a moment.

"It's good." For a moment Ice looked to me.

I nodded. "It's incredible, Ice," I told him, but I could see his building panic.

Arsenal crossed to him, a lost look on his face, and then he got to his knees before Ice, reaching a hand out hesitantly. Ice hunched in closer to Viper.

Viper drew his chin up, still holding him tight.

"They would've given up everything for this," Viper said quietly.

Ice closed his eyes for a moment, and then he reached out for Arsenal's hand.

Arsenal tugged Ice forward. There was one moment of hesitation, and then Ice moved, falling right into Arsenal's arms. At my side, both King and Malakai relaxed.

Ice's voice was choked. "Thank you." He looked up to Malakai and King for a second, letting them know it was for them, too.

"Are you alright?" Arsenal murmured.

Ice wrinkled his nose, tucking his face back into Arsenal's chest then shook his head. "I think I just need... a moment."

FIFTY-TWO

ICE

"Are you okay?" Arsenal asked as we closed the door to the nest.

My breathing still wasn't right, but I didn't care. He'd barely turned to me, but I was already launching myself at him. And this time it wasn't for a hug. His back hit the door as I pressed my lips to his.

There was one moment in which he was clearly startled, and then his grip was digging into my waist dragging me against him, the other hand tangling in my hair as he spun us, pinning me against the door now as he drove his tongue into my mouth. A growl rose in his throat that sent stars shooting through my veins.

"I want you," I breathed, the moment his lips broke away. "Now."

His eyes darted between mine in one lingering moment of uncertainty, and then he was carrying me across to the bed. Before I knew it, he was caged over me, my wrists tight in his grip as he pinned me to the bed on either side of my head.

I stared up at him, lips parted, my chest heaving. I felt safe.

Completely safe. I wasn't back in my nightmares because he was the one who'd pulled me from them.

Lust seeped into my veins, into every pore of my being.

I needed him.

I watched his pupils dilate as his gaze traced my body, down to the half open buttons of my shirt, to the evidence of my want of him. He leaned down, crushing his lips to mine more aggressively this time, and I released a growl of my own, straining against where he had me pinned, desperate to touch every part of him.

He gathered my wrists in one hand and pressed them above my head. I hissed, a snarl on my face as I bucked against him furiously. I wanted to explore his body just like he was so clearly wanting to mine.

A cocky grin lit his face as he watched me struggle, and heat coiled in my stomach.

He undid the buckle of my jeans with his one hand as I tossed my weight against his grip, but he didn't let up.

"I want you." My voice had devolved into a whine.

His eyes met mine, then he kissed me once more. His touch slid down my stomach.

Briefly, he paused on the scars across my chest. The ones I'd shown Onyx the day we'd met her. Claw marks across my torso.

I saw his eyes darken for a second and panic gripped me. But then he pressed his lips to mine again, and his hand slid to my cock, getting a breathy moan from me. I fought the grip he had, trying to kiss him, but he didn't let go.

It didn't take long before he'd tugged my jeans off completely. I tangled my legs around his waist as I tore his t-shirt from over his head.

I felt his finger first, pressing into me and stretching me open. We didn't have prep in here, but it didn't matter, I was wet with slick. I whined at the burst of stimulation from the alpha I'd dreamed of for years.

His gazed traced every inch of my face as he began pumping into me with two fingers.

"Fuck me," I panted. His eyes flashed, already blown pupils dilating further. "I'm ready."

He withdrew his fingers, then flipped me over with ease. There was a moment in which I heard a rustle of his jeans, and then I felt his chest against my back and his cock press against my entrance. I let out a gasp as he pressed past the tight ring, my fists bunching on the sheets.

He let out a breath of pleasure as I bucked back, needing more, and my own slick made the movement easy. I groaned as I felt him enter me all the way.

"I love you, Ice," Arsenal breathed in my ear. "So fucking much." His kisses trailed my shoulders, but I shifted, exposing my neck to him so his lips brushed the bite. The one he'd given me after he'd claimed pack lead all those years ago.

There was a moment's pause, and then I felt his teeth there. I moaned, bucking back further against him, feeling his knot. His grip on my hips tightened.

"I love you," I whispered. "I'm yours."

It was in that moment that I wanted more. I wanted a bite from more than Viper and Arsenal. My chest tightened at that thought, the bond opening with my own lust and joy.

Arsenal's teeth dug in, just enough to send a thrill of pleasure through my system. He pressed me down into the sheets, teeth still grazing that bite as he began fucking me hard. I moaned loudly with each thrust, and I came the first time when his hand circled my waist and gripped the base of my cock.

But Arsenal didn't stop. I didn't want him to. Heat was already building again as he slammed into me harder. His aura wasn't out, but through the bond I could feel it shifting. I tensed, panicked momentarily. He was only days out of his rut. What if he—?

But then his lips brushed my shoulder and his palms pressed

against the sheets on either side of mine. He slowed his pace, a low, rumbling purr vibrating from his chest and right to where our bodies were connected. His aura was shifting, but not into a rut. It was the opposite.

If anything, it felt more stable than before.

When we were spent, I lay in his arms, breaths heaving and a deep sense of peace in my heart. I hadn't asked him to knot me. I was eager to ask Onyx to come in and didn't want to overwhelm her.

"I want them..." I whispered. This was my nest. I felt closer to Arsenal than I ever had, and I needed the rest of them here.

Arsenal sent a text, then lifted me in his arms and carried me to the shower. I didn't argue, happy to hold onto him as he turned on the hot water. He kissed me as water cascaded around us, the full beauty of his massive tattooed body caging me in. I wrongly assumed I was spent on energy and orgasms, because it didn't take long for me to get hard again. It was his fault for being too fucking hot, soaked black hair sticking to his forehead, reaching his eyes.

He noticed my hard-on instantly. I knew my pupils were blown, and roses and cookies probably warred with the shower steam for space in the air.

"How many times can you come for me, Little Omega?" he asked, nipping my ear as he gripped my cock hard in his fist. I arched toward him, but he held me harder against the shower wall by my chin, holding me in place as he worked my cock so he could watch my expression tense up as I found release again.

When I sagged in his grip, he kept holding me up, kissing me deeply once more as I held onto his wrists to stay steady. "I love you," he murmured.

He could say those words a thousand times and I don't think the butterflies would stop taking flight in my stomach. He drew back, water still cascading down the rugged edges of his tattooed face. I found my gaze drift to the small black knife just to the left of his eyebrow. Then his next words drew my attention back to his hazel eyes.

"You deserve that card," he said. "And the whole fucking world that comes with it."

FIFTY-THREE

VIPER

Arsenal and Ice vanished.

Their connection through the bond was shut off.

I was feeling shaky.

My relationship with Ice was important—there was something between us I couldn't explain—but sometimes I worried it might create obstacles with the rest of the pack.

At first, the others were worried, but then we felt a few faint spikes of lust from Ice and Arsenal. I wasn't the only one who relaxed. Malakai had a faint trace of humour on his lips, and King's purr, which had picked up when he began holding Onyx, intensified.

"So... about the bite?" King asked after a while. "Does that mean you aren't a duchess anymore?"

Her brows pinched for a moment.

"Technically, I think your aura still stays all... siren-like," Mal said.

"But no pack will want me," she replied. "Not with a bite on my neck."

"Shit... I guess that's your whole job..." King muttered, his arms coming around her tighter.

Still, I swear I caught the faintest smile on her lips as she looked at me. "I never *wanted* to be a duchess," she said, finally. "The job was just... there, with my aura. I didn't really have anything else."

Her hand crept up, tracing my bite on her neck.

"For the record, *we* want you," King said.

She swallowed, and through the bond, I could feel her nerves, but they were less frazzled than before. After a moment, she sank further back into King's arms, and his fading purr picked up once more.

I couldn't help but smile. They were so cute together.

After another short while, we got a text.

> Arsenal: he wants company

A grin spread on Mal's mouth as he read it.

"I think..." Onyx stood from King, still clutching her half finished glass of wine. "I think I'm going to wait out here for a bit before..." She didn't finish, not making the promise that she would join them.

"Me, too," I lifted my beer to them. "See you in a bit."

They deserved a bit of time with Ice alone. Mal nodded, but King looked torn.

"But we have..." King trailed off, clearly not wanting to push it. He'd been the worst of all of the pack, unsure of why he couldn't just go down and demand she listen to how much she was wanted.

"Maybe we can peek in soon?" I said.

I knew how much they wanted to show her what they'd done. He was just as impatient as Hart used to be...

I shook the thought as soon as it came, but it didn't hurt like those thoughts used to.

Besides, Onyx was out here with us. Tonight was going well. I could feel her softening around the edges. King's eyes drifted to me, and I nodded. His tense expression relaxed a little, and then he was hurrying after Mal.

When they were gone, Onyx returned to sit beside me.

It was hard to explain how complete I felt knowing that she felt safe near me; an ancient ache finally satisfied.

We didn't speak for a while, both taking a few more sips of our drinks in silence but for the light spitting rain on fresh tiles.

"You offered me the bond," she said, at last.

"Yeh."

She frowned. "But only pack lead can offer a bond."

"Well, uh..." I said. "We chatted on the drive over to get you back. Once we'd figured it all out, we thought we needed to close the loop. The best way would be for me to offer the bond."

"So... Arsenal gave you pack lead?" she asked.

I nodded sheepishly. "I mean, I tried to give it back to him."

"But?" she asked, frowning.

"He, uh... didn't want it." Actually, he'd laughed in my face, then carried on watching the soccer, beer in hand.

"Oh. Weird. Well, you were lead... with... our old pack." Briefly, when she spoke, her voice weakened, but she finished anyway. She was so strong, and I could see she was trying to face her monsters.

We sat for a little time more, and I just held her before my phone buzzed.

It was the group chat.

> King: He's asking for you guys
>
> King: Especially Onyx

I caught her staring at it, chewing her lips in concern. The phone buzzed once more. I glanced back down to see the next text from King: a single sad emoji.

"What do you think?" I asked.

Onyx sighed, shutting her eyes for a moment and setting her glass down. "Okay." She swallowed. "Yes. Let's do it."

ONYX

I drew up as we stepped back into the garage.

Okay. I'd heard the construction, but this was much more than I'd expected. It was, I realised, what I'd drawn out for Arsenal at the mall.

There was a balcony overhanging the huge garage, which easily fit under the tall ceiling. A whole half floor had been put in.

"How many days was I down there?" I stared, stunned, at the floor ahead where we'd stopped. There were three doors.

That wasn't all. I could see active renovations on the rest of the garage. I thought they might even be installing a proper kitchen.

But Viper was leading me along the balcony. "Maybe a week? But I can pay for rush jobs and Arsenal didn't believe I could do it in five days."

I halted in the doorway, my pulse thready as I looked in.

A nest.

It was a vast room with an expansive circular pack bed. It was a little bare—as if Ice was just starting to fill it—but the ceiling and walls were hung with fairy lights and there were piles of colourful chunky knit blankets across the bed and floor.

More than that, it was filled with their scents, and most of all, *his*.

Roses and cookies. Content. Safe. More even than in the makeshift nest in Malakai's room.

And they were all on the huge pack bed.

Arsenal and Ice both had wet hair as if they'd just climbed out of the shower. King had been cuddling Ice, while Mal lay on his back on Ice's other side. Arsenal was propped up against a pillow beside him.

The moment the door opened, though, Ice leaped up and crossed the room toward me.

"He's complaining there's too many alpha hormones in here," Mal grunted from the bed.

"Ice..." My words were stuck. "This is... It's amazing. Everything you deserve—"

"Fuck that shit." Before I could do a thing, Ice had picked me up by my waist and was carrying me into the room. I gripped his shoulders, steadying myself right as he dropped us both onto the bed.

"This is *our* nest. I'm outnumbered, and these alphas are stinking it up."

I heard a snort from the head of the bed. I pushed myself up, eyes darting around to the empty half of the room.

"Ours?" My voice was faint.

"And it doesn't smell like brownies." Was Ice *pouting*? My gaze snapped back to him, but he was already glaring back at the door.

"Would you get in here?" he snapped. Then he was shifting back up to the top of the huge bed, glaring between me and Viper expectantly.

I swallowed, hesitating one moment longer, and then following him to the top of the bed.

He wrapped his arms around me. "Okay," he declared. "Now I'm good."

King didn't hesitate, shifting to our side and throwing his arms around Ice. But it wasn't long before I was in the centre of the whole pack, the warm honey and chestnuts of Arsenal at my back.

Something loosened in my chest as I felt Ice's contented purr. My eyes burned all of a sudden, this time with something kind.

For the first time since I danced in the rain with Viper, I was home.

FIFTY-FOUR

ONYX

Neither me nor Ice had ever indulged in a real nest before. Even before Devin died, the nest in my home had been quite empty.

Still, I had more nerves than I'd admit to now it came to actually building one. But Ice was the same, so we were bumbling about it together.

Ice was anxious about setting up the mug cabinet, so I helped him put it together. I was nervous about filling the plant pots, so Ice helped. He turned up with the dozens of seed packets the rest of the pack had bought.

When anxiety had prevented me from accepting them, he came up with a foolproof method of finding my favourites. One by one, he threw them in the trash over the course of the day, knowing I could see and if he heard a growl from across the room, it would stay.

The whole nest had warm fairy lights, though Ice's half was also draped in massive chunky knit woollen blankets of all colours. He'd chosen vintage couches and chairs so he had more places to arrange them. The floor was a plush carpet, but Ice had picked out a bunch of colourful rugs to brighten it up.

My side was simpler. I had dozens of pillows, a couple of jade throws, and a few reading chairs. The rest was shelves beneath the window with carefully arranged pots with soil.

The start of new life—if I could ever build the courage to start planting.

Nash's knife was framed on the wall on Ice's half of the nest. On my side, I framed the last things I had of my old pack. Hart's bracelet, Vik's keyring, Jake's fountain pen. It had been long enough that their scents were gone, but sometimes if I looked long enough, I caught a trace of sugar and spice, of sweet grapes and ocean breeze...

It was better to have them here, where I could see them. I didn't want to spend one more day of my life burying pain. And I could look at them now without feeling like the breath was sucked from my lungs. Most of the time.

I had been worried my pack would be hostile to them, but they'd come through. King even complimented me on the choice of frame.

We had small bedrooms attached on each side—since sometimes nests could get rowdy. But I hadn't wanted to use mine yet, and neither had Ice.

Instead, for the first few nights, I'd tumbled into sleep with Ice's arms around my waist and his purr rumbling at my back, wrapped up safe in his roses and cookies. The alphas were giving us space, but we were both getting antsy with it.

And horny.

I could be honest.

I wanted them.

Ice's heat was coming soon; it was perhaps a few weeks off, but we'd both decided that we didn't want the first pack fuck to be heat.

So now we were both laying on our stomachs on the pack bed, staring at Ice's phone.

"What do we say?" he asked.

"You've known them longer."

"You knew Viper longer."

"That's one quarter."

"You're a duchess, how do you ask guys to bang you?"

I took the phone out of his hands and began typing.

> Me: Attached below is a contract. Please have your lawyers read it over and ensure—

Ice grabbed the phone from my hand with a snort. He deleted the message and typed:

> Me: Anyone around?

He pressed send.

"It's 10pm, where are they going to be?" I asked. Sure enough, four texts came piling in almost instantly.

> Viper: Yup
>
> King: Yeh, what do you need?
>
> Mal: Sure
>
> Arsenal: Just in the shop, what's up?

"Okay. Now what do I say?"

I took the phone back and typed the next message out before tossing it back across the bed.

> Me: Come to the nest.

Ice grinned, nerves dancing in his golden eyes for a moment before he dragged me against him, running kisses along my neck.

"There's only one problem now," he murmured as his teeth grazed my nipple and my back arched against him. "*You* are wearing far too much."

KING

Neither me nor Malakai waited for the others. Viper was just jumping in the shower, and Arsenal was furiously scrubbing bike oil from his hands, shooting us dirty looks as we'd rushed up the stairs without him.

We walked into an ocean of omega hormones. It was freshly baked chocolate cookies and lavender and roses.

Holy crap.

Onyx and Ice were on the bed together. Onyx's golden legs were tangled around Ice's hips. Black lace panties were at her thighs, and he was sliding into her while he squeezed her breasts. Her head was tilted back, a look of absolute pleasure on her face, lips parted and her eyes holding his.

They were, I thought, the two hottest omegas in the universe; her golden curves a contrast to his pale, lean form.

A growl slipped from Mal, and Ice looked over. Neither had even flinched at the door opening.

My cheeks heated. "I... Shit, we didn't... Should we leave?" I asked. Malakai swatted me on the head as Ice choked out a laugh.

"They want the audience." Mal crossed toward them and climbed onto the grand bed, eyes fixed on Onyx as Ice drove into her again.

"We want more than an audience," she managed through a little moan of pleasure. She bit her lip as Ice's fingers twisted her nipples. Her eyes found mine.

A low rumbling sound came from my chest, halfway between a purr and a growl, and I followed Mal on pure instinct.

"Are you boys just going to watch?" Onyx asked. "Or join in?"

Join?

My heart sped up.

Mal was already adjusting himself beside Ice, leaning forward and weaving his fingers through Ice's hair.

"Shall we give them a show?" he asked, tilting Ice's head back.

Ice's pupils blew, and he stopped, cock buried deep in Onyx. "Yes." His voice was a low whine.

I'd never heard him like that, and it was hotter than any dream I'd ever had. Onyx's eyes were wide with lust as she stared up at them, her chest heaving.

"Do you want King to fuck you?"

Ice's eyes darted to mine and my heart tripped in my chest as he nodded, eyes roaming my body like he could think of nothing better in the world.

ICE

King pressed in behind me and I was smothered by the scent of apricots and champagne. My heart rate picked up, even more lust burning my veins. I hadn't thought that was possible with Onyx beneath me, letting out little breathy moans every time I drove into her. But King... I wanted him so badly.

I could also scent riverside and clove. Mal at my side. It was comforting and damn hot. Always had been. They had given me the option of going to clinics for heats, but I never had. Malakai had always been safe, and it was so far beyond the twisted idea that I'd held onto—that he didn't want me.

"Ready, Little Omega?" That was Mal. He was right here with me, and it settled my nerves.

I nodded, and then felt King's fingers press into me, stretching me open. I moaned. I was wet for him, my slick making it easy to slip in. Onyx's fingers caught my chin. She drew me back to face her. I realised I'd bowed my head, overwhelmed with sensation for a moment.

Staring into her glittering sapphire eyes in the low, warm light, that was when it all came crashing in.

My pack was here.

Me and Onyx were connected, her body beneath mine, still squeezing me tight.

"Keep fucking her," Mal murmured. A command. It was enough to get me moving. As I drew out of her, I felt King's hard cock against my entrance. I paused.

"What did I say?" Mal asked, his voice almost a taunt now. Onyx's fingers still gripped my chin, forcing me to look right into her eyes. Her pupils were blown wide, and she bit her lip, a sultry look on her face as if she knew exactly what King was doing.

I shifted back another inch, feeling myself stretch over his tip with a little groan.

"Fuck her," Mal said again, fingers weaving through my hair.

I moved again, a little moan coming from my lips as I drew out of her tight pussy. King pressed in deeper.

"You can do better than that," Malakai groaned.

I whined as I pulled out of her, King's massive cock buried deep in my ass, his swelling knot pressing against my entrance. I was panting, I realised, completely overwhelmed with sensation.

I couldn't help looking up at Mal for a moment. His dark eyes were lost in lust as he watched, loose strands of dark hair swinging in front of his chiselled face.

"Don't stop," Onyx breathed, the words a plea.

Fuck...

"Mmhmm..." My chest heaved and I took a breath. Then I drove back into her, groaning at the feeling of her clenching around my cock and King sliding out of me. He was already soaked with my slick, but the burn of his stretch was overwhelming. He was really goddamned thick.

"Fuck..." It was more whine than curse, and my cheeks heated, but it was going to be hard not to come too soon.

I moved at a slow rhythm, pushed onwards by the low, breathy noises Onyx made every time I entered her. King's hands came down on either side of us, now not in danger of slipping from me. My pleasure was spiking faster than it ever had with King stretching me open as Onyx's tight body clenched down on my shaft.

King joined at last, slamming into me and pressing me into Onyx. Onyx moaned, a beautiful sound that made my veins hot. My climax was coming, my body seizing. I heard King groan from behind me as if he was nearing his too.

"Knot," I gasped before thinking, my mind stolen by a million guilty dreams of having King claim me.

He let out a growl, taking over completely. He crushed me against Onyx and I only just managed to catch myself on the mattress, my face an inch from hers.

She kissed me as King began driving into me ruthlessly.

With the addition of Onyx's tongue driving into my mouth, I came, overwhelmed. My body shook as I spilled inside of her and she groaned in pleasure, squeezing me as I filled her. My body tensed with my orgasm. King let out a low growl, coming as well as he held his knot against me. I bucked against him, needing it. As he stretched me open to accommodate it, Onyx trembled, nails digging into my waist.

The moans coming from my chest as King's knot pressed into me were wild and desperate, and Onyx drove her tongue into my mouth more aggressively as I trembled between them.

"Bite me," I moaned.

I felt the shock through the bond with King.

"What?" Even Mal sounded surprised.

I lifted my gaze to him.

"Claim me."

Arsenal's bite had been the only one that was needed when we'd bonded. Viper's had been, too. Now I knew I wanted theirs on my skin as well.

King barely hesitated, and I shuddered when I felt his teeth against my neck as his knot still locked me against him. There was just the briefest hesitation.

"Do it!" I gasped. When his teeth bit down, ecstasy soared through the bond and I suddenly felt King there, more present than he'd ever been. I didn't realise I'd come again until I felt Onyx trembling and her nails digging into my sides.

"Your cum feels too fucking good, Ice," she breathed.

I felt the cocky grin slide onto my lips. "My omegas," King purred, pressing a kiss to the bite, and then to Onyx's lips. She reached above me, dragging King into a deeper kiss, before letting him go and pressing her lips to the bite.

FIFTY-FIVE

ONYX

King held me against Ice as he sat us up so Malakai could shift behind us.

Since Ice was an omega, he was still completely hard, and the movement sent another jolt of pleasure through my body.

Malakai's touch brushed my waist, lips pressed to my shoulder.

I hadn't realised that Viper and Arsenal had arrived, but they were both here. I should have known. We were joined by the scents of honey and chestnut, mint and mist, and the room had become complete.

Arsenal settled on one side of us, Viper on the other. For a moment, I couldn't take my eyes from Viper. He was topless and wearing a pair of sweats. His lean body was everything I remembered, and for the first time, memories came without pain. How many nights had we spent together, falling in love? Even before I'd perfumed.

"I missed you." It was one piece of my past I hadn't had time to process. Now it all came tumbling back. A smile crept onto his face as he leaned close and pressed a tender kiss to my lips.

"I love you, Onyx," he murmured. His eyes darted to the others, tracing our bodies. "And you are so—" He pressed another kiss to my shoulder. "—So beautiful getting ravaged by our pack."

Our pack.

My heart swelled. I looked back to Ice to find him watching me intently, desire in his golden eyes. I kissed him, then leaned up, also kissing King on the cheek.

Mal was there, solid chest still pressed against my back, and Arsenal drew my chin toward him. "You ruined us, Onyx," Arsenal murmured. "Our turn to ruin you."

I was suddenly breathless. "I want you all."

King.

Malakai.

Arsenal.

Viper.

They were mine. Mine and Ice's.

"You haven't claimed him," I told Malakai. A growl rumbled in Malakai's chest, vibrating down my spine.

"Ride him for me, Duchess," Malakai murmured.

My hands ran down Ice's chest as I followed Malakai's command, sliding again over his slick-covered length. We'd both come so many times I could feel it seeping between my thighs every time I took him in. He moaned, eyelids fluttering, head pressed into the crook of King's neck. It set my veins on fire, seeing him like that. Behind him, King's head was tilted back, the messy waves of his blonde hair almost obscuring his emerald eyes. He groaned, lips parted as I rocked Ice over his knot.

As Malakai pressed his teeth to Ice's neck, Ice wove his fingers through my hair, dragging me close. I felt, in a moment of shock, his own teeth against my flesh.

"Bite me," I whispered.

I hadn't thought I was ready for a bite beyond Viper's. When I took their bites like Ice was, I wanted to be well. But I wanted Ice's, even if it wouldn't last.

I felt both claims burst to life in the bond as his two sharp omega fangs sank into my neck. Malakai's renewed bond with Ice, and Ice's bond to me. He moaned against my neck and came again with a shudder, filling me once more. I felt it, a hot stream that sent shivers across my whole body. It was enough, alone, to send another mini orgasm through me.

And I was so far from done. The pack bond was a live wire of lust and I was perfuming across the room as much as Ice was. *I* was turned on by the roses and cookies, which meant the alphas in here were next to feral.

Malakai's grip dug into my waist, and he dragged me from Ice. He was still wearing joggers, but his swollen cock was grinding against my back. I moaned, pressing against him.

"You're going to fuck Arsenal and Viper first," he breathed in my ear. "You'll be filled with their cum before I make you cry my name."

I shivered just as he released me, and then Arsenal was there instead. I could still hear Ice's low pants and groans—King must be teasing him. Then Viper was in front of me, dragging me up into a kiss as Arsenal's fingers found my wet heat. I ground against them, clutching Viper's face so I didn't break our kiss.

"Ready for me, Duchess?" Arsenal asked.

"Fuck me," I begged, my veins alight with the need for him to take me in front of them all.

Malakai seized my hair, kissing me as Arsenal moved. Next thing, I was straddling Arsenal's powerful hips, and he had his length gripped in his fist as he watched me over him. Viper's fingers gripped my waist, lifting me. Malakai didn't let up on his kiss, still fisting my hair, and I had to grab him to steady myself as he continued driving his tongue into my mouth.

I felt Arsenal's tip against my entrance as Malakai broke the kiss at last, instead running his lips hungrily down my cheek and neck, nipping my skin just as Arsenal pressed into my heat. I moaned, trying to sink lower, but Viper held my hips in place, pressing against my back, sending shivers down my spine as his lips also brushed my neck, finding the bite mark he'd left.

My nails dug into Malakai's arms, my eyes on Arsenal. His head was propped on pillows as he watched me while he slowly drew out. I whined desperately, all dignity gone for the thirsty creature that had awoken. Ice's lust—and all of their scents—was enough to push me over the edge. I tried again to shift downward, but Viper's grip became vice-like.

"Impatient," Malakai murmured, his fingers dropping between my legs and circling my clit. I bucked, another whine loosing from my chest, my back arching. I clutched at Viper's arm in an attempt to free myself from his hold, desperate to be fucked.

My mind was blank but for frenzied omega hormones as Arsenal slowly pressed into me again. But I knew how big he was, and he was only giving me half—if that. Malakai still circled my clit, setting my nerves alight as Viper gripped me tight, holding me in place so I couldn't claim anything they weren't ready to give.

"Fuuuck." I shuddered, feeling a surge of pleasure as Malakai got another orgasm from me, just as I heard Ice moan. Then Ice was there, with his sweeping ash blond hair and pale freckled face with pink cheeks. His golden eyes were blown wide and he hadn't caught his breath from the orgasm King had just given him. He didn't care, seizing my chin and drawing me into a deep kiss just as Viper loosened his grip and I sank onto Arsenal's entire impressive length.

I let out a contented moan, and it was drawn out by hands exploring my body. Malakai's fist was still in my hair, his finger still working my clit. Slower now.

By the time Ice broke the kiss, I was out of breath. Arsenal set a pace, and each movement of his length was bliss.

King was there too, his touch trailing Ice's waist as if he wasn't ready to let go.

"More..." I moaned, fumbling for Ice, for any of them. "Viper..."

He was pressed against me, and to my hormone riddled brain, it was a taunt.

"You want me now, Love?" he asked.

I nodded desperately as Arsenal drove into me again. His eyes were fixed on me, watching every touch of his brothers along my body.

I felt Viper's finger find my other hole, pressing into it gently as Arsenal's knot rocked against my entrance. Someone took my nipple in their teeth, and I shook again, instantly pressing back against Viper.

I didn't want to wait.

He switched from one to two fingers, and I gasped as he worked me with them.

"Now," I moaned, but he didn't stop pressing his finger in.

"Wait till he knots you," Viper chuckled, nipping my ear. "I think he's close."

I groaned at the word knot, my breaths coming faster as Arsenal picked up his pace.

Ice's hands were still roaming my body and his cock was in King's fist once more. Mal continued to work my clit. I kept my eyes on Arsenal as he sped up, his teeth biting down on his bottom lip, the muscles along his tattooed neck tensing.

I was so close to the edge when Mal growled in my ear, "Come, Duchess."

Overwhelmed with sensation, I gasped, my whole body shuddering as Malakai sped up against my clit, and Viper added a third finger. The stretch, along with Arsenal slamming into my core, and Ice crushing my lips with his, sent me right off the edge. More of my drawn out moans filled the nest.

Arsenal let out a low growl, and I felt his knot pressing against me. Soaked with slick, it pushed in with ease, and I was sure that I drew blood from whoever I was clutching, my head tilted back as he sent my orgasm into another stratosphere.

I felt him spill into me, filling me with hot seed just like Ice had.

I was panting, muscles not working as they held me up. I was aware of Ice, fingers still winding behind my neck, but his weight was on me. He was also breathing deep as King fisted his cock slowly, keeping him stimulated.

Mal was still circling my clit gently, and the smallest, low whines came from my chest with each movement. But I wasn't done.

"Good girl," Malakai breathed into my ear. "Look how well you took him."

When he drew back, I was swallowed by his dark eyes.

"You think you can handle Viper?" he asked.

I nodded mutely. Viper's stimulation was gone, but his chest was still pressed against my back, waiting.

"I want to see when he fucks her," Arsenal said, his hazel eyes fixed on me, his breathing heavy. King tugged Ice back from me, trapping him against his chest, running his lips along Ice's neck as he continued to tease his cock. Ice never looked away from me, but a breathy moan came from his chest as King grazed teeth against Ice's flesh.

Then Malakai pressed me closer to Arsenal, one palm tracing down my back, squeezing my flesh along the way. Arsenal took my chin in his hands and tucked my hair behind my ear. "Ready, Duchess?" he asked, shifting his knot further into me as he slid in. My breath caught, and I found myself nodding again, not trusting my voice.

I felt Viper behind me, his cock nudging my entrance. I shifted back toward him, eyes fluttering at the sensation of Arsenal's knot moving again.

"Are you wet for him?" Mal murmured.

"Yes," I said. Viper's fingers had entered with ease, my slick in abundance with how turned on I was. Mal's hand was back in my hair now, keeping it from my face so Arsenal could see me. Good. I wanted him to see me. I wanted them to enjoy all of this, every reaction they were getting from my body.

I was theirs.

I squeezed my eyes shut for a moment as Viper pressed in, stretching me around him. Arsenal let out a growl, his fingers tightening at my chin. I snapped my eyes open, back to him. My lips parted at the momentary burn as Viper pressed deeper. Arsenal's finger dragged across my lips, squeezing them down as my grip tightened against his tattooed pecs.

"More," I moaned.

Viper pressed in further, and I never looked away from Arsenal's hazel eyes as I finally felt Viper's knot rest against me.

"Does it feel good to be filled up, Little Omega?" Mal murmured in my ear, his palm still running up and down my back, pressing me deeper into Arsenal just slightly and getting a little moan from me. My eyes fluttered, my teeth instinctively biting down on Arsenal's fingers before I took them into my mouth.

A purr rumbled in Arsenal's chest, sending vibrations through our connection and stars through my veins.

"Not full enough," he said.

Mal breathed a laugh just as Viper began pulling out of me. My body tensed with the overwhelming sensation, but Malakai arched my neck until I was looking into his beetle black eyes that were lit with lust.

He pressed his finger into my mouth just as my grip fumbled for his wrist.

Viper drove back into me and I panted. Malakai pressed two fingers in and out of my mouth to Viper's rhythm. I couldn't help but close my lips around them, trapping them against the roof of my mouth with my tongue. Stars were still dancing in my veins at each movement against Arsenal's knot. I felt like I was constantly existing on the edge of orgasm.

"Would you like one of us to fuck that pretty little mouth of yours?" he asked.

I nodded once more, which was all I could do between the low moans I was releasing as Viper fucked me.

He grinned, white teeth flashing in delight before releasing me and lowering me down. Then King was pressed behind Ice, forcing him up so his shaft was right before my eyes. I groaned as Viper drove into me once more. I reached for Ice's cock without thought.

Ice's fingers dug into my scalp as I took him down my throat, a gasp escaping my lips.

"I can't..." Ice moaned. "I'm... too close."

"Don't come yet, Brat," Malakai murmured, quiet enough that the weight of his aura behind it was almost unnoticeable. Ice whined, and it might have been the hottest thing I'd ever heard, especially looking up into his golden eyes as I had his cock deep in my throat.

When he drew out, I gasped for air, finding it almost impossible to catch my breath as Viper continued to drive in behind me.

"More," I pleaded. I didn't want them to go easy. I was ready to be completely overwhelmed.

King took my hair, keeping it from my face as Ice began driving into my throat.

Viper picked up his pace behind me. Indistinguishable sounds were coming from my chest as they fucked me like this. My pleasure began to peak again, even as tears blurred my eyes from the roughness at which Ice was face fucking me.

"You're doing so well, Baby," Viper murmured as Ice's cock hit the back of my throat. A little purr stuttered to life in my chest at the praise.

Ice's whine rose, his body shaking with the command not to come.

"Finish, Little Omega," King commanded. Just like last time, it seized me too.

King dragged me forward so Ice's length was squeezed by my throat. It was like a rose and cookie bomb went off in the nest, and his hot load shot down my throat. He came as I seized with wave after wave of an orgasm. I heard Arsenal let out a breath of pleasure, and I felt him unload into me once more, just as Viper groaned behind me.

"You're so tight," Viper nipped my taut neck, still held in place by Ice's throbbing cock, as my body shook with another wave, jolted onward by Malakai twisting my nipple. Viper slammed into me once more, and I felt him finish too.

I tumbled into oblivion with them, sagging onto Arsenal's chest as Ice pulled out of my throat. With his last orgasm, Arsenal's knot had loosened.

Viper withdrew from me, tugging me back into his arms and holding me tight, pressing kisses against my cheek and neck. Then King was there, too, his lips against mine.

"Shall we go clean up?" Viper whispered.

"In a moment," Malakai murmured, tugging me out of Viper's arms until I was straddling him. "You guys go, we'll catch up."

Arsenal had drawn Ice into his arms and was walking him over to one of the bathrooms.

"You... never fucked me," I breathed, trying to keep the whine from my voice as I looked up into his dark eyes.

Malakai's grip was tight on my hips as he drew me closer. Why was he still holding out? I'd been desperate for him since the night he'd played bodyguard. And... my hand drifted down to his crotch, feeling the solid tent in his sweatpants.

"I wanted to wait until they were spent," he murmured. "But after that, I don't know if you—"

He cut off as I let out a little growl, my fingers digging into his chin as I gazed at him.

"I want you."

That cute, crooked smile appeared on his lips, and before I knew it my back was to the sheets, my wrists pinned. "Well, in that case..." He moved both my wrists to one hand. His free hand drifted down between my legs. I let out a little moan as he brushed my clit. "I loved watching them fuck you," he murmured. His touch found my entrance, coated with slick and cum. His finger circled it, scooping it back into me. I moaned, bucking against him. "Let me see it first," I said, catching myself by surprise.

"What?" He cocked his head.

"Ice said..." I felt the flush rising on my cheeks.

Malakai let out a low laugh. "On your knees, Duchess," he said as he released my wrists, sitting back.

I was up in a moment, heart rate quickening. Malakai was tugging his sweatpants off, and my eyes widened. Sure enough, at the tip of his considerably sized length, was a piercing. Two, actually. Like a cross.

I reached out before catching myself, running my palm along his length. He tensed, a low growl rumbling in his throat. Then I leaned forward, pressing my mouth to his tip.

His hand stroked my hair as I looked up at him. His dark eyes glittered as he stared down at me.

"Tongue," he murmured.

I listened instantly, sticking my tongue out of my mouth,

butterflies in my stomach as he pressed the pierced tip of his cock to my lips.

He slid it in slowly, fingers tangling in my hair until I felt the edge of the piercing tickling my throat.

He rose up, pressing it further with a low groan. I gripped his thighs, dragging him deeper, more heat pooling in my core as I felt his thick length choking me.

His palms pressed along my shoulders and down my back for a moment, both coaxing and rewarding.

"Good girl," he breathed, one palm lifting to my head, gently pressing me against him as he began thrusting into me steadily.

Riverside and clove filled the air, omega hormones drawing a purr from my chest as he slid into me with such ease, as if we were made to be together. Eventually, he groaned again and drew out. He tilted my chin up, the glistening tip of his cockhead still brushing my lips.

"Don't make me come before I've taken you."

FIFTY-SIX

KING

I came out of the nest's bathroom to find Malakai was a lying little shit, and they were absolutely not done.

He had her pinned to the bed, wrists trapped over her head as he thrust into her. Malakai was a bit of a fucking specimen, and right now I could see he was deliberately taking his time. His dark, muscular body was stretched over her, making her look much too small. His hips forced her knees apart as he slid his massive cock into her slowly.

She writhed against him, perfect, full breasts heaving as she panted, desperately trying to increase the slow rhythm he was maintaining. But with each thrust of his hips, he crushed her against the bed causing her lips to part, and giving her no wiggle room until he chose to slide out.

Her eyes found me as I approached, and Malakai turned too, a much too cocky smile on his face.

"You haven't taken his cum yet, Duchess, have you?" Malakai asked, driving into her again. She let out a little moan, shaking her head against his grip. One of her hands reached out to me in a demand.

Uh…

There was no way I was arguing with that.

Malakai flipped her then pressed his cock back in, his grip in her hair arching her neck so she was looking up at me. Her thick mane of chocolate hair was wild, and there was a faint sheen on her skin from exhaustion. Her sapphire eyes were dilated with lust, her lids heavy.

I'd thought I wouldn't get a chance tonight. I wasn't upset—fucking Ice was a dream, and we had time—but I loved her, and wanted her so fucking much.

I neared, tugging off the fresh boxers I'd just grabbed, and in a second I was before her. She reached out, soft palm rubbing my cock.

"Treat him like you treated me," Mal told her, his touch running lovingly over her hips.

Her lips parted, and she stuck her tongue out as lustful sapphires held my eyes with need. My cock jumped as blood surged to it in record time.

She was a different creature with Mal. When she'd fucked Ice in our living room— and even earlier when I'd trapped Ice against her—she'd been demanding.

Here, she was putty in his fingers.

Her lips pressed over the tip of my cock, but Mal, who was still holding her hair with one hand as he continued to fuck her steadily, was giving me a look as if I were screwing something up. I didn't think you were supposed to roll your eyes mid-fuck, but he basically did.

"You want him rougher, Duchess?"

"Mhmm…" It wasn't a word, since my shaft was still in her mouth, but it was clear enough.

I'd been a bit rough earlier when I'd helped the blowjob she was giving Ice, but I wasn't going to tell them I felt shy when it was my own cock.

"She wants you to fuck her face, King."

Her nails dug into my thighs as Mal upped his pace. With each of his thrusts, my cock buried deeper into her mouth. It was pure bliss.

I ran my fingers through her hair, and then began to rock into her. I swear her lavender perfume heightened the moment I did, her moans getting louder.

Mal let go of her hair and instead dropped his hand below her waist, reaching for her clit. I knew the moment he found it because she shuddered, her blown pupils looking up at me dazed, lids heavy all of a sudden.

She was beautiful with the slight sheen of sweat on her golden skin, her hair just a little frizzy at the roots now from the exertion of fucking all of us like she had. I couldn't take my eyes away from the way her plush lips pressed against my swelling knot as she took me in all the way.

I pressed in deeper, quickening my pace to match Mal's. I already felt my climax on the way.

"Good girl," Malakai purred, quickening his pace. The moans had devolved to whines, her nails likely drawing blood where she gripped my thigh. Fuck.

I was definitely going to—

"Come for me," Malakai commanded, slamming into her now. I pressed my shaft all the way down her throat as I came with an orgasm so strong it wiped my mind utterly blank. I watched as her eyes rolled back slightly. Her throat clenched me so tight, her body convulsing.

Mal groaned, still pounding into her. One of his palms was on the sheets to hold himself up, his other worked her clit furiously as she squeezed him with her orgasm.

When I finally let her go, she collapsed into the sheets. Malakai, on the other hand, didn't miss a beat.

"*Now*, Love," he murmured, gathering her liquid body into his arms with a gentleness that contrasted the fucking he'd just delivered. "Now we're going to get washed up."

ONYX

Arsenal and King sandwiched Ice in cuddles. Malakai was at one of my sides and Viper at my other. Malakai had his hands propped behind his head, eyes closed as he lay on his back.

"Does he look... unhappy?" I whispered to Viper. He was at my back, clutching me against him.

"He doesn't feel unhappy," Viper said.

He was right, there was nothing off about Malakai's part of the bond at all, though he seemed to keep it pretty locked down at all times.

My question was answered, however, as I heard the rumble of a strange noise. At my back, Viper breathed a laugh as the sound of Malakai's contented purr rumbled through the nest.

MALAKAI

I woke briefly in the middle of the night. Ice was still curled up between King and Arsenal. I could spend the rest of my life like this, laying here between everyone I loved.

I turned on my side, hoping to find Viper and Onyx still clutching one another.

They were, but not how I had been expecting.

Onyx's eyes were squeezed tight shut, her fist curled in the sheets, her lips parted just slightly as Viper made love to her slowly from where he spooned her. His fingers bit down on her hips as he dragged her back against him, moving in a slow rhythm. Her breathing turned into the little pants she was so clearly trying to keep quiet so as to not wake anyone.

Her breasts pressed into the crinkles of the soft white sheets, her smooth, golden skin darkened by the low light of the room—lit only by faint rays of moonlight. Everything about her was divine—the perfect pink lips, the squeezable crease of flesh where her hips met her waist, and the lion's mane of wavy, chocolate hair that tangled across the surrounding sheets. She hadn't straightened it since the moment I'd told her how beautiful I thought it was.

"I love you so much..." Viper's teeth grazed his mark on her neck. "My beautiful omega."

I let my eyes flutter closed, just enough that I could see, but not enough that I would distract them. I didn't want to look away.

What came through from her side of the bond, it was something beautiful. Something whole and full and loving. There was a vulnerability to it, the aching part of a wound that might never truly go away, but she had opened it to us. She had let us in to help her patch it up.

She wanted the love we had to offer, and it started with him.

I listened to hushed sounds of her soaring pleasure—the cutest little low moans she was trying to stifle—as Viper brought her to her climax, whispering his love in her ear the whole time.

His bond was still open and raw and vulnerable, and the love that blossomed from him every time he laid eyes on her, it was enough to sweep us all away.

It was reverence and passion and disbelief all at once, and sometimes when I caught him looking at her, it was as if he couldn't believe she were real.

It paved a path for something so much better.

Not just for her.

For all of us.

It took a lot for me to fall for someone, but I realised I felt the same as he did—the same as everyone else in the pack.

I loved her.

EPILOGUE

ARSENAL

I felt like I was living through one of those house renovation shows they always played in Institute waiting rooms.

The garage was cleaner than I'd ever seen. The kitchen was updated, and there was now actual wooden flooring across the space.

Onyx finally made King and Mal take the money she'd promised them. King had surprised us all, using the money to do up Ice's old nest as a recording studio. Still not totally confident in working in public, he'd wanted to go for something he could do at home. The money covered the cost of the equipment.

It had started one night when he'd flicked through her fairy book. He began reading it out loud to us all when he'd discovered it was full of smut. Instead of blushing, Onyx had told him she wanted him to read the whole thing to her.

Ice, too, still had reservations about going out, despite Nash's death and his registration. We'd talked about moving away from the Gritch District, but he was set on staying in the garage. He *had*, however, commandeered a slice of the workshop to make into a piercing—and one day, tattoo—shop.

Then he'd shocked us all last night by announcing he wanted to host a party.

The news had blown us all away. He'd been reclusive and terrified of anyone outside the pack for years, so for him to suggest that we invite people into our home was massive.

And he'd banned anyone from helping—with the exception of Onyx—since he wanted to see how well he could host.

The party was a week away, but they were apparently *practising*. There were dozens of Pinterest recipes and designs scattered across the couches.

Currently, they were hunched over the kitchen table. Onyx was trying to decorate cookies with roses. The first batch had been long trashed. It had been Ice's idea to make brownies—so of course Onyx had told him rose cookies were just as necessary. But *surprisingly* enough, sprinkling rose petals into cookie mix in hopes it would magically meld together in the oven wasn't the way to go about it.

Onyx—at least—was wearing an apron. Ice had discarded his with a comment about it being stupid, but he was currently covered head to toe in flour.

Onyx had always wanted a pack to look after and never had one. And Ice had always had one and never wanted to. Turned out, neither actually knew what they were doing.

King was the only functional one when it came to sorting the house out. He was not-so-subtly tailing them around, trying to fix disasters waiting to happen when they weren't looking. Every time they turned their back, I watched him edge closer and crack an extra egg into a bowl, or sprinkle a little salt in. He'd retreat as soon as they were done.

Right now the space was filled with the scent of burned brownies. That happened to be their most recent mishap.

"Did I hear one of them say lemon icing on brownies?" Mal asked from where he was working on his bike. I winced, but pressed my fingers to my lips.

"I don't understand." Viper's frustrated whine sounded from behind me. "How do you tell if you did it right?"

"You get a feel for it," I said, turning my attention to him. I'd set him to work on his own bike after it had come out that *he'd* been the one to break it.

My eye twitched just thinking about that.

How? *Why?!*

Who would do something like that to a Hound?

Viper frowned. "I'm really no good at this. Couldn't we just pay someone to—" He cut off at the flat look I gave him. My eye might *still* be twitching. He cleared his throat. "Noted."

I dragged a stool up beside him, peering at what he was doing. "Your family is rolling in it. Do you work?"

"I dabbled," he said quickly.

I snorted. "So... no?"

"I took a few uni courses, but none of them were right." He scratched his head. "Alternatively, you guys don't have to work anymore. I mean my dad is shit, but he hasn't touched my funds—"

"No one in this pack is freeloading. Makes for lazy pricks that no one wants to be around. And that includes you."

"Technically, I'm pack lead now, so..." He trailed off as my eyes narrowed. "Soooo... we'll all be working."

"Good. Well, looks like you're getting the hang of it." I nodded to the bike. "Keep at it and it'll be good to ride in the next week."

"You trust me to fix it up enough to ride it?" he said, clearly thinking I was joking.

"No," I laughed. "Your bike. Your fix. Your ride."

Viper's face paled. "But I'm new..."

"Better make sure you're paying *super* close attention when I'm teaching, then." I clapped him on the shoulder.

It wasn't until I'd turned to walk away that I saw Malakai watching us. I grinned at him and winked as I felt Viper through the bond since he still couldn't shut it down: anxiety and absolute focus.

He was put out of his misery in the next moment, though, as takeout arrived.

It wasn't long before we were all tucking into his favourite Chinese—delivered by his dad's chauffeur.

"So, about the party... What do you think about inviting the Saint pack?" Viper asked.

"That's the one with Havoc Saint, right?" Mal asked. "That gold pack omega you were supposed to dark bond?"

Onyx froze.

"What did you just say?" Onyx asked coolly, looking between Malakai and Viper. Even in a dusted apron with flour on her nose, she managed to look intimidating.

"I was never biting in," Viper said instantly.

Her glare did not stall.

"Her pack helped me get back to you."

"Her?" Onyx's voice dropped a few tones. The scent of charred brownies was suddenly much stronger than one abused batch could possibly be responsible for. I abruptly found the oil under my fingernails extremely problematic.

Viper, clearly sensing danger, got to his feet and crossed toward her. "I burned a whole mansion down to get back to you, Love," he murmured, tugging her against him from where she sat on the barstool.

"Wait, is that the pack with the hacker you used to keep tabs on Onyx's phone?" Ice asked, the only one unphased by Onyx's rather charred condition.

I winced.

"Uh..." Viper's voice was hoarse.

But it was too late.

Lavenders rotted and brownies turned to coal.

The following fallout lasted three hours and ended in Onyx wrapped up in Ice's chunky, rainbow knit blankets, weeping that the fresh pack hormones were out of control. Ice held her tight while Viper tried to bribe her affection back with brownies King had rushed to the bakery to buy.

"We're inviting th-the Saint pack," she finally sobbed.

"We really don't have to—"

"They're coming!" Her voice turned to a snarl.

"Okay." Viper nodded weakly.

"They're c-coming." Onyx wiped her eyes, doing a poor job of gathering herself. "And Ice and I are going to—" She hiccupped."—h-host them, and I'm going to be b-best friends with the waffle girl... Y-your ex."

"She's not my ex." Viper's voice was barely a wisp.

Malakai, who was lounging on one of the vintage couches watching the entire episode with poorly hidden amusement, snorted and tried to pass it off as a cough.

ICE

Later, we lay in the nest. Onyx had fallen into a deep sleep in my arms.

"Hormones were bound to catch up to her eventually," I said.

Omega hormones were no joke.

Viper nodded, still laying at her side, arms wrapped around us both as she slept. He looked a little shell shocked and I was fighting the smile tugging on my lips.

"She was actually *very* rational."

Most of the meltdown had been her hiding in the nest, fretting that everything she was upset over was silly and she just needed to ride it out. It had been a cycle of her weeping, then drying her tears and declaring it was over, reapplying her makeup, and then breaking down in my arms again. All the while sobbing that she didn't even know what she was crying over anymore.

"She just found and bonded a new pack, she was taken by Riot, and she got all her memories back. Plus, she might deny it, but her heat's on its way too." I could feel it. "She just needed a good meltdown to get it all out. She's going to feel way better when she wakes up."

I knew it. I'd done it.

Though admittedly, having Onyx wrapping *me* in blankets to see me through would have made for a much better experience than hiding alone in my nest and trying to pretend hormones weren't real.

Like the time I'd demanded they toss me down five consecutive tubs of ice cream over two days. They'd been worried I was ill, but I'd just discovered King's gym wasn't alpha exclusive. I'd wept a stupid amount of tears, imagining he might run into a sexy, ripped omega. And I'd been *furious* about it the whole time.

"Hold on. Did you say her heat's on the way?" Mal asked, still seated on my nest couch, phone in hand. He liked to be around us when he could.

"Yeh."

"Wait. But yours is too."

"Yup."

"But... Then..." I could see the comprehension dawn on his face. We all knew what it meant. If we were close, one heat was likely to trigger the other now we were bonded.

"Damn." Mal had the cheek to look a little ashen.

"Don't think you can handle us?"

"I absolutely fucking can," Malakai snapped. "It's the other old codgers I'm worried about."

Viper snorted.

My mind drifted for a while before returning to the thing that had been nagging at me. Since we seemed pretty set on the Saint pack coming to the party...

"I did have a question, though, about the guy from the Saint pack that helped you?" I turned back to Viper.

"Kai?" Viper asked. "He's good."

"Where we got taken... The, uh, trafficking ring. I was there before."

Viper propped himself up on his pillow, watching me seriously.

"Do you think... he can help me find someone?" I asked.

"I can ask. He got the Institute's information about this pack when Onyx matched you."

My pulse thundered in my ears. He was good enough to get into the Institute? That was where she'd been taken.

It was a question that haunted me, something I'd never had the resources or courage to fix, not when I'd been so afraid of ending up back in that place. "She was an omega too. She was taken from me..." My voice threatened to give out. How long had it been?

How old was she now?

Where had she ended up?

"Sure," Viper said. "I can text him. What do you know?"

Not nearly enough. Her age—at a guess. That it was the Institute that had taken her.

"Her name is Hannah."

THE END

WANT MORE?!

BONUS CONTENT?

> But I want more :(

> Didn't get enough happily ever after? GO HERE for 31,000 words of fun! Or to MarieMackay.com

> What's in it?

> Double heat! Spice warnings: group scenes. Orgasm denial. Oral knotting, and triple knotting scenes.

> Will they meet Havoc and crew?!?!

Absolutely! The final episode is a PoisonVerse pack collision, where Havoc meets Onyx and Ice!

And remember to Join my Facebook group and let me know how you felt about it!!

WHAT'S NEXT IN THE POISONVERSE?

Hannah's story will be told by Olivia Lewin! Read Now.

MARIE MACKAY

Want to see my next PoisonVerse book: PreOrder Now.

THE POISONVERSE

Havoc Killed Her Alpha - *Marie Mackay*
Forget Me Knot - *Marie Mackay*
Pack of Lies - *Olivia Lewin*
Ruined Alphas - *Amy Nova*
Lonely Alpha - *Olivia Lewin*
Sweetheart - *Marie Mackay*
And more to come...

POISONVERSE SHORTS

His Gold Pack Omega - *Miyo Hunter*
Something Knotty, Something Blue - *Lilith K.Duat*

Go to PoisonVerseBooks.com for more. Find happily ever after novellas, and pack collision bonus content!

FIFTY-SEVEN
AFTERWORD

A quick note on a choice in this novel: Onyx's infertility.

Onyx's infertility was originally a bigger part of the book. As the plot shifted, I considered taking it out as I didn't want to fail to give it justice. But I decided not to.

I realized I was already giving it the voice I needed it to have.

I'm adding this note to say this: I would never want to minimize the journey of those who experience the <u>grief</u> of infertility.

However, I rarely see infertility represented as a purely societal issue. Instead, most often it's both societal pressure compounding existent personal grief.

Onyx's issue was simple: without society making it so, her infertility would be a non-issue. Nervously, I say this: Onyx doesn't care about her condition, *and that's okay.*

Everyone *else* that cares so much it's impossible for her to voice that. *What if it's just... present, yet not something she wants to be important, but she lives in a world that makes it front and centre?*

My relationship with this issue isn't an exact parallel, but this storyline was cathartic to write. **Thanks for reading!**

-Marie

Printed in Poland
by Amazon Fulfillment
Poland Sp. z o.o., Wrocław